Turlough

by the same author

An Evil Cradling
Between Extremes (with John McCarthy)

Turlough

BRIAN KEENAN

JONATHAN CAPE
LONDON

Published by Jonathan Cape 2000

2 4 6 8 10 9 7 5 3 1

Copyright © Brian Keenan 2000

Brian Keenan has asserted his right under the
Copyright, Designs and Patents Act 1988 to be identified
as the author of this work

This book is sold subject to the condition that it shall not,
by way of trade or otherwise, be lent, resold, hired out, or otherwise
circulated without the publisher's prior consent in any form or binding or
cover other than that in which it is published and without a
similar condition including this condition being imposed
on the subsequent purchaser

First published in Great Britain in 2000 by
Jonathan Cape
Random House, 20 Vauxhall Bridge Road,
London SW1V 2SA

Random House Australia (Pty) Limited
20 Alfred Street, Milsons Point, Sydney,
New South Wales 2061, Australia

Random House New Zealand Limited
18 Poland Road, Glenfield,
Auckland 10, New Zealand

Random House South Africa (Pty) Limited
Endulini, 5A Jubilee Road, Parktown 2193, South Africa

The Random House Group Limited Reg. No. 954009
www.randomhouse.co.uk

A CIP catalogue record for this book
is available from the British Library

ISBN 0 224 04151 7 (hardback)
ISBN 0 224 06122 4 (airport edition)

Papers used by Random House are natural,
recyclable products made from wood grown in sustainable forests;
the manufacturing processes conform to the environmental
regulations of the country of origin.

Typeset by Deltatype Ltd, Birkenhead, Merseyside
Printed and bound in Great Britain by
Clays Ltd, St. Ives PLC

TO ALL THE MUSICIANS OF IRELAND,
ESPECIALLY THOSE WHO ARE
RETURNING TO THE WELL, DRINKING
DEEPLY FROM ITS DEPTHS AND RESHAPING
AND REDEFINING THE MUSIC OF A NATION

A word has power in and of itself. It comes from nothing into sound and meaning; it gives origin to all things. By means of words, a man can deal with the world on equal terms. And the word is sacred. A man's name is his own; he can keep it or give it away as he likes. Until recent times to speak the name of a dead man would have been disrespectful and dishonest, the dead take their names with them out of the world.

N. Scott Momaday, *The Way to Rainy Mountain*

For Audrey, who wouldn't let me give up, and Cal, who makes music for me.

Part One

GEANTRA
Music of Sleep and Dreams
The Early Years, 1670–93

One Remembrance of Things Past

From the journal of Mrs McDermott-Roe, lifelong friend, patron and confidante of the renowned harpist, Turlough Carolan

January 4th, 1738

There is great consolation to be had from Religion and so I write these words in my journal to comfort me in the days ahead: 'For death is the destiny of every man; the living should take this to heart.'

Since Turlough arrived with us and his sickness filled the house, I have been reading through these yellowing pages to find some memories to comfort him. But it seems his memory is clearer than all my scribbling.

It has been more than fifty years since I began this journal and in that time I have witnessed too many deaths. Our nation's history has given death a hideous face, but since I have been nursing Turlough I find that the true face of death is infinitely loving.

I know I should not be, but I am surprised at how much this man has involved my life in his own. His name appears on too many of these pages. Reading them again has exposed emotions that an old woman should not have. I am glad no one else will read them! Less than a decade in years divides us. His closeness to death forces me to contemplate my own, but when I am with him my fear leaves me and when I am afraid, I am afraid for I shall miss him so.

January 7th, 1738

I am left to do too much in this house. Turlough's illness gives our servants an excuse to absent themselves from work. God knows, they do little enough. They avoid the sickroom as if death is waiting there for them, instead of Turlough.

Martha, my maid, has been complaining about his language. She

thinks a dying man should not use such words when, at any minute, he might be standing before his maker. I have some sympathy for her, though it's a poor excuse to refuse to clean his room.

I must find more help. My house is full of strangers eager to pay their last respects, but not one of them wants to dirty their hands in the place where death sits, waiting.

January 2nd, 1738

God forgive me my thoughts, but sometimes I can bear no more of him. Today as I sat with him I felt strangely overcome. I had been reading the psalms when I noticed he had fallen asleep. As I lifted his hand to take the cup he had been holding, his body looked cold and weary, as if the pain was too much to endure. For a moment I prayed that Turlough would leave this life. Suddenly I felt cold myself, it was as if I was being sucked into the body on the bed. I began to curse this man, who has so consumed me, but as I was about to release his hand, I had the feeling that this was not really him. I felt that the real Turlough was standing by the window and that he seemed to be glowing.

Was it our Lady? Was it Turlough's guardian angel?

Tonight my prayers will have more passion in them.

January 5th, 1738

Turlough's condition seems to improve daily and, with it, my own troubles increase. He can be like a wilful child at times. If he is not making demands, as if some things are his God-given right, then he is wheedling sympathy out of people. I have little time for his petty indulgences. But, as this has been too long a part of his nature, even the nearness of death will not change it.

Today Dr Bunting chastised me for refusing to allow Carolan any drink. He tells me that the man is so used to the stuff that it could make his condition worse to withdraw it. He even had the audacity to quote St Paul at me, 'A little wine for the stomach's sake.' The look with which I returned his words informed him what I thought of him and his quotations from scripture.

January 22nd, 1738

For the last few weeks Turlough's vitality has encouraged us all. He seems like the old Carolan, although there is a quiet in him which makes me anxious. I thought at first it was simply resignation and acceptance, but there is something more there of which he will not speak. We walk in the garden for short periods when he feels able, which confuses me because he wants me to change it, although for years he has loved this place.

I explained to him how over all these years I have pressed flowers in my journal and how their shape or colour transports me back to some incident that my memory had overlooked. He stopped and turned to me, then said curiously, 'Yes, I know, colour has memory, everything has its own colour.' Then he asked what colours meant to me. I was confused by the question. I take Turlough's blindness for granted, indeed I never think of him as blind. When I tried to answer his question I felt blind myself and lost for words. As I write this, I am looking at some of those pressed flowers in my bible. Before they comforted me, like old friends telling stories, but now they seem to sit there asking questions.

I am too old to have the comfort of my memories taken from me. I am angry with Turlough and his unanswerable questions.

January 26th, 1738

That a woman of my years should be given to dreaming is too much, and to wake and not remember or understand the apparitions of the night doubles my desperation. I want to talk to Turlough about these things.

I remember those nights, many years ago, when he used to confide in me and we felt that the world was ours alone. He is often delirious these days. It is strange, almost as if he has already gone from us. But I feel his presence always there, invisible but real, like these dreams.

It is comforting how he confides in me even now. We have become so close that not even death seems to frighten us. But there are moments when I feel anxious for him. When he talks of his family, memory seems to pain him. Sometimes when he is talking, he seems oblivious to my presence.

January 30th, 1738

Last night in the very room where Turlough lies dying I was transported, as though I had to bring these memories to him, like frankincense and myrrh, to ease him. I will not call it an old woman's foolishness.

The servants look at me and dismiss me as if I am a mad woman. Even my friends urge me to spend less time with him, for fear they may bury us both; but they will not dissuade me. There is some wonder in dying, but how can I explain it to them?

For weeks now Mrs McDermott-Roe had been visiting Carolan's sickroom. She spent many hours there, oblivious to the daily needs of her household. From the moment she woke her whole attention was focused on his room. One of the maids commented that she was like a squirrel, darting back and forth with a store of winter nuts. But everyone knew the close ties that bound her to the musician. It was not only age, friendship or patronage, but all of these and more. She loved him as if he was part of herself.

She felt helpless when she entered his room. There was nothing she could do for him but be with him. It eased her own anxiety and loneliness. She made the sign of the cross and moved quickly to his bedside, where she sat wiping the perspiration from his face. Carolan sighed as she lifted him and cradled him in her arms. Her face was expressionless, but her eyes seemed to look right through him, as if she was listening to something inaudible. His chest heaved and, as it did, he turned his head into her breast. The deep-throated, body-jarring cough of the previous hours had exhausted him to this half-gasp. Tenderly she wiped the saliva from his mouth.

She was always struck by his impassive face, totally absorbed in his own imagination. For a moment her eyes searched his. They were a mask to others, but not to her. She knew the meaning of every moment of animation in them. She knew how he sometimes turned his deformity on those he wanted to dismiss: he would thrust his grotesquely rolling eyes towards them and stare, his eyes flashing with the bitterness of his words. She smiled and wiped his face and mouth again. So much of this wilfulness she had dismissed. But it was all gone now.

There had been occasions in the last few days when the man she nursed seemed a stranger. She could find no resemblance of Turlough Carolan in the face that confronted her. He was often delirious now and she wanted to ease the turmoil she saw in the dreaming face. 'Mother,' he whispered, his eyes suddenly tortured. His anguished expression sent a shiver of pain through her. She pulled him closer to her breast. The great Carolan was calling out for his mother as he stood on the threshold of death. She, who had loved him in more than motherly ways, could only be a substitute. The years between them were so few and even now he could not release that fearsome child hunger which haunted him.

As she nursed him, rocking herself minutely, she looked from his face to the single candle on the bedside table. He always insisted on a lighted candle in his room. She remembered his words from yesterday, that the light was near God, but the darkness was where God was. She shivered at the thought and clung to him more tightly, not wanting to understand. 'Mother,' he called out again, his voice weak and childlike.

She recalled the stories his mother had told and the brooding, moody silences and fierce anger of his father. She had befriended them while they were alive and had attended them both in their dying and knew more than most: Death was the great confidant. She had received their intimate confessions and built them into the texture of her own life. They brought her closer to the man lying in her arms.

Gently she eased herself from under him and laid him back on the pillow. His body seemed incredibly light. She pulled the covers around him, leaving his arms free. He insisted on this. 'There'll be little enough room in the coffin,' he had declared.

As if she too had become light, she moved across the room and bent her head into a bunch of wild flowers that stood on a small cabinet beside the glowing candle. She enclosed her hands around them and, as she breathed in their scent, her hands moved up her face making a washing motion. She knew each of the separate smells. Turlough's mother had taught her and had brought flowers to the house every few days after her son had come to live there. She had insisted they be left in his room and also that he should not be informed who had brought them.

Mrs McDermott-Roe had grown close to his mother. It was a friendship that the bond of fostering had begun, but which had deepened over the years. She knew each moment of Turlough's life, for his mother had spared her little of it. She had confided so much of her feeling and beliefs that a part of her would always be with him and Mrs McDermott-Roe felt her close now.

From the bed Turlough made some childlike moans, then fell silent again. Mrs McDermott-Roe knew about his birth better than anyone living; when she had wiped his mother's dying body she had a strange sense that his motherhood had passed to her. She folded her arms across her breasts and hummed a lullaby she had frequently heard his mother sing. For a moment her weak voice found new life. The soft melody floated around the room – it seemed to still and hold everything in there; it was as if the moment existed in its own time, disconnected.

Physically exhausted and with emotional numbness tightening her stomach she sat and watched the candle flame. Its movements were like the movements of his eyes. Memories rushed back at her, half-remembered, half-reconstructed by her own needs. She felt the soft light draw her into itself. The confines of the room seemed to fade around her . . . she was being transported.

Turlough's father, Sean Carolan's voice roared out of his grave and she was back there at Turlough's first moments of life: 'Ah, howl your whist. There's pain enough here without the lot of you roaring and screaming. I've delivered more life from these hills than the lot of you have years on you. Now sit silent or shelter yourself in the barn and make your music there, the noise of you might be cold comfort to the beasts.'

The rough voice trailed off to a threatening whisper. The faces that filled the room froze. The yellowing candlelight gave them a haunted look. Only the laboured face and heavy breathing of the woman on the bed animated the frozen room. The women mourners shuffled together, their low voices mumbled words about unholiness and defilement.

Sean Carolan turned from the bedside. Emotion punctuated his words: 'Enough! I have known the holy places of this woman as she has known mine. And what's of me is returned to me and, by Christ, this life will be delivered into these hands alone.'

The women sat, silenced by the man's speech. He turned back to his wife and whispered in her ear. His movements about her were equally quiet and knowing. Two of the old women left the room like shadows fading in a lowering light.

Outside a small crowd waited. Some clicked beads in anxious prayer. The priest stood, indistinguishable from the others. His long, unkempt hair sat like a mantle on top of the heavy overcoat. His boots were of good quality, but had obviously been retrieved or stolen from someone whose lifestyle was not of these people. That they were too large for him was obvious as he moved toward the approaching figures. Only the paraphernalia of the last rites glinting in the darkness distinguished him. He listened attentively as the two women spoke of what was happening in the cabin.

Standing away from the women, the men held their own counsel. The glow from their pipes lit their tough features intermittently, tobacco smoke seeming to freeze in the night air and then evaporate. Their conversation was a chorus: they spoke of the wickedness of the night, its bone coldness, the dark clouds that filled the sky, and of a first-born and the fortunes of life. Occasionally muffled cries of pain and curses from the house blazed out across the landscape, stopping their talk.

Inside it was hot and stuffy. The fire cast amber shadows on the yellowing walls. 'Hush now, woman, rest,' said the man, with authority breaking in his voice. 'The lad's fine.' There was a silence between them as they looked intently at one another.

'My God, woman, you've a tongue on you that would scald the feet of angels. It's well seen why priests cower before the mother of God.'

The woman's hands beckoned him to her. Her voice was low but determined. 'Take him quickly, give him the air of the hills, let the stream cleanse him and let him see and taste this life before my love shields him from it.'

'Do you know what you're asking, woman?'

'Even so, take him.'

Her voice was dismissive in its urgency.

As he dressed, he called the waiting women to him. 'Attend to her and wrap that child safely.' Puzzlement marked their faces as they scurried about, unsure of what was being asked of them.

The father stamped his feet into rough hide boots. As he stood, one of the women, afraid to look into his face, pushed the bundle towards him. Encasing the child under his coat and throwing his wife's shawl around his shoulders, he left. Only his wife's eyes did not follow him. The other women looked from him to each other, confused.

He emerged into the night, a solitary figure. The people gathered around, looked at him and waited. They were like crows feeding on a harvest. He wanted none of them and he strode forward. Only the priest moved toward him.

'There's no work here for you this night, Father.'

The priest stood unmoved. He was unsure. The eyes of his parishioners seemed to burn into him. Almost pleadingly, he addressed the man by name. 'Seaneen,' he said.

The man who had made himself a midwife, moved closer, but the low autumn wind could not cover his words but carried them to the assembled neighbours.

'The last shall be first, and the first last isn't that what you preach? And so it is with this one, the first and also the last. It's fitting you carry that vessel of holy water, to bless the living and the dead, for the night has breached them both. I've enough knowledge to know that my wife will never carry another child. But this one will taste and feel the raw sting of the life from these hands which gave it life. I'll be about my business in peace, priest. Let your ministrations be for that woman who has had life removed from her and must live with a new wilderness within her.'

Sean Carolan was caught up in his words, and the priest knew the power of them. The moment eclipsing life and death was greater than him, and a womb made barren by birth was more powerful in the minds of his parishioners than the tenets of faith he tried to teach them. There were moments in the lives of these people which humbled and frightened him. Then his need of faith was greater than theirs.

'Be careful,' he said. Admonition was in his voice, but inside he felt himself quake: pity and dismissal met him as the new father turned and walked away. In minutes the landscape swallowed both man and child. The priest stood enveloped in Sean Carolan's fierce determination. Brooding under the shelter of the house gable someone muttered, 'A man who will not bend to faith will bend to no man.'

Mrs McDermott-Roe heard the words, as if someone was calling to her from the far end of a great meadow. Then they were in the room with her and the room itself was filling up with the smells of old age and death. The candlelight dazzled her back to consciousness. The words had engraved themselves on her mind, as it seemed they had on Turlough Carolan's. He had inherited the stubbornness, arrogance and independence that were so much part of his father, Sean Carolan.

What had happened between father and son that night had been witnessed by no one. But she knew, as she also knew the meaning of his mother's insistent plea. The child had been long desired and his birth had been difficult. That he had lived at all was a blessing and one which only those who had brought it into being could return.

Mrs McDermott's reverie became clearer now. She wanted to fill the room with his life and squeeze out death's imminence. She wanted to revisit that moment and give it to him. What she had been told as she sat at the bedside of his dying parents helped her recollection. She began to spread out the tapestry of memory about the room. Her recollection was so clear, she could have been telling a bedside story to a drowsy child.

Sean Carolan walked sure-footed into the darkness with his newborn child clutched to his breast like an orphaned lamb, while the priest called the anxious neighbours together with the words, 'The night has been hard on all of us. Let us find a prayer of comfort for those who have suffered and a prayer of thanksgiving for the new life that has been given to us.' Obediantly, the villagers gathered round him.

Sean brought his son to where the river made a natural pool and the noise of its movement was softened and hushed. It was a small, natural amphitheatre enclosed by boulders and high banks of wild gorse. The moon was bright as crystal and made the yellow gorse flowers burn like candles.

The father knelt by the poolside, cradling his son, and dipped his hands in the water. Gently he touched the head, then eyes, nose and ears of the softly whimpering child. Dipping again, he carefully washed his feet and hands, then he stood and held the naked child up to the heavens. The bright waters of the pool were reflected in the father's eyes. Whatever words he spoke only the wind received.

The wrap of dreaming fell from her. Automatically Mrs McDermott-Roe went to her patient's bed and laid his head in her lap. She felt his fingers search out and probe her features. Delicately he fingered the dry wisps of her fine grey hair. Her face was wrinkled as a walnut, she was overcome with girlish embarrassment. But his fingers were insistent. They brushed across her eyes and flowed down the lines of her neck. It too had a lacework of wrinkles and thin folds. Her embarrassment grew, but was not noticeable in her words, 'There are more nooks and crannies here than the whole coastline of Connaught, Turlough.'

She spoke, not knowing if he was sensible or not. His hands suggested he was. 'I still see the face I saw too many years ago. Memory is never blind. Is it night?'

Her smile now was open and filled with relief. 'No, the night has passed, and you are still an old charmer. Where were you, Turlough? I was trying to find you.'

'Is the candle lit,' he asked anxiously.

'Yes, it's lit.'

She held a glass of water to his lips. As he swallowed, little rivulets ran down his chin. She began to wipe his mouth.

'Leave it. I like the feel of it, and I like your smell. Did you put some flowers in the room? The odour of death is not a pretty one.'

It was as if he had read her earlier thoughts and was teasing her.

'Hush now, hush,' she said, trying to dismiss the sudden pangs of guilt.

'We were looking for the bittern. Did you hear it?'

'Who was looking for it, Turlough?'

She had known these moments before. He would move from moments of clarity to a state of semi-oblivion and incoherent rambling.

There was a long silence, Carolan's face grimaced and his eyes revolved in agitation, as if he was trying to look around him.

'Father,' he answered finally. 'Father and me – and Seamus, Seamus was there – and – '

Turlough began coughing again. It seemed to bring him back

from his imminent slide into delirium. 'Sit me up and open the window, there's a sun today. I can feel it and I can hear Seamus calling, "Turlo, Turlo, come on will you, come on now!" '

'There now,' she said, propping him up. For a moment or two she looked at him, relieved that he did not see her wipe the weariness and tears from her eyes with her fingertips.

'Do I make a handsome portrait? I may not have eyes, but my ears rarely deceive me. You haven't moved from that spot for some minutes!'

'Ah, Turlough,' she answered tenderly, 'you must eat, you look so wasted, and you're as light as a feather. I'll open the window for you.'

As she moved away from the bed, he listened to the rustle of her skirts. 'My mother used to brush my eyes with a goose feather as she sang me to sleep.'

There was a long pause as if he was about to drift back again. From the window she called out to him, 'Your mother loved you so.'

As if he had not heard, Turlough continued, 'When I first went blind, I used to lie with my head on her lap and she would caress my eyes with a goose feather. Sometimes she would sing, and sometimes she could not, for her voice was choked with tears. I could not bear her sadness.'

She heard the anguish in his words and tried to lift him out of it. 'Childhood is a wonderful place. We are taken from it too soon.'

'I'm a little tired now. Maybe I shall sleep for a bit.'

She came to his bedside and anxiously began fluffing the pillows and adjusting the covers.

'Leave them off me, for the room's hot enough. But sit by me while I sleep.'

Quietly she returned to a chair by the window. She lifted a bible from a small oval table and turned to the psalms. The pages held pressed flowers and pieces of coloured ribbon. Here was a garden that only she and Turlough knew. She would walk in it now, alone, but safe in the knowledge that he was here with her. Even when he was gone, she would still have this secret garden to walk in, and where she would always find him.

Turlough had lied. He was weary, but it was not for want of

sleep. He wanted to be alone. 'Childhood never leaves us,' he thought as shards of memory pricked at him, demanding his attention. He lay still, sensing the fading scent of the wild flowers, the smells from the open window perfumed the room. Rooms were always too full of smells, but the clean air uncluttered them and let his mind breathe.

Suddenly the room felt hot. He felt the need to itch. His skin was dry like an old snake's and he wanted to scratch it off. He began to draw his long fingernails feebly under the undersides of his arms. It was no good. Every part of him itched. He wanted someone to take a coarse horse brush and rub him down. He smiled at the thought. 'A bag of bones', so many times he had heard horses described as such, and here he was, himself, a bag of bones. The room became hotter.

Cabbage, potatoes, buttermilk, the smells of long ago seemed to fill the room. The smell of wet earth and animals' breath. His mother's voice came softly to him, 'You're a strange one and too quiet by half.' The back of her hand touched his forehead. 'There's no sickness, that's for sure. But what's going on inside that little head of yours?'

He liked it when she spoke of 'his little head'. When his father came home and ruffled his hair with his huge hand it seemed to confirm the littleness and bind all three of them together. 'You're too much like your father, and if you grow up as contrary as him, God help the woman who has the handling of you!'

She would say this sometimes to herself, or to scold him if she was angry with him. For a moment he thought of the women who had had the 'handling of him'. But as he heard his mother's scolding voice again, the women faded.

'He's off far too much on his own, Sean Carolan. What does he do for hours on end out there?'

His father's voice was calm and steady. He would hear it passing through their small cottage as if it held the walls together. 'He's up to no mischief, that's for sure. Isn't he always off with a line, fishing!'

'Either the fish know he is coming or he throws them back, for there's few enough he brings home!'

'I've told him often enough. Fish with your fingers and the fish will fly to you, but fish with a hook and they'll only look at you!'

'Well, that's quare wisdom from a man who spends more time looking into the river than fishing in it!'

Carolan could hear them now, as when he was a child. He loved to hear them talking about him as he pretended to sleep.

In his mind he began to inspect his childhood home. Against the wall was the well-scrubbed deal table and round it, like sheepdogs pinning it to the wall, were the chairs and rough stools his father had made. Above the hearth, which was littered with black pots and fire logs, a few cracked and patterned plates which his mother loved were displayed on a shelf. Even now he heard her voice as when he played with them, 'Careful, Turlough, you don't want to be eating off the floor.' Near the door he saw the great weight of harness hanging on the wall and lying in coils on the floor, like black, shiny eels.

But as the familiarity of the room came swimming back to him he began to feel waves of pain cramp his stomach. A slow but searing ache boiled in his head, fogging and shattering the images. Suddenly everything was changed. The warm dim half-light of the cottage was gone. Now he saw himself, a child, in a field. In front of him stood all those familiar things that had made up his home. In the open field they looked strange, even frightening.

He knew this scene. He had long carried it, buried and half forgotten, inside him. Now it was back. With pains in his head and in his stomach, he was being dragged back. Anger, confusion and remorse locked on to him. It was as if he had returned, a stranger, to watch and understand what his childish mind could not.

Wrapped in his mother's arms, he watched his father move in and out of the house. Each time he emerged carrying something – a table, a chair, pots, a bundle of clothes. All the familiar objects that had made the house seem safe now looked strange, piled haphazardly in the open air. He wanted to play this new game, but was afraid. The things of the house were smaller now and their shapes had changed. His father had changed too. He recognised him, but he didn't seem like his father. His mother felt cold too. The breeze blew her hair in his eyes, but she didn't comfort him. She used to dangle her hair in his face and make him laugh, but now she was looking away. Away from his father, away from the house, away from him. He wriggled in his mother's arms until she set him down. He stood holding her skirt and tried pulling her towards the house and his father.

He wanted to be with both of them, together. But she was rooted to the ground. Silently he watched the strange men load his home on to a cart. The family dogs barked at the men and his father shouted at them to be quiet. He was frightened; his father's voice was like a snarl.

A neighbour came up. 'There, child,' she said, 'you'll soon be in your new house with lots of new friends to play with.'

'Is my father coming too. I don't want to go to a new place. My mammy's sick!'

The woman looked at his mother, who stood unmoved, her gaze fixed into the distance. The neighbour wiped a tear from her eye and whispered, 'Life was never meant to curse us so. This is too cruel a day!'

As Turlough disinterred this incident, he began to see it with a new clarity, as if he sensed, rather than saw, the event and could feel what people were thinking. He remembered his father talking to one of their neighbours and he could hear their words again. Slowly, but clearly the incident began to unfold.

He now noticed the faces of his parents' friends. Men stood with their arms about their wives. They wanted to help his father, but were afraid it would insult his dignity. Somewhere someone said, 'There's no one deserves this and no man is less deserving of it than Sean Carolan.' The child did not understand them or why they were here. His father was silent. Again someone whispered, 'A man who stands his own ground will have the ground taken from under him!'

Another voice answered, 'Shut up man. Do you want to bring the same on your own head?'

Turlough asked his mother again, 'Why is father bringing our things out? Is our house going to fall down?'

A neighbour spoke softly to his mother, 'Take comfort from the child.'

As she spoke, his mother lifted him in her arms. The sun

dazzled his eyes so he could not see her face. Only her voice touched him. It was hot like the sun. 'Let them take what they will. Be your own man always, Turlough. No one can take that from you.' Then she pulled him tightly to her.

There was neither defeat nor resignation in her voice. It was quiet and assured. Her husband looked to her. He knew her resolve was greater than the hills around them. He looked at his neighbours, who looked away or dropped their eyes. One of them came forward and spoke, 'It gives me no pleasure to ask if I can help.' Then, dropping his voice, he continued, 'There's a fierce pride in that wife of yours.'

'Aye,' Sean Carolan answered. 'And there are some here who could be doing with a fist full of it.'

'Hurry up there!' roared an English voice.

'And there are those who think they have some – ' Carolan's voice was slow and cold and he stared fixedly at the man on horseback who had called out to them.

The rider saw the glare and goaded his horse forward. 'Take no more of my time and I'll take no more of yours.' The words had the clipped precision of a man who wanted to say no more than he needed, but knew he must say something. 'Come on, man, best get it over with,' he continued, almost pleading. Then, feeling the mask slip, he said, 'I've other plans for this land now.'

Sean Carolan's eyes showed the tiniest of movements. His pupils constricted to piercing pricks. Slowly he walked forward. The horse shied at his approach and the rider seemed unwilling to rein it in. Sean Carolan grasped the harness. 'This land was here before you, and will be here long after you and I have gone our separate ways. Be careful of your haste, for you might be buried in it before you change much of it.'

The rider looked down at the great hand holding the harness and knew that it controlled the horse. For a moment he felt powerless.

'Come, Sean,' his wife called. 'There's nothing to keep us here. The sooner gone, the sooner settled.'

Sean Carolan let go the harness and walked towards her. The rider felt himself shrivelled. He had come to oversee an eviction and yet he felt himself evicted. These were a dark people and their ways were strange. For a moment he felt as if he didn't exist. He was master of nothing.

As Sean tightened the last ropes that held down the scanty collection of belongings he turned to his wife and asked, 'Will you take a turf from the hearth?'

'We'll build a new fire where we are going. Ashes are for the dead, but fetch some water from the well. That's all I'll take from this place!'

'It's already done. Get you and the lad up on the cart, now.'

'No, Sean, I'll walk from this place. I'll not be carried.'

Sean Carolan nodded to the carter. The man slapped the horse on its flanks. 'Get up, girl,' he uttered needlessly.

The cart moved off, with Carolan, his wife and young son walking alongside. They had gone no more than a few yards when the mother thrust Turlough into the arms of his surprised father. 'Hold him and halt that horse,' she called out. Then she ran to the side of the stacked cart and began rummaging anxiously.

'What is it, woman? What are you looking for?'

In silence she hunted furiously along the sides of the cart. Her husband was confused and curious. Young Carolan's eyes followed his mother. His father cast an eye over the cart. He had forgotten nothing and he wanted to be gone. It was hard enough to crush down his anger and humiliation and now they were being delayed. He began to itemise the things he had packed. He was about to chastise his wife when he saw her walk back towards the neighbours and the landlord's agent, who was nailing up the door of their abandoned home. She had something clutched at her breast. Curiosity calmed him and he watched.

She unfolded a white cloth to reveal several loaves of fresh baked bread. She handed some of them to her neighbours. 'God bless,' she said softly and they returned her blessing, some with tears and others simply nodding.

One loaf was left when all had been served. She walked up to the agent, who was standing surveying the scene, and placed the bread in his hands.

'May your house and your heart never be without!' she said.

Incredulous, he said, 'You would give me this?' and looked at her to see what insult was behind her words. But he could find none as she answered, 'And why would I not? I can make again what I have had before.'

With that she turned and walked away. He felt the heat of the bread in his hands and knew he had been given the last thing taken from the house. But equally he knew something had been taken from him. For the second time that day he felt diminished. He looked anxiously towards the neighbours. They, too, were walking away. By her gift she had reduced him to their equal. His power, his authority, his lordship, was only a token thing, like the bread in his hands.

Turlough was fascinated by the clarity of his memory. Its immediacy was frightening, but like other visitations of previous days the images melted away quickly. The moment had been so intense that he felt drained of energy. It was as if he had been part of everyone and everything that happened. He felt the neighbours' pity and fear, his father's steely anger, his mother's pride and resolve and even now his hands were hot and stinging. Something in him made him feel more akin to the land agent than he could bear. Regret overwhelmed him. He felt his own power, authority and reputation were only tokens. Uncontrollably, a great sigh of exhaustion and pain poured out from him.

Like a mother bird, Mrs McDermott-Roe flapped to the bedside. Tears and perspiration had soaked Turlough's face and body. She thought he had been dreaming and silently set about wiping his face and laying cold towels on his forehead.

Their coolness pulled him out of the emotional discharge of his memories, but could not heal the open wound inside him. Even as she wiped his face he felt the compress of guilt against his skin. His mother's face turned Janus-like in his imagination. At once tender and loving, then fixed and admonishing. Her assurance terrified him. Beneath his breath he mumbled, 'Forgive me, mother.'

The words were hardly audible. His nurse could only take them as a prayer of contrition from the dying. She did not understand that his anguish was not at the fact of his dying but at something that his living had wrenched up in him. As she fixed the bedclothes and pillows about him, he took her hand and slowly in a voice, part child, part wonder, part desperation, asked, 'Was I equal to my calling?'

She was perplexed. The days of delirium had thrown up many things, but never this doubt and insecurity. Death was not fearful to Turlough. She sought to reassure him. 'Neither this house nor I myself have ever doubted you, for you have honoured us both and brought the light of life to many more. So what is this dark talk I hear?'

Turlough only half-heard her. He lay silent and unmoved as if caught between two worlds, listening for other words of comfort. His mother's voice came to him, anxious but reassuring.

'There now, don't fret, It's only a growing pain. Put your head on my lap for a while.'

He could feel the light touch of her fingers stroking his forehead and clearing the pain, which came and went when it would. Yet being here, with her, at moments like this seemed to lessen it. In silence he lay and looked into her face. She gazed back, then remonstrated softly, 'You do too much thinking, Turlough. Your head's not big enough for all the ideas you have stuffed in there. No wonder it gets sore at times!'

She smiled and gently tweaked his ear, as if scolding him. He was glad of this, for he found it difficult to answer questions about what he thought so much about. It was too confusing. All his senses seemed to get muddled up. Sometimes he didn't see things so much as hear them and the noises made pictures in his head, which became long stories. He wished desperately to be able to talk about this but it was too difficult. Anyway they were only growing pains and would soon leave him. Sometimes he wanted that to happen and sometimes he didn't. His mother's voice came again, 'Why don't we go outside? The fresh air and sunlight will do us both good.'

Turlough saw himself sitting by the open door. The day was bright and fresh. As usual, his mother came out from the house with her shawl across her arm. She wound it around him, telling him that he must keep himself well wrapped up. He watched her move about, taking wood or newly dried clothes inside. If the day's promise of fine weather held, she would tend her garden. It was a garden she had never cultivated, but whenever she found wild flowers or herbs growing near the house she would protect and nurture them.

Sunday was the birthday of saints, she told him, and he should remember he was born on the Lord's day. She usually collected her wild herbs and flowers on a Sunday, insisting that their powers were more effective then. He remembered her favourites. The white-fringed, puck petals of the bog-bean shone out from the dark undergrowth like a star. The squat, stumpy, deep purple marsh orchid with its slender stem and long pointed flower spike.

Once she showed him a slender white flower. She called it the grass of Parnassus. The waxy, transparent petals seemed too delicate to touch. Its name fascinated him, and this fascination deepened when she insisted that anyone who drank the flower's juice would be enabled to write poetry. In his imagination he saw fields of words stretching out into the distance. When he told his mother she laughed and said he was already a poet without drinking any flowers. The names of the blossoms were poetry themselves: milkwort and wild thyme, bugle and bitter vetch; others were mysterious, St Patrick's cabbage with its tiny flowers leaping up out of flat thick rosette of leaves and St Debeoc's lanky, purple, bell-like flowers. His head was full of names and colours, all held together by his mother's teasing voice.

Often she left great bunches of flowers with him as she wandered about collecting herbs. The smell of her shawl and the fresh picked flowers eased the pains in his head. But when the sun was particularly bright he could only see her as a shadow. Though the distance between them was a few feet, she seemed far away. It was as if she knew his thinking in these moments, for she would always come to him, her voice soft and reassuring. She taught him how to make garlands and crowns with the flowers.

'Now you make one for me, young man. Don't you think I deserve it?'

He asked her what colours she liked best, but she only replied that he must choose. He studied the colours and shapes before him and after much thought selected the deep, almost purple butterwort and bright white and yellow wood anemone.

Smiling, she untied her hair and bent her head toward him. As delicately, as a dressmaker sewing lace, he wove the flowers through her hair and across her head from temple to temple.

When he had finished he leaned back, almost frightened of his handiwork.

Her eyes looked deeply into his. 'What does it look like?' she asked slowly, aware of his apprehension. He shrugged his shoulders, confused. 'Tell me,' she insisted, teasing him again. 'Tell me, Turlough, or are you afraid?'

'It's . . . it's . . . it's like little blue flames dancing on your head!'

She began laughing, and her hand gently touched his face. 'What flowers have you been chewing? I think I look like a bridesmaid, because you've made me feel like one . . . I'd better not wear it home or your father might get jealous!'

They both laughed at this as they made their way to the house, talking of where they would put the flowers. 'When they are picked on the Lord's day, they feel no pain and will last for weeks. But they must have light.'

Turlough remembered that he had never seen dead flowers in the house. He remembered also the wounded bird he had brought home and how she chased him and his bird out of the house, scolding him that he must never, never do such a thing again. Even as a child she hid nothing from him.

'Death waits for us all, but you must never invite him in.'

The memory of her words jarred him. He wanted to be rid of it and instinctively called out to his companion, 'Bring me a drink. It's so hot I feel as if I am suffocating!'

The cold water refreshed and cleared the haziness from his thinking. But his sickroom could not contain his wandering mind.

He thought of his father. His mother seemed to come to him effortlessly, but when he thought of his father it required a more conscious effort. He remembered little of his first home, until now. Many years had passed and its memory had left little imprint on Turlough's mind. His mother spoke rarely of it. But, for his father, it had been the end of something, and when he spoke of it his wife would sit in watchful silence. If she was busy with some chore about the house, she would occasionally chastise him. 'You're broody like an old hen that can't find its eggs,' and then she would turn on Turlough. 'You see what happens when you steal eggs!' She was never really angry with them. Her passion was always to protect her own. Turlough laughed and teased her, 'You're a broody mother hen yourself!'

He was comfortable with her and loved her more like an adult than he did his father. There was a distance between father and son. It was like a silent understanding, yet in his father's presence he felt more of a child. He watched him as he washed himself before the fire. 'Can you not do that at the pump, Sean, instead of turning this place into a stable?'

Sean Carolan's reply was slow and patient. 'I've no mind to stand half naked for the world and his sister to gawk at.'

Their conversation was affable and automatic, a simple acknowledgement that they were together again and at home with one another.

Before they moved to their new home his mother used to take him to his father in the fields. Sometimes, if it rained, they would shelter under a tree and his father would hold up his greatcoat like a roof over their heads and they would run home. 'Without water there would be no life, so we don't complain,' he would say as he dried young Turlough before the fire. 'Hot and cold, day and night, wet and dry, you can't have one without the other. Without the opposite nothing would be right and nothing would get done!'

But his memories of his father after they moved home were the opposite of those childhood memories. Turlough never went to him in the fields and there was no laughing in the rain. Sean Carolan always dried himself by the fire and cursed the day he learned to blacksmith. When Turlough went to him at work he was surrounded by noise, with great hammers banging and steam blurring up as hot metal hissed into cold water, and animals whinnying as the forge roared and sparked. Father shouted when he spoke now. He said he had brought the noise home with him in his ears.

Turlough remembered when his father first came home from his new work. He was black and frightening. Turlough ran to his mother. Charcoal was a new word he learned then. 'It was charcoal that did it,' his father told him. At first he thought charcoal was the name of some other man and that he was a black man too. But as he settled into his new life more new words crowded in on him. They were hard words like his father's hammer blows: coulters, shovels, rakes, reaping hooks, spurs and bits, stirrups, springs, spits, hooks and bolts. All these new words and their associations drove into his childhood memory like nails. They seemed to shut out the light. They were dark words . . . like his dark father.

Often now Sean Carolan would come home from work and sit moody and silent for hours. Some nights he would drink too much. Other nights he would drink with friends and Turlough would hear words like the law, the anti-Christ. They talked of heresy and apostates and of people turning, and all the while his father said nothing, but sometimes stared with burning eyes at his son. It was an old communication and Turlough knew it from before. When the others had left his father would continue drinking alone. His mother would long since have retired from what she called the conversation of fools.

In the quiet and dimly lit room, with his mind loosened by alcohol, Sean Carolan drew his son into close intimacy. 'We inhabit another world other than this and it is with us always. In our language, and in our song and music. Never lose sight of this, Turlough, for whatever the world presents to us we have our own.'

Though his words seemed sad and tinged with regret, there was a quiet reassurance in them, 'Look around you, Turlough. There are those who would see only stones and rocks and trees. But we behold a vision of people of great deeds, of songs and stories that holds the whole together and give it meaning. There is a presence in everything. Each rock, each stone and tree, and the river there, is a landmark built by our past and our people and everything in it beats with its own pulse.'

When he spoke, the young Turlough was only vaguely aware of his father's meaning, yet he understood the sense and he loved the intimacy of it.

He would listen to his father talk of such things for hours. Afterwards they would sit together in silence, as if absorbing the mysteries his father had laid bare. Sometimes, overcome by alcohol, his father would lie back in the chair and sleep. To Turlough these confessions were a sacred gift from father to son. When he listened, he felt there was no age between them. He was less a father and more a confederate. And when Turlough went to bed, his mind was restless with the secret knowledge his father had shared with him.

In his sickroom, Carolan sipped from his cup. He was restless again and felt his stomach clenching. He needed to be reassured. Had he entered through the gateway his father had shown him or had he simply looked and walked away? The question puzzled and saddened him.

'Did my father talk of me when he was dying?'

Mrs McDermott-Roe was perplexed by the question and hunted through her memory for an answer. But before she could find it, Turlough announced, 'I think there were no two people more suited than they were!'

As suddenly as he had made the statement, he dismissed it with another, 'I'm tired now. Do you mind if I sleep? It's a long road I have been travelling!'

She was only too glad of it, for she was as weary as him.

'Aye sleep easy now,' she said, opening the door. 'I'll sit with you later.'

She closed the door behind her. He was alone and for a moment felt the room's silence.

The noise of children's voices coming through the window held his attention. Obviously there were more people about the house than usual. He listened to the incoherent laughter and shouting, and smiled to himself. It was like an echo of his own childhood.

Devlin, Corcoran and Shaw were his constant companions. They were at that age when their parents were glad to have them out from under their feet. Whatever reservations his mother had about their new home, she was happy to see him settled with new friends. Devlin was taller than the others and had a particular fondness for young Turlough, but his games were rough and the river was their playground. The race to it was always the start of their adventures. Devlin would pitch Shaw into the river, complaining about the smell of his father's pigs. But Shaw was fast on his feet and called Devlin a great fat carthorse, slapping him across the backside with a stick: 'Get up there, fat arse!'

Their banter was harmless and rarely ended in a brawl;

Turlough was the peacemaker when it did. Because Turlough was new to the area, each of the other lads vied for his attention. But he was drawn to Devlin. Big as he was, Devlin was also moody. He was the poorest of them all and his one ambition was to be a soldier. He was impatient with Turlough's absorption in the wildlife about the river bank. 'Sissies can't be soldiers,' he would chant at Turlough when he found him studying the blur of yellow pimpernel and cow-parsley stretching along the river. 'Here, take this sword I've cut for you and we'll give Shaw and Corcoran a pastin'.'

So in they plunged. Turlough mounted piggyback on the great carthorse. While Corcoran and Shaw charged towards them, screaming and squealing, they splashed through the water. Devlin snorted and roared more like one of Shaw's father's boars than a battle horse, while Turlough slashed and poked at his opponents, half-choking Devlin as he goaded him on. Turlough was merciless in his attack. 'Come on, Devlin,' he urged, his voice deep and thick with emotion, 'get in close and I'll cut their miserable heads clean off!'

Turlough's screaming drove into Devlin's senses as he ploughed through the water, roaring in unison with his rider, but Corcoran and Shaw swung around him and Shaw landed a blow across Turlough's back. Laughing and giggling he swung again at him. Infuriated, Turlough hissed into Devlin, 'Turn your fat arse round, Devlin, for Jesus' sake, turn around.' Devlin turned and lowered his head to charge his opponents. Corcoran was too close to allow him to charge. Kicking out at Devlin's knees, Corcoran soaked his opponents while Shaw wielded his wooden sword across Devlin's shoulders. 'Kill the horse and kill the rider,' shouted Corcoran.

The anger in Turlough broke. This was no longer a game. 'You skinny runt' he yelled and threw himself from Devlin's back, with his hand tightening about Shaw's neck. Both boys plunged into the river, their horses stumbling beside them.

Turlough surfaced still shouting, but his words and abuse were smothered by his anger. He dragged Shaw up out of the water and, an imaginary weapon in his empty hand, thrust deep into his victim, then plunged him back into the river. Abandoned to his anger, he turned on Corcoran, and growling out Corcoran's own words, 'Kill the horse, kill the horse,' threw himself on his witless friend and dragged him down, lashing and kicking, as the astonished Corcoran floundered toward the bank. Devlin was already there and pulled Corcoran up beside him. When he had caught his breath and stopped shivering from the nervous seizure the attack had brought on, he cried out, his voice quaking, 'You're a wild bastard, Carolan!'

As he spoke, Shaw shivered beside him. His ear was dripping blood, but he seemed unaware of it. The three boys looked at their friend as he stood in the middle of the river. The silence was thick with fear, confusion and anger. Turlough eyed his friends as if they were strangers. He felt he was not part of them, but also that he desperately wanted to be with them. He looked around and, seeing one of the wooden swords trapped between two large boulders, walked towards it. He climbed up on the stones and, sword in hand, called to the bank. 'Shaw!' Shaw and the others looked at Turlough's solitary figure standing on its rock plinth with his sword hand raised in the air. 'Shaw!' his voice boomed out again.

The boys watched as Turlough plunged the stick mockingly into his body. Then, rigid as a board with his eyes gaping madly, he fell backwards into the river. A sudden silence met his splash and then was shattered by bellowing laughter. Simultaneously all three plunged into the water again and dragged Turlough's corpse back to the bank, where they sprawled out, laughing and cursing one another.

As his friends spread out their clothes to dry and prepared to do some fishing, Shaw complained that his ma would skin him alive if she saw the state of his boots.

'You mean your da's boots!' bantered Devlin.

Then they argued about whether to go hunting for birds' nests instead of fishing. Turlough offered to stay behind to watch their clothes if they shared the eggs with him. It was agreed, much to Turlough's relief. The day had had more excitement than he expected and he was happy to be on his own for a while. He lay back in the sun and closed his eyes. The soft sounds of the river eased him. He was frightened and unsure about what had happened in the mock battle in the river. His childhood had been full of stories of wars and great heroes. Devlin wanted nothing more than to be a soldier, but he was too fat and too feeble in mind to be a hero, and Turlough was drawn to his gullible ignorance.

He bent his knees and rested his head on them. For a moment he thought he was drowsy, then he recognised the slow numbing pain starting in his head. He had become used to it now and knew it must take its course. He thought again of the battle in the river in an attempt to dispel it, but it was as if the pain surrounded his thoughts and intensified them.

The noise of the water, rolling and flushing over the stones, was somehow transformed. All around him was the distant roar of war. He saw the river churning a reddish brown over the stones, turning and twisting round the corpses of men and horses. Everywhere were screaming and the high-pitched whinny of frightened horses. Voices cried out to God, while others blasphemed and cursed him. In such a cauldron of hate, killing was the only survival. Racked by the intensity of these images, Turlough opened his eyes.

For a moment the full glare of the sun burned deep into them. He rubbed them fiercely with his knuckles and tried to look again. The fields beyond the river were not as he remembered them. They were a battlefield of horses' flesh, torn and gnawed by rats and dogs, like some horrific plague land.

Once more he rubbed his eyes. It was as if his own imagining had thrown up a screen against the reality about him. Now as the screen began to fade he looked about him not for reassurance against the horror, but to find his friends. With them there were light and laughter.

He stood up and without looking back walked to the trees, where there was shelter. He knew now why birds lived in them and knew also that he would take no share in the boys' booty of eggs. Their shade calmed him and the startled cry and flight of frightened birds distracted his thoughts. Cautiously he walked away from the imaginary carnage.

When he found his friends they had precious few eggs to share; why, was the subject of some debate. Turlough decided to resolve the problem. It was a convenient escape route for him.

'Those are wrens and them two are black chafers and your ma will do more than skin you if you bring any of them into the house. There's a curse on them who bring those eggs into their home!'

Turlough's authority was enough. None of them wanted anything to do with the eggs of such despised birds. Instead they insisted on getting back to their clothes before some thieving tinker helped himself.

As they made off, Turlough held Devlin back, 'They're neither wren nor chafer. Quick, gather them up. Only the winners get the trophies!'

Feeble as he was, Devlin was no fool. He simply shook his head at Turlough's cunning and hid the eggs safely so he could collect them later.

This recollection lifted Turlough's spirits and relaxed him. He couldn't remember what had happened to the eggs. He laughed at these curious gaps in his memory and for a moment was glad of them. He felt sleep close now.

As Turlough lay back in the empty room, he thought that it seemed as if Mrs McDermott-Roe had taken with her all the questions his insistent memory had thrown up. Being alone, he was able to confront disturbing memories without being troubled by them. There was something joyous about his childhood that overwhelmed these odd moments. With the last residues of his companions still in his mind, he listened again for a noise. But all was quiet. People had left or perhaps been chased away. He let the quiet seep into him and imagined his sickroom transformed into his childhood home. At ease now he let the memory flood towards him, and with the flood waters came that grace-filled rediscovery of life that he thought life itself had forgotten.

Journal of Mrs McDermott-Roe

February 9th, 1738

It is dull today and there is a fierce coldness in the air. I worry about Turlough in his sickroom. He refuses to allow his fire to be lit. Though the last few days with him have been demanding they have also been quite wondrous. Turlough's memory is so acute at times. It has made me light-headed trying to keep up with him.

His remembrance of childhood is so clear and makes us both laugh. I seem to be learning new things about this man whom I thought I had known better than anyone else.

He has been talking about Seamus Brennan lately. I hope he never finds out that Brennan has been to the house, but that I refused to allow him to visit. In all the years I have known him, Seamus Brennan has not changed. He has a coarse mouth which he is inclined to exercise too much, and when he is not stealing fish from my river he is smoking and drinking enough for six men.

Turlough and he were inseparable. I remember the stories Brennan used to bring back when he had been off travelling with Turlough, as his guide and groom.

I am sure Carolan got his quick tongue from Brennan, and Brennan has made himself famous by declaring, 'Turlough Carolan was the queerest creature it was ever my good fortune to know.'

The hypocrisy of the man. He is responsible for Turlough's drinking and smoking and his frequent contempt for the cloth. There are those who would have it that Turlough Carolan's 'strangeness' was due to his nocturnal dances with the devil. But Seamus Brennan had more hand in it than the devil.

I fear it will be impossible to keep Brennan away. No matter how much I refuse, Turlough remains determined. He talked of nothing but his 'great friend'. His every waking moment is filled with talk of Seamus.

Seamus and Turlough always went to the same spot on the river. Turlough loved the way the sun sliced through the trees and set up bars of light and dark along this stretch. He called it the keyboard. He had seen a harpsichord once when his father took him to the big house. He remembered overhearing the music man's words from the next room, 'Touch the keys lightly so that your fingers can move to the next note. Remember you are releasing music into the air like a bird, not dropping it on to the floor like a dead goose for the pot.' In his young mind he thought you unlocked the music with a set of keys, and asked his father about this as they walked home. Sean Carolan looked at him, his brow furrowed. His son's questions came out of the blue. It always took him a while to understand exactly what he was referring to. He explained what a keyboard was. Turlough watched his father's fingers dance in the air. After that he always thought of his father's fingers when he watched dragonflies dart and hover on the surface of the river; and he remembered his words, 'Music's not a gaoler, son, there are no prison keys in music.'

The two young men separated. Seamus, too, had his favourite spot and was quick to claim it. Turlough watched his friend move stealthily through the water. Seamus insisted the salmon did not like the deep channels. They preferred the shallows, where there was more light and where it was easier to shake the lice from their scales. To Turlough, Seamus's hunched, slow-moving figure reminded him of an ancient, bedraggled heron. But the water was extremely cold and after only about twenty minutes Turlough abandoned the labour of fishing and took himself to the comfort of the riverbank. For an hour or so he watched his friend's meticulous movements, occasionally calling out and bantering him about his lack of skill. But more and more his thoughts drifted aimlessly from Seamus as he scanned the wider riverscape.

His eyes moved slowly over the expanse of his great silent keyboard. The soft noise of the morning seemed to settle on the water. When the sun got brighter it would be difficult to look at the river. The tones of brightness and light got more extreme and made his eyes sting and his head hurt. Yet he insisted on scanning this stretch of water. As ever, a fish would suddenly hurtle out of a dark patch of the river, and as it threw itself into the bright glare of light bouncing off the water it seemed to disappear at once in midair. Only a distant splash told him it had returned. Turlough was intrigued. It was like a candle being blown out suddenly. He watched the little circles of water appear and disappear. He thought of the fish disappearing in the blinding sunlight. He began to laugh. The idea of catching the leaping fish excited him.

'Hey, Turlo, you off with the fairies again? Come on, give us a hand with these two, will you?' Turlough looked round. Behind him stood Seamus. He was laying out two fishes he held hooked through the gills. He wiped each hand on his sleeves.

'The way you sit looking at that water. Do you think the fish are going to jump into your hands?'

'That's exactly what I was thinking. I wouldn't have to be standing up to my arse in freezing water and my fingers going numb as I try and tickle the belly of those boyos.'

Turlough looked down at the fish laid out on the grass. They looked like two slabs of slate; lifeless and almost colourless, their big brown eyes were balls of dried clay. He thought of watching them move ponderously through the water, silent grey ghosts pausing and flicking in and out of the shadows. They seemed impervious to the force of the current running against them. Yet they felt so smooth and comfortable when you cupped your hands under their belly. They always gave a nervous twitch when your hands first touched them. 'Gently, lightly,' he could still hear his father whisper every time he took a fish. You could feel the whole life in them in that first twitch, then they would sink back into your hands as if they were receiving your touch. 'She'll come to you only if she wants you,' his father had said. He thought of his father's gnarled and callused hands hammering at the anvil and knew he would never again tickle and take a fish.

'I still say it's unkind to take them before they spawn. They have waited their whole life to come back here.'

There was an edge of anger and even desperation in his voice that Seamus hardly perceived.

'They're lifeless, and only fit for the sow bucket when they come down the river again.' Seamus looked at Turlough. 'Holy Jesus, Turlo, they're only fish. I didn't rob the poor box. Here! it was my arse that froze getting them, you can carry them.'

Seamus thrust the two fish into Turlough's chest.

'All right, all right,' said Turlough, taking the two fish up with his fingers. 'And what are you going to carry? The five loaves, I suppose!'

Seamus looked puzzled. 'Five loaves?'

Turlough smiled and sighed in mock exasperation. 'Is that all your heathen hand could manage?'

'No, there's a few more down below. You can carry the big ones,' said Seamus moving away.

Turlough held up the two fish to look at them more closely. Seamus shouted to him from where he was gathering up the remaining catch. 'You look like the priest on Sunday!'

The walk home was always shorter. The day on the river, its

failure or success encouraged the inevitable banter that ate up the miles. But there were only two of them today and as only one of them had fished, the conversation was more subdued.

'Do you ever think about where they go? The salmon, I mean. Where do they go when they leave the river?'

'The sea.' Seamus answered, annoyed by the flies that seemed more interested in him than his fish.

'But where? The sea is so different. It tastes different. There are no banks and turns to mark your way. It's just a big black emptiness. What do they eat out there? There's no river food. And how do they cope with all that salt? Do you think they're afraid of all the strange creatures they meet?'

Turlough turned to find he was talking to himself. Seamus had gone off and was rooting at the foot of a hazel tree. His fish had been left on the trunk of an old fallen oak. Turlough dragged himself and the two salmon to the tree. He was still preoccupied by their mystery. He looked at them lying arched across the tree. He thought about their life journey: from the river to the sea, and back again after many years to the same river, where they would lay their spawn then head down the river to die. The simplicity of it was inspiring. He wasn't sure why, yet he knew that somehow these fish were holy. And maybe because they were holy they could survive the sea and all its strangeness. He sat on the grass and rested his back against the oak.

He closed his eyes and tried to imagine the emptiness of the sea and the strange shapes moving slowly through it. 'Only if you really believed could you be unafraid. If you knew for sure that you had to return to the river of life, that it was your fate, then the sea was only like a kind of dream.' Turlough pressed his finger and thumb on to the balls of his eyes. The pressure threw up various moving shapes of red, green, blue and bright yellow; they moved about, changing colour and shape, slow and luminous in the dark.

The pressure became painful and he stood up, blinking his eyes in the glare of the sun. After some minutes, when they had adjusted, he lifted the fish, his hands cradling them. The thought of ramming his fingers into the gills and up through the back of the fishes' throats seemed offensive somehow. Delicately he laid them side by side on the ground. Now it was not their eyes, but the great gaping mouth and gills that held him. Everything seemed fixed in a final moment of exhilaration. It was as if the fish were even now filling their lungs. Propping them side by side on their stomachs, Turlough lay flat on his own and looked them full in the face. Nervously he began chuckling to himself. The idea came into his head that the fish were singing. Somehow a great outburst of life was coming from the silent fish. He jumped to his feet and hoisted the fish, one in each hand, on to his shoulders. Walking solemnly, his head turned to the heavens he began chanting a sonorous 'Te Deum'.

Seamus stood in awed silence under the hazel. He watched his friend's performance. At moments like this he was unsure whether to laugh or run away. But fear and fascination rooted him to the spot.

Turlough was oblivious of Seamus. The pomp and solemnity of his ritual had disappeared. There was an odd quiet and grace about his movements, his body bowing and weaving like grass in a summer wind. He felt himself swimming languorously with the fish. Slowly he moved off until he was standing in front of a great rock. Lichen and moss had mottled and softened the harsh brittle greyness of the surface. Turlough looked like a sapling before its bulk.

Crouched in his concealment, Seamus smothered a nervous laugh. He wanted to call out to his friend, but something held him back. He did not want to be seen or heard and squatted lower in the undergrowth.

Carefully, Turlough removed the fish from his shoulder and laid them head to tail, one above the other on the great stone. Without thinking he ripped up some nearby foxgloves and cow-parsley and spread them in an arc about the two salmon. He stepped back to admire his handiwork. The shape and colour had released life from the stone. He was enraptured. Caught up in his fantasy, he bowed his head and raised his hands heavenward. For some minutes he embraced the heavens, then slowly he crossed his arms on his breast as he lifted his face to the sky. The cloud cover was still, but glowing from the sun behind. For a single moment he thought he could feel the heat of the huge boulder radiating on him. A strange notion that he could lift the boulder flickered into his mind. Slowly he laid his hands on it and stared into the lifeless eyes of the salmon.

The symmetry of their shape had cut into the stone as if permanently imprinted there. There were words in Turlough's mouth, but he could not find them. In dizzy confusion he sank to his knees, then rolled on to his back watching sky and land fuse. The energy inside him felt like laughter that had been quenched to contentment.

Seamus could bear his friend's antics no longer. He burst out at him as he began moving towards him. 'Turlo, you must have baked your brains or something. You're daft as a brush. The priest would have you roasted on the stones of hell if he saw you.'

Suddenly Turlough could not contain himself and roared with laughter. The reference to baked brains and hot stones was ludicrous. Its unintentional mockery drove his laughter into hysteria.

'You mad bastard, you're away with the fairies, that's for sure. Come on, let's get these things home. What the hell were you doing, anyway?'

Turlough's laughter subsided as he noted the irritation in his friend's voice. He shrugged his shoulders at the question. Even if he had known the answer, Seamus would never understand it. He wasn't so sure he did himself. He felt a rising annoyance and embarrassment with himself. There was a world inside him that he kept hidden, but there were moments when he forgot. He felt foolish and tried to make a joke of the events.

'I was just blessing the Fish for Friday, Seamus.'

'Jesus, Turlo, your tongue is going to get you crucified someday.'

'All right, all right. Take these and let's be going. Do you ever get sick of fish on Friday? I don't think they are so clever though, I mean about finding their way back to the river. Maybe, the water itself has memory! Think of it Seamus, if all the rivers and oceans had a memory of their own!'

But Seamus wasn't listening. He had already set off.

The pleasure of these childhood memories eased Turlough and seemed to bleed away the anxious questions that his fevered mind had thrown up. His eyelids closed with the weight of sleep. As a child he loved to dream and he wanted to dream now. He lay back and surrendered to the pull of sleep.

Two First Love

Journal of Mrs McDermott-Roe

February 16th, 1738

An exhausting day, listening can be more demanding than doing.

When I entered his room he had managed to raise himself on the pillows. He was holding a statue of the blessed Virgin. His fingers were gently caressing the statue's eyes. I wanted to leave, but he insisted I remain.

He asked me how many years he had been coming to the house. Before I could answer, he said it was a kindly and gracious refuge. I corrected him telling him that this was his home, not a refuge! He answered me as if he had not heard. 'There are some places we can't go back to. Do you think "can't" means never?'

Then he began speaking softly in his confessional voice. He has always been obsessive and this has been an irritation and a curse. I have had little time for the affectations this produced in him. But I began to feel ashamed of these thoughts as he spoke. I have never heard him speak of his parents with such intimacy. Yet his memories are full of the turbulent emotions that he brought with him when he first came to live here.

He complains much of pains in his head. It is a sickness he has carried all his life. But the pains are accompanied by fearful flashes of memory that I only half understand.

I remember those years. They were difficult for everyone who was close to him. He was intense and restless and sometimes he could be dismissive. His delirious ramblings make me think he is trapped in those early years, alone and afraid. I shiver each time I hear him calling for his mother or cursing old Manus McCormack. He's too close to the dead.

February 19th, 1738

God forgive me, but sometimes I cannot wait to be out of his room. In the mornings I am afraid to enter it.

These last few nights have been strange and frightening. Sometimes I hear him laughing to himself. There is something horrible about it; it is unkind and mocking laughter. At other times I have stood outside his door trembling and terrified. I hear him whispering and talking to himself. At times he shouts and curses and calls out the names of people I had almost forgot and who are long dead.

It's as if they are all there with him in the room. Yesterday, when I took his hand to comfort him, he called me Bridgit Cruise! I will not have my home haunted by these ghosts, no matter how much he loved them. Bridgit Cruise never loved him, but even in his last days he clings to her. Her surname should have been curse, not Cruise.

> *Holy Mary, Mother of God,*
> *Pray for us sinners now*
> *and at the hour of our death.*
> *Amen.*

Home was no longer a refuge for Turlough. He felt suffocated and more often now he wanted to be away from it. His love for the place and his parents had changed. The years had changed them also. His mother had always been light and gay in the house. Though she still had a bright spark of determination, her instinctive quickness was gone. Her presence now had an air of grace and slow beauty. She was the harmonising element in the lives of the Carolans. Often Turlough would notice her silently watching him and his father. Though time had aged her, her blue-green eyes retained their youth. She would smile at him as she noticed him looking at her, and then her eyes would light up and seem to dance in her face. For Turlough, they were unchanging signs of confidence and assurance.

His father rarely noticed these looks between mother and son. Equally Turlough never sought out his father's eyes, which were cold and fixed, and seemed to stare through everything. Turlough was afraid of their intensity, for he did not know precisely what lay behind them. They were two perfect circles of polished granite, set in the whites, lustrous like pale opal tinged with the pink blur of bloodshot at his tear duct. He was afraid of their hidden power, but was drawn to his father by the deep hurt that lay hidden in them. Resignation and despair seemed to be his father's constant emotions. Turlough could not bear the tensions of these two pairs of eyes. It seemed that he could not escape them when he was at home. Yet, though they were there, they asked nothing of him. Sometimes he wished they would, and yet dreaded that they might.

It was his mother who was more aware of the restlessness in him. Turlough had lost the awkward coltishness of young adolescence. His curious, introspective nature, which had once made his father remark, 'There's a want in that one,' was gone, and was replaced by curiosity and enthusiasm. In his mother's eyes Turlough was becoming a handsome young man. The angularity of his face was resolving and his unkempt shoulder-length hair emphasised his growing masculinity. Sometimes she saw shadows of his father in his face. When he was bothered by his frequent headaches, his expression became intense. His mouth fixed itself into a thin line, as if he was trying to prevent himself from speaking. His eyes simultaneously became hooded. On such occasions he would make an excuse to go off alone, just as his father had done.

He was glad to be away from the house. The pain in his head seemed to grow in its contained atmosphere. He could explain this a little to his mother when he was alone with her, but he was fearful even to approach his father. His mother was sensitive to his dilemma and knew there was no medicine for what she called 'soul pain'. She told him that everyone feels sad to leave their childhood behind and is afraid of what the future may hold. The only remedy, she confessed, was of his own making: he must take hold of whatever life presented him with and use it to his own purpose. She suggested that he visit old Manus McCormack in the village and perhaps become his pupil. McCormack had a fine mind, lacking only a listener, and anyone who listened enough could learn much.

At first the village was strange to him and he did not look forward to his visits with McCormack. But as time went on he felt less need for his childhood companions and looked forward to his visits. One day he brought Seamus Brennan with him. Seamus, being more garrulous than Turlough, felt no discomfort and enjoyed the village but after only twenty minutes at McCormack's he left quickly, arranging to meet Turlough later for the journey home. When they met, Seamus's breath had the smell of cheap whiskey on it.

'Christ, God Almighty, Turlo, that oul one smells of piss and sour soup and on top of that he is crazier than you are. You're a fittin' pair, all right, but I think I'll stay on the outside of his door.'

Turlough only laughed at his friend. Seamus lived in a small world and had no desire to complicate it by listening to a 'smelly old man telling stories'. But Turlough loved them and the old man's enthusiasm made the stories all the more intriguing. At first his infirmity upset Turlough and he would not look him in the face, but as he listened and watched him move about the room he became less concerned. For hours McCormack would fill the young man's mind with stories of the ancient Greeks and Romans with such enthusiasm that they seemed to live only on the other side of the mountains. He would quote long passages of the scriptures in Latin and compare Christ's teaching to the ideals of men called Plato and Socrates, but not before he had taught his pupil how to read and write. Turlough's fascination with the stories made him a fast learner. He became a daily visitor, and McCormack never wasted the opportunity to 'spread his wisdom to the wanting', as he often said.

For months Turlough sat entranced, only half understanding the torrent of words that came like a flash flood from the old man's mouth. Half the time he knew the old man was oblivious of him. He talked often of cities and the people who lived in them, and to Turlough they seemed more foreign than the Greeks and Romans. Above all he loved the old man's reminiscences about his own life. He was, for Turlough, the grandfather he never had and he introduced him to life in a way that his father never could. There were echoes of his father in old McCormack, and yet there were times when he thought his father was much older than his teacher.

'I didn't always look like a shrivelled old mushroom. I had my day and I could tell you things about life that no book can teach you.' As he spoke, a mournful silence enveloped the old man as he became lost in memories. His big brown eyes rolled in his head.

'Like you I always wanted to read and write. I was a sickly child and too feeble to do any kind of work. The priest from the neighbouring village took pity on me. I would disappear for hours to visit him. One time I nearly froze to death travelling home. My uncle had no time for these excursions.' The tenor of his voice changed, he became gruff and chastising. ' "We got on well enough without learning. There's no sense in you dirtying your hands on it," he would say, but I persisted. When I had learned all the priest could teach me, he laid his hands on my shoulders and, looking straight into my face, he said, "I've nothing else left. I have done my best by you." I was sad and afraid that I might never see him again. Because I was fit for no other kind of work, my mother had been teaching me to sew. As an excuse to continue seeing my priest, I sewed him a confessional collar.'

McCormack paused to remember the moment more fully. Turlough waited patiently. Then the old man showed him an elaborate confessional collar he had made. The rich tracery and fine needlework were full of vigorous invention and colour, with tiny birds and beasts and strange holy symbols. To his youthful mind it was soft and warm and more full of love than all McCormack's sermons and lectures. The old man paused and thought for a moment, then turned slowly to Turlough. 'You know, when he draped himself in it you felt he was immersing himself in something that transported him.'

The old man seemed to slip back into his reverie. Turlough turned away and looked out of the window. He opened it and felt a cool breeze stir the hair from his face. He breathed in the heavy smell of sun-baked iron and stone, mixed with the scent of damp thatch and burning peat. The village seemed to seep into the room. On a small stool he noticed a crumpled piece of his teacher's sewing. The patterns on the material were like childish abstract hieroglyphics. Overcome by pity, Turlough looked outside.

There was an austere simplicity in the low stone houses and cabins as they spread out from the village over the hills. The heat was sultry and cast a waxy yellow veneer over the distant vista. In a doorway a woman sat chopping roots. Beyond, in the pub, the men were clinking jugs together. Turlough thought of the priest poring solemnly over some holy book, readying himself for his weekly castigation. The village seemed to be submerged in resigned frustration. Perhaps he was, himself. The many months he had been visiting old McCormack had created an unease and expectation in him. But he was unsure – for what?

Turlough looked at the river glimmering dully beyond the village. He wondered what its destination was and then about his own. Where would life take him and what other lives would merge with his? The village was so small a world to grow old in. The old man had filled his head with questions he only half understood. And when Turlough approached him in search of answers, the only one he got was that answers were for fools. 'Everything changes,' McCormack would declare. 'And the only thing of any value, is the question.'

Behind him Turlough heard a noise like rustling paper. The old man's shoulder blades twitched sharply beneath his heavy woollen waistcoat.

'What's taken you?' Turlough asked.

'I was thinking of my young priest. He must be all withered away in the ground. He died after he had shown me how to read and write. I suppose I'll go the same way.' Turlough touched his forearm gently.

The old man smiled. 'Age makes us foolish with longing.' He paused, then sighed deeply. 'I can see neither the needle nor the thread and yet I go on sewing, lad, and see nothing. But my fingers don't deceive me.'

The old man fell silent, then began again. 'At prayers this morning I found I had lost another tooth. I had precious few as it was,' he laughed. 'But I don't remember losing it. So I suppose I am starting to wither away myself.'

Turlough moved back to the window. He felt that even now, without knowing it, the old man was telling him something about meeting death calmly. Turlough gazed out. Behind him, the old man said something about being washed down and laid out. Turlough felt embarrassed and began to study the street.

A window in the two-storey house opposite opened, framing a display of wild flowers tucked into an old, cracked jug. The delicate blue of wild hyacinths was mixed with wood sorrel. The heart-shaped trefoil leaves and white flowers were a perfect accompaniment. The faded dull wash on the walls was lifted by them. Turlough thought of old McCormack and his colourful embroidery and of the wild flowers his mother collected daily. But his thoughts were suddenly distracted as a girl appeared at the window.

Letter from Bridgit Cruise

Dearest Cousin,

I do not know what I would do if I was unable to write to you. I miss the companionship of someone my own age. When I say so to my father, he only complains that if I want company then I should marry and not be bothering him about it.

My God, marriage indeed. I'm hardly seventeen yet, but sometimes I think I am older than my stupid father.

Do you remember the mischief we used to get up to before you went away to Longford? We had such fun then. I have been so bored trying to be a young woman and 'well behaved'!

Well, I refuse to be 'well-behaved' and 'placid' like one of my father's geldings. I am going to misbehave several times a week lest I become an old woman before I have found out what it's like being a young one.

I must tell you about something that happened a few weeks ago. I was sitting upstairs arranging some flowers in my window. Do you remember that hideous jug that we almost smashed and then blamed it on your brother?

Well, just as I was arranging the flowers, I saw someone watching me from Manus McCormack's house. I didn't recognise the face and it just stared and stared. I stuck my tongue out, but it was as if he didn't see me. Believe it or not, I think he was staring at the flowers.

I was about to close the shutters when I saw our tabby cat on old Manus's roof. Do you remember her? She had big white patches around her eyes that made her look more like an owl than a cat. She was perched on the edge of the roof with a young pigeon clamped in her mouth. The poor thing was flapping its wings furiously and I was terrified the cat might unbalance and fall to the ground.

I flung open the window and began shouting and clapping my hands. 'Shoo, shoo,' I kept shouting and then ran back into the room, where I found a petticoat and started waving and flapping it from my window.

My shouting roused the face and soon I saw a young man crawling through the tiny gabled window and up on to the roof. It was Turlough Carolan. I knew him, as his father shoes our horses.

He slid down the roof like a snake, if you can imagine such a thing. For a moment he hesitated. He had a curious look on his face, more puzzled than afraid.

Tabby seemed bored, unconcerned by the slaughter she had committed and by Turlough sliding towards her. In an instant he grabbed her. She pawed the air in protest, but held fast to the pigeon. Her rescuer stood and held her up like a trophy, just as the cat had the baby pigeon. Man, beast and bird were perched on the roof, with plumes of turf smoke curling round them in the soft afternoon sunlight. It was a strange sight. I could hardly contain myself.

Suddenly Turlough became aware of his perilous position. He flailed his arms wildly to regain his balance. The cat screeched and the pigeon fell at his feet, to be trampled as he stumbled to find a firm foothold. I was furious and hammered on the window sill with my palms: 'Let her go, let her go, you'll choke her. Do you hear? Let go of my cat!'

Turlough seemed dumbfounded and let go of the cat, who disappeared with a loud hiss. Then guess what he did. He lifted the dead bird and stood looking at it. Then he set it down gently and looked over at me. He had the most pathetic expression on his face. I swear if I had commanded him to fly up into the sky he would have done so and no doubt ended up like the pigeon, hanging from the eaves.

Well, I must admit his antics confused me. Instead of wanting to laugh, I felt embarrassed and guilty, so I opened the window and called out, 'What are you staring at? What kind of halfwit are you, anyway? I wanted you to rescue the cat, not strangle the creature. If the poor thing's hurt, I hope you fall and break your neck.'

Believe it or not, he shouted back at me, 'Don't lean out so far. And mind what you wish on others doesn't happen to yourself. I'm done with saving stupid creatures!'

I slammed the shutters and window and laughed aloud. His cheek surprised me. And what do you think? Turlough Carolan was still sitting on Manus's roof at sunset.

I think I might see more of Mr Carolan, though I have heard it said he is the oddest creature.

Your favourite cousin, Bridgit
(Hide this letter from my aunt.)

The evening air was cool on the roof. He gathered his clothes about him. The village below looked different from this perspective. 'Who was that cheeky hussy, anyway?' he thought to himself. Suddenly, and for no reason he could understand, he felt awkward. He turned to position himself more securely. As he moved, his foot came out of his shoe, which had lodged itself between the thatch and the roof timbers. He felt the trapped shoe was mocking him. His naked foot was another indignity. Furtively he glanced at the empty window, then scrambled up behind the chimney stack.

From his vantage point he followed the immense loop of the river as it snaked across the land. It glowed red in the sunset. To the east a great cloud moved slowly like a blue rag being pulled over the sun, giving a purple tint to the evening. Enervated and uneasy, Turlough sat squashed against the chimney, caught up in the nightscape and fascinated by the strangeness in it and in himself.

He began to visit McCormack more frequently. Often now his old friend would ask him to read to him from a book. If the old man dozed off, as he frequently did, Turlough would leave him and go pottering about outside. Several times he saw the young woman leaving the house opposite and she would nod to him. If he saw her leaving from inside McCormack's, he would make an excuse to leave himself. Then he would hang about the village waiting for a glimpse of her. He had learned her name from McCormack. When he pretended to meet her accidentally in the village, he would nod and greet her with a shy 'Afternoon, Bridgit Cruise.' He was delighted when she returned his greeting, using his own name.

For weeks Turlough was restless. He wandered about the countryside near his home, but now it seemed like a vast empty space. He remembered McCormack telling him about a Roman who had written about farming in the hills somewhere in Italy and how McCormack had impressed on him that he must see the essence of how people lived. He thought then, as McCormack spoke, that he had understood what he meant. Now he wasn't so sure. Things were not simple any more.

Restlessness drove him from home and he took to disappearing for long periods. At other times his mother would watch him fidgeting about the house. She knew something was worrying him, but she also knew she could not speak to him about it. She sat close to the fire mending old shirts or patching coats and watching him. Occasionally she would turn to ask him something, but his look pained her and the question died in her mouth. She wanted to draw him out, but she felt helpless. Sometimes she thought it was her questions which forced him from the house. He always left mumbling, 'Goodbye, I won't be long.' The door would close quietly and his mother would look at it and then back at her handiwork. The emptiness of the room pressed in on her.

Like water blown by the wind, Turlough became more agitated as he tried to resolve the disturbance within him. The more he tried, the more the water broke and rippled out in ever-widening circles. At the centre was a woman's voice and teasing laughter. Turlough's body felt heavy and awkward. Love fired his imagination and his body demanded it. But it was only a notion and its meaning frightened him.

The autumn air pierced through his worn shirt. He wanted desperately to see Bridgit again. The thought of her made him oblivious to the growing cold. Occasionally a distant noise – cattle lowing, the noise of door slamming or more often the mournful sound of booming corncrake – called his thoughts from their preoccupation out into the landscape and the dimly lit houses spread through it. He remembered bits of conversation he had heard from people who knew only pieces of news. These fragments created another world, where whole villages had been emptied of their young men. He knew that many families from the outlying farms had rarely visited the village of late, and when they did there seemed to be fewer of them and less of their produce to sell in the market.

He remembered on one market day a drunken stranger roaring about men being burned off the face of the earth and how the land was melting like wax and rotting with shame. He remembered an old farmer embracing his son in a tearful goodbye and when the son had left the father cursed the land that demanded the blood of its own. Turlough didn't understand it then and only half understood it now. He tried to imagine the din of distant battlefields. Blood and slaughter were in every conversation and he didn't want to think they were waiting for him, too.

Fine rain enveloped the village. Turlough found himself walking to McCormack's house, where he would make him some thin soup and listen to his stories until he fell asleep. He entered, and was met by the familiar greeting, 'Well lad, back again.'

The room was pungent. About the fire hung old vests and socks, which the old man was forever washing. He had told Turlough many times he had no intention of going into the cold earth unprepared. The smell of the smouldering fire and the two dogs which sat steaming in the ashes filled the room. Age had its own familiar odours and he was comfortable now with McCormack's dishevelled home. There was something permanent and familiar here. It was a refuge to him.

'How's your day?' Turlough asked.

'As always,' came the reply. 'Have you any news?'

'I thought you might have some.'

Turlough fished in the hanging pot and tossed a few bones into the corner. The dogs moved off towards them, reluctant to move from the heat.

'I'll put in some water to loosen this. Where have you put it?'

The old man gestured in the direction of the window ledge and as Turlough picked the jug up he looked out at the house opposite. A movement from the window threw him into a panic.

'I'm going to fix that window upstairs, there'll be draughts enough this winter without inviting more.'

'Aye,' the old man replied. His voice heavy with sleep. He knew that having someone in the room with him was a comfort and the old man would doze now while the soup cooked. Turlough threw some wood on the fire, then stole silently up to the attic and towards the small window. He wanted to open it and call out, but he was afraid. He knew Bridgit would leave instantly. He cursed the growing darkness and the silence that made his every noise seem like a cannon roar. Within minutes she was no more than a moving shadow. Turlough was resigned. But then a soft glow lit the room he had been staring at.

He saw her lay out some clothes. He was edgy with excitement as she moved about the room. Finally she gathered a small white bundle into her arms, and lifting the candle left the room. Turlough raced to the room below. The old man was snoring deeply. One of the dogs looked up. He ignored both and went to the fire, where he lifted the bubbling broth from the hearth. He set it away from the flames and then took himself to the door, where he stood silent and intent. For some minutes he waited, but no one emerged from the house opposite. He watched and waited until he could wait no longer. With a last furtive glance at the old man and his dogs he stole silently into the damp and darkening night.

The village seemed sodden and his footsteps were heavy, as though he was walking through a winter bog. Unperturbed, he moved stealthily round to the rear of her house. Perhaps she would be in the kitchen. The land had been cleared at the back of the house to allow a small cart to be moved and provide enough grazing for a few animals. Firewood was piled near the door and beside an old rainwater barrel a small window glowed.

Turlough stood, unsure whether to approach, as if the glow would burn him. A movement from inside made him doubly anxious and doubly compelled, and like a young animal being teased towards food he moved slowly towards the window.

Bridgit stood with her back to him at a small table near the deep, pulsing red of the fire. Slowly she poured steaming water from a large black cauldron into an old cream basin. With some effort she replaced it by the fire and with the palms of both hands wiped the beads of sweat from her forehead and temples. Then, from a jug beside the basin, she added more water to cool the first. She took a taper from the hearth and lit it in the fire. Her eyes scanned the room, and finding a candle she lit and placed it on a shelf above the table.

Unlacing the strings about the neck and front of her white nightshirt, she slid it off her shoulders. As she raised her elbows to extricate her arms, her back arched and her head turned upwards, revealing her profile. She seemed content and had lost the animation and anger which she had when he first saw her. She shook the long hair back from her face, blowing away the last stubborn strands.

With one hand clutching the garment about her waist, she began carefully to bathe her body. Her movements as she washed her shoulders and arms were slow and languid. Every few moments she would take up a small cloth and pat herself dry. Rolling her nightshirt about her waist like a garland, she raised her hands to her neck and gathered up her hair, rolling and pushing it on top of her head.

The wispy hair at the nape of her neck was a revelation to Turlough. His thoughts were becoming confused. He thought of a baby's downy head, of young birds in first feather and the smell of his mother's hair. He had never experienced such confusion before. He shivered, but not from the cold.

The fine rain had built up a skin of water on the window and in the growing darkness it had become silvered and opaque. The glow of light behind was a tarnished yellow. For an instant he thought to wipe the window, but he was afraid. A feeling of guilt, and possibly shame, mixed with desire, immobilised him. He felt he could not touch the window. He looked at the sky and saw the dull pewter moon glowing. The window was a mirror of the moon and burned into his eyes in the chill night air.

Inside, Bridgit Cruise was oblivious. She was kneeling before the fire as if to take its heat into herself. She turned her head so her long wet hair could dry against the flames. A towel was draped about her shoulders to keep the cold, wet streaks of hair off her back. She looked at the small window, shining black and silent, and got up to cover it with two wooden boards, which lay on the ledge. Clasping the towel to her throat she pattered across the floor. In mid-stride she recoiled and jerked one of her bare feet into the air. She cursed quietly and looked over her shoulder at her upturned foot. She saw nothing, but dusted her foot as she searched for what had stabbed her. Nearing the window she saw her reflection. At first frightened and then intrigued, she stared. A young slip of a girl with boyish features stared back at her. The two figures looked at one another and then away, as if they were afraid.

Bridgit lifted the towel from her shoulders and scrutinised her reflection. Her damp hair in the candlelight accentuated the bones in her face. The girl in the mirror of glass had small breasts, timidly pointing upwards. She lifted her eyes as embarrassment broke into a smile and the girl smiled back. For a moment she looked questioningly at the glass, then pouted her lips as if to kiss the window. The girl in the glass anticipated her and offered her lips in return. Without thinking, Bridgit kissed her.

The cold of her lips against the glass made her start. She recoiled back into the room and quickly extinguished the candle. She stood bathed in firelight and listened to the night pressing in on her excitement. Laughter bubbled up inside her as she pulled the nightshirt up from her waist and struggled into it.

Outside Turlough heard her soft, incomprehensible laughter. He slouched off, confused, cold and sweating. What had happened this night he was as yet unsure; he was only sure that it would remain with him for ever. The glistening silver icon of the window burned into him, scattering his understanding.

For several days Turlough moped about. The night he had stood before the window troubled him. There was no one with whom he could share the moment, although he wanted to desperately. He could not rest content at home. Even old McCormack's house was no longer the refuge it had been.

Letter from Bridgit Cruise

Dear Cousin,

I am well and have much to tell you since I wrote to you about my admirer on the roof.

It seems he is as 'curious' as people say. I see him regularly now in the village. I must admit he is not as brave as he was on the roof. He is awkward and shy, but very different from the other village lads.

Yesterday I asked one of our stablehands if he knew him. He described him as a 'queer fish' and said he had a fierce temper. When I asked when he had last spoken to Carolan he answered that he couldn't remember. 'He only talks to the "others" at the "rath",' he informed me and when I asked him what 'others', he looked at me as if I was simple. 'The spirit people,' he said, almost whispering the words.

Can you imagine anything more exciting!

Remember to keep these letters to yourself. My father would not be happy about me conversing with someone who consorted with 'ghosts'.

Write to me soon. I am desperate for some news from the world beyond our village. My father talks of nothing these days but war and slaughter, and when he is drinking with his friends he roars like an old tyrant about a holy war. Even the young men in the village are full of such talk.

Your cousin, Bridgit

The rath sat squat on the landscape like a huge abscess. The land about it was low-lying and provided an uninterrupted view for several miles. To one side and near the lower slope several whitethorns grew, confirming to everyone around it that this was a special place, to be revered and avoided for fear of offending the spiritual inhabitants who were believed to live there.

But for Turlough it had a compulsive attraction. For as long as he could remember he had been drawn to it. He found nothing to fear and laughed at those who avoided looking on it, whispering a protective blessing or making a sign of the cross as they hurried past. He was happy that they should avoid the place and leave it to him. Contrary to what the local people thought, he found it a place of peace and healing. He always went there when the pains in his head attacked him. The quiet and remoteness of the hills seemed to kill the ache. All too frequently his mind would drift off into a kind of waking daydream and somehow there he could absorb the stories McCormack had told him and engage his imagination with those ancient civilisations.

Once while meditating at the rath he had imagined it as Golgotha. In his fantasy he witnessed the savagery and anguish of the moment. He saw it not in the way someone recollects a story, but felt it happening with such intensity that he was sure he could see it. He heard the screaming and the weeping. He smelled the blood and the sweat and the fear and looked down on a sea of faces around him. The faces were brutal and inhuman. They laughed and humiliated him.

He felt his body shiver and then felt hot blotches on his skin as if he had been spat on. Somewhere in the horror women were weeping. He looked down on them and saw their faces buried in their hands. Heaving great sobs of fear and desperation, he called out to them and they lifted their eyes to him. They were filled with a pain that seemed to draw out his own. He thought he was beginning to understand what old McCormack had meant about understanding the essence of how people lived.

Now, however, the rath could not work its magic. Everything was in pieces. His thoughts flew in and out of his head like startled birds. And her face was everywhere. When he tried to capture her image and hold it she disappeared. She had become his tormentor.

He saw her veiled face look up to him. Her eyes were like his father's, deep earthy brown, and the white in which they were set was almost crystal in its brightness. The oval of her face had a tawny hue and it, too, glowed. There was a conspiracy in her face which he could not fathom. When he turned to walk away she called after him and when he pursued her she fled, taunting him. She had invaded his special place, his refuge. He tried to discuss this with Seamus.

'So, you've discovered underskirts! You'll be taking to drink next! But that Bridgit Cruise. Jaysus, Turlo, she's a bit rich for the likes of us! Anyway, she's barely sixteen and the two of us aren't much older, so I . . .'

'Of us?' Turlough interjected. 'Have you some notions in that direction yourself?'

'No fear. I'd rather tickle a trout's belly than try and tickle that one's fancy.'

'Seamus, I'm asking you what I should do, not what I shouldn't. Now talk straight.'

Seamus looked at his friend for a moment, took a long swallow out of the bottle at his feet, looked back at Turlough's face, and then said slowly, but with grave authority, 'Well, that's your answer then.'

'What the hell are you talking about, Seamus?' asked Turlough exasperated.

'Straight talk. Just walk straight up to her and tell her whatever it is you want to tell her. If she takes the bait your shoes are well and truly buckled, and if she doesn't, you're footloose and fancy-free and you can fish again where you want. There now, straight talk.'

Turlough laughed as he looked at Seamus. Though his long woollen overcoat had been neatly patched, it would not see many more winters. His grey flannel breeches were a fitting accompaniment, but the bright yellow stockings and ill-fitting shoes that completed the outfit were incongruous, but perfectly Seamus.

'So, you're an authority on matters of the heart?'

'No! But I see no point in muddying the waters. Between McCormack and your secret communication with the spirits at that unholy rath, and now this Bridgit Cruise business, you're in serious danger of losing your mind completely. Not that you're not half cocked already!'

He loved Seamus's earthy honesty and assurance. He envied Seamus because he would never find himself in the state of confusion in which he now found himself. He was so confused that he began to consider whether Seamus was right. But how? he wondered.

He took this problem home with him, but could not resolve it. McCormack was no help, as his advice was strangely similar to Brennan's. 'Fix your mind on what's in front of you and get it done,' he advised Turlough, who was aware that this was no recommendation for courtship.

On one of the nights that he sat at home trying to find the right way to speak to his mother about his concerns, his father suddenly said, 'Mrs McDermott-Roe has been asking after you lately. She has heard you have been studying with old Manus McCormack in the village and thinks you might make a good companion or some such nonsense. What do you think?'

'I don't know what to think. What does she want me to do?'

'I'm not sure I rightly know. Old McCormack, who you think so highly of is supposed to be a distant cousin.' His father paused. 'The bonds of blood and family were somehow severed by these precious laws that think more of property than of people. Perhaps she's trying to bridge the gap.' He smiled and continued, 'Anyway, it will do no harm. Times change and it's best to be prepared.'

There was much more in his father's thinking than his words conveyed. But Turlough was more impressed by what was not said. He felt his father wanted him to take up the offer. It was another of those unspoken gestures of intimacy and Turlough was happy to comply.

He knew Alderford House well, having been taken there on many occasions by his father. On several of these trips to the big house he had met the family. They were congenial and seemed interested in him, Mrs McDermott-Roe especially. But he had thought little of it and assumed this was simply because his father worked for them. As he grew older, he was often sent alone to the house with a message or perhaps with some sewing his mother had completed for Mrs McDermott-Roe, so he knew the property and the grounds well enough not to be intimidated by what his father proposed. As he thought about it the idea of living at the big house for a while held a curious attraction for him.

Three Smallpox

Alderford House sat back on the low edge of the hillside. A plain house, its only concession to grandeur was the view of the lake which it overlooked. Although it was the biggest house in the area, the McDermott-Roe family made no attempt to promote themselves above their accepted station. The house sat squarely and solidly in the landscape, a landmark to all who passed by it, and many of those who did took advantage of its open and generous hospitality.

Over the months following Turlough's decision, Alderford became his second home. He forged an uneasy friendship with his new patrons and more often than not he took himself to the kitchen. It was large and airy and the white rough-cast walls, which were flooded with light by two large recessed windows contrasted sharply with the dimly lit home he left behind. Above head height a deep wooden shelf skirted the entire room, adorned with plates patterned in brown and blue and green. A great arched fireplace was sunk into the wall furthest from the entrance and a collection of well-worn but sturdy chairs was set out around the rest of the walls. A shelf by the fire carried a range of cooking pots, creating a black shiny tower against the white of the walls. The room was suffused with the aroma of fresh herbs. Turlough felt safe here. The voices of the cook and servants were familiar to him. Their language was his own and was not complicated with words he did not understand. As time passed and his visits became more frequent, he felt himself part of the family.

The McDermott-Roes had notions of hospitality which did not discriminate between family, friends, guests and servants. Each person was an integral working part of the house and each knew their place and their responsibilities. There was a warmth here, less intense and less isolating than at home with his parents. To Turlough's thinking the house seemed to fit his growing self-confidence; it provided him with new interests and a sense of release. Curiously he was beginning to feel more at home here than with his family.

Soon he was moving freely about the house and each new room he discovered was a revelation. These rooms, each one with its own predominant colour, rich in pictures and ornaments, were rooms he could breathe in and confirmed what his father had said to him about times changing and being prepared.

Mrs McDermott-Roe was anxious that he should feel comfortable and encouraged him to take advantage of the tutor she had employed for him. She wanted him to make something of himself. All this attention, and the ability to move about the house as if it was his own, pleased him.

Mrs McDermott-Roe was not unaware of his fascination, but it was his introspection that interested her most. To her, he wasn't simply curious about the new world he found himself in. He seemed always to be questioning the significance of things. When he listened to the tutor he was pensive. He never asked questions. She felt he was locking everything up inside himself and that sometime later, when he was alone, he would take all this information out and examine it. She was puzzled by him. He was handsome and finely made. He was also intelligent and unintimidated by new people. Yet he was solitary and part of him remained remote. At times the idea that he was not really of this world crossed her mind. One day she mentioned this to him.

'It's all the time I spend with the nobles.' Turlough's answer shocked her for a moment. She thought he was referring to her home and her family. Turlough smiled again knowingly, but there was mischief behind his smile. 'I mean the spirits of the rath!'

She did not know how to reply. She waited for some confirmation of humour or seriousness. But his answer confused her even more. 'I know only four places in this world. My home, this house, the village and the rath. And each of them is home to me.'

Turlough, in turn, waited for her to respond. But she did not. For a moment he felt a little stupid, but there was something about this woman. Although she inhabited a different world, he felt at ease in her company. He wanted to tell her things.

'I mean, the tutor talks of France and Spain, of England and

Italy, and though I love to listen and sometimes wonder deeply about them, yet these four places, my homes, I mean, compel me more.' He looked at her again anxiously, not for an answer, but to assure himself that she was listening.

'I love it best of all when he reads poetry or plays music. You know, I sometimes go into the library alone and read to myself the poems he has read to us; and then I go to my rath and I hear the words and the music again . . . only different. I don't know how, only that it's different, like an echo coming back, changed.'

He stopped abruptly. He had surprised himself. He had spoken to no one in this manner before. She smiled at him. 'You have a strange mind, Turlough. But I am sure there is something wonderful there. You must never be afraid to share it. But you must excuse me, we are expecting company.'

As she left the room Turlough felt both relieved and pleased. For an instant the image of Bridgit Cruise flashed across his mind, then selfishly he thought, 'I might yet take the prize that's out of reach of the likes of us, Seamus.'

Letter from Bridgit Cruise

Dearest Cousin,

I swear my father gets more childish as he grows older. I am sure he is more in need of a wife than I am of a husband. And how am I to find one if I am to sit at home and keep him company?

He is constantly anxious about 'the state of the times' and insists that people's minds are poisoned and that nowhere is safe.

I admit there is an atmosphere about the countryside and we hear constant rumours. If I couldn't get out I would suffocate.

I see Turlough Carolan several times a week. It seems he is someone I can talk to, but when I tease him he becomes irritated and embarrassed. One day I suggested to him that he might make a good priest. Well, he went into such a tantrum you wouldn't believe. It's so confusing. Sometimes when I am with him he talks about everything at once. His mind is like a hungry bird furiously hopping from one crumb to the next. He makes me dizzy with his enthusiasm. But on other days he is so quiet and looks sickly. He suffers from severe headaches and it takes him days to recover. I feel sorry for him.

Bridgit

As he thought of it now he was surprised how little Bridgit Cruise had been in his mind since coming to Alderford House. But as his friendship with Mrs McDermott-Roe grew, the idea of Bridgit started to percolate into his thinking again. He had seen her many times in the village. At first he felt unable to muster any more courage than to acknowledge her acquaintance. But the familiarity of Alderford and the people he met there encouraged him. Now if they passed in the village he might pass some throwaway remark. 'How's the pigeon killer?' or, 'Have you tamed the tabby yet?' At first she feigned shock or made some rebuke, but this only encouraged him more. She obviously enjoyed his banter, for in her own time she began to return it. 'Are you still sleeping with the fairies, Turlough?'

One afternoon as he sat on the low bridge waiting for Seamus, she came up to him and said simply, 'I was almost drowned in that river once. It was my own fault, I suppose. I was quite a tomboy when I was young.'

Turlough looked at her, surprised by her sudden appearance and easy conversation. Her voice was full of laughter at his embarrassment.

'I often played with the boys and was better than many of them. Every year when it snowed we had this competition. Each of us would build a snowman along the river bank to see which would last the longest. Every day we would come down to patch and repair them, only to watch them being washed away or disappearing into the ground as the first spring wind rode down the river.'

'And who won?' Turlough found himself asking.

'Me, of course,' she answered, her eyes brightening and her face becoming animated. Then she burst into a full hearty laugh. 'I used to get up in the middle of the night and throw on an old tattered cloak and shawl in case anyone should see me. Then I would sneak down along the river, knocking the heads off the snowmen or kicking the nearest one into the water.'

As she was talking she spun round to Turlough, slapping him on the head and almost pushing him headlong over the parapet. In their panic they grabbed at one another. Bridgit burst out, 'It's a wonder I didn't fall in and drown in the dark.'

'My God, Bridgit Cruise, first you have me nearly killing myself on McCormack's roof and now you're after trying to drown me. There's a bit too much tomboy there yet for my liking!'

Bridgit walked a few steps from him and sat on the wall of the bridge. Traces of laughter were still in her voice, but it was low and apologetic. 'Oh no, that all ended when some of them trailed me into a shed and wanted to pull the clothes from me. They were like young dogs fighting over a scrap of meat. Somehow I wasn't surprised, nor did I cry, and when I drew blood from the most persistent of them they all cleared off, shivering and frightened, like the young dogs they were!'

Turlough stood dumbfounded and shocked at the confession. The intimacy of it was unexpected and he saw himself, standing shivering and squinting through a frosted window. Bridgit could not understand the hurt expression on his face.

'Don't worry, I wouldn't have let you fall in the river. I have to go now, but next time we meet you must tell me about the nights you spend on the rath. You are the talk of the village with your weird ways. Goodbye now, Turlough Carolan.'

For the next few days Turlough was buffeted between emotions of excitement and guilt. He was back where he had been months ago, restless and irresolute. Even the pleasure of Alderford had little effect on him. The classes with the McDermott-Roes' tutor became less inspiring.

Journal of Mrs McDermott-Roe

May 11th, 1686

Our tutor, Mr Crooks is adamant that Turlough has no aptitude for study. His mind, he insists, is rarely in the room with him. Apparently he has the habit of asking odd questions and then leaves the room before the tutor can answer. If there is any answer!

When I spoke with Turlough about this, he said he couldn't stand Mr Crooks' dreary voice, then abruptly declared that he's got more wisdom from his father's silence than all Mr Crooks' jumble of words!

I truly think our Turlough understands things with his feelings rather than his mind. But whatever he understands it is of no consequence unless he can explain it.

However, his surly disposition irritates me so!

Even McCormack seemed to be part of the conspiracy to confuse his emotions and make him too dumb to articulate his thinking. He still visited the old man, but more for companionship than learning. On his last visit McCormack seemed acutely aware of his condition.

'You're very excited today. You're as hot as if you had come out of an oven. Have you looked at that book at all?'

'Every single word. There's an awful lot about love in it. It's as if they had nothing else to think about but falling in love and parting.'

The old man smiled knowingly, then continued more gravely, 'Perhaps everything in life comes to that, young man, and you're quite right, there is nothing else to do. Those who love are happy. You may gain the whole world and it will disappoint you, but love. . . .'

'Will save you.' Turlough stole the words from his mouth. Then he continued, 'But if love disappoints you it's much worse than if the whole world should.' He took another long pause then concluded, 'Only I'm not so sure of the truth of all this.'

As he finished he gave a sceptical laugh. The old man smiled back, 'Surely you don't think I would deceive you. You are too indecisive and hesitant. Remember, when a man begins a journey it is unlucky to turn back!'

'You're one to talk, McCormack. You never married yourself.'

'True, but I never said I never loved. And who has the right to refuse the gift of love?'

As Turlough walked towards his home, he thought over his old friend's words. It was the biggest problem his introspective mind ever had to deal with. Should he ask someone, a guide, to help him through this confusion, or should he leave it to life itself to determine his course for him? Every night for many months Turlough mulled over the possibilities as he trudged through the rain, wind and hail, between the big house, old McCormack, Bridgit Cruise and his home. Was one love worth the sacrifice of the rest? This was the question that constantly confronted him.

His mother, as always, was aware that he was not at peace with himself. She knew from experience that she could do nothing until he chose to come to her. But she knew also, that it was a new Turlough that came and went like a shadow from the house. 'You're fretting like a stray mongrel, Turlough. Remember this is your home and whatever you're looking for, you'll find it here.'

He pretended it was just a return of his headaches again, and this was in part true. Sometimes he even preferred the headaches, as a relief from his other torments.

Perhaps it was the idea of torments that took him to the church. He knew she would be there, but part of him wanted to go regardless of her presence. The church was empty and cold when he arrived. Mass that evening was being held in one of the parishioner's houses. He was annoyed that she wasn't there but glad that no one else was. He thought prayer might answer the questions he didn't know how to answer.

But asking God was even more difficult than asking anyone else. In the cold emptiness of the church he felt that God was not listening because he wasn't there.

Letter from Bridgit Cruise

Dear Cousin,

I am breathless as I write this and when I tell you what has happened you may be breathless also.

I was just coming out of Mass, which was being held in John Healy's house. The priest had been sermonising on war and death and I was desperate to get home. There's too much death in this place of late.

Anyway, as I came out and was wrapping my cloak around me, I saw Turlough Carolan sheltering in the doorway. He was dripping wet and shivering and looked to all the world like an old, homeless tomcat.

He came up to me and was about to speak when Aunt Aileen linked my arm and whisked me out into the night. Turlough followed after us for a few moments, until Aileen loosed herself from me and took him by the collar, telling him to be off with himself. But he was having none of it and informed her not to be so free with her hands and tongue. He looked so bedraggled that I took pity on him and asked Aunt to leave us for a few moments. She, of course, wasn't pleased with this and mumbled under her breath something about wanting to kill both of us for insisting that she should have to wait in the cold! Turlough was furious and told her to take herself away on home and save herself the slaying! Aunt Aileen froze where she stood. She was as much afraid as she was amazed by his effrontery.

I was angry and wanted to laugh. So I took him by the arm and walked on, asking him what he wanted. He looked at me as if I had asked him to solve the riddle of the universe, then answered in a halting, childish voice that he didn't want anything.

There we were, standing in the rain, looking at one another and saying nothing. It was ridiculous and I told him so, and walked off, leaving him with Aunt Aileen. But he quickly caught up with me and walked in silence beside me until we reached our house. I was exasperated with his silent antics. I turned on him and told him that if he had a head for thinking but could get no words out of it he might think of becoming a priest, for the soulless words I had heard at Mass made as much sense as his silence.

Just then Aunt Aileen caught us up and stood waiting. I told her to go on in and inform Father that I had stopped behind to speak with the priest. As she closed the door I told Turlough the same thing as he had told my aunt, to take himself on home.

Well, I am not sure what exactly it was, but the expression on his face changed as if he had been whipped. I couldn't bear it and was about to go in myself when I heard his voice hissing behind me, 'Priest, priest!'

Instantly he grabbed my arm and pulled me to himself and placed his mouth full and hard on mine. I thought he would devour me. I was terrified.

When he pushed me away from him he hissed at me again, 'There's a priest's prayer for you to think on.' His voice was deep and thick and he stared at me, then simply turned and walked into the dark.

I watched him disappear and waited to get my breath before entering the house. Father heard me come in and called out into the hall, 'You've got very godly all of a sudden. Your aunt's already home!'

I ran up the stairs, laughing to myself. If he only knew! It was some minutes before I could compose myself and begin this letter to you.

My God, if father knew what had happened. But can you imagine me and Turlough Carolan? It's impossible – his head is too full of fantasies and now I have become one of them!

Your cousin, Bridgit

All the way home he felt elated. He hardly considered the consequences of his action, but he didn't care. It was out in the open, if only between themselves. He felt sure that she would not reject him completely. In fact, he didn't even consider it. Another thing struck him. For the first time in many months he wanted to go home. He wanted to talk to his mother, but he wasn't exactly sure how to! He seemed to cover the miles from the village in no time. He entered the small cabin with a cheery 'hello', but the response was a stony silence.

Turlough looked confused at the faces of his parents. Anxiety and despair marked them both. His mother was the first to speak. Her voice was angry and she barked at him, 'Where were you, Turlough? And tell me no stories!'

Before he could answer his father crossed the room to her and in a comforting tone said, 'Whist now, there's nothing to be upset about.'

Turlough was doubly confused. He had never been met by this type of reception before. More surprising was the reaction of his parents. He had never seen his mother so angry or his father so tender. It was as if they had changed roles. For a moment he stood stunned. It crossed his mind that they perhaps knew about Bridgit Cruise! Nervously he walked towards the fire. His mother's eyes never left him. The atmosphere in the room was tense.

'I was in the village,' he said sheepishly.

'Well, it's the last time you are to go there and, what's more, there are to be no more disappearances from the house.'

His mother's voice was fearsome in its determination. He wanted to say something, but didn't know what. Instead he looked questioningly at his father. Sean Carolan seemed to understand his confusion and moved towards him. He told him to hang up his coat and bring a stool near the fire. As he did so, he watched his father sit his mother in another chair. This time Turlough wondered if she was ill and he asked her.

Instead of answering, she looked at her husband and he turned to his son, 'No, lad, she's not ill, but there's many about these parts that are. We think it's best you stay at home for the next few weeks until whatever it is moves on.'

Turlough was at once relieved but puzzled. He brought the small stool nearer to the fire and sat on it, all the time watching his mother. Her face was softening and the tension ebbed out of it. 'You don't feel ill do you, Turlough?' she asked.

He replied that he didn't, but that he had heard some of the villagers were, and that the priest had been busy lately visiting farms where people had died. His mother said again that Turlough should stay at home.

'What about Mrs McDermott-Roe,' he asked.

But he was not thinking about Alderford House. The excitement of his stolen kiss was backwashing on him. He desperately wanted to see Bridgit again. This time, when his mother answered, her voice was less demanding and almost matter of fact, 'It's the kind of sickness that doesn't discriminate whom it chooses to visit. We will each have to look to our own. Alderford will have to look after itself.' She paused for a moment, then continued, 'If the priest is visiting the sick, then you are to stay away from the church.'

As she concluded she crossed herself, then moved to the pot sitting in the hearth, saying that she would make something hot for them all.

For the next few weeks the Carolans remained at home in imposed isolation. His father made occasional forays to the forge, and when he did he returned with news of another family stricken with the illness.

But whatever his original worries about not being able to visit the village, Turlough soon forgot them. Being at home again for a prolonged period enabled the family to re-establish the intimacy that had been missing for a while. But this time Turlough found himself turning to his father.

'You know, Father, many of my friends have gone off to the war and the last time I was in the village, people seemed to talk about nothing else. They were angry and defiant like I have never seen them before.'

'Aye, anger's in all of us, lad, and it fills some of us more full of words than we have the sense to understand. But anger can be a good thing. It can restore a sense of dignity and honour to a man. But why, in the name of all that's holy, he would want to take such precious things and spill them with his blood on the land that made him is beyond me.'

Slightly surprised at his father, Turlough told him about old McCormack's regret that he would never have the opportunity to die for his country. Sean Carolan turned his head slowly towards his son and looked deep into his eyes, as if he was searching for something. As he spoke he smiled, 'It's the habit of old men to look back on their youth with regret.'

Before he continued he leaned forward and raked the fire. Turlough knew he was thinking about McCormack's words: 'All of us are born with greatness in us. Many of us never find it or even know what to do with it when we do. Sometimes it's easier to get carried away by great causes than to deal with the greatness within us. War is a bloody madness. It destroys the greatness in men.'

Sean Carolan turned again to his son with the same searching eyes. Quietly he asked, 'Why have you been thinking of this?'

Turlough was about to answer when his father suddenly spoke again. His voice was firm and authoritative. 'You are an only son and your first duty is survival. Your second is to find whatever greatness is in you and to live it!'

His father's words struck Turlough with the force of a commandment. He was almost afraid to speak. But he knew that behind the authority of the words was a huge tenderness. He began to speak, at first hesitantly, then with a hasty assurance, 'I sometimes see things and feel things, strange things that I don't understand. I feel them so much at times that they make my head hurt.'

His father's eyes never left the fire as Turlough told him of his strange vision by the river. He wanted to speak about other similar moments, but he stopped, waiting for his father's response.

His father sat for what seemed a long time, staring into the fire. Then finally he got up and walked to the door, where the harness hung. He bent down for a moment and returned with stone bottles and a broken bowl from the table. Slowly he poured some liquid in it and took a deep drink before handing it to his son. Turlough drank, not knowing what else to do. Then his father said simply, 'You were born in water and I bathed the birth bloods from you in river water. Water will always have a meaning for you.'

Then he fell silent. Turlough knew he would say no more. This was one of these moments he remembered from many years ago, when he was a child, receiving the silent knowledge of his father.

Lettters from Dr John Blakley, Physician to the Parish at Ballyfarnan

To, Richard Sheridan
Royal Infirmary
Kilmainham

Dear Richard,

I knew it was foolish to write you about the illness that has befallen us in the county and especially in the parish of Ballyfarnan. My head knew it, but my heart did not want to speak its name.

Too many unconnected deaths in a short period and all with similar symptoms mark it for what it is. Some call it the scourge or curse. Some whisper about a plague and others simply call it the pox. But whatever name they give it they address it with fear.

Even the priest's prayers as he recited over the dead and dying had a sense of awestruck wonder and majesty about them, but it was not the priest alone who has found new energy for his prayers. Everyone in the village and the outlying hills has made time for their devotions.

The 'Hail Mary' is instantly on everyone's lips and in their minds. The Queen of Heaven's arms are heavy with the dead and the dying and her ears are ringing with urgent and dread petitions being hourly sent up to her. For some the unseen threat and imminent death has been too much. Every day Maura Fagan takes up her position on the bridge that marks the entrance to the village and every passer-by is met with an exhortation to flee the wrath of God. But from the wrath of smallpox there is no flight and none are exempt from its arbitrary touch. Though the village has been the worst to suffer, the outlying homes and small farms were no less subject to its contamination. There is little we can do but wait and save what we can.

Your friend, John Blakley

To, Richard Sheridan
Royal Infirmary,
Kilmainham

My dear old friend,

They say that great suffering brings people together and is the proof of friendship. Though years and many miles separate us, I am grateful that our friendship has survived through the barbarous history of this pitiful land.

I cannot give you any better news of our desperate plight. Indeed I can only state that things get worse by the day. Thank you for your offer of help, but you will know there is little anyone can do. We have run out of coffins and what wood we can find is used to burn the dead. I have been cursed and abused relentlessly for this unholy act. One woman tore at my face and screamed that it was a sacrilege against God when I ordered her dead son to be burned. People do not seem to understand that the only sacrilege against God is this cursed plague. It is a hideous irony to me that people who never in their lives knew the comfort of bed linen are delivered to their maker in a winding sheet!

The most difficult duty is not burning and burying the dead but separating families. It causes me great pain to separate a man from his wife or a mother from her sick child, when we know that neither will see the other again in this life.

The war and the slaughter that have tormented this land in previous years have left our community, like many others, devoid of meaningful numbers of men and it is again a pitiful sight to watch women and children carry the dead from their homes.

I tell you, Richard, this is the landscape of Hades. I have heard too much talk of salvation and grace of late, and when I hear it now my anger bubbles and steams like the lime pits in which I have had to bury my friends and acquaintances. All our years of study together have not made me immune to this sight.

It is not enough that the disease destroys our bodies before it finally kills us. It eats even at the souls of the living. A few days ago I spoke with some of those who had lost a loved one in the early days of this curse. It was an effort for them to remember or even imagine the person they had loved and lost.

If I live through this it is only because I have made myself as blind as they have become.

This is all I can ask of you, Richard. Help me to remember and to imagine life beyond this horror.

Your dearest friend, John Blakley

Even the Carolan household could not escape the smallpox. His mother was the first to sense its presence. She knew the coughing and the constantly running nose that had been bothering her son for some days were more than a seasonal cold. She knew that no poultice of herbs or burning of incense would cure what she dreaded was brewing in her son's body. One evening, when the coughing had been worse than usual and she had heard her son curse the cold, she informed her husband that for the next few weeks he should spend his nights at the forge. He only nodded his agreement, for he knew. But neither of them was stoic enough to resist the need for prayer. His mother sat at his bed, her husband beside her, while both of them poured the words of their prayer over Turlough with a fearful enthusiasm not usual to this family.

After a week of moping about the house wrapped in a blanket, under his father's greatcoat, Turlough was felled by the first blow of the illness. For four days he writhed and sweated in a high fever. He talked incomprehensibly and occasionally screamed. In his lucid moments he complained of a tortuous backache that would neither let him lie nor stand, and his head ached worse than he could remember.

His mother could only listen, wipe the sweat from him, and ensure that the fire was well banked and that he had plenty of covers when he broke into shivers. But after these four days

Turlough felt better. Though his face and body were drained by the stress of his illness, he drank a little of the herb soup his mother had prepared and asked after his father.

Mrs McDermott-Roe had heard from Sean Carolan of Turlough's illness and sent a doctor to visit him. He brought blankets and food and assurances from Mrs McDermott-Roe that should the family require anything else they only had to ask. Then, looking directly at Turlough's mother, he confirmed what she already knew, 'He's in God's hands now. There is little more to be done but fall on his mercy.'

To console her, he explained that not all die from smallpox, but none who are visited by it are left unscarred. Time would tell and she could only minister to him as she had already.

Turlough was worried by his father's absence. The house seemed strange without him and thinking of him, he asked his mother to boil up some water and fill the basin his father always washed in. 'I feel as if I have been sleeping in a bed of nettles. If I had the energy, I would strip this skin off me with my bare hands!'

By the open fire and in the glow of candlelight Turlough's mother gently bathed his rash-reddened body. There was neither concealment nor embarrassment between them. When he asked her if she was afraid, she answered, looking into his wearied face, 'Only for you.' For several nights they repeated this ritual in silence.

Every morning, if the weather permitted, she would leave the house while he slept and gather great bunches of wild flowers and herbs. When she returned she would press the juice out of the flower heads and add it to the water with which she cooled his body when she had washed him.

Soon the itch began to disappear and the rash erupted into small pimples, which continued to grow until they resembled blisters on his skin. Turlough told her he looked like a plucked hen. She smiled and brushed his hair, telling him he was much too handsome for that.

For most of the time he was too exhausted to make conversation, but she was aware that his mind was restless and his sleep was filled with dreams. Strange words and names poured from his mouth. Sometimes he sobbed and sometimes he swore. There was a deep anger in him that frightened her. Occasionally he would sit bolt upright, with his eyes wide and staring. He would curse and roar and attack the dark with flailing arms and then fall back exhausted. Some nights when she heard him sob like a child, she would lift his head on to her lap and stroke his forehead with a goose feather and croon quietly to him. Her voice seemed to pass through the torrent of fever assailing him.

Weeks passed and though he grew weaker the fevered onslaughts lessened and his lucid moments grew longer. Considering the worst to have passed his mother sent word for her husband to return. Standing at the door, his eyes scanned the scabs that had formed over the pimples on Turlough's face. His son's body was emaciated and when he looked at his wife he could see how the past weeks had drained her also. He complained to her that she should have come to him sooner. Her answer was quiet but fierce. 'If God demands flesh, he'll only have one man of mine!' And his answer was equally quiet but reassuring, 'You drive too hard a bargain, woman. Come now, sleep, and leave him to me.'

Over the next weeks, his father's ministry to him was no less tender than his mother's. Never before had he witnessed such harmony between them. He had never seen his father's quiet smile so much nor heard his voice so often. He began to understand that it was his father that vitalised the marriage and to feel less distant from him, perhaps because his father began to tell him about his childhood. He told Turlough about the night of his birth and how he had chased the priest. He spoke of how he had bathed him in the river and held him up in the moonlight, and as he spoke he laughed loudly and Turlough laughed with him.

But as life and hope crawled up out of the bowels of despair, Turlough's headaches returned. They were so deep and searing that his eyes began to water and he lost all vision in them for a period. He said nothing for a few days, but finally he complained. His parents turned to one another, wondering which of them could deal with this. They knew, but did not want to admit, what might be happening to their son. His mother first broke the silence, suggesting that his father might ask the McDermott-Roes to send their doctor again. It was a breathing space, a way of putting off for a moment the inevitable.

When he came, the doctor commented on Turlough's remarkable improvement. Then he listened as Turlough explained his headaches and the momentary loss of vision. The doctor looked briefly at his eyes and said authoritatively, 'You have to expect this, young man.' Then he walked to the door with his father. They spoke briefly before the doctor left.

His father was about to speak when his mother interrupted. 'There'll be no deceit between us.' She went quickly to where Turlough lay propped up in his bed.

'You must be strong and unafraid, Turlough. Death has been in this house and has walked by your bed. But he's left alone because you would not go with him. The illness you have lived through has affected your sight – how badly we cannot know, but it will never be the same and it will get worse.'

She ended abruptly. He knew it was to choke back the emotion that was waiting to break into her words. But whatever emotion was there instantly disappeared. Her face took on the familiar mask of angry determination and pride. For a moment it seemed as if her whole body glowed with it. She was willing it to her son and he felt the power of it enter him.

'Will I be blind, Father?' he asked matter of factly.

'It seems likely,' his father answered in the same manner.

This confirmation should have devastated him, yet it didn't. He felt instead that somehow he had been prepared for it. Perhaps the new intimacy that had developed between his parents and himself had diminished the impact of the news. For the next few days their ministrations continued as normal.

One afternoon as he sat by the open half-door watching his mother feed some food scraps to the pig they kept, his eyes slowly glazed over. It was as if someone had smeared cold duck fat across them. He could still see her, but only through this greasy surface.

He wiped his eyes automatically, but the haze remained. He wiped them again, with more effort. As the first throes of panic began, he rubbed them again with the cuffs of his shirt. He sat for a moment and felt himself becoming breathless. Nothing was happening. Instinctively he creased his forehead to lift his eyelids and pulled the underside of his eye downwards with his fingertips. He felt only the coolness of the air enter them. His mother's words came to him again, 'It will never be the same, it will get worse!' He was about to call out to her, but was too frightened and embarrassed. Suffocating panic smothered the words as they fell weakly from his mouth, paralysis and fear clamped him to the chair.

His mother had witnessed the moment, but she held back to see if he would call her. She knew what might be happening and there was little she could do. He must find his own strength. She could support that, but she could not carry him. If he found some measure of inner strength and independence then she could build on it. Blindness was a fearful loneliness and he needed to find his own independence. But even as she thought it, she desperately ached for him to call her. She heard nothing, but an irresistible urge brought her to him.

'Is there pain, Turlough?'

'No, Mother, there's no pain. It's just misty.'

That evening, when she thought her son was asleep, she sat lightly on his bed and brushed his eyes with a goose feather. Turlough was not sleeping, but he did not want to wake up. The room was heavy with a warm silence; it made him drowsy. He dreamt. Sleep was like the land, heavy and black, but curious: dreams were always waiting for him. They pulled him down into themselves. He waited, like someone harbouring a great secret, to be gone into the dreaming dark.

About him the room absorbed the soft low pulse of his breathing and he remembered his mother always telling him to look on the figure of Christ, that he would bless the night. The weight of his father's coat pressed down on him as his mother fitted it gently around the contours of his body. Her warm voice whispering a blessing. He waited to hear it again.

Through the folds of sleep he heard a noise, direct, rhythmic and insistent, pulling him into itself. A confusion of strange images moved across his dreaming mind. A blade, blue against the yellow-green stalks, a woman's hair, the stubble of the field, hard and sharp against his child's feet, like his father's razor scraping across his face. He felt the cold terror of it and he sought the reassurance of his father's huge workman's hands.

Instead he saw a scythe shaft, and a hand clamped upon it. It was like a great still snake. They were women's hands! They were frightening. The great curve of the scything shaft and the soft white hands filled his sleep. He felt giddy; a loathsome taste, as if he had been eating stale tobacco, made him gag. The dream confused his senses. Strangely, his hands and fingers seemed to burn. He opened his eyes. The darkened room felt like a cellar and he shivered. It was all so new to him. Dreams had always been precious secrets that somehow released him. He welcomed them. But this was different. He had never wanted to wake before.

He waited for the familiar room to come back to him. His leaden eyes took in the bowls and jugs glistening dimly; the sticks and spades lying like awkward drunks in the corner; his mother's homespun shawl; the fire softly glowing like a sleeping animal. Somewhere he heard his father breathing, hoarse and slow, and with the reassurance of things familiar, sleep returned.

Suddenly it was back. His own breathing became fierce and tight, as if his chest was a threshing board. His consciousness grew dim, he looked again at the walls, they seemed to move lazily. They swayed towards him as if they wanted to lean over him. He thought he saw his father's boots and heard a shuffling, scraping noise.

And then the wall was gone and a bright meadow stretched out before him. The day was hot and the women bent and moved like grazing cattle as they cut hay. The sun poured down on the crown of his head. The sky was blue, but in the heat it seemed almost black. Rain was coming. In even rows, the women and chattering girls carried on mowing in rhythmic oblivion. He thought he heard singing voices.

A young woman, unlike the rest, was moving among the rows and picking berries. She looked up. Her mouth was like a red wound on the pallor of her skin, and her hands were marbled with the berry juice. Her eyes seemed to follow the line of light that fell on him. They narrowed, then swelled in her face. He could see no colour, only their brightness and their bigness. Slowly she moved towards him, shoulder and breast swinging in gentle rhythm. Beyond and around her he could hear the grass sigh under the strokes of the scythe and fall in neat piles at her feet. Turlough watched her approach. He felt like the grass and was fearful of her.

'Get away, you bad boy.' The woman's voice was like his mother's, but it was threatening. He was rooted, wanting, but unable to run.

'Get away, do you hear?' The voice was more questioning than assertive, then suddenly, 'Go! or I'll mow you down.'

Turlough, frightened but defensive, cried out, 'No. You will not!'

He watched the woman's shoulders arc. The scythe shaft burning in her hands, her body formed a black silhouette against the sun. Only the white flash of her mouth was visible. Then he heard the hollow swish of the blade's silver crescent.

Turlough screamed, with the high-pitched whinny of a frightened horse.

Her eyes, vacant, but still bright, peered at him. It was as if they were burning into his own. Turlough's senses dimmed. Out of the darkness he saw a body laid out on a door. Night was gathering about and the body was bathed in light, but he could not define its source. Everything in him recoiled and he wanted to hide, but he felt he was being drawn mysteriously to the body. He was being forced to look it in the face.

His senses would not submit to the darkness. The room came back to him. It was stuffy and smelling of calves. Flies were buzzing about the ceiling and a face with black and swollen lips was fast disappearing in the dark. Turlough could not forget the wild swishing scythe which had lacerated him in the meadow. He heard it spinning slowly away from him. With a huge effort he tried to rid himself of the delirium, but the girl, the berries, and the burning flesh had eaten into him like rust into iron.

'It's nighttime,' he said to himself. Believing that the sound of his own voice would dispel the dream. Somewhere a disembodied voice spoke inside his fevered head, 'It's always night-time.'

Four Purgatory

Sermon given by an itinerant priest at Mass Rock, Keadue, 1687

What can we say of this stranger that has come amongst us? This stranger that is unwanted by us yet is everywhere with us; seated at our tables, by the bedsides of loved ones and walking constantly at our side.

This stranger has turned many of us into prophets. It has made great theologians and mathematicians of many of this congregation. Soothsayers and chroniclers are everywhere among us.

But such piety and religious fever are the poisonous offspring of those who in ignorance and fear have flirted with this stranger.

I tell you now this superstitious folly cannot and will not usurp the revelations of the true faith and the holy word of God.

And before this congregation loses itself in a sea of superstition let me remind you that all suffering is purposeful to those who are committed to our Lord and his blessed mother. Our saviour's example on the cross is the only prophecy we need believe in. In the moment of his greatest trial he beheld the face of God and knew beyond all question the power of good to overcome all evil.

Our faith is manifested in that great symbol of all suffering, Christ's tortured body on the cross. Great testing will always call forth a great faith.

The stranger that is amongst us is the result of a faith that has gone from us. This has come amongst us because our faith is weak. We must restore faith. There must be no doubt in our belief. It must be absolute. Unless we take this chalice of affliction to our lips, unless we know the raw sting of vinegar and hyssop in our mouths, our souls will be like shriven corpses within our skin and we will die in the spirit as we most assuredly die in the flesh.

In the face of this evil pestilence that is growing in the heart of our community, how many of you even yet have turned away from and closed your ears to God's voice?

Is it not enough that we are put to the sword, that our lands are forfeited, that our priests are banished and that many who were baptised with us have eaten of the bread of apostasy?

God's love is never easy and to be part of his awesome and fearful vision we must surrender without hesitation or reservation to his divine will and purpose.

To stem this contagion, each and everyone one of us must make a journey of repentance and return to the embrace of Mother Church. For there is no one more deserving of the Lord's grace than he who is willing to lose his life for it.

That misting in the doorway was the first of many similar occasions. Over the following weeks and months they increased in number and duration. Turlough dealt with them in silence. His parents were not surprised at his reaction, yet they were anxious, and though they carried on with their daily life they were both separately watchful.

Turlough was watchful in his own way. At first he would examine the scabs on his skin and note how they were declining. Soon this became an obsession. He had no interest in talking to anyone about them and more and more his mother found him talking to himself, 'Another one, you see, you see, they're going!' When he wasn't so preoccupied he would ask if his friends had called to see him. His mother simply answered, 'No.'

When she tried to coax him to talk, he was either too tired or too busy reading; if she asked him what it was he was reading, he would answer that it was uninteresting and that he was bored with it anyway.

He was able to move about the house now and was eating regularly. But if she asked him to come outside with her, he would complain that it was too cold. 'But the sun's shining,' she encouraged him. 'I don't care about the sun, I'm cold,' he answered sourly. After some time she gave up trying and Turlough retreated into himself. It was difficult for her to watch him in his silences, but her own resolve was as great as his and she would not succumb.

There were days when he seemed animated and euphoric. He talked enthusiastically about going to visit old McCormack, and when he was informed that the old man had died during his illness he seemed unmoved. He talked about going for walks in the fresh air and maybe swimming in the river. At other times he seemed to be completely absorbed by the past. He remembered insignificant things with great enthusiasm, like riding on his father's shoulders as he ploughed the small field at their first home. He hummed snatches of lullabies and songs his mother had sung to him as a child and which she had long forgotten. He even hinted in his ramblings about going to the rath to see what the people there thought of his miraculous cure.

This was too much for her and she chastised him and told him to guard his tongue. But he only laughed and pouted his lips to kiss her from across the room. When he was in these moods he would call her to sit while he read to her from the psalms. 'Aren't they wonderful, mother?' But his mother knew he wasn't listening for an answer, his mind was elsewhere. However euphoric he became, these flights of fancy were sure to be dashed by the return of the pains in his head. Long silences and his staring eyes marked the moment. As always she took his head on her lap and wiped away the beads of perspiration.

At these moments she was close to tears herself. She knew the fear and panic that he was holding inside himself. But even as she tried to comfort him, he retreated further into himself. 'Leave me, I'm all right,' he would tell her.

Gradually these moods seemed less intense and less prolonged. Turlough confirmed this when after sitting and reading quietly to himself he suddenly slammed the book closed and stormed towards the door. She waited for a moment before following. He was standing still, his eyes scanning the landscape before him. They stood side by side for some moments. Neither spoke, as each stared out across the landscape. For several long minutes she waited and watched with him, then finally he spoke. 'I've seen it so many times before, but never like this.'

The next day, and for many days after, Turlough was awake at first light and gone from the house. He left a room heavy with the smell of burned candle wax, for it was a ritual with him now to light a candle before going to sleep. In the night he would lose himself in the glow of its flame. On other nights he would sit and talk with his father.

'His questions sometimes confuse me. I cannot answer them. He seems to be travelling in so many directions at once. Once he asked what real darkness would be like.' Sean Carolan shared his troubled thoughts with his wife.

She was pensive and could only answer that Turlough must find that answer himself. 'He thinks with his eyes too much. He must learn to see without them. He needs you now. I want you to take him to St Patrick's Purgatory.'

Sean Carolan was surprised, but nodded.

For the next few weeks Turlough remained at home, stealing off occasionally and returning in silence. He had renewed his acquaintance with Seamus Brennan and the two of them spent a lot of time at their favourite spot by the river. Some humour had returned to Turlough, and Seamus's genuine concern was quickly rebuffed.

'I've seen corpses in their coffins look better, Turlo, honest to God, I have.' Seamus stopped abruptly, aware of what he had said.

'You're not looking up to much yourself, a bit bloated, seems to me. Do you still booze the way you used to? I would have passed you in the lane. You'll be growing mouldy soon!'

They both began to laugh and as Seamus was about to speak, Turlough asked him simply if he thought he had changed much. His voice was calm and serious. Seamus felt puzzled at first and then a little inhibited. He looked at Turlough's face. There were small patches of purple, remnants of the last scabs, and his face was specked with the familiar small pockmarks of the final healing of his illness. The gauntness of his features exacerbated the scars. Seamus took a long drink from the bottle he had placed before them, and said, 'I see you have discovered vanity while you were ill.'

'Curse you, Seamus. What do you see in my face?'

Seamus was direct and compassionate.

'You're a changed man, Turlo! And who wouldn't be? You were at death's door and slammed it in his face. That would change any man! Be easy with yourself.'

Seamus's words were hardly comforting and Turlough was too unsure of himself to confess what he was really thinking. He had begun to accept what might lie ahead of him, but he still desperately needed the assurance of others to accept it fully. He felt a new urgency about Bridgit. Althouth he accepted that in his condition there could be nothing lasting between them, yet he desperately wanted to know if she loved him. So great was his need that he half-believed that knowing alone would satisfy him. Looking at Seamus poking about the river bank, he remembered his advice, 'Talk straight.' Seamus's life was uncomplicated and Turlough used to envy this in him. But now the envy turned to anger and Turlough began to despise his friend. As if Seamus had been reading his thoughts, he said that Bridgit Cruise had been asking after him. 'She says you're to come and see her and I'm to leave the message as I'm passing on the way home.' Turlough's answer was as Seamus expected. 'Tomorrow night. I'll be waiting at the bridge!' He had tried to hide the excitement in his voice, but Seamus could not be fooled.

That evening Turlough's head swam with fear and expectation. She had asked for him. She wanted him to come. She must have been thinking about him over all the months of his illness. But what would she be thinking now? His thoughts were overwhelmed by her; even the solitary candle flame which had so often calmed him in his confusion was useless now. He stared into it, but only saw her face.

The following night Turlough trudged through the frost-filled night. He reached the bridge exhausted. It had been a long time since he had walked so far, but his breathlessness had more to do with the tension inside him. As he neared the bridge the pressure seemed unbearable.

He stood and watched unaware of the puddle that was soaking through the worn sole of his shoe. Then to pass the time he paced up and down, but still she did not come. He wondered if she was ill or if perhaps someone had died. There had been too many deaths in the past months. But what did she want then? His thoughts gave him no peace and to add to his impatience he thought of Seamus's ominous hint that he was a changed man. Nervously he paced up and down.

He could stand it no longer and walked towards her house. There was still some life in the village, but it was all locked inside, behind closed doors and shuttered windows. The windows and doorways were blank and soulless. Etched crosses and black drapes were everywhere. The occasional chinks of light leaking out from some of the tiny cabins provided no relief to the sombreness.

As he trudged through the empty street he heard a cart behind him. He stopped and turned toward the driver, whose face was covered by an old scarf. His two eyes stared at Turlough for what seemed like a long time. Then he spoke, 'Are you lost or are you looking for someone?'

'I'm just waiting,' Turlough answered.

For several minutes the coachman stared. It irritated Turlough, the way the man sat silently watching him. Then he spoke, 'Aye, that's all any of us can do, wait and hope. But for some like my passengers here, there is no more waiting and no more hope. Say your prayers, lad, while you have breath to do so.'

With that, he moved off with his cargo hardly moving as the cart bumped over the ruts and hollows. Turlough could see the blackened feet and fingers of two or three corpses under a filthy hessian tarpaulin.

Letter from Bridgit Cruise

Dearest Cousin,

How desperately I wish you were with me and yet I pray fervently that you never come to this place. Though the plague seems to have gone from us, no one is prepared to admit it. It has left a village full of ghosts. People barely speak to one another. It is as if they don't want to be reminded of what it has done to them. Perhaps everyone is tired of remembering the dead.

Oh, how I hate this place. I hate it! I hate it!

Father is convinced that the worst is over and tells me I can leave as soon as he has made arrangements. And such arrangements. He is even more eager for me to marry so that I can be safely away from here, and I have agreed, for I am too terrified to stay. And what is there to stay for? I swear, cousin, I have forgotten what happiness is and all expectation has left me. I accepted father's ridiculous ideas about marriage because I have forgotten how to hope for anything.

When I come to you, I want you to hold me and hug me until all this misery leaves me. I hope you are not afraid? I thank our Lord that I am whole and untouched. But I am drowning in pity and pain.

Do you remember I wrote you that Turlough Carolan had been sick with the plague? He has survived. My emotions are so confused. I prayed when he was ill that he would not die and now I am afraid of him. It was painful to tell him I was leaving. I shall never forget his words or his face. If Satan has been amongst us, as our priest tells us, then I am sure he has left his mark on Turlough.

When I saw him a few days ago I could hardly believe my eyes. I didn't know what to expect, but whatever it was it was not the Turlough that I remembered and loved to tease. He was so thin and feeble. His eyes were surrounded by great black circles and his face still bore the hideous marks of his illness.

God forgive me, but I couldn't touch him and I didn't want to be seen with him. I made him come to the end of the bridge and climb down under its arch. As soon as we got there I realised I had made a mistake. We were alone and I was frightened and he just stared at me like a puppy dog. All I could do was cry and look at the river. He tried to comfort me, but I wouldn't let him. Instead I just moved away and told him of my father's proposal, that I would have to move away.

I swear I spoke as softly as I could, but I know my words cut him to the quick. Whatever life was in him seemed to leave him and I thought he might topple into the river. Then with a tone of voice I shall never forget he seemed to spit at me, 'Well, good luck to you, Bridgit Cruise.'

It was brutal. I knew the hurt he was trying to conceal, but he seemed so spiteful. I tried to explain that father had been planning things for months, but he wasn't listening. He simply slouched to the edge of the bank and whispered that he would have given me his soul. His voice was low and as he spoke he kept staring at the black sluggish water.

I wanted to comfort him, but I was afraid, and when I asked him what he intended doing he snarled at me, saying, that a bride-to-be shouldn't be worrying about another man 'It wasn't as if you loved me!' he demanded and when I told him I didn't know, that I was confused, he simply stood looking at the waters. Then, with a voice that was softer than a lullaby, he said, 'I can't see myself, Bridgit. I'm not in the water any more!'

Then as if he was talking to his invisible face in the river he said how he had wanted one great love to encompass all his loves. He wanted a single object in which he could believe and through which he could find out love's meaning. He had made me that object and now in a single moment everything was in smithereens!

The softness of his voice paralysed me. We stood in silence, watching the water flow through the long birch shrubs.

Suddenly he turned on me. His hand flashed up to his cheek and he lunged at me. With the flesh of his face nipped between his finger and thumb, he pushed his face into mine and hissed, 'Is it this?' Then he rammed both his hands into his eyes and hissed again, 'Is it this?'

I was frightened of him and his words and I pleaded with him to stop. 'Stop yourself!' he roared. 'Keep your confusion to yourself, Bridgit Cruise. I have enough of my own!'

I cannot describe his words to me. He spat them out as if they were bile in his mouth. His eyes were black and dull like the river and when I looked at them, the pain and the anger in them was unbearable.

He stood tearing me apart with those eyes for what seemed like an eternity, then suddenly like an apparition he turned and was gone. I stood shivering and was afraid to move.

I don't know how this plague has affected him except that it has left a monster in him. I don't want to see it again.

I can't wait to be away and to see you. Say a prayer for us all, we are in great need of it.

Your loving cousin, Bridgit

Perhaps the time was right. Fate had its own timing. For too long since that confrontation Turlough had retreated into the deepest part of himself. He came and went from home in silence and when he stayed there, he was constantly irritated and offhand.

When his father informed him that they would leave the next day for the pilgrimage, Turlough simply answered, 'Yes.' He had known the day for their departure was near. For many nights his mother had spoken to him about Lough Derg. It was a place of healing but also of illumination. 'Nothing happens in this life that is not meant to happen. Everything has its purpose,' she told him. He carried these words and her gift of a rosary with him on the long journey to the lake shore, but the fog in his own mind was too thick to find any consolation as he waited to be rowed over to the holy island.

The crossing was short and the small boat moved through the water as if something other than the power of the oarsman's limbs moved it. Father, son and boatman sat motionless like pieces of cargo rather than persons. The noise of the water beat against the tiny hull, its monotony throbbing in his head while the rain lanced his face with chilling pinpricks. The dampness and smell of wet clothes seemed to deepen Turlough's apprehension. He desperately wanted to hear a voice, or some noise other than the water beneath him and rain above him. As if in response to his thought a bird's cry tore through the air like a knife wound. He shuddered against the cold and cursed the journey and the days that lay in front of him.

His father and the boatman would not be drawn into conversation. They stared at one another, each trying to fathom the other. The boatman's single tooth glinted between the blue-grey lines of his lips, his wet hair ran down his face like old tobacco stains. He was wholly at home in his watery world. His glassy eyes had the look of wet scales.

'What kind of place is it we're going to?' asked Turlough, anxious to know more about what lay before him.

The boatman answered with sulky disinterest. 'The island on which you will land holds the church. Its reputation for holiness is what brings you here. Some say it is frequently visited by angels and that the local saints have been seen.'

There was a pause and the boatman looked curiously at the passengers. 'Dabeol has his seat on Seadavog Mountain to the south-west and the Goddess Bridgit's chair is on the north shore. You'll find her penitential bed and stone cross near the wall of the church. Few make this lonely vigil without seeking the comfort and assurance of the Goddess. The other part of the island is a stony and abandoned place, where the gatherings and processions of evil spirits can be seen by all, and any who dare to spend the night there are surely tormented by demons that leave them at the very edge of life.'

The boatman fell silent. He spoke to his passengers as though throwing food to a dog, not because the animal was hungry but rather that it was his responsibility to feed the creature. They moved on wordlessly. Turlough's apprehension had only been increased by the surly boatsman. He gripped the boat's sides and sat silent until he heard it grate upon the shore. Awkwardly, his father began helping him ashore, and then he searched through his bag to find some money. Turlough heard the boatman's weak, high-pitched voice, 'Best to make arrangements for the return journey now, lest you are unable when the time comes.' The statement was neither ominous or demanding, nor was there interest or compassion in it. He was merely completing a duty begun earlier.

'Be here at the usual time. You'll find us waiting . . .' his father answered, looking into the boatman's face. After a short pause he finished his instruction, '. . . just as you leave us.'

The boatman made no answer and pulled the boat back into the lake. He turned once to seek some point on the far shore, looked at the man and shivering youth and rowed off into the mist. Only the distant dipping of his oar told them that he had ever been with them, then the silence and the island engulfed them.

They watched him for some minutes. Then, before they made their way from the water's edge, Turlough's father knelt and picked up some stones from about their feet. Turlough felt the cold roundness of the stone his father pushed into his hand.

'Offer this at the well of Cullion when he has returned for us. Come now, lad, let's get ourselves to some shelter.'

Turlough sensed that his father placed more faith in this small round stone than in the church they were making their way towards. He took curious comfort from the cold stone in one hand and the soft warmth of his father's great hand in his own as he guided him up from the lake. The two men walked off, barefoot and with their heads uncovered.

There was little to soften the hard line of the shore. What trees could be seen were bare and spiny and afforded no shelter. Near the edge of the path a few feeble weeds clung in the crevices between stones. Their feet bruised against them, but were already too numbed to feel anything.

As they turned away from the shore and began their climb towards the shelter, they found they were not alone. Before them the hill was moving like a great slothful animal, covered with pilgrims, bedraggled and stumbling. Their breath steamed into the cold air and they mumbled prayers or obscenities as the sharp edge of the cold stone cut into their feet. They looked to Turlough like a filthy rag rolling and boiling in a pot. Father and son joined them and were swallowed up on the groaning hillside. They walked, stumbled and clutched at one another, trapped within this holy procession. Turlough was unmindful of the distance they walked. Only the nearness of these strangers affected him. He had never been in the company of so many people bent on a single purpose before.

Before them loomed a barn-like structure. It was not the end of their journey, rather the beginning, a place of respite before the ritual of pilgrimage began. Yet there seemed no rush to claim its shelter. The nearer the pilgrims came to the building the more they wanted to help those less able than themselves. There was an air of solicitude that the harshness of the evening encouraged.

Inside no one complained. Children were being comforted by their mothers and the old and infirm found willing hands to guide them. A great fire burned in a recess on the far wall and oil lamps about the walls reflected its glow. People moved in and out of a side room where they deposited their wet clothes. Around the larger room groups sat, some unwrapping what meagre food they had brought, others passing a thin hot broth amongst themselves, which they ladled from a great cauldron beside the fire. There was warmth beyond the heat of the fire. No one was a stranger. Here and there laughter bubbled up and in quiet corners some prayed undisturbed.

His father found a clear spot among the throng of people and deposited their belongings, while Turlough walked towards the fire. About him the talk was hushed. People spoke of the distances travelled or asked questions about the townlands of strangers. Some shared a recent grief without seeking pity. As he passed, some amongst them offered him a blessing. Turlough felt he had never been in the company of so many felicitous strangers. He looked back for his father. He saw his blurred figure rubbing the feet of an old woman and telling her that her age was shaming them all. She smiled and said she could do with this sort of comfort without having to come to prayers for it. Her smiling face was impudent and his father was grinning broadly. In this atmosphere of mutual caring, Turlough felt the apprehension of the boat journey begin to fall from him. He moved closer to his father and watched him. The island was working on him too. Turlough could not remember when he had last witnessed such tenderness from his father towards a stranger. He drank in the moment and then moved off towards the heat. For a brief second he was jealous of the old woman, but it passed quickly.

As he squatted at the fire, a young woman touched his arm and held out a piece of bread that had been dipped in the communal soup. 'There are more hungry mouths than mine,' Turlough said, embarrassed by the proximity of this young woman in a roomful of strangers.

'Hunger is a common grief. Here, take it,' the young woman insisted, pulling at his sleeve. He turned, grateful for her insistence and the opportunity to look at her more closely. She smiled at his searching eyes and then broke into a subdued laugh. He realised that his eyes had been more hungry than his belly and laughed in turn at his own embarrassment.

'The fire will mark you if you sit too long. It's better to let the cold leave you slowly.' She chewed the bread as she spoke, but her eye never left him. He sensed her gaze and he moved away from the fire to a space beside her.

Hiding his embarrassment behind bravado, he asked, 'What great sin has brought yourself here?'

'None!' she answered quickly, without losing the smile. 'The priests tell us we are born in it, and some of us do it without knowing; so I don't think any of our sins can be so great! For if we are born to it then we can hardly be blamed for it!'

Turlough felt the life in her was more warming than the fire. Her teasing further relieved his anxiety. He felt comfortable near her and she accepted him with ease. She explained, 'It's a duty I promised my mother, my greatest sin would be in not obeying it. Some more?' she asked again, holding the bread out to him.

About them people were making their final preparations before the fast began at midnight. Some had already found a quiet corner to pray in, others slept. Everywhere the room hummed with the gentle click of beads and whisper of prayers. Here and there a mother sung softly to a child.

In the corner, against the fire wall a small group had gathered about an old man. As he spoke people moved nearer to hear him.

His voice was low, but ageless. His eyes moved slowly across the faces of his audience. Occasionally he winked or smiled, pulling the young ones into his story.

The air was filled with the smell of drying clothes and soup. Somewhere a rasping cough began and crumbled away like old stones as the old pilgrim's story wove about the room.

'The hag knew every herb and could brew a powerful poison,' he said, rolling his bowl of soup round in his crippled hand. 'And her son would dip in his arrows and then kill everything his eyes lit upon.'

Slowly he pointed his finger and moved it about the faces turned to him. 'At this time the king of Ireland called his druids and asked them to find a means of getting rid of the witch and her son. The druids answered that it was only one of Na Fianna who could kill the hag and that she would have to be shot with a silver arrow. So Fionn MacCumhaill, who came with his companions, undertook to hunt the pair. They found them gathering deadly herbs on a hill. The hag had with her the pot in which she boiled them. Goll MacMorna shot an arrow at her, but missed and overturned the pot, spilling the poisonous mixture. To escape from the attack the giant threw his mother on his shoulder, but not before Fionn shot a silver arrow which pierced the heart of the old woman. Carrying his burden, the giant flew with astonishing speed until he came to the mountains where, stopping to take breath, he discovered that all that remained of his mother were her legs, her backbone and her two arms, the rest having been torn apart in his flight through the woods. With a great roar the giant threw down the remains of his mother, and continued his flight and was never seen again.'

The old man looked around at his silent audience then continued.

'Many years later Na Fianna came hunting in the part of the country where the bones of the hag lay. While Oisin stood preaching over her remains, a little red-headed dwarf made his appearance. He told them not to touch the old hag's bones because in the thigh bone was concealed a worm, which, if it once got out and could find enough water to drink, would be likely to destroy the whole world. Then the dwarf disappeared. But Conan

Maol broke the thigh bone with his hunting spear and a long hairy worm crawled out.'

The old man's arm moved in imitation of the worm. 'He took it on the end of his spear and defiantly threw it into the lake. Immediately there rushed out an enormous beast,' his arms suddenly flashed into the air, then he continued, 'so terrible was it that all the Fianna hid themselves from its fury. Then the monster overran the country, spreading destruction everywhere and swallowing hundreds of people in a mouthful.'

This time the storyteller gestured as though shovelling food into his mouth. Then with the stubs of his wrists he mopped imaginary blood from his lips.

'But Fionn MacCumhaill sucked his magic thumb and discovered that the beast was vulnerable only in one spot – a mole inside its body. Swiftly he attacked the monster and jumped into its throat. Inside the beast he met two hundred live men and women, and soon he found the mole below the beast's heart. With his weapon he opened a hole about the size of a door and came out with the captives. He left the beast struggling and bleeding on the shore of the lake, ever since named the Red Lake.'

He took a long pause, looking into the faces of his listeners.

Then he began again, 'The beast lay writhing and bellowing with pain until St Patrick came and found it and, to show the power of the faith he was preaching, ordered it to the bottom of the lake, where he secured it for ever. But', he paused, 'when the lake is ruffled by a storm, the monster is still sometimes seen rolling among the waves.'

Turlough looked at the faces of the children. They were rapt and frightened. But the story had sparked other thoughts in his head. He thought of his boat trip and the lake waters washing over the rocks, making them shiny and smooth, folding one on the other like the entrails of the great petrified sea serpent. He wondered as he looked about the room what unquiet ghosts and nightmares had been brought to the island to be exorcised. The story was older than history and older than the faith the pilgrims came here to take refuge in. But in the faces and the silence about him, Turlough felt part of an unbroken order of life and belief, in which the spirit world was always immediate.

He turned again to the young woman. She was sleeping now

and her dreaming face still attracted him. He thought of her zesty rejection of sin and her obligation to duty. Is this what brought all these strangers together? An obligation for which they had forgotten the reason?

He rose and moved among them stepping over and stumbling around the recumbent figures rolled in foetal curls. He found his sleeping father and sat beside him. He looked closely at him, as if to find an answer.

As he studied the face, he felt he hardly knew it. He was a child the last time he was this close to his father. They always talked at a distance from one another and as he grew older the distance seemed greater, yet his father was always a presence in his life. No matter how remote, his father represented security. As he scanned the impassive face, he felt a moment of panic. A time would come when he wouldn't be able to see this face any more. Then the moment passed. That they were here together was enough. It had to be. There was something between them that blindness could not take from him.

He pulled his knees up to his chest and rested his forehead on them. The day had exhausted him and his head ached dully as if a bee was trapped inside it. He looked up after some minutes, his eyes tracing the rise and fall, the contour and colour of the bodies around the room. Soon it would be midnight and the sleepers would wake and begin their fast. The room would hum again with their prayers and the night would be long.

It was a night full of words, with half-heard voices pleading urgently, whilst others droned in emotionless recitation. Somewhere someone choked and their prayer dissolved into sobs. The velvet clicking of beads was soporific, but Turlough's mind could not be restrained to the necessity of prayer. He had to free the hurt in his head and he was preoccupied with the old man's story. But he was weary, and his head dropped again, felled by sleep.

Stifling in the heat of prayer and the low-burning fire, Turlough imagined himself inside the monster. He could smell its hot, stinking saliva burning against his skin. His clothes were torn from him as he moved through the animal's entrails. He felt himself smothering and drowning as he fought his way out of the creature in a monstrous parody of birth. He saw himself standing naked and bloody beside the dying, witch-born serpent. He felt sadness and desire, as if the creature was now part of him and he of it. For a moment he was filled with anger at the saint who had created the red lake from the creature's blood.

Shaking himself out of these childlike imaginings, he listened to the mumbling pilgrims. He despised their submission and self-denial. Would they be forever crawling barefoot and penitential? His father, the old storyteller, the young woman, all flitted through his head. Why was there no guide to free them from this half world? Turlough's prayers through the fasting hours were for answers. It was a prayer of hunger. It was a prayer in his spirit that words could not shape. He looked again at his sleeping father and his calm features reassured him. If he was about to fall into some black emptiness, he wanted to take all the precious things of his life with him.

Morning was marked by a single chime on a small hand bell. Everyone moved towards the doors. Outside the horizon was mottled with sphagnum and sedge, broken by dark patches of turf, all held together by the lifting mist. In the frost-blurred golden light the alders were damson coloured and the willows aflame. Here and there firs and junipers anchored down the island with the weight of their greenness.

Turlough walked quickly towards the water. A band of rooks and gulls was ransacking the shoreline, their startling black and white seeming to stitch together the orange of the lake and the brown of the land. Slowly the mist began to clear. Patches of white and cream smudged the landscape with the last of the meadowsweet, and other wild herbs he knew would be there but his eyes had not the strength to discern.

He seated himself on a pile of fir logs. His fingers felt the amber beads of resin and he raised them to his nose, their sticky pungency cutting through his senses. He lifted one of the logs and held it near his face. He saw the bright pinks and reds of the severed heartwood spin and multiply. He recalled the red lake, blood tinted. Death underlay everything here! What was the attraction to those who came? Trying to rid himself of his thoughts, he glanced up from the log.

The new day was a revelation. The features of those about him began to sharpen and the murmur of devotion was fading with the mist. The shock of so many bared feet made him search the faces about him. He felt himself strangely excited. He wanted to see through their features to understand what had brought them together on this island of death. Only then could he begin to make sense of his own reasons and expectations.

At first he sought furiously for the young woman who had teased and warmed him. It was as if the sight of her would calm his excitement and provide him with a vantage point from which he could fathom the island. At this moment his senses were being buffeted like storm clouds. Then he saw her, but the cheery companionship of the night was washed out from her, she seemed vulnerable and terribly alone. Around her glinting crucifixes were everywhere, reflecting light on old, gnarled hands busy with silent prayer.

Near him sat a penitent, rolling his eyes and thumbing his rosary beads rapidly. It was as if he were trying to smother nervous laughter. There was something final in the urgency with which he prayed. Turlough thought there was more fear in him than faith. Still haunted by the confusion of the night, he felt himself unnerved and fearful, but he would not admit to the ignorance and superstition that he was sure underlined the faith of these pilgrims. They came here because they needed to. They were the maimed of the earth and he did not want to be one of them. Yet he knew, with a desperate anguish, that very soon he would join them. His eyes had lost their keenness but not their hunger.

Behind him a mother was teaching her child the words of a prayer. The child repeated the meaningless sanctity and shivered. Turlough shivered himself. He was lost like a child. A passing pilgrim stopped before him and with a careless admonishment whispered, 'Beware the mote in your eye, for its lust will leave you sightless.'

Then he passed on, fingering a sign of the cross. Turlough smarted at the words, but the man looked demented. Religion had washed all reason from him. The deep human sincerity that was everywhere here did not need to clothe itself in all this holiness. Abject contrition was smothering him. He wanted the warmth of these people. There was no sin so great that it could separate him from them or them from each other. Turlough's heart was loud and quick. Anger and compassion were fusing inside him. He felt lost and knew he could only retrieve himself through the reality of the fleshy, sin-filled people about him.

His father's hand rested on his shoulder. 'The night was long for all of us. I watched you listening to the story. But there is an older name for the lake. Derg means a well, a hollow, like this part where your eyes are set.'

Gently his hands brushed over and ringed Turlough's eyes. He felt the wetness of his father's hands. 'Water's a blessing, we were born in it. Come, let's join the rest of them, though, God knows, this is a journey we each make alone.'

Turlough stood, lifted by his father's words. As they walked through the crowds, his father's voice echoed his thoughts, 'Even in the faces of men you might know the mind of God.'

They walked towards where the ritual was to begin. Turlough looked at his father's white feet and the blue-grey marble tracery of veins. His own feet were numb now against the flint-edged stones, but his father's silent assurance and presence comforted him. Above them a flock of martins careered in irresolute flight, darting to and from the eaves of the church.

Sean Carolan absorbed the scene about him. In the distance the mountains seemed like a watermark against the lurid sky. The silent shapes of the people, more shadow than form, stood in contrast to the benign but elemental energy of the place. It was a landscape which moved him to sublime contemplation. Its natural beauty combined with the quiet within him to lift his spirit beyond the confines of the flesh. The closed sanctuary of Christianity could not move him. Looking at the rocks and water, the clouds with the last glint of morning stars, he turned to Turlough. 'I find myself in a world were reality does not fit. It is a half-world and I feel no softness in it. It does not caress me and it seldom inspires me.'

For a moment Turlough thought of Bridgit washing herself through the rain-frosted glass. Then a solitary waterfowl cut a line across the surface of the water, its curling and flapping wing resonating. In the still air his father turned and looked at him. Turlough was squinting, trying hard to follow the bird's flight. Prompted by the grimace of his son and the image of the bird, his father said, 'There were those before who chose exile and abandonment, who in elemental madness and desire set themselves afloat, oarless, but at the mercy of God,' he paused for a moment and looked about him, then continued, 'while we are reduced to this sun-wise circling of stone and endless repetition of prayer in a language we only half comprehend.'

Turlough listened to his father's discontent. It was balm to his own unease. About him he heard the whispered prayer of the litany of our Lady, 'House of God, pray for us, Ark of the Covenant pray for us,' and in it he heard the word music of his childhood. Suddenly the faces about him were the faces that had inhabited his boyhood. As the prayers continued, he remembered again how his susceptible imagination had been intimately involved in the suffering and death of Christ, when he imagined the rath as Golgotha.

He found himself in front of the broken, rough-hewn, column of St Patrick's cross. Pilgrims knelt and rested their heads in weary observance, and as they rose, they offered the rusted cross their lips. Turlough's eyes were fixed on the small, cold symbol of stone and iron. Beside him his father whispered. 'See, this is what draws them here. But be assured there is something greater than this, something more than this confused ritual. There is something laid down before speech or mind could give it meaning. And it is with us always, son, if we seek it.'

His father fell silent again while around them the words of 'Our Father' followed by 'Hail Mary' and the Creed were mouthed by the pilgrims.

He turned and walked the few steps to St Bridgit's Cross, etched on the outside wall of the church. About him, with outstretched arms, the pilgrims turned their blank faces to the blustering sky. The ancient words of renunciation were quietly affirmed, 'I renounce the world, the flesh and the Devil.'

Suddenly horrified and afraid, he turned his back on the cross and looked out on the lough. He remembered old Manus McCormack's words, 'When a man begins a journey it is unlucky to turn back.' A momentary flash of his mother standing unmoved and defiant outside the home of his birth came into his mind. She, too, would not turn back! The meaning of the words choked him as if his throat was full of pebbles, weighing him down. He tried desperately to say them.

Broken by the need to belong, he felt the island slip through his outstretched fingers. He wanted to be anywhere but here. He turned again towards the pilgrims.

He watched them crush themselves against the wall as they kissed their renunciation into it. Then they genuflected like broken birds. He wanted to be away from them and he wanted to lift them from their wet knees, to be embraced by them. He became aware of shards of flint cutting into his feet. With a deep and exhausted sigh, the words gushed out of him, 'I rejoice in the world, I rejoice in the flesh and I curse the darkness that will take them from me!'

His oath of defiance did not sink unheard into the waters of the lake. There was nothing here that could be hidden. The severity of the island stripped its penitents down to their naked souls. Anger, arrogance, conceit were no defence against it, and Turlough Carolan was no exception. That curse against the darkness was spoken by a voice broken with emotion.

That night his sleep was racked by the thunderous clap of birds' wings as they hovered about his head, their high-pitched caw and screech cutting into him. He felt the darkness of their wings on his eyes. Their closeness extinguished everything and he was suffocating with panic. Suddenly he heard a single, loud, sharp, chiming bell. The black birds evaporated slowly and a luminous whiteness filled his eyes. It exuded a pulsing, comforting melody. It was intoxicating and seemed to be filled with the scent of incense and woman's hair. Turlough felt he wanted to fall into it.

But as he tried to drink it into himself he saw standing near him a large, bald heron. It was black as soot and its wings were outstretched before it, shielding something. Slowly it drew back its wings and in hideous harmony with the melody of the whiteness he watched as it rhythmically tore at the eyes of its victim. He was frozen with fear, but continued to stare. The whiteness and the melody wrapped around protecting him, yet still he sweated and moaned and shivered throughout the night. His anguish didn't go unnoticed.

The young woman who had fed and teased him came to comfort him. Even without waking him, she seemed to ease him. Quietly she whispered to him and with her fingers she gently inscribed the words, 'Jesu, filii dei, miserere mei,' then marked his face with ash before kissing him.

Five The Bird Woman

Whatever had happened at Lough Derg, Turlough was a changed man. There are people who say that those who enter the soul of the island fall into an ecstasy and see all things with their mind's eye. But it is also said that no one leaves purgatory without loss.

Since he had returned from his pilgrimage many who knew him suspected the latter had happened, but those who were closer to him accepted a more logical but no less traumatic reason for Turlough's behaviour, for his sight was fading rapidly now. It was replaced by a complicated surliness. He spurned solicitude, which he saw as an unwelcome intrusion into the world he had to create for himself. He once complained to the priest that he could send up novenas to every saint under the sun, but the truth was he was blind, and if the priest could not explain the colour of the sea to a blind man how could he convince him of the power of prayer to cure or change anything? The truth was that he didn't want to talk about his blindness, nor did he want to talk about his vigil at Lough Derg.

He despised his own increasing dependency. Being dependent on others angered him more than he could endure. They were making a child out of him and he hated it. The worst moments came when the hatred turned inwards. When he was suddenly abrupt or dismissive to his mother or father he would be overcome later by waves of guilt and self-reproach. On those occasions he stole off to be alone so he could release the weeping in him.

Didn't they understand that his darkness made things bigger? No matter how many times they walked him around the room, nothing was familiar any more. The place where the fire was, the deal table against the wall, the doorway to his bed and his room – none of this was his now. Sometimes he hated their touch as they guided him about. They were pulling him back into their world and he hated the place. When they placed his hands on the furniture, on the walls and doorways, everything was too big and he was as afraid.

He refused to wear boots. He didn't know one from the other, or his from his father's. Too often he had pulled on his father's shoes and hobbled about, unaware of the error until his father would say, 'I must go out now, Turlough, and need my boots.' In a fury he would kick them off and as his father tried to help him when he stumbled he would scream, 'Leave me alone, leave me alone!' Many times he fell deliberately, so that when they came to his aid he could vent his exasperation on them.

'Remember this, Turlough?' his mother would say as she walked with him outside their home and pointed out potential obstacles. But Turlough didn't want to remember. He hated it when she asked him to 'come outside'. He had to wear boots and walk with his thighs pressed tightly together and his hands reaching out into emptiness. It was hard to adjust to 'outside'. That word was now enormous. Outside made the hugeness of the chairs and walls of his room insignificant. More than that, there was a different pressure outside. It was threatening.

For months he stayed at home, moving only between the fireplace and his bed. Every time he stumbled he cursed, but the more he did so the less his parents tried to help him.

Sean Carolan's silence challenged him. Turlough could feel him watching. At first he despised it and returned the challenge by stumbling unnecessarily, but his father stopped catching him. His mother, too, ceased being a crutch. Instead she coaxed him. 'Tell me, what do you smell?' she would ask casually when she brought fresh flowers into the room. Without thinking, she would call out the names of the blossoms. But she didn't always need to cajole him.

As his mood eased, he was sometimes careless and demanding. If he tripped, he cursed loudly, but not out of frustration. It was as if the offending item should not have been in his way in the first place. His mother had little sympathy. 'Be careful of your tongue, Turlough. That will make you fall, more than anything in your way!' Her chastisement made him feel smaller than his handicap had. Sometimes he turned on her, proclaiming, 'It's not my fault!' but she was unrepentant, and answered, 'Few of us are faultless!'

Sometimes her rebuke made him sulk, but she ignored him and days would pass with silence between them.

His father's silence seemed to overwhelm their antipathy. Even though he did not know what had passed between them, Turlough's self-indulgence was lifted by his silent presence. There was an aura about his father that drew him out of himself, but still it did not encourage his son to confide in him.

Instead he turned to his mother. One afternoon as they arrived back from the well and Marie Carolan scolded him for spilling more than he carried, he answered, 'What else can you expect?'

'I can expect more, but no more than you can yourself. You seem less afraid of being away from the house.'

Turlough was already raking the ashes in the fire and answered almost without thinking, 'Everything comes from outside me now and it makes my head feel heavy. I hear everything differently. I seem to hear everything separately, but at once.'

'I know, I have watched you. Your head jerks and twists like a curious sparrow, but you seem more sure of yourself now.'

'I don't know. Does it seem that way to you? I'm still confused. I use my feet like hands, but my hands feel things differently.'

Marie Carolan listened. She had spent months listening to her son. She said nothing, his intemperate abuse offended her, especially when he would thrash out against the walls and curse with obscene profanity. She watched and listened to it all and sometimes cursed to herself. But this was something more and she listened again. 'What do you mean?'

Turlough was silent for a few moments, but the silence could not conceal his struggle. 'I don't know what I mean, except that things feel different somehow. Sometimes I know something is there before I touch it. And where I touch it, it's the same, but yet not the same as what I saw, or feel I saw. And I don't know what I'm talking about!'

His last words had a tinge of anger in them and Marie Carolan was quick to stem it. 'Everything in life has a cause, as it has a purpose, and you only think you don't know what you're talking about because you haven't found a purpose for what you feel. I think . . .'

The edge of desperation had not left Turlough and he

interrupted her. 'Don't say any more, Mother. You sound like my father.'

As abruptly as he had spoken, she said, 'No, you sound like your father!'

Although the months had improved Turlough's confidence, his blindness had created confusions which he could not explain. His headaches were returning again and there were days he sat kneading his forehead with the nub of his thumb as if trying to rub out all the questions in his head. But if he couldn't erase the confusion, he was learning something else. Blindness drew people to him. He could hide behind his infirmity or he could play on people's sympathy.

Sean Carolan was not immune to his son's troubled mind. It worried him, but he was no more ready to talk about it than Turlough. Yet he was not content to wait for his son to unburden himself. One evening, after watching his son's troubled habits, he went outside. Returning after some minutes, he placed a heavy staff in his son's hands. 'This house is not the whole world, for there is much of it outside. It's best to make your own way in it sooner rather than later. This is not a crutch I am giving you, Turlough. It's your guide.'

That night Turlough sat alone in his room, fingering the gift. It wasn't simply a stick, nor was it a crutch. Sean Carolan had spent many months carving figures and symbols on the shaft and horn handle. If this stick was a guide, it was also a talisman. Turlough could not decipher what the carvings meant, but he knew that whatever answers he sought he could not find them in this house.

He turned to Seamus most. He felt easy with him. Seamus didn't treat him like a child. He accepted the simple fact of his friend's blindness. But, above all, Seamus maintained his dark sense of humour and fascination for Turlough. And there was another reason. Seamus went nowhere without a drink of some description and it was the only kind of medicine Turlough cared for. The drink was like Seamus himself. It didn't ask any questions and was its own comfort.

The two of them lay flat on their backs, passing the bottle and staring up at the sky.

'I can't really see much more than you, Turlo.'

'What can you see?'

'Stars . . . too many to number.'

'I once learned a bit about stars but I can't remember it. Do you ever notice how you can look at the stars for hours?'

'It's true. Do you think that before the birth of Christ there were no stars, and the night he was born the very first one appeared – my grandfather told me that.'

Turlough listened to Seamus's speculations. He wanted to laugh, but instead he explained the heavens as his father had explained them to him. The stars moved in their courses in a great gloom. They had done and would always do so. There wasn't, to his thinking, any set time for them.

Seamus was unconvinced. 'You may be telling me a lie, and how would I know?'

Turlough ignored the slight and continued, 'When I look at the stars I feel as though something is about to burst in my heart. The first time I saw the speckled moon, it looked like wax poured on snow. I wanted to look at everything, to see what else was queer and unlike itself. Look up, Seamus, forget the bottle and drink in the heavens.'

Obediently, Seamus stared wonderingly at the sky.

Turlough's voice whispered to him, 'Can you see it, Seamus, how amazing it is?'

But Seamus was staring at Turlough, tenderly, and with a frightened, childlike voice he asked, 'Is that what it's like, Turlo . . . being in the dark all the time?'

Turlough thought about Seamus's question. The naiveté of it moved him. His blind eyes stared upwards and he asked himself if that was what it was like, growing into a black starless abyss in which he had to find a meaning. 'Yes, Seamus. It's like . . .'

But before he could finish Seamus lay back beside him and they both faced the stars. Seamus's voice was low, 'Don't answer that, Turlo, 'cause you're a big liar anyway.'

But Turlough could not evade his mother and even in his blindness he could feel her watchful eyes on him. She was concerned about his long nights and his drinking. His drunkenness was not like his father's drinking, an escape into memory and reverie. Sean Carolan was pensive and thoughtful, but his son's drinking was different. A destructive melancholy lay at the back of it. And she was sure it was not because he was blind. There was another inner darkness which only Turlough knew and in which he floundered with drunken excess. In his drunken sleep she sometimes witnessed his racing mind unburden itself.

She heard his teeth grinding fearfully against the desperate low moans of a mind terrified by itself. She knew something had happened on the holy island, but not even her husband could tell her what. When she had asked him, he explained only that Turlough had taken himself off from the main body of the pilgrims, saying that he was tired and wanted to be alone. Sean Carolan was used to his son being on his own and watched him sitting on a pile of firewood looking at the lake. During the ritual of prayers he saw him once or twice, then forgot about him until the morning. He knew Turlough was tired and thought he had gone off to sleep alone, away from the others.

In the morning he had found him sheltering in a hollow of rock. He was staring blankly in front of him and his face had a deathly pallor. He sat absolutely motionless as though he was a piece of the rock itself. As his father tried to lift him, he felt as if he was touching a piece of cold pig-iron from his workshop. But when he embraced him, to warm and comfort him, he felt a huge and terrified trembling, as if Turlough was desperately trying to hold himself together against impossible odds whilst his being was being shaken and broken into pieces.

For a long time his father held him, until, finally, Turlough collapsed into a fit of dread-filled weeping. Sean Carolan remembered that he mumbled something about the earth being dirty and full of lies and that only the blind were holy. When they walked back to the shelter Turlough moved in a kind of trance, and he remained in that state throughout their journey home.

If he could not lift this state from himself, his mother determined that others must. But Sean Carolan was adamant and she could not break through the invisible wall Turlough had built around himself. Night after night he sat at the fire in his room. He always had a bottle of his father's rough whiskey, to relieve the pains in his head he claimed. No more priests' craft, he insisted.

Mrs McDermott-Roe wanted Turlough to return to the big house, and his mother thought she could help. Mrs McDermott-Roe knew his fascination for music and poetry. She had often seen him listening to the musicians and poets when she entertained her guests. She believed there might be better medicine in music than in prayer.

Marie Carolan was anxious about handing over the care of her son, but she also knew that he needed a stimulus to pull him out of his self-imposed apathy and growing alcoholism. Her compliance had only one condition. She insisted that Turlough could learn what he might in the home of the McDermott-Roes, but it would have little meaning until he spoke with the *calleach*, Fionnuala Quinn.

At Alderford House, a room had been set aside exclusively for Turlough. It was a short distance from the small library and overlooked the garden. The room was spartan in its furnishing to help him negotiate it, but to everyone's surprise he asked that some wild flowers and a candle be left in it for him every few days. 'I might not see them, but that does not mean I do not need them,' he said after spending his first night there.

In the days that followed he was often visited by his patroness, who was anxious that he should feel at home. But, at his own wish, he was left to his own devices. His previous visits to the house had fixed an image of every hall and room in his head and he thought he would quickly be able to negotiate the house without much assistance. But he rarely went to the kitchen now. He felt he would be an encumbrance and besides he didn't want people hovering about him making noise. He hated loud noise. It was an unwanted intrusion that frightened him as it shattered the distance that alcohol and emotional emptiness had thrown up around him. He had developed a new harmony in his senses, through which he could receive an impression of his environment, but noise was like a hammer blow that smashed up the order he had created. Whoever slammed a door in his hearing received a cursory dismissal or fierce rebuke, and the language in which it was delivered would have shrivelled a saint, as Mrs McDermott-Roe once informed him.

When he wasn't roaring abuse, he could be seen moving about the house like someone suffering from rudimentary paralysis. His body leaned into the walls as he walked. His footsteps were tiny again, as they had been at his home. But instead of pawing the air in front of him to direct himself, he attacked it with his father's stick. Any time he walked into a door or some item of furniture he demanded aloud, 'Why does no one tell me?' No one dared, for fear he might attack them. Only Mrs McDermott-Roe was unafraid of him. She spoke softly and evenly to him, like a child.

After many weeks and more effort he became less perverse, but instead he expected people to pity him and thus to serve him. He treated the servants contemptuously. Even Mrs McDermott-Roe and her guests were occasionally expected to dance attention on him. And many of them did. Mrs McDermott-Roe watched him 'play' with her friends. Turlough was learning how to be cunning and manipulative. At first she didn't mind, thinking that he might need these attributes to help him become independent, but, as time passed, instead of 'using' people less, he manipulated them more.

Each morning when she saw him, he would ask, 'How do I look today?' At first she thought he was enquiring about his wellbeing, but the hospitality of Alderford House was creating another Turlough. He was becoming obsessed with his appearance and was only delighted when she fussed about his clothes, fixing a button here or arranging his cuffs. He told her he had been too much inside of late and should be dressed in light greys and soft blues so as not to highlight any pallor on his face.

There was little she could do about this 'new' Turlough. If she remonstrated with him or teased him, he would be moody and petulant. So she played along with him for the entertainment it gave her. One day she overheard him say to Seamus Brennan, who had pretended to call about some harness-mending, that he felt like Moses in Pharaoh's house, to which Seamus answered mockingly that he looked more like Joseph in his coat of many colours. Turlough, surprisingly, accepted the banter in good humour, but when Seamus turned on him and said, 'Be careful, Turlough, lest you lose the run of yourself. You may be blind, but it does not mean you can't remember where you came from, and if you ever forget, Seamus Brennan will remind you.' It should have been a salutary lesson, but it only served to turn Turlough sulky and unpleasant for several days.

When he emerged from his room the smell of alcohol and stale sweat that clung to him was repugnant. For months Mrs McDermott-Roe and the rest of the household had watched him spin an invisible spider's web as he tentatively found his way about. He would pace back and forward along the same pre-fixed route. It was as if he was weaving and enclosing his own invisible space. But now he lurched around the rooms, insensibly attacking the air with his stick and cursing everything. No matter how much she disliked Seamus Brennan, she had learned something from him. She caught his stick in midair as it was about to flail a chair and commanded him to 'settle himself'. For the first time she looked closely at the words cut into the horn hands and read them aloud, 'A river flows by the power of its current, not the confinement of its banks.' For a moment both of them stood in silence, then she enquired if he understood the significance of the engraving.

Quiet and suddenly sobered, he replied, 'Aye my father has a curious way of saying things.'

The change in his demeanour puzzled her for a moment, then she said, 'If it's from your father, I would take heed on it, for your river is overflowing with alcohol and you're drowning fast.'

She was about to say more, but the expression on his face stopped her. He looked weak and defenceless and without another word he slouched off to his room.

Curtains and carpet were new to him and he loved the feel of them against his feet. These luxuries absorbed noise and he could pace up and down barefoot, talking to himself. They were the only adornments he accepted.

He would frequently ask Mrs McDermott-Roe to read to him when he had cosseted himself with some drink. It was at this time that he developed his love of the psalms. Mrs McDermott-Roe was delighted to read for him, and was astonished when he could repeat what she had read the next day. She was beginning to sense that some part of him remained unaffected by his drinking and this ability encouraged her in her mission. As they sat quietly together, Turlough confessed his interest in the poetry of the psalmist. The plea for redemption, for liberation from suffering, appealed to something deep in himself. He admitted he had trouble speaking about it because he was still unsure why he was so drawn to these images. To Turlough all things were transitory, but the psalmist's resolution in joy and praise elated him. This was the psalmist's redemption. Life was meant to be full and happiness was its goal.

Sometimes Turlough would speak of these things for hours

with the urgency of the half-converted. It was his inarticulate enthusiasm that intrigued her. She wanted to harness it in some way, to give it a voice. One day she entered his room and placed a harp in his hands. 'Let this speak for you,' she said simply as she turned to leave the room.

From the doorway she watched as he awkwardly handled the instrument. She wondered what he was thinking. As his hand felt out its shape, she called out to him lightly, 'Be careful Turlough the harp isn't a woman. But you may have to know it as one!' then, laughing softly, she left the room.

Alone in the room Turlough set the harp on his bed and crossed to where a single candle stood. He passed his hands across it to ensure it was lit, then returned to the bed and took up the instrument again. His hand travelled across the enclosed sound box and along the graceful forepillar to where it joined the downward curve of the neck. The carved 'T' section was cut into the form of a serpent or a fish. Turlough was unsure and his fingers lingered and probed its features.

For a moment he remembered his father teaching him how to tickle trout. This carved fish seemed just as fragile to him. He stroked the high-tensioned brass strings and listened as their sound was dramatically distorted in the soundbox. He plucked his fingers across the strings again, with more purpose this time and tried to distinguish the array of bright overtones as they flowed back at him. For several hours he fondled the instrument. As a young child visiting the house with his father, he had often watched the instrument being played. He thought it a curious irony that now he could not see he was given an instrument of his own. Later, as he slept, the black and red of the bog-stained sally and yew wood glowed in the dim candlelight. It would be waiting for him, his first companion of the morning.

For the next few days Turlough spent much time with his new friend, fingering and caressing it, testing the tensions in the brass wire and listening to the varying pitch. Sometimes he would be conscious of people moving about outside his room so he would steal off into the garden. He noticed immediately how the sound of the instrument changed, but he was never deterred from his exploration. On one occasion, as he was engaged in this solitary study, Mrs McDermott-Roe came up to him. He sensed she had someone with her.

'Turlough, this is Fionnuala Quinn. I have told her about you and have asked her to give you instruction. So I am going to leave you two alone. Be patient with him, Fionnuala, this one has a mind of his own.'

He heard her walk off and leave him alone with the stranger. As she sat beside him, he smelled pipe tobacco. After taking several deep draws on it, she spoke, 'I'm glad you have a mind of your own. You'll need it. But when it comes to playing it's best to walk before you can run.'

Turlough was unsure how to deal with this stranger. He was angry and defensive. Who was she? He knew his mother had asked her to come, but she came so infrequently and then spent more time with Mrs McDermott-Roe. He began to feel all his resentment about being dependent rising up in him.

Fionnuala sensed it and reached towards him. 'The first lesson, lad, is the most difficult. It's a lesson of faith and not of learning. It's about believing that what's in yourself is enough to do whatever your dreams have told you; and that, lad, is the key to all knowing.'

Then she spat and sucked deeply on her pipe. Turlough gagged against the smell as he felt his ears being tugged roughly. 'That poison you're blowing in my face makes learning anything difficult and while you're hanging off my ears like a cat with a wet rat, I doubt very much if anything will pass through them.'

Turlough was determined he would not be made a fool of.

'And that's your biggest problem, maybe too much has passed through them already.' The old woman tugged on his ears again. She was equally determined that this young man would learn who was master. Her voice was insinuating. 'Before the light began fading from your eyes you found yourself looking at young girls. Or maybe you were one of those log-heads who thought girls were for knocking down?'

He knew her meaning but his blindness had given him a new boldness. 'What has that to do with anything?'

Her reply was quick and sharp. She had the measure of him. 'First, know how tightly your instrument's strung before tuning it – and in your case it's well strung!'

Turlough was instantly weary of this woman. He felt she wanted to diminish him and to treat him like a dog. And in turn he wanted to snap at her derision. She felt his anger and her voice softened, but the authority was not lost from it. 'You'll have to see the world with other eyes. You'll have to feel it in a different way. But it's no loss to you if desire has warmed the blood. Come,' she demanded suddenly, 'sitting stupefies you, and men are always stupid when it comes to talk of women.'

He heard the rustle of her clothes as she rose to move off. He was unsure. His pride told him to refuse her commands, but part of him was drawn to her because of these demands. He had had enough of people's solicitude.

'Wait,' he called out.

She stopped and turned to him. 'Lean on me and listen while we walk.' There was a finality in her voice, so he complied. They walked in silence out of the house and into the grounds.

Mrs McDermott-Roe watched them from her window. They were an odd coupling, age and youth. Man and woman bound together by their mutual infirmities and each needing the other for affirmation. Against the vastness of the skyline their silhouettes seemed pathetic.

Turlough cursed, swearing that she was without doubt the ugliest hag in all creation. She smelt of stale tobacco and boiled fat. She said nothing as she walked and he followed in silence. His head was full of questions. He wanted to reject her, but he was sure he would not find his way back alone so he followed her in stony silence. As they passed through a tunnel of trees, he could feel the passing light on his skin. 'Sit,' she said, coming to a halt.

'I thought it made you stupid,' Turlough quipped, half innocent, half tongue in cheek.

'Only if your brains are in your backside. Here!' She pushed a small stone bottle into his hands and ordered him to drink. The liquid was pungent before it got to his mouth. After choking down a mouthful, he retched. Its taste reminded him of boiled peas that had been left to sit, undisturbed, for days.

'If your brains are really in your backside, one way or another it will make them work!'

He drank again and cursed the donkeys he insisted she had milked the liquid from.

'Your brains may not be in your nether regions after all.'

'Old woman, if you have brought me here to listen to the rantings of a mind soaked in that poison, I can just as easily . . .'. His words were cut short as the old woman's voice rounded on him, dismissively, but authoritative.

'Before midday and before sunset will be your study times. You must be your own master and pupil. Your first instrument is those ears. Listen and listen and listen again. Disentangle the melody about you, for it will be the making of you. Be quiet and listen!'

Turlough sat restless. His darkness was not fearful to him, but the old woman's commands seemed to be driving him deeper into it. He wanted to fill its emptiness, not look into it. What was he to listen to? Her? The wilderness about him? It was harder to hear things. Everything came to him more slowly now. He needed a picture to fix sound into meaning. There was a long silence and he knew she was making him listen.

'There,' the old woman spoke softly, 'the yellowhammer toasts the day and curses us with the same breath.' Her voice whispered in imitation 'che-e-e-ees' and then chattered quickly, 'divil, divil, divil, take yez.' She laughed, her voice cracking like twigs on a fire. 'Not unlike you, Turlough.'

In the background an old rook coughed and he was about to return her sarcasm when she stopped him.

'I know what you're thinking. Age is my excuse for what I am, what's yours?'

She didn't give him time to think or answer, but asked immediately, 'Do you know the birds?'

Turlough knew this was a game and entered into it. It might be entertaining and it would at least save him from listening to her abuse. 'Aye, I know them, and better than most,' he answered almost aggressively.

'But do you know their note and how it hangs? That old rook you would compare me to sings a different note in flight.'

'Cuckoo,' Turlough challenged.

'Soft, sometimes pleading. Perhaps he is calling someone from a nest he hopes to borrow. You might call his note deceitful or luring . . . like a woman,' she teased.

'The wren.'

'Wonderfully bland and varied for so small a bird and not to be confused with the lay of the robin, sharp and piercing but less joyous.'

'Chaffinch?'

Her voice was high-pitched in almost perfect imitation, ' "Toll, loll, loll, toll, loll, loll" and the great tit answers back, "'tis sweet, 'tis sweet." '

The old woman leaned into him. The odour of her breath washed over him and he recoiled. She crushed his fingers in her own as she spoke, 'But remember this always. Their note is only determined by the urgent wildness of their nature. As a musician you cannot learn that, you can only find it in yourself – and then release it.'

She paused for a moment. He could hear her sucking on her pipe. Then there was silence again and he could feel her eyes on him. He was uncomfortable, but was unable to speak. After some minutes she spoke again. 'All that anger and resentment in you has a source, and that too must be understood and released or it will beat around inside you like a caged bird. There's no life in the song of a caged creature!'

Above their conversation a greenfinch added his querulous note, 'Twe-e-er.' Turlough thought how it fitted his own mood of growing interest mixed with confusion. The old woman was beginning to intrigue him and his resentment was evaporating. He listened as she described the liquid echo of the linnet's 'chucka-chucka' and breathless 'zip-zap, zip-zap' of the chiffchaff. Suddenly an image coursed across his mind of the old woman sitting saint-like, with the birds at her feet. She was weaving their song into some sort of harmony. The thought disturbed him, for it was immediately replaced by his mother's face, desperate with longing. He wanted to touch the old woman's face, to see her with his hands. Instead, as he always did when emotion was close to the surface, he took refuge in humour. 'Come on, old woman,' he said. 'That donkey's milk you have been feeding me is making me stupid. It's time to walk.'

She rose, taking his hand in hers. He felt her age in the bony fingers and loose skin. He thought of an old turkey. 'I might call you old turkey, mother of the birds,' he said.

'And you might not be able to walk as well as not see,' she answered. There was a giddiness in her voice.

'A blackbird! Can you see him?' he asked.

'No, he hates being seen, but his lazy mellow song gives him away. Not like the thrush who stands singing for all the world to hear. But the mistle thrush won't let him dominate. His song is a monologue as if he were telling himself something he only remembered vaguely. The other proclaims to the whole countryside, rapturously, the fancies and the follies which seem to chase one another through his mind. Be mindful of these two. The more you listen, the more you learn, the better your song can be.'

They walked on, but now not with the groping gait of the aged and the blind. There was a long way to go, but getting there seemed less effort.

Fionnuala Quinn left him at the entrance to Alderford, telling him that he had mind enough to find his own way from there. As he began walking up the path, she called softly, 'Remember, it's only a matter of walking into another kind of light!'

She was gone as quickly as her birds, but what she said left a deep impression on the young Turlough. For the next few days he thought of her. She, too, was a creature of the wild. She lived outside rooms and houses. She could find harmony in the wildness about her. At times he wondered if she was also a frequenter of the rath. She had begun to make him hungry for something. But the following months under her tutelage he felt himself like a caged bird.

Fionnuala was a strict taskmaster and she demanded all his patience. 'Keep your back straight, Turlough and bring it to you like a woman. Let her rest on you, not push you over. Don't hold so tight, she won't run away. Be sure now that the strings run straight up and down between the earth and the sky. Now relax and don't hunch your shoulders. If there's tension in you it will travel into the music. Remember the birds – you have to release them to hear their song.'

She called out instructions as if he was a child. The old turkey woman was turning into a demon. 'Remember you have to think ahead and decide whether you need two positions above the note you are on in order to play the two higher following notes, or whether it is better to change the fingers on a long note. Never play a note without knowing that you're secure and confident, and that it will improve the tone.'

At times Turlough felt as if she was disassembling the very bones and sinews of his hands and then resetting them. He found himself working through the exercises involuntarily until he was so accomplished that he could take the harp and find and play the notes he sought as if the instrument was part of himself.

'Now,' she said, 'you can choose to listen to the birdsong or the screeching that you make, now it's time you exercised your ears!'

And for many hours they drank and smoked and talked. Her advice was rudimentary, but now he had acquired a sense of the instrument all her gibberish and chastisement was beginning to make sense.

'First, and above all else, listen to every instrument and align your ear to the time of the music, learn its language as I asked you to learn the language of the wild birds. Melody is first, and when you are able, you can add what decoration and harmony you wish, but do not let it interrupt the flow of melody. Then listen again. At all times hear what you play and ask, is it what you think you are playing? Listen to the harmonies. Do they ring with the melody?'

So intense was she as she lectured him that the words melody, harmony, oration, were driven into him like a dread warning. But whatever music he listened to, he was beginning to understand the value of having first listened to this old woman's passionate ranting. She told him how to incorporate bass harmonies into his playing, but explained that they must be part of the idiom of the music and should be drawn from it, not imported into it.

'Find the keystone moments in the melody and ask if they need to be pointed up and revealed in some way to deepen, and strengthen, the melody. Listen how moving up and down the notes' range you can support the melody. And remember, never let your hands fall into dispute. They should address one another in prayer and in praise. Each must know instinctively what the other intends to do.'

Fionnuala's final admonition surprised him. She had been driving him for months, repeating her instructions over and over until his head was so full of them that it seemed as if no one else in the world existed and that he himself had had no prior life before Fionnuala entered it.

'Think of the room you sleep in, Turlough. It is decorated with three things, as I remember it. A crucifix above your bed, a burly candle and some flowers of the fields. Let your music be as your room. Carry these things into your music. Above all, you should be able to hear every note. And if you play a note that gets lost, then get rid of it, for it shouldn't be there. If the merging strings sound like a muddy river, your composition is too cluttered. Remember. A bird with its crop full of corn may be greatly satisfied with itself, but it can never sing.'

Turlough slept with these words each night and heard their echo in the morning. They had transformed his room. It seemed as if he had entered the hollow of a ringing bell. It was full of the sound of her words and music; and every night as he slept the harp sat glowing in the dark, the bright glow of its brass strings burning like needles.

The more she seemed to fill him up, the less frequent were her visits. The days that she did not visit felt empty and were only relieved by his evenings spent with Mrs McDermott-Roe. She continued to read and discuss the psalms with him and he revelled in them as much as he had before Fionnuala Quinn took all his time. But now he had a deeper enthusiasm.

He associated his growing musicianship with the great harp of David and he felt an odd association with the psalmist. He was beginning to feel what his old turkey woman had meant about understanding the source of anger and resentment inside himself and he spent many evenings in his room trying to find a musical harmony by which he could release it. He was beginning to understand the importance of Fionnuala's first farewell admonition about another kind of light. He sensed it glowing dimly somewhere inside himself.

The months turned into seasons and the seasons revolved back on themselves. Throughout the revolving year Turlough patiently endured Fionnuala's tutelage. With concentration and practice he could play any tune he heard at Alderford's festive evenings in an accomplished manner. Indeed, it was not unusual for him to be asked to play. He had done so, at first awkwardly, and then with growing confidence. Everyone who listened to him remarked on his playing and was quick to congratulate him on his achievement. He soon learned to accept such praise without embarrassment; on several occasions Mrs McDermott-Roe noticed that he had acquired a certain air, as if he deserved acclaim.

'You've come far in such a short time,' she told him as they sat alone. 'The quiet and intense young man is no longer with us. You've made this place your own and you seem to have shed your father's staff.' Turlough did not answer, but instead took up the harp and played on it. As Fionnuala had demanded, he had learned the language of the harp and more and more now he used it. When he played alone with his patroness it was by way of thanks and she received it as such. But when he was alone he used this new language to articulate things he was unable to speak to others about. The quiet and intense young man had not left Alderford House, but remained in the shadows and spoke to Turlough in whispers. In the long evenings musical phrases of strange elaboration would be heard from his room, but they were stilted and unfinished. Turlough's room had become a place of retreat, exclusive to only him, his teacher and Mrs McDermott-Roe. But the two women only saw the burgeoning artist and were unaware of his lonely evening torments.

There was another part of Turlough which he kept to himself. As he became more knowledgeable about the harp and proficient in his playing, he became bored and increasingly restless. His sleepless nights were returning. The pursuit of musical excellence had isolated him.

Sometimes, without any premonition, he felt as if the house was closing in on him. During moments like this he would take himself into the garden or go walking in the small lanes and fields about the house, always feeling his way with his father's staff. He enjoyed the acclaim and applause that the house brought to him, and he now moved with easy confidence amongst his betters, who received him as their equal. But something still sat uneasily with him. Alderford was only a few miles from his home, yet he was increasingly beset by flashes of longing when he felt like an exile. He was at a crossroads and was afraid to go forward for fear of what he had left behind and what he might lose and never retrieve if he didn't lay his ghosts.

The well-trodden path to his home was not difficult. In any case the months spent walking with Fionnuala Quinn had made him sure-footed. He knew every stone and turn, but a manservant was sent with him in any case. He carried his harp and a muslin bag of meats and bread, a gift that made him feel embarrassed and uneasy. There seemed some betrayal in it, as if it was a payment for something. He thought of the harp on his back. Was it a coat he could clothe himself in or was it a shield? Either weighed heavy on him. Briefly he thought to turn back and make this journey another time, but knew immediately that he could not. The end of this day's journey would be the beginning of something. He dismissed the servant, paused briefly at the cabin door, then entered.

'So, they have taught you how to wear new clothes as well as other things!'

His mother's voice came at him, but its meaning seemed veiled. He had forgotten the new clothes he had become accustomed to wearing. They were not the rough homespun in which he had clothed himself before he left. He realised how comfortable his new clothes had made him feel as he moved about Alderford, but now he felt small in them. He wanted desperately to explain, but knew he couldn't. He handed her the gift of bread, meat and cheese and felt smaller still, like a message boy.

As if she sensed his discomfort she came to him and ran her hand gently across his face. 'You've healed well, Turlough, but you're too pale. There's not enough wind in your face.'

Even these comforting words scorched him. He suddenly felt a longing for her embrace.

'Sit,' she commanded. 'We'll leave the food till later. You have much to tell me and time enough to do it.'

Like the messenger boy he felt himself to be, he poured out the story of his long stay at Alderford in a hurried, nervous monologue. She sat quietly, watching. As he spoke of his first encounter with Fionnuala Quinn she laughed. But Turlough wanted to be quit of his story, as it seemed to affirm the distance he now found himself from his family.

As he concluded, her response surprised him, 'Alderford has been a kind fosterage. Don't be in such a hurry to be rid of it!'

'Let me play for you,' he said, needing time to understand what she was saying. But she put him off, laughing and light-heartedly complaining that the Carolan household was a long way from the habits of Alderford and it would be best to leave the music-making until later.

Feeling more at ease now, he found the hours flying past. It was as if his home had stood still in time waiting for his return. He smelled the old smells, felt out everything in its place, smiled at the cool chill of the window pane without any curtains. Quickly he removed the stout boots and stockings he was wearing and rubbed his feet in the earth and ashes by the hearth.

That evening Sean Carolan splashed and washed before the fire as usual. Though he spent all day in front of a roaring forge fire he always found his own hearth more comforting. Sitting with him, Turlough realised how difficult it was for his father to adapt to his work. His own hatred of noise since he became blind encouraged this new empathy. They drank together and he attempted to explain some of the learning he had acquired. His father's dismissal of the works of the Romans and Greeks was more than encouraged by the drink. 'Look first to your own, Turlough, and mind what Fionnuala Quinn teaches you!'

Turlough took the hint, lifted the harp and began to play. His air was light and soft, but he chose to suppress the gaiety that was bubbling under his fingertips. He was anxious that his music was appropriate to his home. It was as if the tininess of the room inhibited the music's flow. He played with restraint, careful not to offend. As he finished, the memory crossed his mind of Fionnuala Quinn chastising him and raging about her wild birds.

'Play another, lad. Then let's hear your mother entertain us!' his father said. Turlough complied. Determined this time to give more volume and throat to Fionnuala's birds, he let the notes fly about the room with their own abandon. He recalled the walls of his home, empty, but for a crucifix, a statue and a cross woven from dried straw. He could not attempt any elaborate fingering, but the gaiety of the tune could not be withheld. He finally forgot the room's smallness and allowed the music to push back the walls and let a little light in.

There was an unexpected quiet when he finished. Then Sean Carolan spoke, 'It's a different Turlough that sits here today from the one I found shivering and weeping and looking like a frightened animal at Lough Derg. There must be more powerful healing in Alderford than there is in this house. But it's served you well.'

Turlough was relieved, but the reminder of Lough Derg made him uneasy. He wanted to forget it. The gift of music which had been given to him at Alderford had placed a thick curtain over the incident, but he had not been able to put it from him completely. As he sat mulling over the memory he heard his mother's voice.

Her song was low and unstrained and filled at first with echoes of the childhood lullabies she had sung to him as a child. So soft was the melody that he imagined he could feel the goose feather drawn across his head. The perplexing memory that his father had unearthed was calmed by this remembrance from childhood. As her voice lifted and filled the room it seemed to impress upon him the distance he had travelled from his roots. He felt again his father's greatcoat about him and the smell of his mother's shawl comforting him. Intimate things were so immediate to him now. It was as if the awe of the melody had returned his sight again and he could see before him the cottage and its rooms, his mother's voice rapt in song and his father's face glowing from the firelight.

It was both comforting and disturbing. It made him feel extremely lonely and pulled him deeper into the rhythm of her song.

For a moment the room fell away and he imagined himself standing in a moving mist broken by sunbeams and golden light, with skylarks carolling in the background. Angrily, he saw again the shoreline of Lough Derg and almost simultaneously his mother's voice became more impassioned. He saw storm clouds gather, blood-red and blue. He heard again the call of suffering and cries of despair, but above this, the plaintive clarity of her ascending voice gave him back the lark's song vibrating beyond the troubled sky.

Here was a music that the drawing rooms and parlours could not teach him. It was something buried deep in him, which he recognised instinctively. His whole body seemed to be vibrating like the strings of his harp. He began to feel breathless. He could do nothing but let her voice wind itself around him.

When she brought the song to its end he felt he had been drowned in a grandeur too great to follow. His voice was weak as he spoke, 'Irish music is too full of weeping!'

Then, turning towards his father, he called out, 'Give me a cup of what you're having, Father.'

Father and son sat drinking and talking while his mother prepared the food he had brought. The conversation dispelled the tension the song had dragged up in Turlough, but it was too poignant, too close to the bone to be easily dispelled. After a while their easy conversation seemed to become stilted.

The alcohol and the heat from the great roaring fire, compounding this sudden intimacy, became too much. He knew he had to leave. His mother's song had made him as drunk as his father's whiskey had. He needed air and silence to restore himself.

When he made the excuse that he had planned to meet Seamus Brennan for a few hours, his father simply said that Brennan's alcohol was not always as good as his own and he should take some with him. Urgent to be gone from the house, he accepted the small jug his father held out. He turned towards them both, as if he could really see them, and smiled awkwardly before leaving.

The cool snap of evening couldn't penetrate the protective skin of alcohol, meat, and potatoes cooked in goose fat. He strode off into the dark, his head becoming lighter. The fumes from the alcohol mixed with the fresh air sent a second charge of drunkenness into his head. He had arranged to meet Seamus much later than he admitted, and he set his course automatically towards the rath, his father's staff tapping out a clear way.

In the moonlight it loomed larger than it actually was and as always he could feel its bulk call out to him. He laughed to himself as he mumbled, 'Even blindfolded I could find this place.' He stumbled, drunken but assured, to the small coppice of trees near the foot of the hill, which provided shelter from the wind. He could hear a gentle wind soughing through the high branches. It didn't have the intense passion of his mother's song, but the power of her singing voice was still with him.

He tried to remember the landscape around the rath. Nothing changes for the blind, he thought. As he sat listening, his mind began to settle on other things. His mother's voice and father's words were pulling him back to his immediate past. Had Alderford changed him? Had his blindness changed him? They were not really questions in search of an answer, but rather ideas looking for a place to fix themselves on. He thought again of his father's words, when he had found him shivering like a terrified animal by Lough Derg. The memory made him shiver again. No one knew what had transpired there and even he had forgotten it, or so he thought. He felt himself shiver again, but not from the cold.

Quickly he thrust his hands into his pocket, pulled out a candle and set it in the hollow of a small altar of stones he had built years ago. He lit it, laughing at the absurdity. He didn't know why, but he felt safer knowing it was burning there. Next he took out the small jug of poteen his father had given him and took a long swallow, then another.

The alcohol was like flaming ether in his head. He thought of himself sitting here in the open and of the pangs of loneliness that overcame him as he sat at home. Immediately his thoughts turned to Bridgit Cruise. In the blur of alcohol he saw her again, undressing and washing herself through the rain-frosted window. He drank deeply. Then he laughed at his rooftop escapades and her voice scolding him. He thought of walking by the river and her story of kicking the snowmen into the water. He remembered kissing her and how it had made him feel funny, like being drunk.

He lurched to his feet and began turning in a circle, kicking at imaginary snowmen and knocking off their heads. 'Love me, love me not,' he shouted as he turned about, knocking over the invisible figures around him. He was laughing and drinking together, and as he did he hummed snatches of melodies. Alcohol, music and memory were beginning to work together. His voice now lost any grace and his body lurched unsteadily. He was overcome by anger and regret as he stared into the dark and gulped down his poteen. With his voice shaky, but rising as he spoke, he proclaimed,

'The past doesn't hurt me any more. I regret only that I remember. The harp isn't a woman, but she'll come to me and I'll make her sing. I'm going to fill the sky with great butterfly wings. I'm going to obliterate . . .'.

But before he could finish he stumbled and fell exhausted. As he gathered himself up the hysterical laughter turned to tears. For a few moments he sat still and silent, listening as the sobs died in him. Then as if someone had placed one of his father's burning rods in his hands he turned his face up to the moon and screamed into the dark, 'I can't see, I can't see, I can't see!'

He clawed at the stones beside him and flung them into the darkness. Almost in a whisper he sobbed again, 'I can't see, I can't see!'

Something had broken in him and he pulled himself into a foetal position on the ground. He was too frightened to get up and leave. He pulled the collar of his coat about his face and closed his eyes.

The night was full of memory, despair and desire. This was his private place and he desperately sought the relief of sleep. But there was no respite and in the hard dark of the rath, exhausted and numbed by alcohol, he dreamed.

He stood before a huge door. Its gnarled oak panels were fixed with great iron pegs and bolts. An inscription was cut into the stone above the lintel in a language he did not understand. And the door panels themselves were carved. Turlough was fingering the carved scenes to know their meaning – they were familiar, with the texture of embroidered cloth. He knocked again and the doors opened. Before him stood the lord of the house, who bid him enter. His voice was like Manus McCormack's.

Turlough was introduced to a beautiful young woman whose voice was soft like the purring of a cat. He fell in love in an instant and they were wed by old McCormack, who enfolded them in a fabulously coloured scarf. But as he lay with her in the marriage bed, she was transformed and he found himself embracing a withered tree trunk. His member was trapped in a hole in the trunk and was dully beaten. Each time he tried to extricate himself its branches gripped him, tearing his flesh. For a moment he saw himself spread-eagled and naked and the old priest with the head of a heron was torturing him with its bloody beak.

He was then brought to the lord, who enquired after his wellbeing. When he complained of the pain the lord told him to bathe in the garden stream. He entered the boiling water as if his skin was melting, then he was doused in cold water by the beautiful young woman. He felt himself pierced by icy points harder than nails.

He was pulled out of the water by hands that had no bodies and laid on a cart. All around him were wide-eyed corpses, their faces disfigured by hideous pock marks, and all of them looked at him. He was brought to a huge room and told to wait. Then they tied him by his feet from a beam in the ceiling and dashed him against the walls. From a gallery somewhere he heard the voices of women laughing. When he looked he saw only a line of black, bald herons looking at him with red eyes. He saw himself hanging, bruised and lacerated, swinging from wall to wall.

Throughout the dream, the sleeping Turlough screamed and moaned. The suffering seemed interminable.

'Turlough, Turlough! Holy Christ Jesus, Turlough!'

Seamus Brennan's voice finally broke through to him.

'Let's get the hell's gates away from this place. Have you been here all night? I knew it, I knew it when you didn't come. What happened here, Turlo? What happened? Holy God, you terrified me when I came down here looking for you. The noise you were making, Turlo, I swear you sounded like an animal.'

Seamus was panicking and his speech was staccato. He was trembling as he lifted Turlough and they stumbled from the silent but morning-bright copse.

When they were about half a mile from the rath, Seamus spoke again, his voice steady and more confident, but still shouting as if he wanted to break through the blank stare of Turlough's face, 'I thought you were joking, I was almost laughing at your antics, but now! Turlough, what happened there? What in the name of all that's holy happened there?'

Turlough's voice answered him, dry and cracked with fear, still slurred from the alcohol. But to Seamus the words were disembodied from the man he was carrying, 'Don't ask, don't ask! The earth is dirty and full of lies and only the blind are holy.'

Six First Compositions

Journal of Mrs McDermott-Roe

July 20th, 1688

I have had enough! He demands that I leave whatever I am doing and listen while he plays some strange pieces of music he has been working on. Sometimes I can only sit quietly, hardly understanding a note! And if this isn't enough, it is becoming a habit of his to answer people's innocent questions with three or four lines of verse. This would be bearable, were it not accompanied by greedy bouts of drinking.

I wonder where it will all end. What will be left if he continues working and drinking and treating people with foolish contempt? Perhaps the husk of a man, scarred, soured and indifferent to others; whose own world is fuelled with self-indulgent fantastical nonsense. I am afraid to think it . . . a drunken dreamer and a failure!

September 2nd, 1688

The scars of the pox have grained themselves into the skin of his face and do not appear so pronounced and disfiguring. When I look at him now there is a handsome symmetry about his features. His shoulder-length hair is full of lavish curls and waves that any woman would envy. Turlough is blessed in many ways! And much changed in a few months!

September 19th, 1688

Turlough is becoming a great favourite (or great curiosity) with many of my friends. They call him my protégé!

Perhaps they are right. I think, in any case, that it is time for him to take his talents abroad. I am beginning to feel that he is smothered here.

Sometimes, he reminds me of a tarnished coin dug up after centuries, black and stained with the dye of years in bog water – but someone has polished one side for him. One side black from the bog and the other glistening in the light!

September 23rd, 1688

Today I made up my mind and told Turlough of my plans to have him travel to the homes of my friends to entertain them. I am determined I shall send him to Squire Reynolds. He is a gracious but lonely man, and a good friend. If Seamus Brennan can keep his mind off the bottle, he will make an excellent guide. I hate to admit it, but there is no better man with horses. Turlough will have no one else about him, and I don't wonder. He can be so dismissive to the servants – if he is not cursing them, he ignores them completely. Not one of them would willingly go with him!

The journey to Letterfian would be a short one, he had been told, but the shortness of it only compounded the dread accumulating in his stomach. He felt awkward and stupid perched on the trudging horse.

'It's the first time I have been on a horse for years, Seamus. I feel out of place.'

'Why so?'

'Well there's little for me to do but sit here.'

'And look stupid, as you say!'

'All right, Seamus, don't overdo it.'

'I might suggest that you should concentrate your mind on your coming performance . . . for on the quality of it might depend the quality of our supper!'

'Do you know this Squire Reynolds? What kind of man is he?'

'Kind enough, I'd say, and a good friend of the McDermott-Roes. Beyond that I know no more than yourself.'

'Well, let's hope his ear is as kind as you say his character is.'

'We'll find out soon enough. I suggest you compose yourself and remember it's not an execution you're going to. It's a job of work and you have a good few of those in front of you.'

Seamus's kindly dismissal struck Turlough. The cosy security of Alderford was behind him. From now on he must make his own way in the world. This first short journey must be the beginning of many. His life was suddenly laid out before him as a number of journeys to unknown places and people. As he contemplated it, his self-confidence felt shaky.

'I've never been away from the house much,' he said to Seamus.

'One place is much the same as another I suppose,' Seamus answered. 'Anyway, it's not the places themselves so much as the journey. The weather can be a killer, and it's not fussy who you are. So rest assured it doesn't matter much where you're going, only that you get there's as quick and as comfortable as you can. Now a bit less talk from you and the sooner we'll be there. Then you can do all the talking you want.'

Turlough felt justly admonished and sank into a contemplative silence. He hummed to himself bits and pieces of melody. He tried to remember the years spent learning the harp, but so much of it seemed tedium. He could remember the songs and tunes without much effort.

When they arrived, Seamus was quick to help him dismount. Turlough listened, trying to gauge the size of the house by the sounds around him. A strange voice said, 'Well, Master Carolan, you're welcome and much looked forward to. Come in and comfort yourself with a glass of something.'

A hand took and shook his own, then gently led him into the coolness of the house.

'Come, I have a fire in the room and after your guide has stabled the horse and unburdened her, he can join us. But until then you can give me all the news of Alderford and the family there.'

'As you wish, Squire, though I might have little enough to tell you.'

'We'll see, we'll see. Sit here while I find something for us both . . . here now, enjoy that!' the squire said, pushing a glass into his hand.

As they drank, Turlough found himself becoming more at ease. Squire Reynolds seemed to take a good-natured delight in Seamus or Turlough relating some misfortune at the McDermott-Roe household. Turlough began to sense a loneliness in the man.

'Enough of the sagas of Alderford. Mrs McDermott-Roe has nothing but good words for you, young Carolan. Let's hear what she's made of you – though I confess I am no musician myself, so don't be intimidated by my enthusiasms.'

Turlough was grateful for these words but another part of him was annoyed. It was as if the good squire were providing excuses for him before he played. The thought bothered him as he took up the harp. He tucked it squat into his shoulder and reached out his arms to find the end string. His long fingernails danced lightly over the strings to ensure the tuning was true, then, with a sharp plucking as his hands and fingernails darted from the strings, he announced that he was about to begin. Almost instantly he launched his fingers back to the strings and played into the silent room. As if every lesson that had been driven into him had come back, his fingers chased over the strings calling sound out of the harp. They moved with a precision learned by rote and he played without thinking. Only the thought that the squire had already forgiven him his mistakes hovered in his mind, so that he had to concentrate the harder to ensure that each note was precise.

His hands set gently against the vibrating strings to declare an end of the music. Then, suddenly anxious lest he had confirmed the squire's worst ideas, he launched immediately into another piece. There was no timing or no announcement. His fingers flew into the strings and his nails skipped earnestly across them. This was not speed but haste. Turlough was trying to race through the tune before any errors or faults became apparent. He knew that playing this way would discover its own errors, yet anxiety compelled him. He could not see the faces of those who were listening and he felt again that awful frustration he had felt when he first began to learn the instrument. He wanted to curse his blindness and curse the harp and curse those who had made him play. And as he cursed his fingers moved faster and his fingernails seemed to pluck at the strings with dismissive contempt. He played with this intensity until the tune was finished. Abruptly as he had began, he finished, and sat back silent and impatient.

'Here, Seamus, fetch our musician another drink and pour one for me and then will you go downstairs and ensure that our dinners are being prepared?' said the squire.

He listened to the drinks being poured, desperate to know what the squire and Seamus might be thinking. As Seamus stood pouring the drink into his glass, Turlough whispered, 'Well, is it a supper of beef or broth after that?'

Seamus laughed and said, 'We shall have to see, won't we!' and moved away towards the door and the kitchen.

'I should think we could manage both,' said the squire, as the door shut behind Seamus. 'Tell me, lad, how does the life of a musician take you?'

'I hardly know how to answer. I've not given it much thought until today, on my way here.'

'Mrs McDermott-Roe tells me you're something of a strange one, much taken with the delight of your own company. She tells me you spend many hours alone, near the fairy rath. What takes you there?'

'I'm out of people's way, I suppose. It sometimes annoys me to be constantly lifted and led by people. I lost my sight, but I never lost my mind, and being blind did not make a baby of me,' he answered with a laugh. This was not the conversation he had expected, and he was feeling his way through it uneasily.

'Many a lad your age has gone to the wars. There must be some fortune in blindness?'

This was a strange subject of conversation and with some impatience Carolan rejected it. He snapped abruptly, 'If I had my sight I would hardly be a soldier!'

'Good for you,' responded the squire. 'But it's your profession now to praise those who would.'

It was half-statement and half-question and he was unsure how to answer either. Instead he took a long swallow and drained his glass. 'Might I have another?'

The squire filled his glass and then topped up his own. 'I think you might be right. There's little honour in a wasteful death. But there's just as much suffering in art and that takes a lot of courage also. Are you up to that, young man?'

'I think I am,' he answered. There was neither arrogance or insecurity in his voice. The question compelled him in a way he had not expected.

'Aye, and I think you might be also. But tell me more about this fairy rath of yours. Some say there might be magic about those places.'

Turlough laughed. 'And some might be right.'

'Is that what takes you, then?'

Turlough was slow in answering. No one had been so persistent before about his visits to the rath, least of all a stranger. 'There is something about the place, call it magic, if you will. I find its stillness somehow full, if you know what I mean. There's a mystery there that pervades the mind. It allows me to think intensely but clearly.' He stopped and seemed to hesitate, then said softly, 'I seem to see things there . . .'.

There was a long pause as he waited for Squire Reynolds's response. There was none and he was relieved. He wasn't ready yet to talk of such things. Still the lack of comment bothered him. After some minutes the squire said, 'There are those who believe that blindness is given to some as a gift.'

'Aye,' snapped Turlough 'and those who say that some of the sighted are blind. For my part, I wouldn't wish this curse on anyone. It's a thief, and in more ways than one. I have to be continually patient with others because they are so overbearingly solicitous of my blindness. So I go to places like the rath. I can be myself there without the fussy attention of people!'

The squire seemed to take his reaction to heart. He began, 'I didn't mean . . .', then quickly changed the subject. 'I've a proposal for you, young man. Take it or leave it as you please, but give it some thought before you throw it away as an old man's fussing. You seem to have little taste for soldiering or for the bloodletting that has cursed this land and its people. But there's another war that you might think on.'

With this Reynolds began a long tale of two hills where two fairy queens resided. Such was their rivalry that a great war ensued between them. 'It was a battle of petty jealousies and ludicrous vanities,' said Reynolds, 'as maybe all wars are.' The squire filled his cup and replenished his guest's. 'Think on it, young man, you might compose something from it. I think that mind of yours might be sharper than those fingernails.'

There was a long pause, then Reynolds, encouraged by Turlough's curiosity and by the alcohol he had consumed, said lightly, so as not to offend, 'And I think your playing might improve if the music was of your own making. Now then, let's eat before one or both of us becomes incapable.'

That night Turlough slept restlessly. Dinner had been accompanied by too much strong wine and whiskey. He had quickly become fond of Reynolds as the evening progressed and he was smitten by the story of the two fairy hills, as Reynolds insisted on calling them. 'Sidh Beag agus Sidh Mor, fairy hills,' laughed Turlough to himself. The squire's anglicised imagination had reduced the spirit world to this childish contrivance.

'A fairy war,' Turlough said aloud, 'with flying horses and twinkling swords, magic appearances and disappearances.' He laughed deeply at the nonsense he was concocting. This was the imagery of a mind which knew no correspondence with the dark but majestic spirit which he secretly believed in. The rath was his spirit refuge, where he moved in harmony with his other world. The war that might be fought here was not the ugly and bloody brutality which had ravaged Ireland and which was the subject of much discussion in Alderford. Alcohol was fuelling ideas in his head. His spirit world was a place of clarity and light, where everything found its place and moved in order and harmony.

He thought of Fionnuala Quinn's words as she taught him the mysteries of the harp. 'The old people', as she called the spirit world, believed the universe was ordered by sound – all things were held together in harmonic relationship. She spoke of the 'harmony of the heavens' and the 'harp of David' as she told him of the tuning tabulator of the Ogham signs, old runic symbols which existed before invented language. She had instructed him in the tuning of two flights of overlapping notes, which gave him the soft warbling and quivering that made the rich embroidery of his harper's art. And now he was beginning to think there might be some truth in all her mumbo-jumbo, some inner secret that he must discover, however long it took. He could hear her words again: 'Nothing is given, it must be discovered. The power of music will not reveal itself without a struggle. The secret code must be searched for. For here is the healing and reconciling of opposites, just as the sun and moon sit in harmony and balance.'

Was this the war of the fairy queens which Reynolds had so little understanding of? Carolan began to sweat, as ideas and memories flashed through his head. Reynolds in all his naiveté had given him something. Such a composition as he was beginning to envisage was impossible, yet his mind would not let go of it; and somewhere in the back of his spinning imagination the fairy queens were dancing. He heard Reynolds's words again, 'I think your playing might improve if the music was of your own making.'

This was a double-edged compliment. He knew he was an infant at the harp, and an old infant at that. His fingering had not the grace or subtlety of one who had been put to the instrument as a child. For a moment he cursed his blindness that it should have afflicted him so late in years. No sooner had the thought entered his head than he remembered his abrupt dismissal of Reynolds, that he would not wish this curse on anyone. Now here he was wishing that he had been blinded years earlier.

The next morning he excused himself to his host, saying that the excess of the previous night had not yet fully left him. 'They say there's a healing in music, Squire Reynolds. So I mean to find what cure I can for this great hangover that's banging in my head like my father's hammer.'

'Feel free to use my house as you wish,' the squire replied.

'Thank you, sir. And I'll see what I can do with the fairies!'

Reynolds laughed, remembering the rambling discussions that had occupied the two of them long after dinner had been eaten. Everything from music, poetry, fairies, the land, religion and the savagery of the penal laws when set against the superiority and humanity of the ancient Brehon Law had been tossed across the table between them. 'A mighty evening, Carolan. That tongue of yours might well play a better tune than your harp! Good luck to you.'

Carolan left the room with things on his mind that he wanted to thread through the strings of his harp. This was the beginning of his epic. The ether of alcohol and imagination was a whirlpool he was determined to swim out of and he had all the exuberance and confidence of youth to buoy him up. For many hours he sat in the garden, oblivious to what went on about him. Even Seamus was given short shrift when he called out, 'Well, maestro, is this the workman at his craft?'

However, hours of tinkering would not show him a path through the previous night's miasma. Nothing seemed to ring true. His fingers could not find the co-ordinates of his thoughts. But he persisted. Hour after hour he attacked the strings, and his frustration grew. He wanted eloquence and he wanted depth, but his bass hand had not the power. He could not find the right quality to mirror and shadow the sunlight in his harmony. The effort exhausted him. Only a mind less preoccupied with its own artistry could even begin to sound out what he was seeking. He had not the capacity to answer what he was only beginning to ask.

'Seamus, Seamus,' he called out and when he came, he asked wearily, 'take me for a walk for my head is mighty sore.'

'And no wonder after the night you've had. Take it easy, Turlo, you'll never find the fox till you've got a scent of him!'

'Aye, and this is a cunning one I'm after.'

The two men walked about the garden and along the stubble-strewn drive leading to the house. At first Turlough was silent, but soon he took delight in Seamus's account of the drunken conversation.

'My God, the fairies were flying last night. It's a long time since I've been so entertained. You teased the man rightly, and he enjoyed every minute of it. And when you promised him you'd bring him fairies in the morning I thought I'd burst.'

'I had those frolicking fairies all night, I can tell you.'

'Well, before we go, you'll entertain him so, and thank him in doing it, for he's a gentle soul after all.'

'I suppose I must, and so I will,' Turlough said, resolved that from all his efforts there must be something pleasing that he would offer: 'Take me back now and fetch my harp into the house. I'll cobble together something from my sweat so we can earn our stay.'

It was many hours after he had returned to his room that Turlough asked to be brought to his host's presence, where behind closed doors he delivered his homage to Mr Reynolds's fairies. His music was light and airy and he played it without the apprehension of the previous evening. The squire listened with curious attention throughout the rendition. When Turlough finished, the squire said, 'Well done, young Carolan. A hair of the dog to the man that made it.'

As he spoke, he pushed a filled goblet into Turlough's hand. He was both pleased and honoured at the gift the young musician had given him.

'It's only an apprentice piece, and I hope I do some justice to the ideas which you have given me.'

'What's done was well done to my poor senses and I'm grateful for it.'

'Well, sir, thank you. I hope Seamus and I may now leave for Alderford. I feel a bit uneasy on that horse while Seamus leads me on foot.'

Some hours later Seamus and Carolan took their leave of Squire Reynolds. But this time both men were mounted.

'Well, Turlough,' Seamus commented, 'I don't know what you played for the man but I'm a horse better off for it. If this is a sign of things to come I think you might do well at this music business. What did you do for the man to make him so pleased and so generous?'

Turlough reined in his horse and sat unmoving for a moment, then he said, 'Well, Seamus, it was simple really.' He paused again, leaning his head back and turning his face to the heavens, and with a great laugh rising up in him, said, 'I conjured up the fairies for him!'

As the weeks passed he was often off on his own, playing or trying out new lines of accompaniment, but the effort seemed fruitless. The words must follow the music and the music must have priority, then the words would find themselves. He had not forgotten Fionnuala Quinn's insistence. For hours he laboured and worried over his fairy queens. He became so distraught that Mrs McDermott-Roe called him to her room. Weakly he tried to explain what was troubling him, but he knew his words and thoughts were as confused as they had been at Squire Reynolds's. She listened patiently until she detected notes of self-pity and then she addresed him quietly. She was anxious that what haunted him had little to do with his music. 'Don't drive yourself so, Turlough. You are young yet and too ambitious by far. When you have lived more then you may be able to explore these dark realms. Entertain us now with what we know. Master the craft that is handed down. The world is dark enough, Turlough, let the music heal – give us light and give us life. That must be your musicians' task.'

Turlough was grateful for the comfort and was about to speak, when she began again. 'There's someone here I think you should meet.'

Eager to get away from this conversation, he rose. Mrs McDermott-Roe took his forearm and guided him across the hall into the large room in which she always received her guests. 'Sit here a moment while I find our visitor.'

Turlough heard her leave the room. There was a musty smell of old books and a fireplace that someone had forgotten to clean. Sitting there, he began to feel anxious about the conversation he had just had. Residues of alcohol had loosened his tongue. As these thoughts wandered about in his head, he heard the door opening and people entering the room.

'Well, here he is, Bishop, our musician, Turlough Carolan. Turlough, this is Bishop O'Rourke.'

Before Turlough could stand, a large smooth hand took his own. 'Indeed a prodigy. I have heard you play often in this house.'

'You two gentlemen sit and be comfortable while I fetch something!'

As she finished, Mrs McDermott-Roe closed the door behind her.

Turlough wished she hadn't left so quickly. He knew of the bishop, though he had never met him, and he felt vulnerable. He was a man whose position and attachment to the Church had made him unwanted and shunned in many parts of Ireland. Those who ranked high in the Catholic Church had been either hunted out of the country or lived a life in hiding. Some, like the bishop, would always be well received in the old family households.

As Turlough sat nervously contemplating what was to follow, the bishop said, 'Mrs McDermott-Roe has great expectations of you, Turlough. She has also told me much about your life here.'

Turlough became more nervous and even defensive.

The bishop continued, 'I know your father and mother.'

Turlough moved towards the edge of his seat. What would this man know of his family and why would he want to know them? Turlough was becoming aggressive. He was unprepared for what this man might say.

'Even the lord took time over his creation!' said the bishop. 'Your patroness tells me you spend a lot of time alone, sometimes at the rath. You have a mind that asks many questions, but sometimes the questions we ask redirect us from our purpose.'

'Bishop,' said Turlough, half-apologetic and half-aggressive, 'if you know anything of my family and myself, you'll know I'm a poor communicant of the church.'

'Yet you read and study and psalms with more zeal than many a priest I know.'

Turlough sat silent. He sensed he had been too quick and too defiant.

The bishop moved closer. 'Don't worry, it's your music I came to speak of, lad. There is much in music, as there is in faith. But perhaps only a few know the truth of this. The chief character of music and what makes it a religion is its purpose to teach and elevate. But to hear and understand men must be brought up with good music. Yet in our circumstances, with things as they are, where men believe so little,' the bishop paused for a moment then continued, 'a life without art is all brutality, the musician must always strive for the beyond in the knowledge that the good in art is always there to be found.'

Turlough's temper shifted from aggression to attention.

'The world is as it is, and for the most part it is disappointing. I hear you are struggling in the dark realms of disappointment also. Yet there are some who would know more. How can they know without a teacher? How can a proper response be drawn from them? As art draws out, so must it direct. It must seek out and express high sentiment. Music is the Mass. Concentrate on this, as there is in people a truer instinct, not simply religious, but shall we say artistic, so we must create a sense of proper relations and fitness of expression.' The bishop paused again, then, with a smile in his voice, he concluded. 'We must create a music fitted to soar into the great vaulted arches of the cathedral. This must be your aspiration.'

As if she had been waiting for this moment, Mrs McDermott-Roe entered the room.

'An apt benediction, Bishop,' she said, 'and here's the refreshment I promised.'

But the bishop had not finished. 'We were speaking of why we must never allow our native art to be tainted and your drink makes me ask, "Are we to drink, a generation late, the dregs of England's Cup? Might we not more trust to ourselves and drink of that more wholesome cup?" ' He paused and stood in thought.

Turlough thought of his talk with Squire Reynolds and his dismissal of a soldier's life. There seemed to be something militant in the bishop's words: 'There is within us an absolute art, even in its faulted remnants. We have capacities and inheritances, though we have not much of the last. But yet we have something.' There was a hint of excited urgency in his voice that fascinated Turlough. 'And when we are ourselves we are not in imitation. There is within our culture something extraordinary. In our music, as in other matters, if we are ourselves, we should be more able to enter the world of art. Art is real and unpretentious, not falsely self-conscious and forgetful of life. It can express everything, taking from what is local. And we must express it with our own individuality.'

The bishop stopped to take a long drink and Turlough found himself smiling as he remembered his own excited thirst. The bishop saw his reaction and smiled, then asked Mrs McDermott-Roe if he had been sermonising too much.

'It's not for me to say,' she answered. 'I wasn't in the room to hear you. But, by the looks of him, Turlough might.'

The bishop's words had inspired a confidence in Turlough he had not known before and the thought of his own drunken evenings had made him giddy. 'No indeed, I have not been spoken to in this manner before and I am wondering what Fionnuala Quinn might make of it.'

The bishop drew his chair close to Turlough. 'She might well curse the manner in which I tell it but she would applaud its essence.'

He laid his hand on Turlough's arm and continued, his voice relaxed and confidential as if he were speaking to a close friend, 'We must refine ourselves from what we are. Never play bad music, and more importantly never listen to it. If those around you have not the ears to hear, then unstop them. Lead them by the sounds that are in them to follow. If they learn and if they believe, then by your guidance you may help them to make a virtue of the life that is so denied them. Indeed, if it's in you, you might inspire a nation.'

The room was held in a stunned silence for a moment. Turlough himself felt breathless and excited. Then suddenly he laughed. 'Holy God, father, if you knew how many times

Fionnuala Quinn pulled and jerked at these ears of mine until I heard nothing but what she said. And now here is the bishop commanding me to do the very same!'

Turlough sat, amazed with his own giddiness. Then he rose. The last few days had wearied him, and he wanted to take the bishop's words back to his room. He felt them already beginning to unravel much that his thinking and imagination had become tied up in.

In his room he lay on the bed. He was exhausted, more in mind than body. Too many things had been happening in too many days. But he still felt that what the bishop had said was of more importance than perhaps even the bishop realised. Something in what he had heard had given form and shape to the purpose of his chosen life's work. He knew instinctively what the bishop meant when he said that music is the Mass. If life was brutal then why, indeed, should art reflect this? Could it go beyond? Could music be a healer of affliction? Turlough thought back to his drunken turmoil at Letterfian. He thought of the endless hours he had sat alone trying to find some musical correspondence to his confused thinking. The bishop's words about creating a sense of proper relations and fitness of expression struck home to him. He knew this rage for order, but now wondered if he had misunderstood its application.

He lay still for some minutes then absent-mindedly stood and removed his boots and stockings, throwing his coat at the bottom of the bed. He walked pensively across the room and pulled the heavy curtains before turning to light his candle. He found it lit and smiled at his patroness's kindness of thought. He lay down again. Undressing had eased the pressure of thought. He felt he might sleep, but something still held back that relief.

The bishop's words came at him again, but this time it was as if someone had laid a cold compress on his forehead. 'If we are ourselves, we should be more able to enter the world of art . . . Art is real and unpretentious, not falsely self-conscious and forgetful of life. It can express everything, taking from what is local.' The words reinforced their stamp upon him. 'We must express it with our own individuality.'

He sat up slowly. That was it. This was the resolution he had been looking for. He squirmed at the words 'self-conscious and forgetful of life'. He had been looking into the dark too long and, seeing only himself, he had become obsessed. The thought began to stir up anxiety. Yes, he had wanted to look in and recreate what the bishop had called the coloured dome of eternity, even in Letterfian. But he had not looked to find it first, in life. His thoughts were coming faster now and he began to feel the knots untying, like snakes writhing away from a sudden flame. Then he heard again his words of defiance and despair called out to the wind on the shore of Lough Derg, 'I rejoice in the world, I rejoice in the flesh . . .'.

The morning was bright and fresh and Turlough threw back the curtains with relish. His sleep had been deep and untroubled. He dressed quickly and took himself into the garden. This morning and for months to follow he was to be found lying in a shaded corner, for hours, drinking in what Fionnuala Quinn had taught him of the melody of birdsong and the universal harmony of nature. The garden became his daily retreat and the rath, which had been a secret compulsion, now intrigued him less and less.

As the weeks passed, he seemed less intense and less troubled. All the urgency had washed out of his face. Even Mrs McDermott-Roe noticed an easiness and steadiness about him. His sudden long disappearances from the house became less frequent. She still visited him in the evenings, but found to her surprise that he would now ask her to read from the Song of Solomon rather than the psalms. Sometimes he would simply sit silent when she ended. At other times he engaged her in discussion about musicians who had lived before him. Had they a sense of purpose beyond the playing of music? And if they had, how did they explain it? How did they reconcile their music with whatever they thought was its purpose?

It was obvious that he had, over the months, been carefully considering the bishop's words. He had a growing sense of music's social value. He once asked Mrs McDermott-Roe if she thought music existed, in some mysterious way, in the people themselves before it came to the musician. These were questions she could not answer, but she was convinced that he might find the answers in the company of others. Increasingly the shy, defensive, self-impelled young man was casting off his adolescent vanity. He was becoming a man, a social creature, who was beginning to understand his need of others and more importantly was beginning to enjoy their company.

'You can't sit here each night, Turlough, pestering me with these questions. I have provided you with horse and leader, and Squire Reynolds has given Brennan his own mount. So you must take to the road and find your answers from whom you will. I will arrange some visits with my friends over the next few months and if you're up to it, no doubt they will recommend you on to their friends. It seems you may be firmly on the road.'

For all his openness and ease, Mrs McDermott-Roe noticed that one aspect of the old Turlough remained. She would see him on occasions in the garden, with his head in his hand and the knuckle of his thumb rubbing against a spot between his eyes. She remembered his mother telling her of the head pains that Turlough had experienced from his childhood.

In the meantime Mrs McDermott-Roe had arranged for him to visit Denis O'Conor, the O'Conor Don, at Bellanagare. The O'Conor Don took to Turlough immediately and was soon to call him 'Bard'. This was a special honour. The bards of earlier years had had a special function, to uphold tradition. Turlough was learning quickly what his function might be.

Between his stays at Alderford and Bellanagare 'the Bard' was busy with musical excursions with his guide, Seamus Brennan. On one occasion he visited a family at Longford. Here he was asked to compose a tune for their daughter. She was a young creature and as innocent as his own composing skills, but the curiosity and kindness with which he was received encouraged him. When Mrs McDermott-Roe asked him how he had fared at Longford, he simply replied with a smile, 'My song was full of wind and trees and innocence, but it pleased them mightily.'

That evening as he entered his room and went towards the candle to ensure it was lit, he found on the small cabinet on which it sat a goblet, a rosary of coral and a handful of buttons. He fingered the items curiously. He could easily imagine who put them there, but for what reason he could not fathom. As he pondered the possessions before him, Mrs McDermott-Roe's voice answered his thoughts, 'It's not a great many years ago that no bard would leave his doorstep without making sure he had his goblet and beads with him.'

'And the buttons?' asked Turlough.

'A personal gift. I've watched you on many an occasion, silently count out the rhythm of your compositions upon your buttons. Mind you do not lose them, they're silver!'

When they talked that evening, Turlough said that the little composition he had made for the family at Longford had encouraged him to another piece. He had the remnants of it in his head, but every time he sat down to play it it seemed to change and take a different direction. When she asked him what the inspiration for the tune was, he answered at once, 'Bridgit Cruise'.

'That tune might take some taming!' she replied, and as Turlough turned questioning towards her, she explained, 'Your sleep gives you away. This is not the first time I have heard her name on your lips, and if you have the skill I think you have, I hope it will not be the last.'

And it wasn't. Turlough set himself to the task. Perhaps because he was addressed as the bard, perhaps because he had been given the gift of bardic amulets he began to compose with what he had learned and heard as well as what he felt. He toiled over many weeks to find the right musical form for his memory that would allow him to share his emotion.

He wanted the music to convey a sense of the person and of the musician's response. There would be no tortured plucking of the strings, no bitter regret. He wanted the harp in his hands to be Bridgit. The music was to be about acceptance, a celebration of love, another way of loving. 'It seems old McCormack may have been right after all,' he thought to himself.

He was determined this music should be born in the garden. He had never been indoors with Bridgit, so the daylight hours found him propped against a tree or wall, slowly kneading his forehead. Bridgit seemed to him to have too many faces, but he could now think of her and of them both together without being racked by the memory. It was as if he had been set free. He felt he could not yet compose one long piece, rather he thought of separate moments and composed around them, hoping that they would find their own harmony.

He pulled the harp to him and it found its snug place on his shoulder. His nails plucked the strings into a gentle rhythm, coaxing out the images that would direct his music. Slowly his fingers moved across the strings as if they were sewing lace. In his mind his composition moved slowly into focus as if he was seeing Bridgit through her misted window. Like a candleflame flickering, the music lit up as her image warmed and came close to him. He allowed the melody to establish itself as his composition moved to the moonlit riverbank. The music became less evocative. Now it was tender but full of desire. Each note sounded in its own clear space and linked effortlessly with the next, like her teasing voice. The music shifted again. It was a wistful goodbye, but strangely filled with quiet joy. Sadness moved through it but without pity or recrimination. Then it echoed the opening melody in a moment of praise and thanks for beauty.

He played the music over and over again to ensure his timing fitted the emotion it sought to capture. There was no need here for harmony or ornamentation. It had to be clear as the air about him, but not disturb its stillness. An echo of the harp music of the ancients was informing his composition: the tinkling of the small strings lightly sporting with freedom under the deeper notes of an imperceptible bass. Somewhere he heard the mellow voice of his mother wrap around him. He could do no more. He released his hands from the harp and set it beside him. His fingers caressed its carved head.

For the next few days Turlough moved about in a kind of languor. He seemed neither distracted nor contemplative. His mood was light and he responded good-naturedly to those in the household he came across. Some of them thought at first he had been drinking secretly but he was too composed for someone who had been several days indulging in alcohol.

His creativity seemed to have taken flight and it was no surprise that he began reworking his tune for Squire Reynolds. He thought he might compose words for it to give the music more force. And when he thought he had the words he sought, he brought them to Mrs McDermott-Roe.

'I have decided that those "fairies" that people think I spend so much time with should be taught a lesson!', he said cockily. She looked at him with a puzzled smile. 'Listen,' he commanded and began to pluck the notes. Against the lilt and lift in the music Turlough intoned his verse, and Mrs McDermott-Roe listened patiently.

Journal of Mrs McDermott-Roe

January 28th, 1690

Turlough has composed a curious tune tonight, it is a song full of high moral enthusiasm about the fairy war. He declares the enmity between the fairy queens is 'the fight that destroyed our heart'. His composition, he insists, is really a plea for reconciliation and peace. At whatever price, Turlough's song proclaims that peace is better than slaughter.

I wonder at his innocence. This is the blackest year of our history and the land is awash with men's blood. I wanted to tell him that his price was too great and too many had already paid it in full.

I was unsure whether Turlough was playing with me or not. He can be so changeable. One moment passionate and excited, then suddenly sullen and withdrawn. I thought I would test him, so I asked him if he really thought that a mere mortal could teach the spirits anything. 'They say the spirits are the good people and friends to us mortals. Why would they engage in such slaughter?' I asked.

Turlough's answer was quick and dismissive. 'Don't you worry about that. Immortal beings can never be killed. It's no more than a faction fight to them. Isn't it more important we learn some sense of morality from them than all that nonsense about them tippling on heifers' milk and stealing newborn babies?'

But I was as quick with my reply, and suggested that there were some who say that's what happened with you!

The laughter welled out of him at this last remark and I could not help but join him, while at the same time asking if he had finally cast off the fairies and finished with his visits to the rath. His answer was absolute, but I knew he was teasing. 'Never, for we may learn more from what's buried there than all the tutors and priests in Christendom may teach us.'

I hope Turlough is right, but I fear we have more dreadful lessons to learn.

Part Two

SUANTRA
Music of Love and Joy: 1693–1735

Being a collection of letters, conversations,
memories and journal entries
from Turlough Carolan's closest friends

Absent thee from felicity awhile,
And in this harsh world draw thy breath in pain,
To tell my story.

William Shakespeare

Journal of Mrs McDermott-Roe

June 10th, 1697

Turlough is irrepressible. He has taken to the road like it is second nature to him and has become a great favourite with too many of my own friends. The Dillons, the Conmels and the Drurys are forever requesting him to call to them. He is a bit too sure of himself and is drunk with pretension at times. A few days ago he told me that, whatever his life was to be, the road would shape it. He gestured with an outstretched hand as he spoke, as if the world was waiting for him.

Alderford is a base from which he radiates out into the country as though he is on some kind of mission. Who does he think he is? It is dangerous to mistake a profession for a 'calling'. At times he struts about as if the world and everyone in it is waiting for him. The reports I hear of him do not paint such an admirable picture as he would have me believe. Perhaps I made a mistake in taking him in . . . No, I will not blame myself.

I think he is overly encouraged by my cousin, the O'Conor Don, and his son Charles. The O'Conor Don lives too much in the past and addresses Carolan grandiosely as 'the Bard'.

His son is altogether different, bright and studious: I hope he will challenge Turlough. Charles may yet reclaim more for the name of the O'Conors, perhaps even for Ireland, than his father with his penchant for wallowing in the past.

February 2nd, 1698

Carolan returned today full of enthusiasm for the harpsichord. He says its music is airy and gay, like music dancing on tiptoes, but that it needs the enclosed space of a parlour or library. He remembers asking his father about the instrument many years ago – he paused as he recalled the incident. I thought this was another of his newly acquired artistic affectations, but he really seemed possessed by the memory.

I was about to ask about his father, but he quickly read my intention, laughed off the recollection and declared that the music of the harpsichord had no place in the open air. It might be balanced, but it needed soft chairs to rest on or the long flowing robes of women's dresses to roll itself in! He declares he needs something wilder and more elemental. He says the melancholy of the old harp is too maudlin, it weights his fingers. I wonder at his authority on these things. As for his flamboyance, I was about to remind him that it was far from such sentiments that he was reared!

February 11th, 1698

Young Charles tells me that Carolan has been spending many hours at the harpsichord. He is trying to play the instrument and has long conversations with Charles about the music it makes.

Charles explains to me that Carolan uses it as a sounding board. He often tries to play a tune he has spent some time composing. If he cannot manage it, Charles is seconded to the task. Once, having spent many long hours playing and discussing the instrument with Charles, Turlough jumped up in barely concealed rage. Charles laughed as he acted out the petulant scene for me! Charles undoubtedly admires Carolan, but I am not convinced of the quality of Carolan's relationship with Charles!

May 23rd, 1701

Tonight Turlough treated us to one of his compositions in praise of drinking, for which he is becoming overly infamous. One of his dizzy verses runs,

> *A while drunk, a while mad,*
> *A while playing the mistress on my lap*
> *smoking and drinking and going insane*
> *This is the fashion we will practise*
> *and ever play it, again and again and again.*

Apparently it has become his war cry and in every tavern people acclaim it with loud cheers.

There is another song he is often called to play, a tale of a bawdy musician, who, after many days' constant drinking, concludes with the words,

But I was weak, Yea laid low,
Without a stir in my foot, or my hand
And my heart could not even awaken itself
At the sight of a pretty milking girl.

It seems our bard has a habit of looking at his private parts, while delivering these words, obviously suggesting a lack of arousal and his inability to take advantage of the milking maid! I am glad he keeps such perverse performances out of this house.

September 17th, 1708

I revise my opinion of Seamus Brennan completely, but wish I could do as much for our famous harper. His reputation walks before him, and it is not one to take pride in.

I fear that Carolan's gracious reception at the homes of 'the gentry', as Seamus calls them, have set him at a great distance from his friend. In the ale house they are as thick as thieves, but Carolan's fame and status sit uneasily with his friend. Brennan is a man of fixed habit, who is content in his own small world in and around Ballyfarnon. He likes a place that he knows and things that are familiar to him.

Tonight when I asked him how their journeys went, he answered me in an almost apologetic tone that he had never been one for the road and that the last few years he had had more than his fill of it. 'The road is Turlo's place and no doubt he'll find his end on it,' Seamus said, but he concluded ominously, 'he doesn't see it as I do!'

I could get no more out of him, so late this evening I approached Turlough. He was in a fine mood as he had spent the previous hours at Greyfield House with the O'Conor Don and Charles. The bloodshot corners of his eyes told me just what they had been up to.

I asked him about Seamus's confession and how he felt about it. He was at first shocked, then angry. I heard him slur something about betrayal. Then in an almost derisory voice he snapped, 'Manus McCormack told me that once a man starts out on a journey he should never turn back! We each have our destiny!'

I could not control myself and told him that he would drown before he found his own destiny and that he would never see it through the bottom of a bottle! I know some men's natures are more steady and resigned than others, and I can excuse his poetic nature much, but when his arrogance becomes insolence, I cannot tolerate him.

Seven Hayrick

Journal of Mrs McDermott-Roe

February 26th, 1738

The last few days have exhausted me. There is a new urgency of life about him. His mind is focused yet erratic, like a child's.

Today he told me he had had enough of being cooped up in his room alone. Alone indeed! Have I not been tending him like Mary Magdalene herself? He complains that he will be a long time dead and his room has the feel of a coffin about it and he insists on leaving it and meeting people.

I felt guilty for having refused to allow him visitors; but as each day goes by the numbers of people arriving in the village amaze me.

March 4th, 1738

There is an incredible brightness about his eyes, a new strength in his voice and body and with it a terrible impatience. He throws tantrums if I insist he stay in bed and drink only water. Nursing him is trouble enough, but I am to be a wet nurse? He may have his visitors, but I have restricted the numbers and have instructed the servants that only Seamus Brennan, the O'Conor Don, Charles his son, the bishop and Charles McCabe may be allowed entry.

March 6th, 1738

Seamus Brennan has spent some time with Carolan. I pity him, he seems more broken than our patient. When he is not in Carolan's room, he spends many hours in the kitchen with Charles O'Conor. I am not privy to their conversation, but I do not mind this so much because it must be some consolation to Charles, who is hesitant about visiting the sickroom.

'I don't wonder you don't want to visit with him. He's not a pretty sight at first, but thankfully the old Carolan is still wandering about inside that feisty old head of his. The things he remembers . . .' Seamus paused and stared into the fire roaring in the great kitchen. Charles O'Conor waited for him to continue, but realised that Seamus was caught up in his own memories.

'Sometimes I thought it incredible the way he could recall music instantly though he had heard only once. But, typical of Carolan, he then made it his own!' Charles's remarks seemed to have drawn Seamus back to himself. He looked slowly about the kitchen, then glanced at Charles before he continued.

'This kitchen reminds me of the night we stopped in Hugh Dempsey's on the road to Sligo. Jesus, that was one wicked night. I was never more glad to darken his doors. Do you know it? No, I don't suppose you do. We had to climb up that steep stone staircase that was built against the outside wall, like some stone caterpillar with us two fleas on its back! I was always anxious about his hands. The weather could be so bitter. The cold cuts into you and can cripple you.

'We almost fell into the place in our hurry to get out of the sleet. It seemed like half the countryside had taken refuge there. The place smelt like the carcass of a waterlogged boat that had been baking in the sun. Dempsey's customers looked more like skeletons than men. They hung about the walls as if they were afraid to move out of the shadows. In the centre of the room and about the fireside were the small farmers and a handful of drivers and coachmen. They huddled round the fire as if it was their own, their faces half hidden by the smoke from their pipes.

'We seated ourselves by the window, close to the smouldering fire. The sour smell of boiled cabbage and horse sweat mixed with the stench of raw spirits was everywhere and Turlo was in a foul temper. I remember him declaring, "There are a few here with a three-hapenny mouth on them sounding like five guineas!" The weather had put him in one of those moods when he didn't care what he said or who was listening.

'I called for a waiter, who approached us with his greasy apron belling out behind him. The sight of an apron in Dempsey's was something to behold! We were about to order, when a neighbouring coachman called out, "While you're here, I'll have a bowl of boiled pork, and make it hot, no slops mind."

'Turlough bristled and with a sour challenge in his voice, said to the waiter, "Fry us some duck eggs to put with your man's pork, pepper them both well, put two stout crusts of oatmeal bread alongside, and when you have brought that here to us, serve your man there. And while we are waiting, you can bring us both something hot, strong and sweetened with honey and make it a double measure."

'The coachman sneered and spat on the floor, grinding it underfoot. But our Turlo wasn't finished. "There's many a one carries the arrogance of their master without having the substance of it," he said. Then he gulped back his drink and shouted, "Bring another, lad."

'I knew this moment only too well. Master Carolan, here, readying himself for a quarrel. Heaven help any man foolish enough to suppose the mighty Carolan would stand in line behind him. When he was in his cups, he was the worst offender at the very crime he railed against. I watched as his eyes twist in their sockets, and I knew his mind was racing, trying to bridle his anger. I sat silently, dreading the abuse that might gush forth at any moment.

'Fortunately the waiter returned and set up our drinks again. There was little else for it but to pour the drink, and another, and another, with Turlo roaring that a bird never flew on one wing. I tried to warn him, for he had been 'flying' as he calls it for the past few days from that "fortifier" he always carries with him. But he was oblivious to the warning and it was useless to complain further.

'The idea of food, I hoped, would distract him from his violent drinking. But then I saw an old, decrepit organ thrust against the wall, some distance from the bar. I can remember it clear as yesterday. The tall pipes were like huge hunting trumpets and the thin red pipes gleamed in dusty silence. I told Turlough of it, as if I had discovered a holy relic. Then I lifted him and steered him towards the far wall. We must have looked like the pair of bedraggled drunks we were. When we reached the instrument, I placed his hands on it and went to pump the bellows. As he seated himself, I remember him declaring, with a smile spreading on his face, "I dare say the pawnshops in hell are full of the likes of these."

'If people had not been listening before, this loud insult caught their attention and just to ensure that they were attentive he began to paw the ramshackled instrument.

'Almost immediately a great sigh issued from the contraption and a creaking of the rollers followed, but this was brought to a quick stop by a premature squeak issuing from a thin pipe. "A small fart, no more," laughed Turlo. Then all the pipes, large and small, burst into a ferocious wailing, and our musician called out above the racket, that a chorus of blind men, singing and coughing, were trapped inside her and that he was going to let them all out. The attention of everyone in the pub was riveted on him. I was anxious. Turlo sometimes loved to feed the animosity that he had a habit of gathering about him in such places.

'Fortunately, the waiter approached. He explained that the instrument had once been installed in the private chapel in the local lord's house. Before the English armies could destroy it, the estate workers had managed to cart it here. In a lowered voice he told us that this room had been a chapel for the faithful. The organ had served as an altar, and even in its silence had given consolation to many. I could well imagine how the presence of this instrument would have transformed the atmosphere of the barn we were in. But the curious union of ale house and temple made me smile. When I think on it now, I'm sure the man was hinting that we should leave the thing alone, but he was too frightened to say so.

'The organ was in a pitiful state; some stops were broken and the whole thing seemed to be held together by the dust and grime that layered it. Part of it lay behind the counter and was being used as a funnel for pouring liquids. So much for holy relics. I wanted to stop pumping and return to our table. But I knew it was too late to pull Turlo away and I felt myself squirm as he began fingering the thing again.

'The last of the daylight had gone. It was that time when things undergo a curious change and the rapture on drinkers' faces was mirrored only by the intensity of Turlo's own face. The music swirled up and seemed to settle in the rafters. The noise of the faulty reeds and broken stops, was swallowed up by the roar of sound. It was as if the instrument itself had been blown clean and began to yield a clear prospect of what had lain choked up within it.'

Seamus turned his face from Charles and looked towards the ceiling, as if he was trying to hear the music. Charles's answer assured Seamus that he had been following every word: 'His knowledge of the instrument was limited. Many years ago I stood in the great hall of St Patrick's cathedral with Turlough. Dr Delaney had a secret wish that Turlough might compose for the church and he spent many hours instructing him on the great organ that was housed there. I remember him fumbling at the keys and pedals trying to sense out what quality of life was in it.

'He told me some days after that he hoped that he might find in the organ a depth of resonance that he could not find in the harp. But he said it was as if the notes were afraid to fly out of the instrument. I can still hear him declaring with that pompous eloquence he loved to display, "That instrument is for more muscular faith than is in my heart." '

Charles paused and Seamus continued his story.

'He seemed incapable of making much of the old organ. I was too hungry to listen further and returned to our corner and one of the farmhands took up the pumping. His face was bent into his chest as he continued playing, but the music had become stilted and monotonous, as if a tarpaulin had been thrown over the organ. I rose quickly and made my way to the far wall. I pushed a drink towards him, and whispered "Give it a rest now, Turlough. Here's food for thought."

'He lifted his hands, searching out the drink. The noise around us was growing, with people shouting, "Sound, man." "Another before you go, there." But there was a vacancy about him. His voice was almost childlike as he spoke. And he said something that has puzzled me to this day. He complained that his hands hurt him and that he kept thinking of wedding music, but he couldn't play it. Then he said, "You can't forgive a thing like that. It should never be forgiven." '

Seamus looked puzzled as he said this. He waited for Charles to reply, but Charles remained silent and when Seamus spoke again his voice was low and shaky.

'You know, when I was with him today and we were

remembering this story, he suddenly said, "It's the curse of memory, Seamus. The things it drags up and casts in your face." Mrs McDermott-Roe was in the room. She turned to me and with her finger on her lips she signalled silence. Then she went to Turlo and chastised him for talking too much. As she began to wipe the perspiration from him, he sat quietly like an obedient child. Then, after what seemed a long time, he roused himself and declared, "Aye Seamus, alcohol and emotion are two very uneasy companions . . . and it is part of my nature to drown one in the other."

'And it is so, and I told him as much, saying that there was an old devil lurking inside him still. Like the old Turlo, he almost sang out to me, "Many of them! I suggest we invite them all to this party of ours. Shall we make a night of it?"

'I can tell you, Mrs McDermott-Roe gave me a look that was fit to kill, but I was only too happy to encourage him. I leaned across and clinked cups with him, then looking at the unfinished meal on the bedside table, and eager to change the topic of our conversation, I ventured, "Now what about food, man? There's a devil in me too and right now he could devour the leg of the Lamb of God!"

'But his thoughts were still fixed on the memory. "I think I butchered the lamb all over again on that sad instrument." He paused, then said pointedly, "I hate old broken things that have nothing in them but melancholy, and I include myself in that!"

'He took a long slow sip as if to underline what he had said, then said more slowly – and it was obvious that his thoughts were elsewhere – "When faith loses its mystery, it loses its power to compel. But it should be a mystery of light. The black heart of man must be lifted up out of its despair. Music that does not compel us to laugh and dance has little part in the life of men. We live in dark enough times. Religion should have the same quality as music. It should liberate us."

'I wasn't too sure what to say, so I simply answered, "The memory of that organ has brought out the preacher in you." "Never!" he shouted. "There's only one sermon I want to deliver, for there's more joy and life in a full glass than in the dry stony words of the clergy."

'Well, that was enough for your aunt and she gave us both her own sermon. "I am in no mood for sermons. You, Turlough O'Carolan, should not condemn the clergy with a glass in your hand and you, Seamus Brennan, can take yourself off to the kitchen and wait while cook prepares some hot broth. Now away with you! And make sure you don't indulge yourself in my cellar. This is not Dempsey's, you know!" '

'Maybe we should take up our friend's invitation ourselves,' said Charles, pouring a drink for Seamus, who watched and tutted in mock imitation of Mrs McDermott-Roe. Charles smiled and they both toasted 'Turlo' like two conspirators before Seamus continued.

'He loves stories, so I'll finish mine while we drink this.' He paused only long enough to drain the goblet.

'The night didn't end with his organ recital and, as he himself said, he is no organ master or sermoniser and soon he forgot the organ and took up the harp. There was not a person in the room whose attention was not on him. Everywhere feet were stamping and heads nodding to the tempo. Those haunted and emaciated faces that had peered out from the shadowy corners before seemed to come to life.

'Jig followed jig to whoops of delight, as Turlo named them, and threw back his head and laughed as he plucked the tunes out faster and faster.

'He was in his element and the customers responded in a way that he found irresistible. With them he could perform with an abandon that he did not find possible in the homes of the great and noble. Here he was among his own kind. Here he was blind Turlo and not Carolan the Bard. A great gawkish grin spread across his face as his head jerked with every jig. Sweat rolled off him and wisps of hair clung to his cheeks as he tried to toss them from him. There was always a deep red glow to his face that belied the amount of drink that had been taken. Every time he paused, voices would roar up at him to continue or else call out the name of another musician's tune, and Turlo would roar back in mock abuse, "To hell with him, and to hell with you too, for it's Carolan's night tonight." Or else with the same mock contempt he would stand up and berate whomever had called out, "If you're not fit for listening to what I'm playing, then you're not fit to be sitting drinking with us. So you can take yourself off to hell's gates away from amongst us."

'When he finally stopped playing it was as if the music was still dancing about the room. The place was busy with excited voices laughing, swearing and shouting for more. No matter how he had abused them they loved him for the music he brought to them.'

Seamus stopped to take a breath and Charles poured again.

'But he was the moodiest of men. One minute he is crying at an old broken organ about wedding music and the next he is chasing after barmaids. Let me tell you about Mary Kelly, for I'm sure he never will.'

Seamus laughed to himself as he acted out the barmaid in Dempsey's banging the drink down on their table. 'There so!' The master of the house say's I'm to see you don't go thirsty tonight.'

Seamus explained that he had not seen the woman approach and he watched her as she sat the drinks before them. She was older than her voice had at first made her seem. She smiled at him, but kept her eyes on Carolan. 'Your music has certainly warmed a few hearts tonight!'

Seamus remembered the directness and honesty in her comment, and he noticed too the rough hardness of her hands. He was about to say something when Carolan asked her name. 'Mary,' she replied. Carolan, though blind, still had an eye for the women and a tongue that could be as laced with honey as it could be with abuse. Seamus mimicked Carolan's voice as he acted out the scene.

' "A blessed name, Mary, thank you for your compliments. I may have warmed many a heart here tonight, but who is it will warm mine?"

'Mary answered with a familiarity that made us both smile. "If you finish what's in front of you, I don't think you'll feel cold tonight . . . or anything else come to think of it!"

'Her familiarity only spurred Carolan on. "Come, sit beside me Mary, for I have had only this man's company for too many days now."

' "And I will so, for I've been on my feet for too many hours to refuse."

'From somewhere across the room someone called to Carolan

to mind that he keep his hands on the harp and off the woman. Carolan ignored them. "Well, Mary, what would a pretty young woman like yourself be doing here? I'd have thought you'd be at home with a husband or a lover."

'Mary laughed and slapped Carolan's knee. "I'm neither young, nor am I pretty, and as for a husband, I've not seen or heard from him in years. And as for this place, it's provided me work and company."

'She was staring across the sea of faces as she spoke and didn't notice Carolan lift his harp again. His fingers caressed the strings gently. As he did so, he spoke softly to her and about him the room quieted and listened. He told the story of a woman whom he knew well. When her husband died, his brother dispossessed her of what land and wealth her husband had left for her and she was forced to return to her own people, penniless, to seek work to support her young family.

'Carolan began to recite, intoning to the graceful notes that slid out from the harp. The words flowed like a litany.

"Black head, black head, darling black head
  move your head over me.
O mouth of honey, on which is the scent of thyme,
He is a man without a heart that would not give you love.

"She is the Queen of Connacht, Miss Mary
  of the bright white mouth.
She is the loveliest and the best of woman
  that I have seen.
Her side was like the swan and her eye like
  the green grass.
Her cheeks are like the rowan berries at the
  rising of the day.

"If you forsake me, madness will possess me,
This land of Erin I shall see no more.
For I gave love to you as Naoise loved Deirdre
And for whom hosts of men laid down their lives.
Move head, move your sweet darling head upon me,
Put your smooth white hand over across me

O mouth of honey, on which is the scent of thyme,
He is a man without a heart that would not give you love."

Charles noticed how Seamus seemed rapt in the words as he repeated them.

'The room was hushed as the last notes fell from the harp. But Mary broke the silence. "If a man loved a woman as strongly as you make it seem, I don't think even his dying could destroy it."

'Carolan took a long drink and smiled curiously towards Mary. "If love were always so, then perhaps you would not be as lonely as you are, and I wouldn't have the pleasure of you at my table."

' "You're an old charmer, Turlough Carolan," Mary answered, without any hint of coyness or sentiment.

' "Charms!" laughed Carolan, then lowering his voice, he whispered, "Charms are the ploy of deceitful women, I'll give you charms and deceit and the death of great men!"

'And with that Carolan's harp rang out the first notes of his lament for Owen O'Neill. Instead of singing the words of the lament, he told its story, of the death of a great man at the hands of a woman.'

It was an old story and Charles had heard it often, but Carolan had a curious way of telling it and Seamus insisted on relating it again as if Charles had no knowledge of it. Charles, for his part, could not disabuse him.

Owen O'Neill had been given a pair of dancing shoes by the daughter of General Monroe. She pretended to care for Owen, so he was delighted with the gift and wore them to a ball which he and the young woman attended. Little did he know of her perversity, for she had impregnated the shoes with a lethal poison.

As he spoke, Carolan had conjured up the young lovers, dancing in a ballroom brilliant with gold and gilt and crystal chandeliers. But even as young Owen embraced the woman he loved, the poison was seeping into his flesh and slowly leaching the life out of him. 'Here, indeed,' said Carolan, 'was a hideous dance of death, disguised by love's embrace!' As he spoke his voice and music dropped a register and the tempo of the music changed. Carolan sat silent and let the lament for the fated hero being slowly consumed by poison harden in the minds of his audience. Even Mary was moved by it and laid her head against the musician's shoulder. The music was compelling against the background of the story and the audience hung on every word.

When he thought he had brought them to the edge of expectation, he continued with his story. When the young man returned home he was in great pain and his feet were swollen, so much so that his attendant had to cut the new shoes from his feet.

He described the young woman on her knees, weeping and bathing her lover's blistered and swollen feet. 'But there was no remedy for love's deceit!' He suddenly affirmed, tearing notes out of the harp. The volume was deafening and for a moment it seemed as if the notes bounced off the walls as if he had struck the strings with a blunt hammer. Behind the music he went on, 'And in a short time the beauty of life left him.' The sudden conclusion had the same effect as the fierce fingering of the harp. But if the story had finished the music had not. It softened and found a more even pace. The death dance became a funeral march, which ended as an oration and elegy.

'The whole place sat stunned,' Seamus said. 'The bard stood and, laying the harp across his outstretched arms, he handed it to me and I took it from him with equal ceremony. Then he lifted his glass and continuing the pomp and ritual declared, "A toast to those, our countrymen, who have gone before us but left their greatness with us." He tossed back his drink and as he did the room was shattered with the noise of everyone jumping to their feet. Chairs and stools scraped and tumbled backwards. Bottles, glasses and tankards rattled and clashed as voices chorused the toast. I jumped up and cheered as well. I swear to God, I don't know whether I was acting it or I was as carried away with his performance as the rest of the room!

'Then he sat back regally and sipped slowly at another drink. I sat speechless. This was a performance I had not seen before. He had played without restraint, finding his cue in the men and women around him. He had taken a room full of strangers who had little in common with each other and had moulded them according to his fancy. "By Christ, Turlo," I remember saying to him, "that was a performance and a half. You've drunk them under the table, scourged them, laughed with them and hurled abuse in their faces. Then you lullaby them with love songs and finish them off with a story and a lament that destroys them – and they sit there loving it, and adoring you. How do you get away with it?"

'But his answer was directed towards Mary. "I'm not such an ogre now, am I, sweetheart?"

'Mary leaned back and studied him closely, before looking at me and then back to Carolan. "I'm not so sure about that, Turlo Carolan!" she said.

'Turlo laughed and turned to me, but his words were intended for everyone in the room, "Do you think I'm some sort of conjuror, Seamus? No, my friend, I know these people. They are as close to me as the blood in my veins. We are a race of people in search of our soul, which seems to have got lost or is in hiding somewhere within us. I only remind them that they still have a soul and that it's a proud and glorious one and that it's capable of great love and great passion. And what happens when a man finds his soul? He wants to rejoice, he wants to celebrate. That's the hunger in everyone of us. To find our soul again and rejoice in the discovery." '

Seamus paused, and turned to Charles, 'When he wasn't making up fabulous stories, he was sermonising and everybody in the room was believing him, and half the time I think he believed it himself! His arrogance was excused by the alcohol he had consumed, but it rankled with me. I was uneasy with the way he played with people's affections. God forgive me for speaking unkindly of the dying.

'Anyway, across the room the barman was barking out orders and banging half-eaten food into a slop bucket. As he passed, the dogs crawled up from the fire and trotted after him. Three or four young children darted towards dishes he had not yet collected and rifled what the customers had left. But I remember one particular sight. An old couple hobbled across the packed room. The man's greatcoat was patched and threadbare. The seams at each armpit gaped, exposing his filthy undershirt. His wife's long grey hair was tucked under the shawl about her shoulders. Her wizened face was toothless and had the buttery white pallor of age. Their feet were wrapped and tied with rags. I had seen their kind so many times before. The roads were full of these destitute creatures but what was odd about these two was that they shared a single walking stick between them.

'Hand upon hand, both clutching the gnarled stick, they shuffled across the room. As they passed, I noticed a hessian bag, held by a piece of worn rope, strung across the woman's back, the tops of an old pair of leather boots poking out. The old couple passed by the gambling coachmen. One turned and swore viciously at them as he spat at their feet. I heard Mary's voice trembling with passion behind me, "Keep your abuse to yourself. Their custom's as good as yours, and their manners could teach you something!"

'I turned and saw the anger on her face. She looked ready to leap at the coachman's throat. The coachman knew it and looked back sheepishly at his table. I must admit I was moved and angered by the pathetic sight. I turned to Carolan and downed a large measure of the rough whiskey before I spoke, and when I did I let him have it.

' "Christ Almighty. It's well for you, you're blind. Hungry souls. Holy Jesus, Turlo. The only thing I see is hungry bellies, bare feet, poverty, greed and a bunch of drunks sitting out there! And every one of them swallowing the lies you're feeding them. God love them and God forgive you Turlough Carolan." I must admit I was shocked at my own voice.

'But Mary was not finished. She admonished me for my words, though the bitterness with which she had challenged the coachmen was gone. "Ah, hush, man, will you? He's not deserving of such harsh words – especially not between friends."

'Carolan said nothing in response, but simply asked Mary to fetch his harp. As she handed it to him, he said to me, "If they're drunk out there, then they are indeed blessed and we should join them!" As his fingers trembled across the string, the clean notes seemed to lift the animosity that hung about the table.'

Seamus was struck by this memory. Rarely had he ever allowed his irritation with Carolan be overheard. But he confessed to Charles, there were times when the bard's performances were more than he could bear. But the thought of Carolan lying dying upstairs made him feel guilty and he laughed nervously.

Charles had enjoyed the story and could well understand it. The Carolan he knew was more refined, though there were moments when he thought the man half mad, yet maddeningly irresistible. He told Seamus that he had heard some mourners in the village say that Carolan was the greatest womaniser in Ireland and had made more music with women than he ever had on the harp. Seamus smiled and said that women were certainly drawn to him, and that perhaps the thought of a blind man's hands upon them enticed them. 'But however much he loved women,' he said, 'it was with a dark kind of love. Turlo played with women, but whether he really loved them . . .' Seamus let the statement hang in the air and ended, 'If he loved them all, good luck to him, for he's in a lonely place now and heading for a lonelier one. Drink up now, for I must go back to him, or your aunt will have me horsewhipped for sure.'

When Seamus returned to his friend's sickroom with some soup, he found him fingering the harp, while Mrs McDermott-Roe sat silently beside him. His own thoughts were still fixed on the evening in Dempsey's. The recollection of Mary Kelly, the barmaid, had raised a devil in Seamus. He said to Turlough nonchalantly, 'I'm told to leave this, and leave you alone to eat it, for the cook says you'll eat nothing while you have company. Talking of company, I have been sitting in the kitchen remembering Mary Kelly. Don't tell me you don't remember her, or perhaps there are some things men don't want to remember.'

'Away with the both of you for I have things to do that would not be fit for either of you to see. And you leave Mary Kelly to me, Seamus Brennan.'

As the door closed Carolan sat back and smiled at the incident Seamus had reminded him of. He could hear Mary's parting words to Seamus as he left them to make their way to her home from Dempsey's.

'Well, good on you, I'll be along in a while or so. Are you sure?'

'When there's no audience to play up to, he's no bother.'

He wanted to recall the evening Seamus had unearthed for him. There was something about that night on the road that no one else knew about, not Seamus or even Mary Kelly herself.

He remembered the cart piled with hay. It made a great soft earthy mattress as he lay on it, covered up to his eyes in sheepskin. It was warm and soft and the bumps in the road rocked him gently. The smell of the skin and the hay, combined with the languorous heat in his body, was pleasing and lulled him into a dreaming sleep.

At first the dream was nonsense, fragments of conversation and shadowy faces all flitting at random in and out of his mind. But then everything settled down. He loved this moment. He could not be sure if he was in a hayfield or a field of grain, but it was huge and a host of women were working it. Their sickles and their scythes made a gentle wind sound as they worked. Turlough thought he recognised the field. He knew he had been here before. He saw himself walking freely among the women. Their presence and the smell of cut grass seemed to excite him. He walked through their stooping forms, supervising their work. He would occasionally call out to them, 'Take it tight, take it tight.' It was as if there was no other man in the world except himself, and he was the axis around which the grateful female world moved and bowed incessantly.

Everywhere about him women's buttocks were moving and undulating in the great meadow. He stood in the centre. His hair was chestnut and flowing, his eyes bright and shining. He was a conqueror. He turned to one of the women and pinched her, 'Don't wag your tail, woman, get down tight,' he said masterfully. The woman turned to him and looked at him, silent. He was stunned and could only look back helplessly. The woman's face was placid and expressionless and he felt he knew it intimately yet could not recognise it. 'Down woman,' he wanted to say, but the woman's face weakened him. The power of her silent expression was drawing the energy out of him. He sensed he knew this woman, but her features would not reveal themselves.

He looked desperately around, wanting to be out of the meadow. He was afraid that all the women might turn and look at him. Now he was running through the fields looking for a way out, but his every exit was blocked by a fast-flowing river. He was exhausted and sweating. The stooping figures were ominous. He wanted to reach out and touch them, but he needed to find the way out first. The day was becoming hotter and hotter. Standing off from him he saw the woman who had turned to him. She was raising her hand. He watched, but did not know whether she was waving a farewell or calling to him.

Suddenly he was jolted awake. At first he was unsure where he was. The wind in the roadside bushes and the crisp night washed away the dream's potency. Night and dreams, dreams and night, they were a maze of delight and confusion and he shivered as the darkness chilled into him.

He recalled the evening, the music, the talk, the arguments, the drink. Everything had been served up in double measure. He smothered the memories in the warmth of the sheepskin and thought of Mary. She laughed like a rainbow and had a provocative coarseness to her voice. He wanted to speak, so he pawed the air to find something to pull himself up by. 'Mary, are you still there?' he said as his hand reached her backside. 'Yes you are,' he finished, pulling himself up and pressing his back into the cart's sides.

'Back with the living?' she asked.

'Where are we? It's cold enough to freeze a body alive!'

'We've a bit to go yet. Snuggle down if you're cold.'

'Up and down like muck in an ice hole,' Turlough complained to himself. 'Tell me, Mary, is it a widow you call yourself now?'

'Neither maid, nor wife, nor widow!' she answered, the huskiness of her voice teasing him.

'How's that then?'

'Men have no conscience at all, men haven't. They think shoes and shawls will keep a woman happy. But I find no pleasure sleeping with a shawl and it's too many years I've been doing it.'

Mary's answer was direct and Carolan had the feeling she was talking to herself as much as him. He was curious. He felt playful and the alcohol encouraged him.

'How long?'

'Four years or more. Gidup now, Maeve, it's no night for slacking.'

'My God, Mary, the man's deranged. Now, if it had been me, I'd have stuck so fast to you, you'd have to beat me with that horsewhip to get me off.'

'Hmph, I wonder!' she mocked. Turlough could not tell if she was pleased or not but he continued, 'I tell you, Mary, you can pack up all the shoes and shawls and pawn them tomorrow and wager every penny on it. Just give me a chance.'

Mary snapped the whip in reply and the big mare trotted into the shelter of the trees that ran along the side of the road.

'It can't be much fun in these parts without a man,' he continued, trying to gain some reaction.

'Don't you think if I sold all the shoes and shawls and any other trinkets I'd have enough money to have little need of man?'

'You no more believe that than I do.'

'And what if I don't, there's not much point in rubbing it in.' Then laughing, she jibed at him, 'A village woman's nothing to you, I suppose. I'm sure you've had dozens of them.'

'Oh, dear Mary, a priest wouldn't be asking what you're after asking!'

'A priest would know better!'

Turlough laughed, there was an easy warmth about Mary's response that made him feel at ease.

'Mary, if you've got a drink in that driver's box you're sitting on, I'll tell you about town women.'

Mary reached down and half-turning handed him a stone jug. 'Here's your drink, but I've no interest in listening to your gossip.'

'Well, have it your own way,' he said and took a long drink, then continued. 'I knew another woman called Mary. Her husband was killed. She just withered away, went as thin as a board and some say went mad as well.'

'Indeed, and I'd go mad if I listened to you!' They both laughed. Then she said poignantly. 'It's all right for those who get killed . . . he stinks for a bit and then it's over. But it's a hell of a life for the women . . .'. There was a long pause then she continued, 'Some days it's like you're not living at all.'

He noticed how all her assurance had gone in those last words and tried to retrieve their earlier teasing humour. 'Well, there you go, Mary. Isn't that the first sign of madness.'

But Mary's mood had changed. 'Loneliness is not an easy thing to shake off,' she continued slowly, disregarding his remark. 'And anyway, what's the idea of getting me worked up? I'm nothing to you. You just go back to sleep and leave me alone.'

Turlough knew he was being chastised but also knew that simply to go to sleep would be a greater unkindness than his foolish remark. Swiftly she came back at him as if she had read his thoughts, 'There's not much point in asking a blind man to take the reins while I warm myself where you are.'

Turlough felt her remark was a plea for pity and comfort, and in her own way she was taking the measure of him. It was a challenge as much as it was an offer. He sat in silence. The minutes that passed were filled with the noise of creaking shafts and the trudging of the horse's hooves. Maeve had given up trying to trot and returned to a slow walk.

'Don't you think that old mare of yours knows her own way home by now?'

Turlough was aware of Mary turning on the driver's box, 'Let me in, I'm frozen,' she said, pulling the sheepskin from him.

'You're a bold woman.'

'Not bold, bone cold, and if your hands are as mighty as you tell everyone they are, then you might be able to do something about that.'

Turlough laughed, but the laughter was soon smothered. Both of them were equally strong and well built, and cold, compassion, need, lust, pleasure all demanded their own fulfilment. The power of Mary's desire overwhelmed him. She dragged the man from him almost mercilessly, but he was suddenly afraid. He felt small and clumsy. He felt her close, smothering him and when she spoke her voice was thick and desperate, 'Your mouth, man, give me your mouth.'

He was frightened like a child and tried to squirm out of her grip and bury himself in the hay. In a panic he heard himself whimper. Then he choked out the words, 'Leave me alone, please, I can't breathe.'

An overflow of panic possessed him. He felt himself smothering in the straw. For a moment Mary froze as she clung close to him. Delicately she laid her fingers gently on his eyelids. 'Hush,' she said and as she spoke, he shivered and wept inside himself. It had been a long time since anyone had touched his eyes with such tenderness. 'Do you miss much in your darkness?' Her voice was soft and shy, but curiosity and kindness drove the question from her.

It was a long time before he answered, 'There are things in this life, that I am glad that these eyes have never witnessed, Mary Kelly.'

She started up, then, playfully pushed him from her, grasping his hands and placing them on her own face she demanded, 'And am I as pretty as you would wish me to be?'

Turlough explored her face slowly. He was silent as he traced the curve of her cheek, his cool fingers flowed up to the hollow of her eyes and broad expanse of her forehead. Then his fingers ploughed their way slowly through the tresses of her hair. The silence and the intimacy of his touch began to frighten her a little. She was impatient and anxious and for an instant feared what might be passing through his mind. She felt the nervous tension in his hands. 'Well man,' she burst out. 'Are you feeling sorry or relieved?'

He laid his hand awkwardly on the swell of her breast as he fumbled to draw her blouse about her and then said defensively, 'You are a lovely and beautifully sinful creature!'

'There is no sin,' she said, returning his tease, 'in exchanging a healthy living man for a dead one.' She leaned into him, and whispered into his ear. 'I don't know how fine a musician you are, Turlough Carolan, though I think you consider yourself fine enough; but I have discovered you. You have made a mistress of the harp, for a woman is an instrument you haven't learned to master yet.'

Turlough mused on Mary's words. Even after all these years they still hurt him. He had forgotten how Mary had exposed him. He had forgotten that dream which froze him in his bed of straw. He remembered he had once told young Charles O'Conor that if he died dreaming he would die happy. But not that night with Mary, for dreams and the flesh conspired against him. Perhaps Mary herself was a ghost woman sent to haunt him.

'Ah, good Christ, have mercy,' he said to himself. 'Don't come back to taunt me with this Mary Kelly. If we all knew then what we know now.'

He paused and smiled. He remembered Seamus Brennan teasing him when he came to collect him from Mary's home the next morning and here he was, more than forty years later, teasing him again. Seamus only knew half the truth and had no doubt made up the other half to suit himself. But that was the way of the world, half-truths would always do if the whole truth did not fit; and was he any better than the rest? He was content with the half-made world people had created for him. But now he despised it and he despised himself that he had not lived more honestly. As if the thought was too much, he dismissed it and once more spoke into the empty room.

'If I couldn't tell you then all the thoughts and feelings that unmanned me that night with you, Mary Kelly, let me tell you now and perhaps you may forgive me and leave me in peace. There was another woman and another night, but there was no dream and no ghostly women to frighten me. Though this woman frightened me also, for she too thought she had uncovered me. But there was something about her . . . maybe I simply wanted to make up for our lost moment. It was in the shell house by the lake, at Dillion's mansion. I have always been drawn to water and that's where she came to me. But she would not let me forget her the way I wanted to forget our fateful night, Mary Kelly.'

Eight Carolan's Devotion

Journal of Mrs McDermott-Roe

March 13th, 1738

Since Seamus Brennan has been here Turlough has improved, but he has made the rest of our lives a misery. First he wants this and then he wants that. I am sure Brennan sneaks whiskey into his room, for the stench of the place in the morning is overbearing. When I complain Turlough makes a witty remark about the smell keeping death on the other side of the door!

When I ask Brennan what they find to talk about into the small hours, he declares, drink and women and dreams, and then he explains with drunken elaboration that to Carolan's mind drink is the only real thing, while women and dreams are both insubstantial.

I feel sure this is Brennan's own nonsense, though sometimes I wonder. Yesterday Turlough demanded that I leave some flowers for him. He specifically asked for yellow lady's bedstraw and some sea shells in his room. When I asked whatever for he simply answered that they reminded him of some very dear friends and when I turned to Brennan for explanation he shook his head. I wonder it didn't fall off.

I refuse to be treated like a servant by these men and I will be quick to show them both that this woman is no insubstantial thing if I hear any more nonsense.

March 15th, 1738

I have spoken with the bishop about Turlough's bawdy behaviour. It is so unbecoming. But the bishop simply tells me to be patient. He has confided to me that sometimes when old men know their death is near and inevitable their thoughts turn to carnal things and their talk becomes fleshy and indulgent. He says that for some men it's fear of what's waiting for them and for some it's a last chance to take a deep draught of life!

I suppose there is something in what he says and if I am honest I must confess to being a little jealous! Does an old woman not need to take a last deep draught of life also – and can she not be afraid also?

March 20th, 1738

Turlough has me exhausted these last few days. He wants to know who is in the village and what they are saying about him. But he refuses to see anyone but the O'Conor Don and Charles, and he demands that I bring the bishop and McCabe to him the minute they arrive.

I may have been his eyes for the last thirty years and more, but that doesn't mean I see the world the way he does. He wants to recall everything and expects me to have all the answers and remember everything. You would think, by the way he has been talking of late, that he was the finest bull in the island of Ireland and that room of his was filled with women every night.

Seamus Brennan Remembers

The Dillion household was one I took no great pleasure in. Maybe because himself liked it so much. But it was more than that. You see, the people made too much of him there and he wallowed in it. He always wore the showiest of clothes when we were there and had me fussing around him like a parlourmaid as he dressed in preparation for a performance. I can still hear him saying that tonight he would bring them the first rays of summer and then he would demand that I found his blue vest and cream shirt and a curious yellowy-gold waistband which was a gift from old McCormack before the pox took him. And he always insisted on hanging his coral rosary from it. He was mad for colour and would pace up and down dressing and undressing like a nervous virgin. Virgin, did I say? I wonder how he would like the description. Already the village is full of stories of what a great rake he was, and most of those who tell them have never met the man and hardly know a tune he played. But I know more than these half-wits and hangers-on. I remember a night at the Dillions' house when the gamecock's mating song turned sour in his mouth.

Carolan was seated amongst a small group of people. Around him the large parlour hummed with whispers and laughter. It seemed the whole house had gathered for the entertainment. But Carolan was in no hurry to entertain. He was master of the moment and he would have his audience wait on him. To put an extra edge on their anticipation, he turned slowly in his chair and with much affected caution set the harp on the ground beside him and stroked it affectionately. Then he called loudly for a drink to ensure that people knew he was there. A young woman came to him and he began his usual game, asking her where she came from.

'This very house,' she answered confidently.

'You may have the manners of the house, but your voice tells me you've different origins. I doubt there was much white linen about when you entered the world.'

He had been drinking with the Dillions earlier that evening and as usual his intake made him dismissive of those whom he thought had climbed above their station. The young woman's voice trembled.

'I . . . I . . . I'll go and . . .'

'Ah, never mind me. I'm just an old dog that barks when he's thirsty. Go on with you now and bring me a good drink. And be sure you come back here and help me finish it.'

Her laughter as she moved away told him he had been forgiven. But I have to admit such behaviour rankled with me. As he sat contemplating the possible origins of the young woman, he was interrupted by another. 'You were a little unkind to her, were you not?'

The woman was older, more assured, with something of a challenge in her voice. He was quick to rise to it. 'There are some here that are too quick to bend the knee,' his voice grew more angry as he continued, 'and there's some who have forgot where they come from or who they are!'

'And what about you, master musician?' The woman's voice was softening but had not lost its confidence. I sensed she was teasing him. Carolan ignored her and listened to the gabble of voices and laughter about him before replying. 'What about me? I'm my own man, madam.'

The woman was not to be intimidated. 'Surely. You musicians

are a strange breed. You make every house your home, and seem to have none of your own. Where do you feel most at home?'

It was not the kind of frivolous enquiry he was used to. I wondered what she meant by it and could see that her question had disconcerted him and he wanted to be rid of it. 'Whichever is the sweetest to my senses!' he answered dismissively. This woman was too familiar and too curious. It was obvious to me that Carolan did not feel himself to be 'his own man' as he professed, but this woman was not going to be charmed, or chased off.

'So you make your own world according to your own pleasures?'

'Don't we all?' he replied.

'If we can – and only if we know what might please us most.'

He was intrigued by her wit and it disturbed him a little. He was unsure if there was a teasing barb in her question, and he decided to end the conversation. 'It seems you are your own creature also!' he said dismissively.

The woman laughed. Her laugh was deep and I could see that Carolan felt trapped, as if he had been cornered and she was savouring her first taste of him. He moved uneasily in his chair. Then he raised his glass to drink, pausing to savour the wine's bouquet before drinking it down greedily. I was becoming anxious, so I went to him and made some remark about the decor of the room, which wasn't much to my taste. He answered me in the same sour tone he had used with the woman, 'Has the liquor addled your brain altogether? What are you saying, man?'

'There's not a wall that isn't decorated with the head or body parts of some unfortunate creature, and the staring eyes on them . . .'

Before I could finish he demanded that I walk him round the room. I thought it a ludicrous proposal and said so to Turlough, 'They're dead blind, you're blind and I'm blind drunk and you want me to show you the corpses on the walls! You have the queerest notions, but let's go and glory in the gaping dead if that's what you want.' And off we went and found some quiet corner to ourselves.

We both stood for a moment as I took in the faces of the decapitated animals and the staring portraits hung opposite. 'An image of eternal enmity,' Carolan called out as I described them.

But it was obvious his thoughts were still with the woman to whom he had last been speaking. I thought another glass of wine might distract him, so we walked to another corner and found ourselves a full bottle. I must admit I was enjoying his discomfort.

Himself leaned against the wainscoting. As I filled his glass he reminded me of a moment in his childhood. Like all his stories it was about the world before he went blind.

He saw six or seven stags being driven towards a lake. He remembered how they burst out of the woods, the yelping dogs streaming after them. The dogs were already up on them and so they plunged into the water. He had watched their heads bobbing and jerking as they swam and thought that the weight of their antlers must drown them. The dogs were racing backwards and forwards on the shore, demented and snapping at one another. To his relief, he explained, the deer pushed through the water, but the hunters were not to be outdone. They piled into boats with some of the dogs and rowed out after the deer. The whole lake, for him, became a great sound box: the roar of horns and the baying of infuriated dogs was accompanied by the huntsmen shouting. Perhaps it was the drink in me, but he made me sweat as he described the scene. He described how they bludgeoned and piked the animals as they swam, then loosed their dogs on them as they stumbled exhausted and broken from the water; all the time they were yelling and screaming and laughing.

He always had an eerie way of telling stories and the recollection it seemed exhausted him. 'May they rot in hell, the bloody barbarians,' he spat out, careless of the people about him. 'And they want me to sing great orations in men's honour, with these ornaments hung about me! Take me back to the women I was sitting with. There's drink there and I can wash the taste of raw offal from me.'

When we returned to where he had been seated, the guests began to gather round him. Carolan the bard was about to entertain them and they were anxious to enjoy his offering. He was quick to address them, his personality transformed in front of an audience. 'Sweeter to me than the music of all the harp strings in Ireland, are the women of Ireland.'

The women either smiled or laughed openly and clapped in agreement. But the bard continued, 'And the day I am unable to cajole a woman may I pack up my profession altogether! So let me now praise the woman of Ireland.' And so he began.

His harp took up its easy melody. There was a charm about his notes that was fitted to his words.

'It is with Dark Moll of the Valley
My love is laid up in keeping,
It is she who never got blame or shame,
She was becoming and mannerly fair.
She said to me in the morning,
"Depart, and see me not for ever."

'I call on thee, O sister,
I call on thee, O secret,
And I call on thee nine times,

'I call on thy locks
That are beautiful and soft, like feathers falling on my face,
And I call on your noble, lovely form
I call on thee again, O love,
My soul is in thy hand,
Protect me from the death
Henceforth forever, for myself.'

At this point the music lifted as if a light wind had blown away its sombre refrain. His hands plucked the strings as if he was pulling away the veil of memory and desire that inspired the song. His voice called out and had rid itself of its morbid intonation. His dark moll was now a heady liquor that he drank it down with delight. As he finished, the harp teased out an echo of his opening but it was more fulfilled. The musician had shared his longing and in so doing had confirmed his love and reclaimed it. His hands slid down to his sides as he awaited the applause, which came quickly and loudly.

After a few moments it died down, but there was still an air of irritation about Carolan which few noticed. He seemed to be brooding silently.

I asked the two women who had talked to him earlier if they

had enjoyed it. The younger one, who was enthusiastically filling his glass, said that she thought it was wonderful.

But the older woman wanted to pursue the conversation she had begun earlier with our old friend. 'Fine indeed, but it gives me no answer to my question.'

'And what was that?' Carolan asked bluntly.

'Wasn't it something about who you are and where you come from?'

As always the applause had begun to soften him and the alcohol was making him garrulous. 'Memory is our only true home. For isn't it there we return to most often?'

'Tell us some of yours,' the younger woman said enthusiastically. 'I'm sure they must be as wonderful as your music and poetry.'

I hated the flowery language he adopted at these times, but I knew that underneath it he had felt the edge of the first question. The woman had made him uneasy and he wanted to answer her, but if she was going to insist then he wanted to make her feel as uncomfortable as she was making him.

'All right then, let me tell you a story,' he began. 'For the curiosity of women is more often satisfied by stories than by answers alone.

'I was a child then and my recollection has only the understanding of a child and years may have faulted my precise recollection, but no matter. Did you ever as a child lie half-awake listening to the conversations of adults? I remember one such night after the villagers had finished gathering the late harvest. In the candlelight I could see the shadowy, hard faces of sober men. They spoke in whispers, hinting at something my young mind found hard to understand.'

Carolan paused to listen to the silence around him. Then he returned to his story. ' "What does he want the land for?" asked one of the men in a spiteful whisper. "Sure, he doesn't know what to do with the soil, whether to make cakes of it or put it in his soup!" And another quieter voice answered, "We're a peaceable, law-abiding folk when the law serves us. We'll not be looking to harm those who have not harmed us." But like all the other children bedded on rough sacks about the fire I was too sleepy to listen and soon fell asleep.'

He paused again and drank deeply, then held out his glass for someone to fill. Behind me I heard a nervous giggle.

'I was awoken by a scratching noise and a loud voice saying, "Well, boys, what about it? Time we were going." They tightened their belts and pulled the caps down over their eyes.'

He took a long pause and drank deeply again.

'Then they were gone. I must have fallen asleep again, for the next thing I can remember is standing on a small hill. Most of the village was there, alarmed and exultant. Before us the landlord's house was aflame. There was no smoke. The beams fell apart heavily as the great red flames licked through them. I remember the sky was a dirty, even colour, with a grey sun struggling through. We stood there, oblivious to the morning cold.'

He fell silent again. Those who had gathered round him were silent and anxious, wondering where his story might lead.

'Then suddenly a huge red bull burst through its enclosure. Its head tossed wildly and blood streamed from where its eyes had been. It stood still, its sightless orbs rolling this way and that . . .'.

As he spoke, he leaned his own face and blind eyes into his audience and in a grizzly mockery of the bull rolled and twisted his eyeballs in his face.

I watched him grin to himself as he continued, 'There he stood, roaring out a great bellow of pain. From somewhere a stout lump of branch was thrown and struck him. Overcome by agony and fury he charged off, stumbling and bellowing. His noise was like an avalanche in the night. I was terrified, but stood transfixed as I watched the creature charge into the river.'

There was a long silence. Turlough neither moved nor spoke. His glass was frozen in his hand and when he spoke again his voice was low, hardly audible. 'There for the last time in his life he gored and roared at an invisible foe. The river was deep and swirling. I remember the great majestic bellowing as the watery chasm closed over the creature.'

For a moment the great hall was hushed, then about him there came up a mixture of sighs and groans and a single nervous giggle. His audience were gasping with relief, but he was not finished, and when he spoke again there was a curious, almost spiteful tone in his voice.

'It was a week later when men on horseback with pikes and

guns arrived in the town. Their horses never stopped snorting and neighing. There was a deadly silence as they took away the five men. Before everyone's eyes they were stripped and lashed. Their wives watched and were afraid to weep aloud for their menfolk. But a more awful silence was to follow. For their children had to witness the terrible indignity of their fathers weeping with rage, pain and shame as they dragged on their old patched trousers and winced as they gathered their shirts about their shoulders. Everyone was afraid to touch them. They were like broken holy relics. The women stood erect and terrible throughout the flogging, barefoot in the freezing rain.'

From where I stood listening I heard muffled sobs and choked swallows. Carolan drew a great deep breath as a warning to those gathered around him. They waited like cornered animals. His closing words fell upon them like blows. Even I felt the smart of them.

'Something had stolen on them like a thief in the night and brought with it the law and the lash. Who then should a young child threaten with its harmless fists or what, with such memories, do we become when we ask ourselves who we are?'

The silence about Carolan was uneasy. Those who had not been within hearing range were drawn to the small silent knot of people gathered about him. Carolan was on his feet again and called me to take him to the far end of the room near to the windows. His audience parted to allow us through.

As we walked off I chastised him, for I thought there was something more to this story. 'My God, man, that's curious entertainment to be serving up. Is there any truth in it at all?'

And he answered me with the same kind of scorn with which he had answered the woman earlier: 'Truth is as truth does. Sometimes I don't feel part of all this and that damned woman scorched my soul tonight. But mark my words. I have her now!'

I was about to chastise him again when he suddenly changed the subject and asked me, 'You know Seamus I've often wondered what it's like to dance. If I could, I wonder if I would enjoy it?'

'God knows, for at times there's no pleasing you!' I answered exasperated.

The group behind us began to break up, talking in whispers.

Some commented on the sadness of the man, others had taken offence but were afraid to voice it. Somewhere a voice said, 'He's a dark angel, that one.' The two women he had been sitting with were deep in conversation. I left him to retrieve his harp. The women had been disagreeing and I overheard one say, 'What have I done? Stolen something from you?'

Meanwhile Carolan returned under the guidance of a guest. He caught the closing words of their conversation. 'Who's stolen what?' he asked.

'I think you may have stolen a few hearts tonight, especially Kathleen's here. But you must excuse me, for I too see some friends I must speak to. I'm sure Kathleen will look after your needs.'

With the older woman gone, Kathleen seemed to gain a new confidence.

'I think it was fine, and it stirred my heart exactly the way I suspect you wanted.'

'Ah,' laughed Carolan. 'Give me your hand and let me see if I can guess your age.'

Kathleen did as she was bid, delighted at his attention. As his hands enclosed about her wrists she exclaimed, 'Well, and what do you find?'

'There's more woman than child here, for sure.'

'I don't know whether that's good or bad,' she said.

'Neither do I. But a bit of both is always best. Come, Kathleen, take me out of this crowd. I need to give my head some peace and quiet.'

At once they both stood up and went out of the room in a hurry. I laughed and thought to myself how like a fox Carolan was. He was into the chicken coop and away with the plump young hen before anyone knew it. But I also remember thinking that these women must be blind. For Carolan was no pretty picture, but if they were fooled by his words, well, then I wished him well.

Less than an hour had passed when young Kathleen returned and ran across the room to tell me that I should go and attend to my charge where she had left him. She whispered, 'He's injured himself.' She gave me directions and I left telling her to say nothing until I returned.

I found him where she had told me to look, sitting alone on the window seat in the long hall. He was nursing his hand as if it was a frightened bird. I have to admit I was too far gone with the Dillions' fine wines to be sympathetic and I remember my voice echoing down the hallway.

'What lonely vigil is this? And what's this about you battling with the stonework and frightening young women?'

'Never mind the questions. Lead me out into the garden for a moment, will you?'

'What? Another assignation!' I could not resist teasing the great womaniser.

'Yes, with myself. Now just do it, Seamus.'

'Have it your way. For you're in a queer mood tonight.'

I unlocked the garden doors and led him into the night air. He breathed deeply and the cool blast seemed to calm his senses. 'Take me away from here,' he demanded and I did as I was bid.

I remember that there seemed to be as much light from the moon as there was indoors. As we walked further into the darkness I became convinced that the owner of the house must be a proper unbeliever. The statues looming out of the shadows seemed defiantly heathen and some of the words written beneath them were in a language no Christian would want to understand. Carolan just laughed and said that when I came to a statue a bit like the Blessed Virgin, only with a name beginning with 'V', to stop and turn towards the lake. At the end of a small path I would find a shell house close to some great spreading trees and there I was to leave him for a while. I was annoyed at having to nursemaid him through his tantrums and demanded why he wanted to be sitting out here in the dark, alone.

'Seamus!' he exclaimed. 'Haven't I been in the dark a long time now and as for being alone,' he paused then lowered his voice to a whisper, 'I won't be. I'll have all these heathen statues to keep me company!' He paused again, then said, 'Now, take yourself off. Come back in a couple of hours and be sure and tell no one I'm here!'

I guided him into the small, shell-encrusted pavilion, where he sat and let his hands feel out the walls.

'Have you ever seen the sea, Seamus?' he asked. I couldn't be bothered answering, for he knew I never had. 'Well then, take your time walking back, and Seamus, be careful, be sure not to look too closely at those statues as you return. Strange things can happen if you look at them. I'm safe, I'm blind. I can't see them.'

I left him, tired of his behaviour and eager to console Kathleen with my company, or myself with some fine ports that our host had laid on.

I decided not to look on the statues even though his warning made me want to. All the way back to the house my eyes never left the gravel pathway. In my drunkenness I imagined their stony eyes following me, and I was glad of the bright moonlight.

When I got back to the house, I spoke to Kathleen and learned what had happened. She had told him that she didn't like the way he talked, as if he were on the stage in a theatre. She couldn't understand how he could be so cruel. Then, feeling guilty I suppose, she had asked him if he was going to stay.

He had replied that he didn't know. And, as for theatre, what was theatrical about watching your friends and neighbours being beaten? It wasn't entertaining to watch the blood run out of your own. His voice was low with passion and Kathleen did not know how to react. She had sat hesitating, her fingers plucking at the threads in the curtains. She had wanted him to go on and she wanted him to stop.

Finally she blurted out, 'I don't want to kiss you either. Your eyes are filled with red when you start talking like that. I don't know if it's pity or anger, or whether it's in me or you.'

Carolan moved his hand across her lips. She noticed the trembling in his fingers was more to do with nerves than tenderness. 'Did you want me to kiss you?' he asked.

'No! You wanted me to kiss you. You play with people . . . just like . . .'

But before she had finished he rose from his seat beside her and stood a moment, then said, 'People's eyes always turn red when they're speaking the truth.' Then, abruptly, he walked slowly along the hallway. He paused as his hand felt out a pillar of rough stone built into the wall. Suddenly he punched his fist hard into it. The rough surface bit into the softness of his hand and made it bleed. He turned towards the seat he had left. In a low voice he asked, 'Kathleen, is my hand bleeding?'

She had already started to walk away, but stopped and called back to him, 'You caused it, you can cure it. You're no better than that snorting bull in that horrible story of yours!'

When I sat with him today and we spoke of that evening in Dillion's house, he laughed as he remembered every little detail. He even related the strange story of the burning house and the blind bull word for word, and then he said there was no more snorting left in the old bull. He laughed too when I told him some of the stories that were being told in the village. But when I asked him what had kept him half the night in the old shell house by the lake, he pulled himself up in the bed and beamed. 'Come on, man,' I said, 'if your mind is so sharp you must remember.' For a moment he sat there, nodding his head ever so slightly. Then he turned to me and told me he had been composing. 'Indeed,' says I, 'well, your memory's not so fine, after all, for let me remind you that you left your harp in the house when I took you out.'

For a moment he seemed stunned, then his smiled returned and he said, 'True, Seamus, I had not forgotten but I had another one to play on that night!' Then he chased me from the room, telling me to find young Charles O'Conor and send him to him. I couldn't find it in myself to tell him how distressed Charles was by his illness and that he was fearful of visiting him. So I left him to his grinning silence.

In the quiet of his empty sickroom Carolan recalled the shell house and that evening Seamus was so inquisitive about. Though Seamus was closer to him than any man alive there were things he didn't know. 'But I'll tell you, Mary Kelly,' he said as he closed his eyes and took himself back to the little house by the lake.

He recalled sitting still and listening to the sounds around him. The silence coming off the water seemed to amplify the night noises. Somewhere the haunting blast of a corncrake boomed out. The heavy flap of birds' wings sounded nearby. 'Perhaps an owl hunting,' he thought. The night world was alive and he too was a creature of the dark. He felt comfortable and safe.

He fingered the shell-like shapes embedded in the walls: concave and convex, crinkled and flat; mussel shells, scooped like spoons, he remembered their blue-grey pearly sheen. Everywhere the walls were a wild mosaic of shell from the fan-like scallop; the tight cup of a cockle and tiny, spiralling, bead-like shells. As his hands flew round the walls he could imagine their brightness. Each one fascinated him. His fingers sought out their form and he remembered their name and colour. Thoughts were racing through his head, but he could not form them as easily as the shells. There were all kinds of thoughts, long or short but always elusive. Slowly words and pictures began to shape themselves in a new loose harmony, and as they did, he rubbed his fingers in his forehead. He hummed almost inaudibly. This was the kind of composition he had no control over. It came to him in fragments, out of nowhere. And as he hummed he listened to the lake. He felt it pressing against him, a mass so heavy and so limpid that he imagined he could have leaned against it.

He touched the wall again and explored the resonance of the shell hollows. Then he stood and fumbled around him until he found a piece of branch. He walked out of the shell house towards the pressing mass of water. He wanted to break up the sounds it sent him and reform them. He stopped and threw the heavy branch out on to the lake and waited to hear it fall.

This was the magic he understood. Sounds never came from a single point in space. Nor did they retreat into themselves. There was the sound, then its echo, then another sound into which the first sound merged. It was the birth of an endless procession of sounds. He listened again until the whole landscape seemed to be swallowed up in the softly booming lake. In empty landscapes he could find music, as if the landscape itself was an invisible composition which only he could read.

The peace of it, its endless harmony, were very different from the house he had left. The hum of words sometimes made him so dizzy he wanted to cover his ears. Sounds that he did not want to listen to were like a blow to the body and spirit. Real sound, music, did not happen outside him, but was a presence passing through him, sometimes lingering until he fully understood it. Turlough sank back into it and let his senses reel and sway. It was like lying back in a voluminous eiderdown. After several minutes he raised himself from his reverie and walked back to the shell house.

Somewhere behind him the scrunch of footsteps biting into the gravel broke into his meditations. He disregarded it until a woman's voice addressed him, 'Your guide said you might be here and suggested I should not disturb you. I told him I had something for you.' A short snuffle of laughter punctuated her speech. 'But for some reason he cautioned me about the collection of statues that line the path to this curious place. Surely it's not their naked bodies that intimidated him.'

As he listened to the low modulation of her voice with its nasal intonation, it seemed different from the demanding voice which had questioned him in the house. 'It's not their naked bodies that bother him, for he's seen enough of them in his day. It's their eyes!'

There was a hint of surliness in his voice, but curiosity smothered it. The confusion told him how tipsy he was. 'Well, don't just stand in the doorway, come in.'

'I imagine you were expecting someone else. Kathleen perhaps! We had a bit of a quarrel. It was over you.'

His curiosity deepened, but he remained defensive. She moved towards him and asked if she could sit by him.

'Sit where you will! What is it you've brought with you, anyway?'

'A bottle of claret from the reception for you and a coaching blanket for myself.' She fell silent for a moment and looked across the moon-bright waters. 'It's very lovely here. It makes me think of your song about dark Moll. That was a curious choice – in a strange way I thought it was directed at me!' There was a hint of anxiety in this last statement.

'You're a queer one to think that. Have you come here with more of your damned questions?'

'Perhaps I've come to comfort you,' she snapped back.

Carolan felt trapped again, but he was not ready to surrender.

'You made me feel like one of those stuffed creatures nailed to the wall . . . and I'm not sure you haven't come here to skin me!'

Their laughter lessened the unease between them, yet he moved away and stood by the entrance to the shell-house.

'You're in a bad humour still. That's a pity, I'm a good-natured creature,' she said.

They were silent for a minute, as if giving each other time to find their balance, then she began again, 'I think you're as much a stranger here as I am, for all your fame and reputation.'

'You're strange enough, that's for sure. What's your name, anyway?'

'Joyce Featherstone. I'm from Dublin and I'm thinking I'd have been better staying there! It's like another world here. It's brutal and savage and inhuman, and, O my good God, it is pitiful.'

The contradictions in her answer made an impression on him. 'We're a queer pair of birds all right, you and I. And what is it makes you so inquisitive? Why so many questions?'

'This place, this whole wild, sad, God-forsaken pigsty of a country draws them out of me.'

Her intemperance made him the inquisitor now. 'You're a nice one and no mistake. A pigsty, is it? That's an offensive remark to a man sitting in his own backyard. If that's the manners Dublin teaches you, then it doesn't sound much more than a pigsty itself!'

For a brief instant he was shocked at his own remark. He was grateful they were alone and that he was too far gone with alcohol to bother much about what he said. But he had not frightened her, only confused her.

'What are you so defensive about? I mean it's so absolutely hopeless here, that's all.'

She paused for a moment and then placed the coach rug around her shoulders, and continued in a quiet voice.

'And even if you don't see it; your stories are only stories.'

He felt echoes of the frustration that she had caused in him earlier. She challenged a part of himself that he rarely questioned. He recognised determined confidence, but also a sensitive loneliness in her remarks. He turned and walked back to his seat beside her.

'Take this thing off me. It smells of horses and God knows what else.'

'What?' he asked, suddenly puzzled.

'This bloody horse blanket, for I'm sure that's what it is!'

He felt her turn and press her back and shoulders in his chest.

'Is that all you want me to take off?' The words came out of him before he had time to understand the reason for them.

'Fool' she laughed softly.

It was a titillating, but cautious laugh, which made him think of a cat's walk. He was frightened by her proximity.

'If I'm a fool, I'll go!' Even as the words came out he knew she could read the weakness in them. He imagined her mouth widening in a sly smile.

'Where to? Not to that slip of a girl you had eating out of your hand? If I were her father, I'd set the dogs on you. I wouldn't take pity on those big blind eyes or your poor sensitive soul.'

There was no way out for him now. Yet by challenging him she was allowing him only one escape route.

'Be careful, Joyce Featherstone, I don't give much warning!'

She laid her head back on his chest. He could feel her eyes looking up into his face. 'And I give a lot!' she teased. 'Are you hiding yourself away here because that young woman chased you?'

He could say nothing. Intoxication lay like a leaden weight on his head. The walls of the shell house started to ring as if each shell had released its own note. The sounds, her presence, his own drunkenness acted like a drug on him.

The blood throbbed in his fingertips as his arms surrounded her body. She turned into him and he felt the heated blood swim up to his temples. He felt loathing and abomination in his soul, but his body was maddened and moved irresistibly. He could feel the brutality in his hands as they moved over her body. Yet she received him and answered him with her own passion. Even as he undressed he thought that all her demanding questions were only a means to this moment. She wanted to find the man in him. Who he was was meaningless, but what he was and what he could be to her – that was all that mattered now.

Their union was animal and resolved into a long silence. They fell apart from each other like rocks loosened in a landslide. The wall of quiet that separated them seemed to encircle Carolan, forcing him to retreat into himself. He felt as if he had been tossed out of his house naked and the door bolted behind him.

'I suppose you're ashamed of yourself, aren't you?'

Her question astounded him not because of what she was asking but because of her opinion of him. He didn't know what he felt. Torn fragments of the evening flashed through his head. And as if she really was inside his mind, reading its every thought, she pulled him on to her breast. He felt the crumpled satin of her open bodice. It was saturated with alien smells. He thought of the house and the anonymous people waiting for him to play. He thought of his contempt as he entertained them. He thought of his flirtation with Kathleen in the passageway. He thought of his delight as he had sat listening to the night sounds and now this. He had some control over everything else . . . but not the smells that poured out of her open bodice. He reached up his hands to feel her heart beat and felt a blemish on the swell of her breast. 'It's a birthmark,' she said. He imagined her breast glimmering with blueness and the mark, tender and pitiful. He heard her voice again low and sensuous like the night. 'It's small and dark, like a leering eye!'

The remark was strange. It seemed to bring all his tumbling thoughts to a sudden stop. For a moment he thought of the white marble statues lining the garden pathway. Everything that had happened during the evening had led to this moment. He felt no shame. He had wanted this woman and had enjoyed the gift of her. But instead of shouting his pleasure, other words came, 'I only feel like other men when I'm inside a woman.'

Her response was a teasing rebuke, gentled by her hand caressing his forehead. 'I never thought to hear Turlough Carolan admit that he might be half a man . . . without a woman!'

'And you never will!' he answered.

They both laughed. Then she stood up and fixed her clothes, ready to leave. 'They might think we have been up to some mischief!'

Her voice still had a ring of childish conspiracy and it seemed she skipped like a child over the gravel back towards the house.

Turlough lay in silence listening to her footsteps. Her body scent was everywhere. He did not want her to go, but was happy to be alone. The moment seemed right, he didn't want to spoil it with awkward conversation. He felt warm, fecund and wordless.

For half an hour he lay still, listening to the lake. Then he too made his way back to the lights and the noise. The half-empty bottle of claret swung in his hand as his feet bit into the pebbled pathway. He wanted to go back and play again and be amongst people, but as he passed the line of statues he stopped. He could imagine them like white silhouettes against the dark empty lawn. He stepped off the grass and walked towards where he remembered they might be. His outstretched hands pawed the darkness until they found their target.

Slowly his hands explored the cold marble stone. Its symmetry was too precise. As his hand cupped a naked breast he chuckled to himself. 'No dark, sinful blemish here.' They were perfect effigies to the greatness of classical wisdom. Divine proportion for divine gods. But they were cold and frigid.

These thoughts were resolving themselves when the silence around him was broken. From out of nowhere a voice blasted, 'Christ Jesus, Turlo, what the hell are you doing?'

It was Seamus. The amazement and disbelief in his voice were obvious. Carolan could picture the ridiculous scene he had come upon.

'What name is carved on the plinth here?' he said.

Dumbfounded Seamus began to spell it aloud, 'V.E.N. – Venus,' he said.

'Well then, I'm feeling Venus!'

The next morning was the sabbath and the guests who had remained overnight were busy preparing either to leave for home or attend the local church. He waited in his room until he was sure the majority of them had gone. As the house quietened he made time for his own prayers. This morning he could be truly thankful, but even as he prayed his mind went back to the shell house. Before Joyce Featherstone arrived he had been composing a piece of music. Since their intimacy he had experienced a strange, almost soporific intensity in his composing.

The stillness and harmony of the night and the cradle of quiet which the shell house provided had unlocked his creative impulse. Music was moving in his mind and he thought of a melody that reflected the nightscape. He wanted a shadow of his mother's sad but determined voice to be part of it. It would be a song of praise and rejoicing in woman, woman as mother, wife, daughter and patron. In the shell house he had heard its first sounds and now their echo was returning to him. Instinctively he began to finger his coral rosary as his mind focused in on his idea.

Nine The Midden

Seamus Brennan Remembers

It seems as if half the world has come to Keadue to pay their respects. But that's country people. They're fast after funerals for the fill of their belly that they can get there. He has not departed this life yet and already the village is full of stories. Stories such as I have never heard before and I spent more time with him than any man or woman. Some loved and some loathed him and I dare say he brought it all on himself. But he would revel in all this for he insisted he loved these people. Yet there was a part of him that was afraid of them. There was another Turlough Carolan which the world didn't see and the great Carolan would hardly want them to.

I remember a queer evening, on the road from Enniskillen to Sligo. Enniskillen is a bog at the best of times, but that evening the rain lacerated us. Our only hope of refuge was a miserable and decrepit cabin at the end of a sodden path. Had there not been smoke coming out of the chimney I would have sworn no human creature could inhabit it and if the road had not been impassable I would not have thought twice about leaving that hovel to sink where it sat. But I knew how much he hated the discomfort of the weather and how he could make everybody else uncomfortable because of it. In our haste toward the shelter of the cabin, I was cursing the animals and was left in no doubt of Carolan's mood. 'Go on, you black-hearted, miserable cur!' I heard him call out behind me.

He knew I would be unsure about what I had heard and whether he was addressing me or the horse, as was his way, and he left me to my indecision. He had other things on his mind. He was always anxious when arriving at a strange place. He knew what to expect as an invited guest, but arriving unexpectedly at these peasant huts frightened him.

As we approached, the owner came splashing towards us. He understood our need for shelter and without speaking began to help Carolan from his horse. 'Bend your head now,' he said, thrusting him through the doorway. Like an obedient old heifer being pushed and prodded towards the milking byre he obeyed. As I followed them through the entrance I found myself suddenly lambasted by noise and by our host screaming excitedly: 'Sally, Sally, quick, clear a place and move these children. Whist, will you?' he roared at a whining dog, then, 'Fetch that stool over here and clear some room near the fire. Shoo, shoo, shoo!'

His excitement at our arrival was as torrential as the rain that had brought us. I was trying to peer through the darkness of this hovel to get some idea of the place when there was a sudden outburst of cackling and a wild flurry of feathers. I saw Carolan trying to make sense of all this pandemonium as our new host began tugging at his shoulders. 'Give me that coat of yours, there's a week of drying in it!'

Before he had finished, Carolan had the coat dragged from his shoulders and a rough cloth flung over his head. 'For God's sake, I'm not a beast you're skinning for the pot,' he complained nervously. But our saviour, as no doubt he thought himself, answered nonchalantly, 'There's many a beast might be happier in that pot than standing there like yourself. It's a blessing you can't see the state you're in. Hurry, man, hurry. Soonest done, soonest mended.'

Poor Carolan was too confused to argue. There was a tender insistence in the man's voice and behind him I heard his wife, saying, 'Pity the poor creature, wasn't it fortunate he found us? Here, you young uns, spread these wet things about the fire there.' Then she came quickly to Carolan's side and began unbuttoning his waistcoat and shirt. He could have been one of her own brood the way she handled him.

I stood on the threshold, dumbfounded, still trying to see through the gloom. When my eyes found him again he was sat before the fire, stripped to the waist and shivering like a beaten dog. Three children, barefoot and filthy, sat opposite him staring. The woman of the house busied herself around him. She draped a threadbare patchwork about his shoulders and furiously dried his head with an old rag. Then she turned towards me and began chastising both of us. 'Is there no sense in the pair of you, to be out on the roads in weather like this? There is probably more wit in that youngest of mine than is in both of your heads!'

I was still too spellbound at the vision in front of me to listen to her remarks. She wore a blue shawl, its ends criss-crossed over her breast and tied in a crude knot in the small of her back. Her skirt was voluminous and brown, tattered and ragged with a crust of mud decorating its ends. Her feet could hardly be seen, for they had their own skin of filth and muck encrusted on them. She was far removed from the elegant ladies our bard was used to being attended by!

The rush lights burned dimly and gave no more than an ochre-like glow. The filthy faces of the children blended into the gloom, only the stillness of their staring eyes distinguishing them. In the quarter-light it would be easy to confuse them with infantile apparitions. The man who had met us was nowhere to be seen and I was uneasy in this house full of women and children.

'Well, don't just stand there, you look big and old enough to look to yourself.' The wife scolded me gently and ushered me nearer to the fire, shooing her children away to make room.

'Where's the man of the house?' I asked.

From behind a screen of hanging clothes, remnants of cloth and a brace or two of birds and rabbits, a voice answered. 'You'll not find me far from the house, this day,' and he emerged from the darkness to introduce himself. 'Paddy-Jo's my name and this is Sally and those three there are mine, Matthew, Mark and Sean . . . christians, every one.'

I looked again at the children now my eyes had become accustomed to the light. Curiosity and fear stared back at me and in the oldest of the faces there was also a kind of defiance. I was about to say something, for I was anxious to break the silence between myself and them, when I was set upon by the family dog. It bounced backwards on its hind legs as it snarled and yapped at me, and for a minute I thought that there might be more comfort drowning in the muck of the road than in this house.

'Matt,' the man barked towards the child who was staring so aggressively. Matt moved slowly toward the dog as if he wanted the animal to give me a further warning. 'Quiet,' he snapped with all the authority of his father. The dog looked at him and again the child addressed it. 'Quiet, boy,' he said, but this time his voice had changed. It was softer, almost tender. I was grateful for this. I thought these children were not far removed from the animals I heard rooting about in the dark corners of the house. They were too close to something that wasn't human. Their staring silence was unsettling and I moved quickly to where Carolan sat silent and shivering. As I sat beside him, I quipped, 'Well, well. How are the mighty fallen!'

His head was bent into his chest. It was still draped in the cloth that Sally had been drying his hair with. She had moved away to clear the impossible clutter of the cabin and say something to her husband.

Carelessly I reached out to slide the cloth from Carolan's head. What I saw shocked me more than the place we were in or the children's unsettling stare. What I had taken to be Turlough shivering with cold and damp was something else, something I was not ready for. As I looked into his naked face I saw that he had been sobbing and his face was wet with tears.

I was stunned and could only look at him helplessly. Then, realising I must do something, I stood up and placed the cloth back in his hand, suggesting I should get something to warm us. 'Aye, do that,' he answered, but his voice was barely audible. Before I could move, Sally called out for me to give her my own wet clothes. I complied, for I was glad to be away from him for a moment.

I undressed and dropped my wet clothes where I stood. Sally bundled them in her arms and shuffled off towards the fire. The dog sniffed around me. Contemplating the sight of my own nakedness amongst these strangers and Carolan's deep dejection, I began to laugh nervously. 'Paddy-Jo, do you want me to stand here looking like Adam in the garden of Eden all night!'

'Take this,' said our host, as unconcerned at my dilemma as Sally had been. 'It's old, but warm even if it won't make a great fit on you.'

I accepted the ragged overcoat he handed me and quickly put it on. Then I picked my way across the cluttered homestead, feeling the ooze of the ground between my toes. I rummaged through the bags, pulling out a shirt and breeches for Turlough and the flagon of poteen that he insisted should be the first item to be packed for any journey. I can tell you I was more than happy that he was so meticulous in these matters, and called out to the housewife, 'I'll hang these by the fire for a moment to air. Have you anything we might heat a drop of water in?'

'Give me those and I'll heat a pot as well,' said Sally, taking the fresh clothes. 'Bring over some more turf, lads,' she said to the children as she passed.

I took a seat beside himself and tapped him comfortingly on the knee as I whispered, 'It's as dark as Hades when you first come in here, but it's a sight better than outside. Here, take a sup of this. It will soon let the cold out of those bones of yours.'

Then I looked again at Paddy-Jo. He was opening a door into a room, or more precisely a hole in the wall. The small door was hinged with rope and withered leather straps. Beyond, was a tiny box of a room and Paddy-Jo was shouting from within it. His voice seemed muffled by the rising smells emanating from the place, 'There now, settle yourselves and remember we have guests here tonight.'

As the smells from the small room hit the heat of the room in which we sat, they seemed to explode. I gagged at the onslaught and turned to Carolan, spluttering. 'It's a bit too pungent in here for me. Christ, give me a drink before I pass out!'

He passed the flagon and suggested that I should invite our hosts to join us. I turned to where Sally was stirring at a pot and offered her and her husband a drink: then half apologetically I asked if we could have some fresh air.

'There's a window behind your friend with a board and a bit of curtain to it. It's wind, wet or warm, please yourself,' Sally said.

I moved around and opened the tiny window. Behind me Turlough sat silent, listening to the voices about him and warming himself from the drink in his hand. He repeated her words, 'Isn't that the whole of it, wind, wet or warm, take your pick?' As I returned he mumbled something about being home again. He recalled when he was young how the walls of his home were refuge for a variety of smells. Always in the morning there was the smell of potatoes from the night before mixed with the stale smell of burned-out candle wax. At midday there was the hot smell of sour milk bread. At night there would always be that inexplicable smell of his mother's plump, bare arm. She always kept a little box of wild lavender and other herbs. After she had washed herself she would rub the leaves over her wet arms and let the smell dry there.

'There are some smells that never leave you, Seamus,' he said aloud to the room.

As he did so, I noticed him lift his hands to his face and with the heels of his hands wipe each eye. 'Did you know that turf smoke can make a blind man's eyes sting?' he asked. 'I think we need more drink. I have almost finished this one and I'm beginning to feel a great drought on me.'

As he finished, Sally approached and put the warmed clothes in his hands. 'There now, can you manage on your own?' I was about to interrupt and suggest that I help when he silenced me and reminded me to go and bring the rest of the poteen and claret to the fire. 'Sally will look after me,' he said. I did as I was bid and felt through the bags and found the bottles . . . There were more than I expected. As I lifted myself to go back, I stood for a moment to watch.

Turlough had removed his wet breeches and stood draped in a colourful patchwork. He looked nothing like the great bard, more like a child who had just stepped out of a bath with a towel thrown around his shoulders. He stood quietly as Sally knelt before him and held his dry breeches open for him to step into. Gently she guided his feet in turn and slid the garment up his legs.

'Now give me the cover while you fix these and I'll fetch your shirt,' she said, and I noted the familiarity with which she addressed him.

I had never seen him so compliant or submissive. Turlough was a man of moods and they were always employed to entertain or admonish whomever he chose, but this silent, accepting child-man was something new.

Sally returned and pulled the open shirt over his head, carefully guiding his arms into each of the sleeves. Only once she looked at his face and, smiling, brushed the hair back from his eyes. 'So,' she said, 'now we're more comfortable, but keep that cover about you for it's a long night yet.'

As she moved off in search of some drinking vessels, I resumed my place and whispered to him, 'And who's not wanting for attention this night?' but he was in no mood for my teasing and answered me back like I was the dog that had been barking earlier! 'Mind your tongue and leave that bottle of claret by me!'

We settled ourselves around the smoky fire and ate a supper of potatoes in pork fat and cups of buttermilk scooped out from the pail. But Carolan would have none of it and stuck to his drink. In the end we all joined him. The more we drank, the more we talked. It's a powerful thing, how strong drink concentrates the mind and can make a philosopher out of the likes of even Paddy-Jo. Inevitably our conversation turned to the hunger for land and the thirst for blood, subjects on which our host was prepared to lecture us. While he gabbed away Carolan sat, concentrating, as I thought, on the drink in front of him. If the rain outside had half-drowned us, then Carolan was determined to finish the job. But as Paddy-Jo paused for a breath and a drink, Carolan broke in, his voice thick and slurred with the drink.

'What we hunger and thirst for will find no satisfaction in either land or blood, but some madness in us makes us think so. When you've lost something dear to you, the want of it never leaves you. It's the loss that makes savage orphans of us all, and we end up looking in every wrong corner trying to find what it is we have lost – and the absurdity of it is that half the time we don't know what it is we're looking for. The other half of the time we are sucking on any substitute to make up for it. Land and blood are no substitute. They're the cheap half-brewed poison of ignorant men with hard heads and pig's shite for brains.'

He tossed the bottle to his mouth and took three long deep swallows, stopping for breath between each one, and as he did he hissed, 'Parasites, damned parasites, every one!' Then as if something had just entered his head he stopped suddenly and called out to Sally, telling her to bring her children close for he had a fine story for them.

Carolan loved stories. He would sit and listen to them for ages and he loved to tell them just as much, but this night he wanted to listen and he shouted to me to give them the story of the gander fight.

I realised there was no escape as the expectant faces of his audience held me trapped. A story was to be my ransom. For a moment I looked at Carolan sitting aside from the family. His face was flashing in and out of the shadows as the fire flared. He had a great fondness for the story and never tired of hearing it, and at this moment he looked as expectant as the children and their parents. I don't know where the story came from, but I knew how Carolan told it and also knew that I should tell it as he liked it.

It was a story about a gander fight between two rival princes. When one of the princes' prize gander was defeated he was so inconsolable that he traded some of his land and its people to the other to obtain the winning gander.

As I told it, Carolan jerked one arm vertically into the air and with another jerk flipped his outstretched hand out at right angles. In the soft light his arm and hand made a grotesque goose-like neck and head. Slowly he moved it, occasionally darting his hand and fingers towards his listeners, in imitation of a gander's chisel-like bill. It was as if he could see the faces around him.

'Cups, cups!' he shouted suddenly. 'The tale's not finished yet!'

I filled their cups and continued the story.

'The people who were traded for a goose loved and had families and died on a piece of wasteland that their new master settled them on, and their families lived and died, and more families on down the generations. Only a great lush watermeadow separated them from their original home. It was known as Goose's Green. And that should have been an end to it.

'But time passes and history changes things, and over the years a great enmity broke out between the descendants of the settlers and the families of their original ancestors and a God-almighty squabble broke out about who should get the land that divided them. Isn't it wonderful how people only remember the history that suits them?

'Anyway, there was a day when one of the factions gathered on the meadow and called the priest to bless the fields. There they were all bowed before the holy Virgin, praying like hell that the river would not overflow.'

As I spoke Sally and her husband blessed themselves at the mention of the Virgin. I was beginning to feel the way Carolan sometimes felt when he played to a silent audience. But this time the great Carolan was my audience.

'As they were all knelt in prayer, in came the people of the wasteland. They had come to make peace in the hope that the presence of the priest and the blessed Virgin would make matters easier. But history does not forget things easily.

'Sure enough, they went at it tooth and nail, murdering each other on every side. While they were fighting, the priest began to pack away the image of the Virgin and all the implements of the sacrament. Now one of those who had invaded the ceremony turned to him and demanded he hand them over and immediately the priest became a raging bear. Into the thick of it he went, swinging his censer and murdering anyone within range with the crucifix. There they were rushing and charging, cursing and slaying, and none of them any the wiser who was friend or foe. Then a strange thing happened. All of them, regardless of which side they belonged to, decided they must claim the Mother of God.'

Suddenly Carolan interjected. 'And wasn't she laughing at the lot of them, beatific smile, my arse. She was laughing – I can see it all now, one man on the hill with the Mother of God and another with the cross of Christ and the whole world ready to butcher his brother in the name of one or the other.'

He stopped for a moment as the others stared at him in shock and confusion. Even I was taken aback. As suddenly as he had spoken he leaped up. 'I'll tell you,' he said, stretching out his arm and pointing it about the room. 'I'll tell you, Seamus. I'll tell you, listen now, listen.'

Paddy-Jo and I both rushed to catch hold of him. It was obvious he would end in the fire unless someone restrained him. We eased him back to where he had been sitting as Sally clutched her sons to her and whispered, 'The drink has driven him mad! God help the creature.'

Her words fell like a cold compress on Carolan as he sat kneading his hand in his eyes. With his voice slurred with drink he declared, 'That's the great unholy truth of it. The great duck war and haven't we been breaking each other's heads for years and for what? All hail, the great glorious goose. The glorious arrogance of kings and prelates. I piss on the lot of them. The great Battle of the Boyne, the great squabble on a duck pond and that awful blood-letting ever since. I'll tell you, Seamus, we're a people before we are a principle and some of us can do no more than live like beasts.'

I must confess I felt myself on the edge of laughter as I looked at the stunned faces of Paddy-Jo and his wife but I could hold it in no longer. 'You're as queer as a goose yourself! What are you getting so morbid about?' I challenged him.

But Carolan was in another world. He mumbled to himself, not caring who was listening, 'Sidh-Beag, Sidh-Mór. The great fairy war, and men are less than fairies. I can't compose music for a great slaughter. I won't compose for a bloodbath, as if there's anything honourable in that!'

I was about to speak, but saw that he had not finished. Drink had him by the throat and the venom was pouring from him like blood from a stuck pig. 'Seamus a chaca, Seamus a chaca,' he kept roaring and 'William, Prince of the House of Orange. There's hardly a man in the whole island of Ireland knows the smell of an orange. But I know the smell of those men. It's blood and lies, Seamus, blood and lies.'

Carolan stopped abruptly, cleared his throat and spat viciously at the floor. 'Damn them! I spit on them all – and on any man who thinks there's merit in them.'

It took us time to quiet him. Even as we got him to sleep he was mumbling about how only the blind can see. It was a phrase often on his lips but I am not so sure I ever understood what he meant by it.

For three days the inclemency of the weather made us prisoners in that squalid cabin. Though I found the circumstances almost unbearable, they didn't seem to bother Carolan. The morning after his drunken raving, Paddy-Jo and his wife were subdued and perhaps a little fearful, but the children were fascinated by the queer stranger. They were drawn to him and he in turn was content to indulge their animal curiosity. At times I watched them and felt as if a secret communication passed between them which was hidden from the rest of us. I am still curious about his outburst. I have never been able to understand what goes on in his head, and sometimes I think that whatever it is should be left where it is, because it's an ugly monster.

Letter from Reverend Horace Plunkett, clergyman of the Church of Ireland

The Rectory,
Castleblaney,
Co. Monaghan

Dear Brother,

This is a curious country indeed that I have landed in and a far remove from the kind of curacy I had hoped for. Ireland might well be a place where reputations have been made and fortunes too. But I have given up hope of the former and as the latter is not consistent with my calling I must not dwell on it, although a little luxury in this God-forsaken place would make my calling and my living more bearable.

I have come to believe that I am simply tolerated here. Many of the locals, in that offhand but seemingly inoffensive manner that they possess, have suggested to me that it is a source of great puzzlement to them why a decent Englishman and man of the cloth should wish to come and live here. I have given up trying to answer them as I confess I suffer from the same puzzlement.

Allow me to relate an incident to you which should illustrate how impossible these people are.

Just last week I was told by one of my parishioners that the famous harper Turlough Carolan had arrived in the townland and could be found at McGrattan's Inn. (I should be hard put to describe the place as an inn, indeed I have never been inside, as those who frequent it would not consider themselves parishioners of mine, and I thank God for such small mercies.)

I had heard much of this man and his music and that he is a great favourite with both the noble families and the likes of those who find more solace in McGrattan's decrepit hostelry than my sermons. I was curious to see and perhaps meet him, though I was daunted by the place.

My reservations were confirmed as I entered it. The room seemed to glow in a yellowing light that gave the faces of the customers a grotesque look. In the strange light I found myself confronted by a wretched and emaciated race. Yet somehow, however aged or ugly they were, there seemed to be little pain on their faces, rather a great weariness. I don't fully understand what I saw in those faces. Maybe I was expecting what I couldn't see. They were like a people that time had left behind and their peering faces made me think of dried-up toadstools!

For a moment I couldn't distinguish the famous musician, but as my eyes adjusted I could make him out, though in physical appearance little distinguished him from the others. His coat was of better quality and gleamed with bright silver buttons. He had a few more frills about him. But his face looked as weary as theirs.

The inn began to fill. The more people that arrived, the greater was the air of expectation. Women and children sat in corners. The men drank and gambled and spat. The air was almost fogged in places with tobacco smoke. Occasionally, someone would call over to the musician to 'play a jig' or call for a particular song, but he would refuse.

Sitting across the room from the harper was another musician known as Murphy. The men around him were noisier than the others and Murphy was the loudest of them all. He was a competent musician on the pipes, but had not made a profession of it. He played when and where he liked, but rarely went beyond the townlands of Castleblaney. He was a slightly built man with an air about him of insignificant meanness. He made gestures with the pipes, affecting to tune them in preparation to play, then he would put them aside. It was like someone calling a dog to heel or to sit each time it strayed. 'Play it, man, don't kick it!' someone shouted. Murphy looked towards the speaker with a vacant expressionless stare, then suddenly began to play. There was unrestrained wildness in the music and the volume he pumped out of the pipes drowned the roaring encouragement of the drinkers.

There was no doubt Murphy knew his instrument. When he finished his spinning reel I couldn't help feeling exhausted. I must admit, if these people have want of talent or intelligence, their music doesn't display it. The crowd called on the piper again, but he refused to listen and settled back to his drink. He had set the place in motion and the customers had no intention of settling for silence. They returned to their talking and arguing, knowing that the evening had just begun.

Murphy drank three more glasses and without any coaxing began to play again. His body was strapped and buckled into the instrument like it was part of a machine. I could see his elbows pumping at the bellows and his fingers releasing the notes from the chanter as his knee damped against it and his foot tapped out the rhythm. The crowd loved it, I could hear that. This music excited them and whatever restraint was in

Murphy's playing there was certainly none in them. The noisy camaraderie of the place affected even me.

'Come on, Carolan,' someone shouted, and then another, then Murphy's name was called again. I saw the piper look challengingly in the harper's direction. 'There are more musicians in the room than me,' he called out sarcastically.

The invitation was clear and I could see that Carolan knew the audience was primed for him. He couldn't refuse, nor did he want to. 'The harp, Seamus,' I heard him announce simply.

A roar of appreciation quickly dissolved into mumbling silence. He struck some chords to check the tuning and then began playing. Soon jigs and reels danced off his strings. His short pieces were airy and light and filled with laughter, like newly released birds. He simply snapped out each title by way of introduction and then let the harp tell its story. The room resounded with cheers and applause as one piece followed after another, until he sat back in his seat and with a light touch of his finger silenced the vibrating strings.

The warmth of the applause was something Carolan seemed well used to, although he seemed touched by it. As he chatted with the guide I studied the establishment.

The room was filled with babbling voices and the banging of chairs. From somewhere I heard a woman berate her obviously drunken husband. The coarseness of her language is beyond my capacity to reproduce here, but I seemed to be the only person in the room to be shocked by it. Even Carolan's guide found some humour in it and commented to the harper, 'Your music will have to be a lot sweeter to suck the sour out of that one.' To my surprise, Murphy the piper answered him, but there was nothing humorous in his words,

'Sweet music's like sugar water. There's no substance to it and them tunes of yours Carolan, are like bones without beef. I could hear a hundred like them and I'd still feel a want in me!'

The rebuke in this man Murphy's remark stunned me and was, I thought, wholly undeserved. Carolan's guide was quick to reply. 'It's a want of sense you have, Murphy.'

He was about to continue, but Murphy would not be silenced and continued his slight. 'Can you not compose a tune that has some body in it, Carolan?' Such public effontery was clearly creating a tense atmosphere.

What was lacking in Murphy's expressionless face, was made up for in the derision of his words. Carolan's guide came back quickly, 'Catch yourself on, man, if you can't hold it, don't drink it,' he called out to the surly piper.

I was hoping that enough had been said, but I was not prepared for what followed. Carolan was too quick. The offence was too public and too personal. Without warning, he sprang up from his seat and stormed past his guide like a wounded animal, making straight towards Murphy's table. 'Sit down before you fall down,' said Murphy and his voice gave Carolan the target he needed. He leaned forward, placing his face close to his antagonist. The words hissed from him, sharp and slow.

'I'll compose a tune before I quit and you, Master Murphy, may put what beef on the bones you please.'

With strength altogether inhuman, he pulled the helpless Murphy through tables and stools, sending drinks and food and anything else that happened to be there smashing and skidding across the floor. 'Meat on my music you say, you foul-mouthed ignoramus,' he bellowed.

Then he threw his hands at Murphy's face, grabbed him by the hair, and trailed him across a table.

'With these fine strings I'll make a tune for you,' he hissed. His voice was heavy and thickening. 'Come on, Murphy, help me now, what name shall we give this tune?'

The words seemed to throb furiously when Carolan spoke and his face clouded over in a deep flush. I stood frozen to the spot. I was terrified and looked for Carolan's guide to intervene, but he too seemed stunned. The whole place fell silent. Only Carolan's voice could be heard booming around the room, 'You have a mind like a pigsty, Murphy, and the noise from those pipes of yours sounds like an old boar that has just had its balls cut off!!!'

Carolan was jerking Murphy's head from side to side as he spat out his words. It looked as if he was trying to pull the man's head off. 'Is this beefy enough, you black-mouthed, fatherless whelp?' he roared at the hapless piper. With each jerk of his head Carolan found another ignominious name to abuse the man with. The barbarity of his language was truly appalling.

Murphy was helpless. His arms and legs were so buckled and tied to the pipes that he could do little to defend himself. Carolan was merciless. He kicked him and slapped him about the head. 'Is that substance enough for you?' he spat at his opponent and lashed out again with his feet finding Murphy's body more easily with them than his hands could find his head. The assualt was merciless!'

After some minutes Carolan stopped, his breathing coming in quick pants, but his abuse continued, 'Put some beef on that air, you insolent mongrel.'

The words were hardly audible and the nervous pitch of them declared the anger that still seized him. His guide now moved quickly and took Carolan by the arm.

'Mother of Christ, man, leave it now. Let him lick his wounds, come on away here.' He whispered gently as if he was calming a wild creature, which indeed he was, and as he did, he led Carolan away from the furore, behind the bar and into the proprietor's living room. As they passed, I heard Carolan ask, 'Are my nails broken, Seamus?' His voice was weak and childlike. I could not make out what Seamus answered, his voice was so full of nervous tension. He looked as if he wanted to scream the words at Carolan. His voice was raised several octaves and almost breaking as he spat out his final rebuke, cursing Carolan's 'black savage soul' with a language that my calling does not allow me to repeat.

Inside the room they had just left people were still recovering. Murphy's friends were gathered around him. Some were lifting him and others were unbuckling the pipes. The room was tense, as if everyone was waiting for Carolan to come bursting into it again.

I am not a man of indelicate constitution as you know, but this incident was too much for me. There's much unbridled passion in these people. They live on the very edge of their instincts and I fear they will never be able to control them.

I have not been back to the place. But a few of my parishioners have kept me updated, though I do not know the truth of what they tell me.

Carolan, it seems, was determined to show everyone that he was not going to skulk off. Each day he sat and talked with his guide and in the evening he played as if nothing had happened. During the day no one spoke to him. In the evening he teased and cajoled them with his music. Soon they relented and as they cheered and applauded, Carolan declared to them all, 'I'll not leave under a cloud.'

Was it arrogance, bloody-mindedness, was it dignity or courage? I cannot say. I only know that I am convinced Carolan needed the acclaim and adoration of his audience. These people were his lifeblood. He needed to be assured of their affection. They surrendered it willingly and acclaimed him boisterously, though no one mentioned the fracas with Murphy, at least not within his hearing.

My parishioner noticed that much of the time Carolan seemed to be in another world. He supped his drink slowly, and although he never refused to speak with anyone who approached him he kept his conversation short. There were long periods of silence when he would pretend he was listening to the other musicians who were there, but when he spoke he said some curious things. He would complain that the road had eaten him up and that he was tired of performing. He was always someone else's man and never his own.

During his last evening he was heard to declare, 'I should quit the road before it swallows me up. You can lose yourself out there and not know it. Maybe Murphy and McCabe were right. And you, yourself, cursed my black, savage soul! There's a dark part in all of us and I have been running down every back road and boreen in this island looking to get away from it. There's a part of me I left somewhere, Seamus, and it's time I went back to find it before it's too late.'

My parishioner remembers, how, as Carolan spoke there was a strange light in his eyes, though there was no animation in them.

His description intrigued me. How can blind eyes be so bright? I was beginning to think that perhaps the harper might be in some degree possessed. Even as the thought entered my head my informant stated that the last thing Carolan was heard to have said was a question to his guide. 'Have you ever been to purgatory, Seamus?'

I wonder what the musician meant. He is indeed a strange creature, full of violent passion and with an arrogance about him. Yet his music is famed for being sweet and even compelling!

Whatever he meant by that curious question, I could have told him and his guide that he need not travel too far to find the place he seems to be looking for! On many occasions I have stood in this parish and considered myself in purgatory. I pray that my sins have not been so great as to keep me for ever in this place. Was I too zealous for that country parsonage? I do hope you will employ your best endeavours with the bishop to find something for me.

Every blessing, Horace

Ten Virgil and the Gravedigger

From the Journal of Mrs McDermott-Roe

November 1717

I have always known that Turlough takes great and sometimes childish delight in playing tricks on people. I have never understood it. If he isn't playing these childish games, he is mocking people by telling them the most outrageous lies. Only the other day I overheard one of my estate workers telling a villager how Carolan has once asked some old men for directions. They gave him the information, then they asked who he was. Carolan duly informed them he was the blind Bishop of Limerick and that Seamus Brennan was his priestly assistant. I would laugh at the notion myself if it wasn't so ludicrous. I questioned Brennan about this and he told me that if Carolan wasn't pretending to be the bishop of Limerick, he was a papal emissary from the Holy See and insisted that Brennan address him as 'your eminence'. When I asked Brennan about the reason for this miraculous ordination, he quoted Carolan's own words, 'The currency of stories is more valuable than coins in a purse.' He even insists that those who believe his fabrications and receive his 'papal blessing' are richly rewarded for the service they have rendered him. I suggested it might be kinder to give them some tobacco, but Brennan laughed and said that those who have been blessed by the blind bishop of Limerick would be chewing on the story for longer than they might on a plug of tobacco.

I informed him that both he and Carolan should learn the difference between humour and blasphemy, for they will surely live to rue the day!

Eyewitness Account of the Churchwarden at Fenagh Church

I was there that day. Charles McCabe is known to everyone in these parts, though few of us have darkened his door. He darkens everybody else's. I thought it odd when he approached me and, without as much as giving me the time of day, asked if any men on horses had been asking after him. I told him I had seen no one and it wasn't my job to be waiting on any friends of his. If he was so interested in who was looking for him then he should wait himself. So I left him to his business, while I went about mine. But I never knew then what I know now, and I am the only man to tell it, for I am the only man that saw it.

I was away beyond the wall of the graveyard, keeping myself to myself when Carolan and his companion arrived. I didn't know them then, but it's my duty to be watchful of this place and two men on horseback was something to be watchful of.

As they approached the gates of the churchyard, a ragged-looking character emerged and walked towards them. He had all the appearance of a gravedigger. His head was covered in an old piece of sacking that draped down over his shoulders and what remained of the coat he wore was patched and held together by string.

Carolan was in fine spirits and called out to the stranger if he had seen Charles McCabe the poet, who was to meet them there. The gravedigger stopped where he stood and lowered his head, shaking it slowly. 'Have you gentlemen come far?' he asked.

'There are not enough miles that could keep me from a few nights' company with Charles McCabe,' Carolan answered with boyish excitement in his voice.

'Are you friends of his?' continued the gravedigger.

'Aye, there are few men I would put before him!' Carolan said.

'I can understand that well,' said the gravedigger, 'for there is no more loved man about these parts than Charles McCabe. So I am heartsore for you both.'

I'll tell you, Carolan's buoyant mood fell from him. His voice was anxious. 'And why should that be? Speak, man!' he demanded.

'You won't find Charles McCabe at home any more. And if you're looking for him you'll find him inside the churchyard.'

'Dead!' gasped Carolan, his voice almost a whisper.

'Yes, and buried. I placed the last sod over him myself.'

I have witnessed reactions like his before, so nothing was new to me. Something reeled inside the famous musician and his companion quickly dismounted, helped him from his horse and leaned him against a gravestone. He stood there and I watched him take long, deep breaths. His companion was helpless to console him. 'Who is that man that has cursed the day for me?' Carolan demanded, with the breath hardly in him. His companion answered that it was the gravedigger and Carolan told him to give the man some tobacco and instruct him to take him to the grave, while his friend waited with the animals. Men should be alone with their grief, I always say.

When he arrived at the graveside, Carolan asked if there was any inscription on the stone. But the gravedigger muttered that he knew no words, so could not read them. Carolan nodded and asked him to leave as he wanted to be alone with his friend. The gravedigger grunted and moved off some yards. I was watching all this and my duty to the dead demanded that I move nearer.

Carolan's voice was unbearably low as he tried to speak, and as the words spilled out from him he seemed to sway. The gravedigger started forward, then stopped as he heard the words, that Carolan spoke. They were heartfelt, and I remember them as I remember every name on every stone, and their sad histories. And what he said might well have been cut on a gravestone.

'I've sung many a lament and praised the dead for the life that was in them, but I can't find words for you, Charles McCabe, for they are down there with you and I hope they warm you where you are. You have left me cold as the stone that marks your grave. I have no more words than this empty gravestone, for my heart is cold and close to yours.'

As he spoke, he stood rigid as the headstones about him and the gravedigger's eyes were more wet with tears than Carolan's own. Both men stood within feet of one another and, I have to say it, even I wept as I watched.

After some minutes the gravedigger moved towards Carolan and turned him gently towards himself. As he did so, he lifted Carolan's hands to his face and said, 'This jest has turned back on me. For whatever pain I have inflicted on you, my friend, I bear it ten times more myself. I never thought I'd see the day when the words of my friend Turlough Carolan would fill me with tears, but this day I am a wiser and more humbled man.'

As he spoke, Carolan furiously fingered the face and his eyes were screwed almost closed. 'McCabe!' he screamed. 'McCabe! You miserable, deceitful son of Satan's own slut out of hell. I curse the day you were conceived and twice curse the day I met you. You should have been smothered in the sheets you were born in.'

Such words spoken in the place of the dead were terrifying to hear for a curse given over the graves of the departed is a dangerous thing. As I stood blessing myself against what I had heard, I saw Carolan's helper rein in the horses and tie them to the gates. Then, leaping the wall, he burst across the cemetery towards the men. As he reached them, I saw the gravedigger bent double across a tombstone choking with laughter, while Carolan lashed out with his hands at the blank air.

'You rotten cur,' he hissed. 'There's not a woman alive would give birth to you. You're the spit of Satan and you surely fell from the arse of some half-dead mountain goat. If I had eyes, by the blood of Christ, I'd put you in that grave you brought me to.'

The scene was incomprehensible to me. I thought Carolan was insane with grief and that all reason had left him, but the cackling gravedigger confused me even more. All Carolan's guide could do was hold him in a bear hug as he tried to calm him. 'God almighty, Turlough, cease, will you?' and, turning to the gravedigger, he screamed, 'Get yourself away from this place whoever you are.' All the while Carolan stood screaming, 'McCabe! McCabe', as if he was incarnating his curse.

Shaking his head in disbelief the gravedigger rolled away from the scene and towards the gate. As he did so Carolan's companion tried to console his friend with the words, 'He's gone, he's gone! Compose yourself now.'

It seemed ages until Carolan subsided into the same manner as he had entered the cemetery, gulping great breaths, but this time with his head thrown back and his eyes rolling. For several minutes I watched until the whole scene fell into silence. Then Carolan broke the quiet. 'That scheming charlatan, McCabe, has been planning this for years!'

Account of Patrick Anthony Nolan, Poet

My name is Patrick Anthony Nolan. I'm nineteen years old and a poet apprenticed to the renowned Charles McCabe. I'm here today because Charles McCabe insisted that I bring him. He's really too old and too feeble to travel, but he says that friendship and honour are more important than any pain or inconvenience that a few days' travelling could cause him.

Indeed, it's a strange relationship these two men have. McCabe always made sure that I was at his house when Carolan was there, for he informed me I could learn much from their conversation. But I was never sure what he expected me to learn, for most of the time they were together they were either roaring drunk or arguing about everything and anything. Though the last time they were together, I learned much, yet I still don't know what I am to make of it.

The walls of McCabe's house are so buckled and swelled out that it looks like an old cooking pot sinking into the lands it sits on. It's a bit like McCabe himself, for his voice sometimes sounds like he has been living off the bramble and gorse that surround it. That's why he always has me there, to read or recite for his guests when he is incapable. And that's why I was there the last time Carolan stayed.

I can still see McCabe bent across the fire, hurling great gobs of spittle into it and coughing like he was breaking stones. Carolan was unperturbed and hummed to himself between swigs from a stone bottle. As I was fixing two rush lights to brighten the place, McCabe joined Carolan where he sat. They must have been talking before I arrived, for McCabe was complaining about music and poetry.

'I tell you, Carolan,' he grunted. 'Melody cannot come before words. The musician must always follow the poet.'

McCabe was determined, but without any sign of aggression. Carolan's mood was amazingly calm and assured. I wasn't sure if he was playing with McCabe, but my ears pricked up. I thought if they weren't too drunk I might learn something and to this day I remember well the turn of their conversation, though, as I say, I'm still unsure as to what it all means.

'Never, McCabe,' Carolan answered. 'Without music words are like stones rattling around in an old butter box. Music gives wings to words. It enriches the meaning of sentiment, for it carries beyond reason.'

But McCabe was not convinced, nor was he the man to bow to Carolan's reputation, though it was obvious he respected him greatly. He challenged him again: 'Play me a lament on that harp of yours and let's see how far beyond reason your music might take us.'

Carolan did not hesitate, he pulled the harp towards him, paused, then began.

The music was lower than I have heard him play before. In the quiet of the cottage the notes seemed to flow out from his fingers and settle quietly around the walls. There was a certain and sure sadness that pulled the mind into quiet reflection. McCabe's face was crumpled in concentration and at his insistence Carolan played one lament after another without attributing them. 'Let the music stand without any great man, or the help of words, to hold it up,' McCabe demanded.

A small candle burned on the table where the men sat and I studied the faces it lit up. Carolan's head was tilted towards his harp. The white collar of his shirt enhanced the light falling on his face. It was expressionless and seemed unmoved by the music, or McCabe's words.

McCabe's silvery head and greying beard glistened and he held his head bowed, but in a half-turn towards Carolan. His features were sharp and lean and his ears were like small, tight buds. His great bony hand cupped the drink before him. His eyes never left Carolan's face, but in their intensity it seemed he was looking beyond the musician. Even then he was gaunt and lean. His brown waistcoat and red undershirt seemed to flow up into the features of his face. It was as if he had been cut out of the stone slabs that made up the walls. And he still looks like that today. But he's slower now, the sap's all dried up in his bones. Carolan's face looked well fed, even bloated and his skin had a sickly pallor that was not usual in someone who had spent nearly thirty years on the road. He looked like a dying man even then.

With his own eyes half-closed, Carolan plucked out the closing notes, and without speaking laid the harp at his feet. McCabe simply nodded and poured them both a drink. His gritty voice was low and he told Carolan that 'his music was like milk soaking into muslin!'

I started in my chair. Carolan sat unmoved. McCabe spoke

again, intimate and urgent. He said that he 'felt no passion, and felt no dread and if there was grace in the music there was no power'.

'A lament is about life not death,' Carolan answered, but his words were feeble as if he was unconvinced.

McCabe was eager to teach his companion the lesson he has been teaching me for years. 'The greater part of any man's life is tragedy. The poet in you must tell you this. Even without your eyes, your years on the road must have shown you this.'

I expected some vehement reply, but none came. McCabe was too taken with his own thoughts to notice the silence of his guest. With growing enthusiasm he asked Carolan if he remembered telling him how he had enjoyed listening to Virgil's words being read to the children at Alderford. He answered that he did and that even now, some forty years later, he still heard the story of Aeneas being read and talked of in many of the great houses where he played.

'Indeed!' affirmed McCabe. 'Priest and pagan alike are drawn to the wisdom of Virgil's story.'

Then McCabe walked to the corner of the room, and opening an old wooden chest extricated an old book and returned to his friend, saying, 'Listen now and say if there's a melody in your music that will fit these words.'

And so he began to read in his gravelly voice. I sat silent and watched. As McCabe read, the words seemed to throw a net around Carolan. He made no movement other than to drink and fill his glass. I have that very book with me, for McCabe made me bring it. He insists he will read again to his old friend those words he read that night. For he thinks there is some mystery in them that only Carolan knows. Here, see, he has marked them with feathers. It starts, 'They were walking in the darkness, with shadows round them and night's loneliness above them,' and goes on to describe a substanceless world that is lifeless and colourless. It is a world filled with disease, 'Fear, Hunger, and Evil, pain and death are everywhere, and death's harbinger, war, rages everywhere.'

Then he described the ghoulish figure of Charon, filthy and repulsive with eyes like sparks of flame, and the souls who stood anxiously on the departure shore. Mothers and strong men, huge bearded heroes and unmarried girls. The souls each stood begging to be the first to make the crossing and stretched their arms out in longing for that further shore. But the surly boatman accepted only some, and forced others back, not allowing them near the riverside.

Carolan continued to sit in broody silence, with his head occasionally nodding as if he recognised the place. But when McCabe spoke of the 'Fields of Mourning', Carolan seemed to start up in his seat.

'Let me see, here now, "Not far thence are displaced the Fields of Mourning, as they name them, and they stretch in every direction. Here there are secluded paths and a surrounding myrtle wood, which hides all those who have pined and wilted under the harsh cruelties of love. Even in death their sorrows never leave them." '

I remember it because Carolan stopped McCabe to ask what sort of flowers might grow in such fields and if McCabe really believed that the dead are forever sorrowful. But before he could answer he dismissed his own question and told McCabe to continue.

Carolan listened entranced to Helen's murderous betrayal and the innocence of Aeneas. He was brought to the 'burning river of hell' with its adamantine columns and its great iron towers from which poured out the savage sounds of screaming and flogging. McCabe was describing the terrible scene, when he suddenly stopped and then declared, 'Be warned, learn righteousness and learn not to scorn God.' He told Carolan to think on that, then continued.

As McCabe's voice rolled around the room, my fascination grew. I have never witnessed a man so subdued and compelled by a story before. But when he read the part about Aeneas seeking the ghost of his dead father, Carolan became agitated. With his voice quaking, he made McCabe read the lines again.

' "Father, oh, let me clasp your hand! Do not slip from my embrace!"

'As he spoke, his face grew wet with the stream of tears. Three times he tried to cast his arms about his father's neck; but three times the clasp was vain and the wraith escaped his hands, like airy winds or the melting of a dream.'

Though I was not sure, I thought there was a watery brightness in Carolan's eyes and even as I made the observation, he broke the silence. His voice was low as if he had just awakened. 'Lethe water, more Lethe water, McCabe,' McCabe nodded to me to fetch some more drink.

I quickly found the jug I was looking for and brought it to the two men. They were engaged in discussion and McCabe posed the question, 'What can he mean that each of us finds a death suited to himself?'

Before Carolan could respond, he continued, 'Now do you see, Turlough? Can you fit a melody that can conjure up Virgil's underworld? For here, surely, is a lament for all of us.'

Carolan lifted his glass then, dragging it, tapped it lightly on the table, 'Lethe water, young man.' His voice was bright for a moment, then dropped to an almost inaudible whisper. 'I'm afraid of the dark!'

McCabe seemed not to have heard or else he chose to ignore it. I myself was not totally convinced by what I heard. The strangeness of the statement was deepened by the strangeness of Carolan's voice. His shaking voice reminded me of my own childish prayers.

But McCabe was undaunted. Fired by alcohol and his enthusiasm for the words before him, he lectured and questioned and recited almost in the same breath. 'The whole story is about overcoming passion in a world where love, war and death rage all around him. Now, Carolan, where is the music that will excite these emotions in us – and yet, mind you I said and yet, a music that will resurrect the desire in us to rebuild this nation that lies hidden and shivering out there? Has your music the power to give us that? No, my friend, only 'the word' has the authority to do that.'

McCabe's excitement had incensed Carolan and seemed to pull him back from wherever his thoughts had taken him. He was angry and defensive and their conversation quickly became an argument.

'You're a drunken dreamer, McCabe. Even if "the word" could do as you say, it would still be useless. For the people you want to rebuild into a new nation can't read your words. But they can listen and be comforted and gladdened by music. Music, master poet, not words will set them free!'

'They can hear words as well as they can hear music!' McCabe flung back at him.

'And there's more lying words than there'll ever be lying music! Now give my head peace and take a drink.'

They both talked and drank long into the small hours while I tossed uncomfortably in a corner. Occasionally in my half-sleep I would pick up snatches of their conversation, but it was all meaningless. Once I heard Carolan demand urgently, 'Stop, stop, read that bit about his mother again.'

McCabe, enjoying the attention, pronounced the words with drunken intensity. 'So Venus spoke, and as she turned away her loveliness shone, a tint of rose glowed on her neck and a scent of Heaven breathed from the divine hair of her head. Her gown trailed down to her feet; Aeneas recognised his mother, and as he vanished his cry followed swiftly after. "Ah, you are too cruel, why again and again dissolve your own soul with your mocking disguises? Why may I not join hand in hand, hear you in frankness and speak to you in return?" '

As McCabe ended, I watched Carolan smoothing the heel of his palm in his forehead as if he was desperately trying to rub out some mark or spot. McCabe reminded him he had read this portion three times and wondered what was bothering him. Carolan answered without raising his head, his voice was slurred by drink and slowed by the emotion behind it, 'In my room at Alderford I keep a statue of the blessed Virgin. Sometimes I take it and hold it; and when I do I can think only of my mother – and I feel incredibly alone.'

Now McCabe is a man of little sympathy. I should know, for as a teacher he is kinder to his dog. He dismissed Carolan, telling him the drink had made him morbid and he should finish what was in front of him so they could both retire. I was glad of it, for no one can sleep in a house full of drunken babble. I was about to turn gratefully into the wall when I heard Carolan's voice again. 'Leave a candle by me, McCabe,' he said weakly. I was too sleepy to realise how strange his request was. But I have often thought about it since.

The next morning I awoke to find McCabe standing in the middle of the room snorting like a horse as he splashed cold water about his face. From another smaller bowl he swallowed great draughts of the icy water. Then he complained to his still sleeping guest that he was as dry as a burnt pot and that his throat felt like he had been drinking ashes all night. He insisted that, as he was up and about, so should others be. Carolan, once awake, answered with sleepy sarcasm, complaining that the rawness of McCabe's throat had nothing to do with ashes or alcohol, but more to do with all that talking he was doing last night. His own head was aching from the verbal boulders McCabe kept dropping on it!

I was thinking how childlike these two men were, with their games, their tantrums and their constant feuding and arguing, when I heard McCabe say, 'How are you this morning? Did you sleep at all?'

Carolan was standing at the door, as if looking across the hills, and he answered as though he was still asleep. 'I'm not too sure. I can't remember when you finished talking and I started dreaming. But I dreamt I saw some people I knew standing on the banks of your cursed river. I was in a boat, but I wasn't sure whether I was rowing away from them or towards them.'

McCabe laughed and said that he wasn't sure himself when he finished talking, but he remembered lighting a candle and leaving it beside Carolan's bed. 'Are you really afraid of the dark?' he asked.

Carolan stood silent by the door, then answered with another question, 'Did I say that?'

'You did,' said McCabe, 'but I thought you were playing with me, so I said nothing until you asked for the candle. But it's a queer notion now, as I think on it, a blind man who's scared of the dark! What in the name of our holy mother did you mean?'

I was about to close my eyes and sleep, for I had had as little sleep as both of them and I hoped they might both go off somewhere together, but the conversation that followed taught me more than all my years with McCabe had. I lay and listened, afraid to move, as Carolan spoke.

'I'm not sure I know. Maybe it was the drink in me. When I was young I loved the light. As a child it seemed to cast a spell over me. I would sit for hours at the open door and watch light flowing over the surface of the land. I didn't really look for the sun. I looked for the light reflecting off everything, a rock, the wall of our house, at how it glistened on our window and threw a long column from the door into our kitchen. I stood in it. I thought it had come specially for me.'

McCabe sat by the fire and listened. He drew heavily on his pipe and studied the silhouette of his friend in the bright doorway. There was something about the way Carolan spoke. His voice was different, I can't explain it, but it was almost as if he was someone else. It certainly wasn't the Turlough Carolan of the night before.

'Even the nighttime couldn't dispel my fascination with the light. Darkness was still light, but it was different. It was slower or something. It was only light in another form. In the dark I could dream even with my eyes open.'

Carolan stopped and rubbed his eyes. Then he turned to McCabe and said brightly, 'You know, children know more than we think! When I was a child I knew everything with the whole of my being. But now I am old, I only know things with my head. Perhaps that's why I am afraid of the dark.

'I'm going to let you into a secret, my friend. Being blind is not what you may imagine. People say that being blind means not to see, but they're wrong. The blind are only blind if they insist on seeing with their eyes. When I couldn't see things in the way I had before, I felt angry and it filled me with despair. And so for too long I lived without seeing.'

His voice changed and became urgent. He raised his index fingers and tapped on his temples beside his eyes. 'But not because of blindness. You see, I was still looking with the eyes I no longer had. No, no, I mean I was looking the wrong way. Then I met Fionnuala Quinn and she began to prise my eyes open. I began to look more closely, not at things, but at the new world blindness had brought me. It was like a radiance emanating from a place I hardly knew was there. Now I think I live too much in my head and I can't find that place. That's the problem with poets too, and that's what I was trying to explain to you last night.'

As he finished, he turned from the door and walked towards the fire, where he stood warming his hands. McCabe sat behind him in silence.

With his back to him Carolan asked, 'Does my secret confuse you?'

'It's queer talk, all right!' said McCabe.

'It took me a long time to understand these things, and I'm not sure I do now. You see, I was already a young man when I became blind. But as I learned to leave my sighted world behind and enter my own new world, I began to feel indescribable relief and happiness. I was filled with confidence and gratitude, as if a prayer had been answered. At first these moments came in short bursts, then they grew longer and slowly light and joy came to me. They came as one sure thing in my experience.'

McCabe could not restrain his words. 'It's like a dream, an enchantment. It's like magic!'

'But it was not magic for me. It was reality and my whole being was filled with it. It seemed as if I lived in a stream of light. And here's what's stranger, McCabe. Colours also survived. This inner light threw its colour on things and people. Everyone had a colour that I never saw before I was blind. It was as much a part of them as their face or their voice. For a long time I didn't understand all this. I only knew I was living it and in time I would understand it. But I couldn't speak to anyone about it. I became confused and angry. I frightened people, I suppose.'

He moved away from the fire and asked McCabe to fill him a pipe as he pulled a chair to the table. 'Does this begin to answer all your insane questions of last night?' he asked.

McCabe seemed perplexed for a moment. There had been much drunken debate and I think he was not sure what Carolan was referring to. He mumbled out his confusion as an excuse, but Carolan would not let him finish. His voice had lost its calmness. 'The dark, man, the dark. That passionate, majestic dark that you believe makes great art. It's not in me.' He took a long pause, as if he wanted the statement to sink in, then he lowered his voice and whispered, 'Though as I get older I have premonitions of it, I feel shadows. Age leaves its shadows on us all.'

At this moment Carolan did not seem as self-assured as his words suggested. McCabe quickly lit the pipe he held and placed it in Carolan's hand, saying, 'As for those shadows, you, my old friend, have less cause to fear them than the rest of us.'

For several long minutes the two of them sat drawing on their pipes. The silence was suffocating. I was about to get up when Carolan asked McCabe if he remembered the Brett family. Before he could answer Carolan told him that it had been ten years or more since he had been to that household. He stopped and sat still as if remembering something, then he began as if he was addressing no one in particular, 'I never went back because I couldn't.' His voice dropped, 'Not even after she died, I couldn't.'

I thought that this was going to be another story specially concocted for McCabe's attentive ears, but as it unfolded my doubts vanished.

Carolan had called on the Bretts many times and had always been well received. They were middling people, with a middling knowledge of music and poetry, he explained. But they were honest, generous and open and he felt obliged to call on them whenever he went into Sligo. They had a daughter whom he had not met before, although he had heard her moving about the house. On his last visit, not having been there for many months, the young girl's father asked if he would do him the honour of composing a piece for his daughter. He was only too happy to oblige and asked if he might meet her. He explained that he liked to hear the voices of the women he composed for.

The father was delighted and showed him into a small parlour, while he found his daughter. But even as Carolan heard her approach the room his assurance became shaky. He did not know why until the father introduced her. Her voice when it returned his greeting seemed sunk so far inside her as to be almost inaudible. But more important, he thought, was its quality. Voices could be soft and low and still have a melody which gave him a sense of the person. Though she was sitting next to him, he felt as if she was not in the room at all.

Then he explained something that confused McCabe and made him wonder if Carolan was telling his tall tales again: 'Everything and everyone has their own sense. There's a kind of pressure or vibration about each of us, as we each have our own colour. It's part of us. But there was no pulse from the child. There was no vibration.' He paused briefly. 'I could not see her colour, only the colour of old rain-washed lime. I tried to see beyond it, but there was nothing.'

At this point he stopped again and tried to hide the sigh rising up in him by smothering it with a cough. McCabe sat silent, afraid to speak, I suspected.

'I played some music for her to see which pieces she liked and she said she liked them all. She said she also liked the sunlight and was sorry that I was blind. It was then I explained to her the "secret" I've just told you, McCabe. It pleased her greatly, but she promised to keep it to herself and skipped out of the room with a cheery goodbye.

'No matter how I tried, I couldn't find any melody in me that radiated from her. Something pressed down on me. Notes fell about my feet. I tuned and retuned the harp, but could find no sweetness in it. Some evil genius hovered over me. There was not a string in my harp that did not vibrate a melancholy sound when I set about trying to compose for her.'

McCabe looked at him, waiting for him to say something. I knew McCabe felt himself on shaky ground at the moment. When Carolan spoke again he said that he spent a long time talking with Mr and Mrs Brett in their garden. Mrs Brett was upset and very soon after he left. All the way from Sligo to Roscommon Carolan said that he never spoke one word. He seemed to be trying to collect his thoughts.

When he spoke again, he said, 'She died, poor child, within six months!' Then after a pause he turned to McCabe, 'So do you see again, McCabe, why laments don't come easily to me. I saw it, and I knew it, that the little girl would not see many more days.'

McCabe was about to speak when Carolan said, 'I have believed since that day that it's a curse to lament the living. But, for your abuse to me yesterday, I have composed for you the lament for Charles McCabe.'

Then he quietly lifted his harp and plucked out a hollow dirge. I didn't know what to do. But after several minutes I got up and made some excuse about getting some firewood.

Some days later, after Carolan had left and I tried to speak with McCabe about what Carolan had said, he remarked simply, 'Maybe the sighted are blind.'

Eleven Death and Light

Memoriam, on the Imminent Death of Turlough Carolan, Last of the Bards; by Father Fintan O'Hanlon

It's been many years since I've been here. I was a frequent visitor when I was secretary to Bishop Thaddeus O'Rourke. He's related to the O'Conors through the marriage of one of his sisters. He always said that the position of the Church in Ireland was one of survival, and it would only survive if it could maintain some continuity with the history and survival of these ancient families. I had many a history lecture from the bishop in my time and there were many times when my services to the bishop were more like those of an historian than an administrator of the church. Perhaps there was something in what he said, for though I have been away for many years I don't feel a stranger here.

Carolan has much changed from the man I knew all those years ago. He has aged terribly yet still seems alert. He knows that he may not have much time left, but he seems unperturbed. When I suggested that he was fortunate to have such friends and be able to find himself in such comfort, he answered me that an old dog always finds its way home, it was only men who lost their way! We talked much about how things had changed. But I sense Turlough had more urgent things to discuss. The O'Conor Don and his son Charles were coming to join the bishop and the poet McCabe, whom I was told had already arrived. I felt my presence was not required, though I am sure the bishop will have much for me to record for him before the week's out. So I have come here to Greyfield House. It may well be the seat of the O'Conors but Carolan had made this house his second home. As I look at it now, it too seems as worn out as the man himself.

As a young priest I was amazed by the grandeur of this crumbling old house's history, which Turlough also sensed and was determined to make himself part of. The name O'Conor is of ancient lineage, tracing itself back to one Turlough Mor O'Conor, King of Ireland, whose son Rodrick was often described by the people hereabouts as the last independent monarch of the country. The house itself is still, in many people's minds, a seat of royalty, such is the deference which the whole neighbourhood accords it and the affection in which they hold its occupants.

Like many of the old households, Greyfield's is a history of brief inheritance and periods of confiscation. Finally the estate fell to Denis O'Conor, its present master, but because of the 'attainting' of his father and brother the lands were forfeited once again. Only his persistence in declaring the honour of his person and the legitimacy of his claim, ensured the restoration of a mere fraction of the once princely territory of his great-grand-father.

Denis O'Conor was fond of saying it was his adherence to the Catholic faith that had turned his hair grey. 'No matter what the law begets a man, his faith will take it from him,' he used to state ironically. For many years he lived in a tiny cottage at Kilmactranny in County Sligo, despairing of recovering his lands. I can still hear his drunken voice booming across the estate as he addressed his sons, 'We are of royal blood and I am the son of a gentleman, but you are the children of a ploughman!'

Those twenty years living in a cottage and fighting for his own had neither hardened nor hurt Denis O'Conor, they endeared him to the people who came to know him. Carolan loved him for his stubborn belief in himself, his faith and the rightness of his cause. Though Denis O'Conor might represent the final eccentric remnants of an Ireland that is being pushed, and crushed and driven into extinction, to Turlough Carolan he represented something else. I remember one evening the bard confessed to the bishop that the O'Conor Don was a living testament to the truth his own parents had driven into him, 'Be your own man, be true to yourself.'

I knew how sentimental and childish Carolan could become when he was drunk: that same evening I heard him explain to the bishop how the O'Conors made him think of the biblical genealogies, an endless chain of all the begetters and the begot. To his mind the O'Conors were like an old patriarchal family who down through the ages had begot chieftain after chieftain, lord after lord to lead and guide the people. Walking these grounds now, a part of me recognises Carolan's drunken sentiment. There is something patriarchal about Greyfield and the O'Conors, even if time and history have passed them by. But I am wrong. It is not the ravages of time that have diminished this household, but something more evil! It is a government's deliberate policy to erase a nation and a culture from this particular piece of God's earth. Perhaps the bishop taught me a better lesson than he knew all those years ago, for while we maintain our ancestral memory the fools can erase nothing. I am sure Carolan knows this in his own way.

He has spent years entertaining in homes like the O'Conors'. Though their glorious histories are often no more than a drunken memory, yet they survive, changed greatly in circumstance yet not in standing. Their owners might be destitute, dissolute and constantly living beyond their means, but to Carolan they represented quality and continuity. The land, he knew, had lasted for ever and would continue to do so, yet these families with their tragic histories imbued the people with an immortality equal to the land's. At Greyfield, as at Alderford, Carolan always felt himself in communion with this stored sense of cultural energy. If he could see it now, what would he say? But some men choose to be blind, for there's comfort in that.

Everywhere the external plaster is peeling from the walls and here and there weeds have found a bedding place between the stones and are already throwing up their first green shoots. The bishop once told me that Turlough's only memory of the house before he became blind was looking up at the façade and thinking how it resembled an old man's port-wine stained face with hairy warts and moles growing on it. Sometimes he imagined that Denis O'Conor looked like this. When he said this to the O'Conor Don, Denis O'Conor laughed with him and said, 'These houses never grow old – they were always old. Old with stories and ghosts and that old sadness that's part of us all.' Carolan only nodded his head in agreement, as if he could hear the stories and feel the old ghosts. But he was happy with them. This was their home and he considered it his, so they could only be his friends. But look at it now. There's sheep droppings and cow dung everywhere. You'd think they would at least keep the animals away off the forecourt! It seems impossible to me that future generations can reclaim or restore this. But the O'Conor Don's son might be equal to the task.

Young Charles O'Conor is a great favourite with Carolan. He is in every point the son of his father. He is a sensitive and cultured young man and has lost none of it in his mature years. Though he is in robust good health, his features suggest otherwise. He's tall and well made, but his fleshy covering seems inadequate to his frame. His high cheekbones and aquiline features are set in a sallow complexion. If I didn't know better, I could mistake him for a Spaniard. His eyes are a deep blue black, like slate.

He has an air of pensive quiet as if he is waiting for things to come to him, but his personality is quite the reverse. He's inquisitive and demanding. He seems to drink books and any learning that is offered him. Though he is relatively young, in his mid-thirties, I believe he can hold his own with any older or more mature mind. He also knows the extent of the estate and the limitations of his father's wealth, an equation not easily balanced. Yet he revels in the challenge of remaking the estate.

I feel that 'young Charles', for they still insist on calling him this while his father lives, is more disturbed by Carolan's passing than he shows. When Charles was much younger Carolan, among others, was his teacher and perhaps his mentor. The young man respected him for what he could learn from him, but loved him for his failings and his frailty. One incident comes to my mind. It had been an evening of great entertainment, when the house overflowed with his father's friends. Carolan had played and recited and entertained in high fashion. But when someone inoffensively proclaimed that the table might better understand what he was talking about if he stopped drinking between breaths, Carolan turned blind-eyed towards the offender and announced with great authority, as if pronouncing the amen, 'Drink adds flavour to the feast of reason and enriches the flow of the soul.' I remember Charles was greatly impressed, but I thought there was an unnecessary arrogance in his words, and I had little time for his showy behaviour.

Yet Carolan's room was empty as a monk's. He preferred it that way and once explained to the bishop how its bareness seemed to push back the walls into limitless space. He felt he couldn't live in a large room. Big rooms demanded to be filled with a clutter of things. Such clutter, he said, unnerved him. I remember the small fireplace in his room, which was rarely lit. The smell of burning faggots reminded him of charcoal and his father's glowing forge and his mother's cooking fire. 'No,' he declared, 'fire is not my element. Fire is history.' It was a curious statement and when I questioned the bishop about what Carolan may have meant he said he wasn't sure, nor was he sure that Carolan wasn't lying, or at least merely saying things for effect. For with our bard you could never be sure.

Both the O'Conor Don and his son Charles called his room 'Turlough's pantry', or occasionally, when they were ribbing him about his drinking, they would call it his cellar. However they joked about it they never invaded his privacy when he was alone there, yet Carolan rarely felt the need to retire into its seclusion. The companionship of the O'Conors was one he enjoyed. In any case, if he wanted to be alone, there was an arbour in the garden which Denis O'Conor had had specially constructed for him. When he took himself off there someone was always sent with a pipe, tobacco and a bottle or two. Denis O'Conor called them 'offerings to the muse' and instructed that Carolan should never be left in the arbour without offerings to stimulate him.

When his patron asked what they might plant round the arbour to provide shade from the sun and shelter from the wind, Carolan said, wild dog rose and ivy, and he seemed so immediately resolved on them that no one argued, and the place was planted accordingly. The latticework of willow that made up the sides of the structure soon became a green wall. On many occasions I have seen him settled back in his snug green compartment oblivious to the world. He seemed happier in that ivy enclosure than anywhere else.

The old library was where I sat taking dictation from the bishop or listening to the conversations between him and the O'Conor Don. It is a significant comment on the times we live in that these two men – one a descendant of the last king of Ireland and the other a prince of the Church, who in his time was chaplain to Prince Eugene of Savoy and on intimate terms with the duke of

Marlborough – are reduced to a condition of practical disinheritance, and are virtual refugees.

Perhaps history has stood still in this household. I remember one afternoon, sitting here in the company of the two men, as if it was yesterday. There was little in the bishop's appearance to declare his high clerical position, even if his clothes are of a better quality and cut than one would expect in this part of the countryside, although they were well worn, like his features. It was impossible not to notice the anxiety, world-weariness and withdrawal that marked his face. Everything about it seemed small. His ears were like buttons pressed into the side of his head and his eyes were small dark amber beads. They had a strange light in them as if they were asking a question to which they already knew the answer. Uncharacteristically he wore a small black skull cap embroidered with gold threads. It was a curiosity which he insisted served only to keep his head warm.

Denis O'Conor sat opposite his brother-in-law in a great throne of a chair. The top of his head was quite bald, but what hair remained was thick and tended to curl about his ears and neck. His beard was deep and full; it was the kind of beard that required its owner to frequently smooth back the moustache from his mouth. Two deep channels ran down from his nostrils and disappeared into the beard's lush growth. His eyes held a quiet resignation. They had their own depth and it was inviting and warm. He wore a great red fur-trimmed wrap, with huge bell-like sleeves running from the collar to his feet. It gave him the look of an old judge. His title of 'the O'Conor Don' suited him.

I remember them both sitting contemplatively before the great stone hearth. The O'Conor Don stared into the fire blazing by his feet as he listened to the bishop. Even now I can still hear the words.

'Conversion will not secure the land to us because it changes our relationship towards it. We can possess nothing meaningfully if we tear up the fabric in which we clothe our soul.'

'Those are fine words and no less could be expected from a cleric, but they will not put clothes on our backs or food in our hungry stomachs. We have to be pragmatic, Thaddeus. We have to have some stake in this nation. Look at us. We are relics, you and I. There are plenty of people around us who do not share our faith, yet they share other beliefs with us.'

'I know what you're going to say before you say it, Denis O'Conor. Render unto Caesar whatever is his tuppence-worth, eh! Isn't that right?'

Denis O'Conor smiled. 'God is not a land agent, however we perceive him. I can't see him doling out land titles according to the colour of our prayers.'

'A nation must have a spiritual and moral centre as well as a temporal one. And the meek shall only inherit the earth when they have the legitimacy of that superior spiritual authority to guide them. We cannot have the authority of the state dictate in matters of the spirit.'

'Thaddeus, your zealot's eyes have blinded you, for the state already has, and both you and I are affected by its decrees. It's no good you and I skulking here and scheming about the past.'

Both men sat in silence. It was an old argument between them, but though their views were different they gave them mutual comfort. That they could debate such things reassured them that they still had significance and that reason and humanity could still find a fitting relationship. It was an ancient dialogue and I suspect these walls have heard it ten thousand times, for I know it verbatim.

I was more interested in Carolan and Charles, who were talking at the far end of the room. Carolan was determined to instil in his pupil the rudiments of musical understanding.

'There are four essentials you must be able to recognise and adapt into your compositions. They are the foundation stones of our music. Let's look at a very simple form of this structure.'

Carolan lifted his harp and let his strings describe in tones what he was explaining.

'First we engage ourselves with the instrument and call out to our listeners. The voice of the strings must be gentle and persuasive.'

His harp sang out a low melody. It was soft and pathetic, any impulse in the music was subdued and restrained.

'Next we lift the music.' As he spoke his fingers easily ascended the scale. The notes became bold and energetic. The earlier sense of pathos found a new impassioned plea.

'Then we repeat this again, letting the new energy find its own voice.' His harp repeated what he had just played, this time with more varied embellishments.

'Now she's found her voice, and her song becomes less energetic and less urgent. It becomes eloquent, graceful and full of assurance.'

He caressed the instrument, allowing the music to underline the core of his words, then he spoke again, 'And now we return to where we began,' and with these words the music returned to the pathos of its opening. 'The music comes full circle, so, like an echo, it deepens its effect on its audience. Remember, the musician is first of all an entertainer and his audience is his first concern. But the composer? Now that's a different tune altogether!'

Charles was an able student. He understood concepts easily and could appreciate their application. His uncle the bishop had meticulously schooled him in Latin and Greek, and every aspect of science and mathematics. 'If you inherit nothing else, at least you'll have enough knowledge to be the equal of any man,' he used to tell him.

Consequently Charles was unafraid to turn his understanding on his companion. 'I understand what you're saying but I think you're lying or at least you don't practise what you preach.'

I was shocked, but Carolan seemed unmoved. 'I'm a liar and hypocrite, is that what you're telling me?'

'I'm saying that you're not telling me everything,' said Charles, undaunted. 'What you have explained produces a music too much haunted by melancholy, but your own compositions are very different.'

'What makes you say that?'

Charles paused, then replied confidently, 'You run away from melancholy. There's little room for weeping in your compositions. Even your laments are more songs of praise than mourning.'

'Explain precisely what you mean, Charles!' Both Carolan and his pupil were surprised by the bishop's voice joining theirs. They had their backs to the fire and were unaware that the bishop and the O'Conor Don had been listening to them.

Charles found it difficult to answer his uncle, but the bishop coaxed him, 'Try, lad. It won't become easy until you begin unravelling what you think you mean.'

'Well,' Charles hesitated, then began, 'I think it's full of contradictions . . .'

But before he could continue he heard his father's scolding voice, 'So the student is master of the teacher.'

'Leave him,' said Carolan. 'I might learn something yet.'

'Well,' Charles began again with this encouragement. 'You have a fondness for the minor keys, which can be wistful and sorrowful, but you do not let them dominate. You cover the full compass of the harp, ranging up and down in an abnormal flight as if you were trying to escape the haunting ghosts that the dominance of the minor keys would bring to the music. Yet your instruction to me seems to encourage the old style of playing, with its retreat into the mists of the past. In your music you are desperately trying to blow them away.'

Charles paused again, waiting to see if there was any response. There was none and the silence encouraged him.

'At first it seems uncontrolled, the fingering seems impossible, yet somehow it always finds a sprightly elevation of feeling. But I don't know how you do it?'

The statement was put as a question and Carolan knew he was required to answer. He was intrigued by the observation. 'I can only tell you what was told to me too many years ago. The secret is in the harp herself. It's as if all the music is already there in the instrument and you have to find it. You can never be the master of the harp. You can only share in its secrets if you surrender to it.'

He was not trying to be evasive, but I perceived he really did not know how to answer Charles, whose mind was too analytical, too sharp.

He was thinking what else to say when Charles continued, 'Yes. That's something, that word, sharing. The way you re-echo the melody from treble to bass and vice versa, and then how you double the notes on any one or all the positions in a new time, produces something incredibly unexpected but yet a wholly harmonic cadence. I don't understand it, it just seems suddenly to be there and perfectly fitted to the music as a whole.'

'Well, that's a relief, Charles. But I must admit that's too great a mouthful for me to understand,' Carolan said quietly.

'It's as if the old music is there but not as a presence, as a shadow. Are you afraid of it?'

Charles's question came like one of the moments in Carolan's music that he was trying to understand. It seemed just to pop out. Before Carolan could even think of an answer the bishop found his voice.

How well I remember, for I had learned always to take note when the bishop was speaking extempore.

'I suppose the simple truth is that all the arts – music, poetry, and even science – are ultimately God's gift to mankind. They cannot be monopolised, owned or isolated. This gift reveals itself through progression, like, for example, the harmonic progression in music itself. Out of the intercourse of all the notes something even and expected emerges which is harmonically suited to the whole work. It is created within the work, but is immediately a significant part of the work. It has all the value and force of the law that reveals to us how "good tends to spread". By this natural law good shall ever diffuse itself and thus re-create itself.'

'Well, holy God, Bishop!' came O'Conor Don's excited voice. 'You were not saying that a while ago when we were talking before the fire.'

The bishop smiled, 'Then I was talking about the law of men, but here I am relating the law of God!'

'So now we're back again, Thaddeus, sitting in front of that fire we have just left, flicking Caesar's coin through our fingers,' said Denis O'Conor.

The bishop was not to be so easily dismissed. He turned his attention back to Charles and asked, 'Do you understand the premise I'm trying to articulate, Charles? If art is God's gift to mankind, and through it we may unite the temporal and spiritual worlds, each giving substance to the other in a new unity, then it follows that no law that sets itself against mankind can ever be successful, you cannot legislate for the annihilation of a culture. No law, no matter how pernicious, savage or inhuman, can obliterate the culture of a nation.'

I could see Carolan drinking in the discussion. Questions were beginning to form in his mind. He was fingering his forehead in that intense way he has when his mind is preoccupied. Before he could air them, Charles said to his uncle, 'Do you mean that the poet's function is to propagandise?'

'No, it cannot be so. Art celebrates life and in so doing ensures a nation's growth and development. Propaganda merely feeds that which it abominates. Its vision is limited. Music, song and story are the undeclared emblems of nationhood. They cannot be taken from us, for our experience cannot be other than it is.'

At this point Carolan interrupted, 'Those are grand-sounding words, but you've lost me altogether. You talk on a scale of ideas that makes my musician's efforts seem trifling. Not so long ago Charles McCabe lectured me with long quotations from Virgil and told me that my music did not mourn enough the tragedy of our race. Between the two of you, I think I'd be better with a begging bowl in my hand instead of a harp!'

Everyone in the room laughed and Carolan insisted on relating his debate with McCabe, which made them laugh even more. He conjured up an image of the drunken poet pontificating on the tragic despair of the Irish people and bemoaning the lack of an Irish genius to expose their plight and give testimony to their ruined greatness.

But the bishop would not let the matter lie there. 'The man's a fool and you're a bigger one for listening to him. He misses completely the whole idea of Virgil. Let me explain, for it illustrates well what I am saying. Virgil stands as a great light shining out from the pre-Christian world across the era of Christianity. His epic poem is a great human saga. It describes the end of one world and how the last of the Trojans fulfil their destiny although beset by hopeless despondency.

At this point the O'Conor Don intervened. 'And that sounds exactly like McCabe in his cups . . . filled with hopeless despondency!' However, Bishop O'Rourke was not about to give way to more humour.

'The thing that led them to their success was how they responded to divine help and encouragement. The temporal world and the spiritual world are allied in the minds and hearts, in the hopes and dreams of some men.'

I thought the bishop's logic might be beyond these men, but Carolan seemed fascinated. I had long since learned that when

Carolan was concentrating he would rub the ball of his thumb between his eyes. As the bishop spoke of those 'Divine communications' I watched Carolan finger his forehead and take huge breaths as if he was drinking in the words.

'Two great imperatives emerge from Virgil,' the bishop continued. ' "Avoid excess" and "Be true" in the sense of being loyal to god, to family, friends, your homeland. Now McCabe's problem is that he sees only the wickedness, the violence and the horror, but Virgil points a way beyond this hopelessness. It points towards peace, humanity and reconciliation.'

The bishop stopped and looked around the room. Everyone was listening intently.

'If Aeneas is prince of destiny, this is assured by his relation to the guidance of the gods. Venus his mother presents him with a set of armour made by Vulcan, god of fire and metal working. With it he is able to overcome his tribulations, and the gift of art is no less God's gift. By its powerful employment we can "be true" to our cultural inheritance and carry it with us to rebuild our future.'

The bishop walked to Carolan and Charles, and laid a priestly hand on their shoulders.

'Venus, the goddess of love, constantly attends Aeneas and advises him. Her advice is neither selfish nor indulgent. It has moral depth. She dissuades her son from all hate and revenge. Virgil is a keen observer of life and of people and his art lies in making what is seen reveal the unseen. He shows us those common qualities of human existence which bind us to our fellow men.

'He can reach through generations to present a world view which belongs not only to himself but to us all. It is condensed and focused by a single genius in a single poetic statement. Now this, I think, is what our friend McCabe is thinking of, but he has to see beyond the past and the tragedy of our present. He needs to find the "truth of art" not the truth of history. You told us, Turlough, that McCabe insisted on dragging you round Virgil's underworld, no doubt frightening the life out of you with all its horrors, but do you remember what Aeneas carried with him? A golden bough, sparkling round with every virtue! I think you have your own golden bough, Carolan, for I have heard it.'

There was silence after the bishop's praise. No one wanted to steal the moment from Carolan.

Then the O'Conor Don broke it.

'Well, bishop, you've succeeded in turning our music room into a seminary and I think it's time to turn it back again.'

Charles was quick to pick up the opportunity this offered. 'Can we leave the entertainment until later.' There's something I want to show Turlough and I don't want you two interfering,' he laughed.

The bishop and his brother-in-law realised they were being asked to leave, and made for the door once Carolan and Charles had agreed to join them later. I looked at the bishop, who signalled to me to remain.

As the door closed behind them, Carolan said, 'Listen, Charles, if you're going to continue where your uncle left off, don't bother. It's too cerebral for me, even though the gist of it may well do to put McCabe in his place.'

Charles reassured him that he had no intention of pursuing his uncle's line of discussion. He was anxious to get back to music and asked Carolan if he had ever heard Italian music.

Carolan said he remembered Dr Patrick Delaney from the University in Dublin being in the house once when he was there and that he remembered him playing on the harpsichord and talking about the popularity of the Italian musicians in Dublin.

'The harpsichord is not my instrument, though what I remember of the music was that it was pleasant enough. I did think of how what I heard could be transferred to the harp and that there was some real merit in the pieces. They reminded me of jigs. Highly refined jigs, but I suppose I only say that because I can't really imagine jigs and Italians and Dublin debutantes having much in common.'

Charles was laughing at Carolan's explanation and complained again that he was a great liar: that he had not only heard the music but he had enjoyed it so much that he had spent time with Charles and Dr Delaney listening to the pieces being played over and over again. He helped Carolan slowly from his chair and led him to a small tub-like chair behind the harpsichord.

'I have been spending a lot of time in Dublin lately. The bishop insisted that I could only get proper instruction in the sciences there. But I learned more than science and I want you to listen to this.'

I left them to their music and joined the bishop and the O'Conor Don across the hall, where they had resumed their conversation.

The bishop stood on the flagstone hearth with his back to the glowing fire. Denis O'Conor was standing in front of a great oak cabinet. I was given the task of pouring both men large measures of whatever they wished.

Two tall windows draped with old and worn brocade allowed daylight to flood halfway across the room. The wall opposite stood in shadows and was hung with elaborate gilt picture frames containing portraits and landscapes that had been too long denied any light. Here and there empty squares, oblongs and circles marked the places where paintings had once hung.

The fire hissed behind the bishop and he remarked on the futility of trying to light a fire with wet and unseasoned timber. Denis O'Conor replied humorously, 'If I had the money and the manpower to cut, collect and season the wood, then I would surely make every effort to warm your Grace's backside in a more fitting manner. But things being as they are, we live as we must!'

Bishop O'Rourke smiled and as he took the glass I brought him he moved from the fire to a seat beside it. The O'Conor Don returned to the huge ancient dresser to fetch a silver salver with his own glass and bottle and then took up the conversation.

'You're a curious one,' he began. 'When we last addressed this matter, you sounded like an angry and aggrieved man, and then, with Charles and Carolan, I listen to your militant catholic loyalty give way to the platitudes of an old pagan philosopher! I wonder what is really going on in that busy mind of yours.'

At this, the bishop's laughter became less veiled. As if the irony of the O'Conor Don's remark had somehow broken him open, he smiled broadly and his air of austerity fell away.

'We're a curious conundrum indeed, Denis, and the answers are more difficult to find the older we become. We each have roles to play in life, and it's as you say, times being what they are, we must live as we can, rather than as we would.'

But Denis O'Conor was not content. He watched his

companion's face soften and said gently, 'Don't give me any of that priestly evasion, Thaddeus! What are you really thinking?'

The bishop sat silent for a moment, then walked across the room to the shadowy wall opposite the windows. Slowly he walked its length, stopping momentarily to examine the paintings. Finally he began speaking, as if addressing an invisible congregation.

'I have travelled the length and breadth of this country for too many years and the catastrophe of our history still haunts me. I cannot remember a week passing that I have not witnessed deep suffering that has no parallel anywhere in Europe. I have performed the last rites so many times that I am now numbed by the experience. I thought I was immune to death. I had drunk so much from its caustic cup that I felt my own soul had shrivelled to stone.'

'Come on now, let's have less of such talk. Where's the man who was lecturing my son and his friend not so long ago?'

The O'Conor Don's words were sympathetic but authoritative, but the bishop's reply was equally powerful. 'Hear me out, Denis. Even the priest needs a confessor.'

For a moment the room was frozen. In the background the fire continued its hissing, but a few flames were struggling feebly upwards. The bishop's words came slow and thickly.

'A few weeks ago I was returning from Dublin. I had stopped at a small cabin to make some inquiries about finding a hostelry for the evening. As I spoke with the owner, his wife came running up to us. Though she was breathless she seemed strangely calm. "There's work for you, Father," she said and then told her husband to fetch some of their neighbours and to make sure they brought shovels with them. I took directions from her and made my way to the scene she had just left. I was a little irritated that I had to break my journey to go and bury someone's dead. But at the spot she had described to me I found not one, but several corpses. A whole family had made a rough shelter under the trees and had been living there for some time. All of them were dead except the father. The mother and seven young children had passed away, perhaps days before. They lay there, an emaciated heap of rags. The children were all gathered about the mother like piglets at a sow. Their father squatted in a corner of their hovel mumbling some gibberish to himself.'

At this point, the bishop stopped and took a small sip from his glass. He pursed his lips and rolled them slightly as if he was rinsing his mouth.

'I set about the grisly task of delivering the dead, secure in my priestly immunity. The words came to me automatically and threw up a wall between me and the horror in front of me. But as I moved from corpse to corpse I became aware of the husband behind me. He was continually repeating, "Happy now! Happy now!" '

I was aware that the sympathy between the two men had intensified dramatically as the bishop spoke, but it suddenly stopped with the pronouncement of the chant-like words, 'Happy now, happy now'. Both men looked at each other as if lost. The room was infiltrated by the dancing sound of the harpsichord from the room they had just left. At first the music was like a irreverent comment on the bleakness of the story, then it became wiry and nervous.

When the bishop spoke again his words faltered, 'I looked at the man. His staring eyes seemed to scream out of his skeletal face and he continued chanting, "Happy now, happy now". I tried to ignore him and perform my duties with his sad hysterical voice repeating the words over and over. I turned to him again, wanting to tell him to be quiet, but he looked back at me like an ancient gargoyle, mocking me and mocking my own immunity before death.'

He paused again. His sombre face could not hide the anguish the memory caused him. Music continued to filter into the room. This time the harpsichord spun out an intense concentration of rhythmic patterns that flooded round them.

'Merciful Christ, forgive me,' the bishop sighed. 'The man's demonic babbling possessed me. I wanted to be rid of him, I wanted to strangle him and thrust his skinny corpse in with the rest of his family. I even wished I had a knife. I would have cut his throat and silenced his insanity for ever.'

The bishop paused again and drank. He had obvious difficulty swallowing. His Adam's apple moved slowly in his scrawny neck.

'I was thinking all these things, and worse, at the very same time as I was reciting the prayers for the dead!'

He bowed his head into his chest and quickly made the sign of the cross. The O'Conor Don remained silent and watchful. He held up the bottle, but his offer was declined.

'Somehow I managed to complete my duties. As I sat back on my knees exhausted, staring into the faces of those I had been ministering to, I was overcome by a sense of despair and anguish that I never want to experience in my life again. I turned to the man again, my face awash with tears and we chorused those dreadful words, "Happy now, happy now!" '

Denis O'Conor knew the moment had come and passed. He stood and walked across the room and, without asking, filled the bishop's glass. Both men seemed stunned and unable to speak. The O'Conor Don looked once more from the glass to his friend's face and turned and began to walk back to his chair. The bishop started speaking again, but his voice was steady, calm and relieved. 'When we went into the room with Charles and Carolan I was suddenly overtaken by the memory of that event. Perhaps it was Charles's youthful enthusiasm or perhaps when Carolan began speaking about McCabe's fearful opus on the tragedy of the Irish people. I kept hearing the words "Happy now, happy now!" and knew that I must impress on them that they must make their happiness and ours now, in this life. But perhaps, as you say, I was preaching!'

Denis O'Conor poured himself a drink and stared into the fire. His eyes were fixed on the fluttering flames. 'Perhaps you should have spoken to them as you have just done to me. Come and sit by me again. It's a strange music they have chosen. Let's listen.'

As he finished, he tossed two great logs on to the fire. Both men sat letting the music wrap itself around them. When the bishop spoke again, it was as if he was cleansing himself with a benediction.

He spoke of how he always felt at odds with himself when he met these people or took shelter with them. There was a quality of resigned acceptance about them; as if starvation, homelessness and poverty were underlined by a greater and more sustained hunger; as if the very hunger for life itself was greater than anything that could diminish life. Yet he had heard stories that chilled him.

Stories that made him doubt his own fanciful resolution about the determined quality of the life energy that, against all the odds, sustained these wretched and brutalised people!

While he spoke, I remember that Carolan and Charles's music was percolating into the room and into our bones, creating its own benediction on that haunted evening.

Twelve Geminiani

Journal of Mrs McDermott-Roe

March 25th, 1738

For years people have been amazed at Carolan's constitution. He could drink into the early hours without ceasing, and when he did he frequently became abusive. I had little time for him in his moods. When I reminded him that he should be mindful of the prayers he presents to the Lord with the odour of alcohol on him he would dismiss me, claiming that the night was no time for prayer and if God could heal the sick, then he would surely excuse him if he could only manage a quick genuflection and prayer to the Virgin.

But on other mornings when he was not suffering from the previous night's excesses, he would kneel in solemn obedience and give himself fully to prayer. It was always a prayer of thanksgiving and of safe keeping. Then for an hour or so he would sit silently by the window in his room with the morning sun warming him. His hand would finger a small gleaming crucifix and thumb the rosary of coral beads I had given him. Sometimes his pose of sanctity was not all that it seemed. Prayer was not always the subject of those anxious fingers. When the night was fuelled by alcohol and passionate conversation, Carolan went to bed restless with ideas. Then the morning prayers were often accompanied by low humming as he counted on his rosary. He had made it a prayer guide and a musical abacus and to his mind each was an accompaniment to the other. At other times he would sit in one of his long silences with the rosary draped around his neck. In his hands he held the statue of the Virgin. Rocking himself, he would finger it and at times his thumbs would gently caress its eyes. At other times he would be seized by some memory and hug the effigy tightly to himself and kiss the holy face. Then he would throw his face back and take the full force of the sunlight on it, and sit as still as the statue in his hands.

But this morning he seemed unusually excited as I read him the psalms. He explained how he wondered at the constant assurance of the Lord's safe deliverance. The emotional triumphalism and assurance of God's grace, he was sure, were the golden model for all music and songs. He was especially fascinated with those moments of deep anguish and despair. He explained how he thought of a great dark cathedral, where the soul shivered in agony of loss and then the moment of golden light. The dancing, flying, bursting moments of aurora-like light; then the light-filled presence of the Lord pouring like fire into the shuddering soul and uplifting him beyond all pain and doubt. Even as I listened to him, exhausted and moved beyond words, Carolan suddenly complained about the momentary pain in his fingers and a numbness in his chest. I was a little anxious and told him to lie quiet, and he did so for some minutes. Then he implored me again with words he has put to me before, 'Was I equal to my calling? Do you forgive me now?' I don't answer him because I can't. I simply told him to hush and listen as I read him the sixth psalm. As I concluded, he said, 'It's hard to think of men as angels!'

Knowing his propensity for mischievousness, and being anxious of his mood I told him not to be too presumptuous, and reminded him, 'It says here a little lower than angels!'

He laughed, 'And thank God for it, too!'

I was relieved but then he made a curious statement. He remarked that practically every time he asked someone what they saw while he was on the road they answered him with the phrase, 'A God-forsaken land that no one could be happy in!', or some equally gloomy remark. The words made him think that everyone in Ireland must be a psalmist! For a moment he grew ponderous, then he explained that only when he himself knew a similar agony could he compose the elegy that even now was haunting him; but the psalmist's conclusion was always the glory of God and in praise of life. He could not let go of this. Music must ultimately be the great healer. It must give us reason for joy. Like the psalmist he must know and claim this first – he must give it voice or let the darkness take him. And he was afraid of that. He was afraid to dwell too long in that forsaken country. Oh how fearful he makes me feel when he talks like this!

March 26th, 1738

I unearthed this letter today. I remember how angry it made me when I received it. I never made any complaint to Carolan at the time, knowing what his reaction might be, but now I think Father Thomas O'Keefe was misjudged in his condemnation.

Dear Mrs McDermott-Roe,

The subject of my correspondence with you is the itinerant harper, Turlough Carolan. I am informed that you are his principal patron and that he makes his home in yours when he is not 'plying his trade'.

As I have also been told that you are a devout Catholic and a lady of charity and dignity. I am sure you will understand and sympathise with what I must relate on the matter of Carolan.

On those occasions when he and his guide arrive in the parish, the whole population seems to take leave of their senses. As soon as he finds the inn, everyone joins him and within hours the entire village is steeped in alcohol and the spirit of debauchery.

I am sure that you know well the hardship that these people must endure. The moors and mountains of Leitrim, Sligo, Roscommon and Mayo are one vast provincial prison where the inhabitants endure utter misery. Such a people require that their spirits be nurtured with the blood of Christ. These long-suffering people are reduced to a condition of complete abandon when Carolan plays them his irreverent jigs and planxties.

I am not seeking to use your relationship with this man to do what I would not myself. Indeed I have had words with him and thought foolishly that he listened to me. But I should have known better, for he answered me with the tongue of Satan flashing in his mouth!

'Dance is the true liberator,' he declared and then spoke to me with drunken bravado of how King David himself was a great dancer. Then he audaciously proclaimed that he, Turlough Carolan, was a messenger and a healer. His music, he said, preaching at me!, was the cup of oblivion by which men could forget and in their forgetting they could remember the joy that lies in the vaults of men's souls. He concluded his drunken apostasy with the pointed declaration that his was on a mission of consolation and liberation and that I should leave him to his work!

The man is possessed, for it is the work of the anti-Christ that makes men think they can usurp the throne of our blessed saviour.

It is my duty as priest and confessor of the people to provide Christ's pardon, but I fear this man is beyond redemption. However, it is not his debauchery or apostasy alone that force me to write. For his soul is his own now and if out of pride and perversion he has cast it away, then so be it. My concern is for those whom he might snare in his own perdition.

When Carolan last brought his dark shadow to our village I watched as he absented himself from the drunken revelry he had instituted. To my horror, he took himself off with the village children. In a quiet corner he sat amongst them telling stories of fabulous and undoubtedly evil contrivance. These innocents were held spellbound and as he finished they arose and danced in a circle around him. Then, one by one, each of them entered the circle and sprinkled water over his head. All of them were laughing and giggling, while Carolan sat also in the throes of laughter!

Suddenly, by the undoubted grace of God and the power of his Holy Spirit, the heavens opened, ensuring that this satanic bacchanalia was brought to an end. As his guide led him indoors I heard the vaunted acolyte say, 'The king should always rise before his courtiers.' What self-proclaimed king is this who thinks that these proscribed and oppressed people are his?

My heart bled with prayers that evening for what I had witnessed. My faith forced me to confront him the next day as to why he had sought out these children. He answered me, with the words frothing from his mouth, 'And why wouldn't I? I enjoy them. I love their enthusiasm and excitement. Their whispering voices and the wild laughter thrill me. They don't bore me with their questions or their fawning applause. I feel comfortable and easy with them. Almost as if I am one of them. Neither do they chastise me with sanctimonious blather. They love me for what I am. And remember, Priest, what the Lord himself said about suffering the little children to come unto him!'

Even as he spoke his face was laughing and teasing the very foundations of our faith. I beseech you in the name of the saviour to gather about you those who are prayerful, and seek out the assistance of the saints and the power of the spirit, that this man and the possession that fills him is rendered without authority amongst the faithful. But if it is within your temporal authority, command this man to absent himself from our parish!

Your servant in the Lord, Father Thomas O'Keefe

Journal of Mrs McDermott-Roe

March 30th, 1738

What a night it has been. I was awakened from my sleep by the sounds of screaming and sobbing. I have been so exhausted these last few days that I thought myself dreaming. But after some minutes I knew it was coming from Turlough's room. I went to him quickly and found him sitting upright and awash with sweat. It was some moments before I could calm him. Then he began to explain his distress to me. He had been thinking back to his childhood.

One memory had isolated itself in his mind. He had been playing at soldiers with his friends by the river. He had left the affray and stolen off silently to the rath, where he lay wet and sweating in the afternoon sun listening to the water and the cries and screams of his friends.

Then, as if a great dark cloud had moved across the sun, he was seized by the nightmare. Looking at the glistening water and the brown pebbled river bed, he saw it running red. Its rocks and boulders were taking the form of corpses. The water itself screamed with the din and roar of dying horses. The river stank with the fleshy offal of men and animals. He tried desperately to push these images from his mind. They had remained locked away inside him for years and now their half-formed horror was revisiting him. He wanted to dismiss it. He wanted the laughter of Brennan and the other boys, but instead he heard the dark gurgling river make its own music and dark harmony. It swirled around him and tried to pull him into, itself. Carolan's knuckles whitened as he spoke and then his hand raised to his head and his head bent to meet it. Slowly, as if trying to erase the images, he began to rub the area between and just above his eyes. The ball of his thumb kneaded deeply into the spot.

The terror on his face, I will never forget as I prayed in silence but with great fervour, for I was sure this was not some memory but that the river was the swirling waters of life and death encircling him.

I did not know how to console him. I can only hope being with him helps, and that my constant intercession with our Holy Mother, her Son and all the Saints will see us through this time.

I hear some rumour that Lord Mayo and his family will be arriving to honour Carolan in his last hours. An honour indeed and a great change from our last visit to His Lordship's. It was an evening that anyone who was there will not easily forget. And that great brute of a house, who could forget that?

An avenue of yews and hollies led up to it and in the grounds around it were several small lakes 'stiff' with brown trout and if I had my way I would have left his Lordship to his entertainments and taken myself off to those lakes. The house looked cumbersome yet defiant, but the imported stone that made up its façade had long since weathered and was mottled with the blue-grey and green stain of the moss that clung to it. Its grandeur was in its bulk rather than its grace: it was a bastion of one of the last of Ireland's ancient noble families. I never warmed to it, but Carolan was in his element there.

Inside the cold hallways were full of long black oak chests and much of the house was panelled in a patchwork of different timbers, most of it the salvage of shipwrecks. Spreading blotches of damp were everywhere and the moudly smell from the upholstery and heavy French curtains and tapestry confirmed, to me if to no one else, that however great the man's title might be, his fortune was far from the equal of it.

There was, as usual, a great number of guests. They were affable enough to me, for I was the great Carolan's companion and I was busy renewing my acquaintance with some of them when my attention was drawn to the doorway. Carolan made an impressive entrance, walking slowly and carefully into the great hall with his blind eyes turned up to the ceiling. Lord Mayo himself rushed to his aid and guided him to his seat, with every eye in the house trained on them. The room was buzzing. Everyone was eager to hear the maestro play the praise song he had composed to honour the host and his family, as I was, no less than the rest of them. I watched a group of men gather around him, and made what excuses I could and moved closer.

Their conversation intrigued me. It was unusual for Carolan to be party to any political discussion. He considered himself to be, first and foremost, an entertainer and above all a special guest of the host. As such it would be inappropriate for him to indulge in debate. Why, then, I asked myself was he seated where he was? I looked about me. Slowly I began to understand. A greater crowd had gathered at the other end of the room around Lord Mayo, who was making much of a man who stood beside him. This was an Italian violinist, whom we had been told of when we arrived, a man of great repute who had charmed the cities of Dublin and London. I could not see much of the Italian for the crowds that milled around him, and it was obvious that Carolan was being dismissed in favour of Master Geminiani. I took it that this was why he had buried himself in this small knot of men intent on serious discussion and I decided to remain near him. I sensed the wound that he was smarting from, and I thought I might be able to bring him away if necessary.

One man was more outspoken than the rest. He was a member of the clergy, and with some learning. His manner was cold and confident and there was an air of dispassion, even contempt, about him. I knew he would not be easy company. At first I wasn't sure what the subject of their conversation was, but it soon became clear, for his words rang out with all the authority of his priestly calling.

'I must do it justice, it is a complete system, full of coherence and constancy, well digested and well composed in all its parts.'

Then he paused for a moment to throw a remark to Carolan, 'Much in the manner of Carolan's compositions, it is a machine of wise and elaborate contrivance, but unlike our musician's art it is as well fitted for the oppression, impoverishment and degradation of people and the debasement in them of human nature as was anything ever contrived by the perverted ingenuity of man.'

There was something in the priest's voice and the soft intensity with which he spoke that gave great weight to his words, and weighty words they were! This was the fiercest denunciation of the Penal Laws that I had ever heard. There was noble blood in this house and his declaration was a challenge to it. From somewhere amongst the faces listening intently, I heard the words, 'Catholics are not supposed to breathe in this land.'

Carolan sat silent. I thought he must be sulking at being overshadowed by the Italian and swept aside by one of his most revered patrons. But it was not sulking as much as brooding anger that spilt over when he spoke.

'Who is it here that seeks to add more poison to our already poisoned lands? I have been a guest in the many houses of our Protestant brethren, Sir Edward Crofton, his lady wife, Charles Coote, Loftus Jones, Lord Masserene, James Plunket, Dean Massey, and I have received honour and hospitality the equal of any. That law which you so rightly despise has given us cause and has united all creeds in common love of country and hatred of oppression. We might better look to the qualities within us to liberate us from the oppressor outside us.'

His anger was obvious. I thought he was trying to mock the sermonising tone of the cleric and I was fearful that he should lose control of himself completely. But before I could intervene, he leaned down and lifted his harp. Gently his fingernails skipped across the strings, and then again while he intoned, 'The good man must all our praise command, even the sage priest will bless his bounteous hand.'

The priest was quick to understand Carolan's challenge and responded in kind. 'Exceptional times demand men of exceptional gifts. Who amongst us in this room can meet the demands of the time?'

Everyone around knew the priest's meaning. The bards in Ireland embodied the qualities of the poet, philosopher and law-giver. And in his time Carolan loved to pontificate as if he was all three rolled into one. I did not catch exactly what Carolan said next, for his voice seemed slurred, but I think he remarked that Christianity might be only more subtle in its subversion of the people than the laws which the priest railed against. I watched him smile and thought his anger was turning mischievous. 'Piety is not the first instinct in man,' he said simply, and leaning into the harp he began to play. The notes were gentle and light and threaded themselves like a flimsy scarf about the group. His voice chanted slowly as the music unwound.

Carolan repeated the tune and then sat silent, letting its effect sink into his listeners. All his music, he asserted, was a rebuke against this kind of piety, for that to him was a 'debasement of human nature as great and as pernicious as the laws which sought to crush the Irish at every point and station in life'. My watchful eye rested on him. I knew how intemperate he could be. Never had the great Carolan been shunned by his patron as tonight, and this little performance was to draw attention back to himself.

It was now obvious that the whole company had turned its attention to him. I smiled and thought however blind the man was he had the cunning of a fox. This playing was not meant for the priest alone. Other ears had heard it and were even now moving towards the harper.

Lord Mayo was first to speak. 'Carolan, my old friend,' he said solicitously, 'this debate is not the entertainment I had planned for this evening.'

Carolan's rebuke was swift. His anger had found its target. 'And friendship demands more than that friends should wait upon strangers. Who is this man that claims our attention tonight?'

Lord Mayo was anxious and apologetic in the same breath. 'Signor Geminiani had honoured us tonight. His violin is spoken of everywhere, but he assures us your own name has been much mentioned to him. He considers it no small honour to be in your company.'

'I am indeed honoured,' Carolan said coldly, 'but it's a compliment I fear I cannot return.'

'Nonetheless, the music of his country is the praise of all Europe.'

The exchange made me anxious for the evening and I looked towards the violin master. Geminiani's expression was quietly inquisitive. He kept his eyes fixed on Carolan and seemed to be taking stock.

Lord Mayo offered Carolan a compliment as a way of inducement. 'It seems your name is as famed in Dublin as it is in our own countryside.'

Carolan would not yield, however. 'I'm glad you make the distinction between Dublin and our own lands. For I'm sure there's little in common between us.'

To my mind Carolan was like a fish on a hook, caught between the puritanical challenge of the priest and the lure of his patron's compliments. He had backed himself into a corner. I watched his nose twitch as if the perfume from the Italian musician infuriated him.

It was the priest who broke the tension. He said something in

Italian to Geminiani, which had the effect of making Carolan more annoyed with the priest than before. As if he had read his thoughts the priest turned towards Carolan, but addressed the room, 'Signor Geminiani has travelled a great distance to join us. He tells me his journey would be without value should he not hear the harp of Carolan. Will you play for our guest, Carolan?'

Every movement in Carolan's bloated face revealed his thoughts. He was incensed. He was not here to play for this stranger, who had already usurped the attentions of his patron and his audience. When he spoke, his words were soft but could not disguise his feelings, 'I'll play with the man. Music has its own language after all, and we might understand each other the better without an interpreter.'

Geminiani took up his position beside Carolan and waited. There was a great composure about his face. The shiny black mass of curls was thrown back off his head and crowded down to his shoulders in full luxuriant growth. His face was long and unlived in except about the mouth. His lips were slender but well formed and made little indents into his cheeks as if he was always withholding a smile. But his eyes were large and dark, a perfect balance to his flowing hair. He stood unmoved by the attention fixed on him. His elegant appearance made Carolan look shabby and even ugly.

The priest approached Carolan again. 'Signor Geminiani asks if you would like to lead or if you would like first to listen.'

'I'll follow his lead until he relinquishes it, then let him follow me if he will.'

Carolan leaned his harp snugly against his shoulders and rested his hands on his knees. A few seconds passed, then he nodded permission to begin. With equal ease Geminiani lifted his instrument to his shoulder and began to play with effortless grace. As he played the audience sat silent and, I have to confess, spellbound. I had never heard such magic before. It immediately dispelled the gloom from that musty old house and for a moment made Carolan even more pathetic.

But our harpist sat silent, letting the rhythms soak into him. There was a quality of stately impersonality about the sound that was surrounding him. Slowly he lifted his hands to the strings and held them poised, awaiting his moment. With clean precision he took up the bass and followed the violin. His accompaniment was in perfect measure. Never bearing down on the music or dragging after it, his fingers flowed across the strings of the harp effortlessly.

Rising to the harp's harmony, Geminiani sent his fingers flying up and down his instrument. His dexterity and accuracy intensified the music without losing its elegance. Carolan's bass, in its turn, became richer and deeper with the intensity Geminiani had set up. The room filled with Geminiani's music. Grandeur and delicacy danced around the audience and swirled about them again as the music repeated itself. This was the music of a nation inspired and assured of itself and its inspiration was not lost on Carolan.

As effortlessly as Carolan had followed, the Italian now handed the lead to him. It was as if someone had set Carolan's hands on fire. The challenge of the priest and the offence of his patron welled up in him. Like a cornered animal finding a bolt hole, Carolan surrendered to his anger. In the full flight of offended power he soared aloft. He would do more than lead, he would conquer. All the old lore and skill of his forebears were suddenly in his hands. The overlapping harmonics of the wire-strung harp echoed and repeated, building up a high wall of resonating notes that Geminiani's violin was powerless to scale. The complexity and speed of Carolan's fingering was as incredible as it was impossible. At times I felt that Carolan was ravaging the harp in his hands. Bright burning half-tones sounded everywhere, but against them Carolan's face was passionless and white. He played as if every note was a miracle in creation. The great hall was silenced as his music filled it. Then, with a powerful final flourish, he stopped. It was as if the room had suddenly stopped spinning and been plunged into a lake of ice. The guests stood senseless.

The applause at first was muted, then, almost in imitation of the music itself, became rapturous. Geminiani, too, seemed transformed. His face was animated and flushed. His eyes were staring and shining. His whole body seemed trapped in a motionless but intense vibration.

Carolan sat exhausted, hearing the heavy waves of adulation come at him from a distance. I walked quietly to his side. For a split second my mind left me and I wondered where I was. Then I heard myself declare, 'Mother of Christ, holy Mother of Christ,' to which Carolan answered only, 'Give me a drink, Seamus, my mouth's on fire.'

The applause began to die and was taken up by a fierce hubbub of salutation and affection. As the crowd watched I poured a drink into Carolan's glass and they too replenished their glasses. There was an excitement in the room that needed quenching. But none of us were prepared for what happened next.

As Carolan was about to lift his glass to his mouth, Geminiani walked forward. Reaching him, he stretched out a nervous hand and stopped his glass in midair. Those nearby who saw the action froze into silence. I looked on astonished as the Italian held out an empty glass. It was quickly filled. Carolan was about to complain, but before he could open his mouth, Geminiani spoke. His voice was low. Releasing Carolan's arm he said simply, 'Hail, Carolianus.' Everywhere about him, outstretched arms saluted him and voices chorused, 'Carolianus, Carolianus.'

Carolan himself knew the significance of the gesture and the deep honour accorded him. This moment could not be surpassed. Slowly he stood. Then he bowed his head towards the Italian and the audience. Lord Mayo walked quickly forward to congratulate him. As he did so, Carolan whispered something. His host nodded and after looking about him for a moment, asked me to help Carolan to his room. As we walked through an avenue of applause and admiration, I noticed that Carolan walked more slowly than when he had entered.

We passed along the dark hall with the last remnants of appreciation dying behind us. As we reached the door of his room I said nervously, 'I think you've set the house on fire tonight.'

His answer was cryptic and left me too puzzled to say anything more. 'It's not my element!' he declared and without another word closed his door.

The rest of the evening passed sedately enough with an edge of excitement always underneath the surface. I could say I was impressed by Carolan but that would not be correct, rather I was stunned.

The next day I made a point of saying to Carolan directly, 'You have the ears of a fox, but you have the tongue of a viper. My God, man, I thought for a moment last night you were about to draw blood from the holy father.'

'I've been told there are no snakes in Ireland, Seamus, though I've been in the company of many in my day. There was something in the priest's words that did not sit easy with me. There was no lack of intellect but I thought his understanding and his sensitivity were in short measure.'

I laughed. 'Well now, Turlough, I'm sure that accusation could never be laid at your door, No, no. Heaven forbid!'

Carolan simply smiled in return. He obviously enjoyed my ridicule. But he wasn't finished with the priest yet. 'Perhaps the seminary where he learned his trade has polished off all his rough edges. There are things he has yet to learn. We are an old and dark race with long and dark memories. We are an Old Testament people. Our souls are close to the land and law cannot exterminate the soul. I have travelled through this emasculated countryside for too many years not to feel its presence. As for that priest, I think a better understanding of the beatitudes might serve his understanding more.'

Correspondence Between Geminiani's Secretary and His Friend in Florence

September 16th, 1717

My Dearest Friend,

I am now convinced that Geminiani has lost his reason. To venture to this unenlightened nation bespeaks a want of sense in the first place, but to pursue his fantasies about Irish harp music to this remote region is an insane indulgence.

Last evening's entertainment, which was specially arranged for Geminiani's benefit, confirms my anxiety about this foolishness of his. Our host, Lord Mayo, had invited one of these renowned harpers, by name Carolan, to the festivities and had assured us that there was no more famous or able exponent of the instrument in the whole of Ireland.

I will not bore you with describing the evening. Imagine a supper with a collection of minor aristocrats and government cronies in some forgotten village in Tuscany. It was provincial and unstimulating, the more so because one did not have the relief of those warm and sensuous

Tuscan hills. My God, the land here is brutal and its unrefinement has effected the manners and the lifestyle of its inhabitants. The 'entertainment' did little to change my views.

I was not sure what to expect, though I expected little enough. The great harper when he presented himself had the face of a bloated monkey and his apparel had all the significance of a second-class merchant. But, to be fair, these people have their own way about them. But I digress. It's the music I want to write of.

The man Carolan played some small pieces for the company he was in. I suspect that's normal in this land. Then there was much fuss when he and Geminiani resolved to play. I could not expect less, of course.

Geminiani played with his usual finesse, but for some reason omitted some bars. I noticed this at once, but given Geminiani's absurd curiosity about the music of this country, I dismissed it.

To my surprise, the harpist engaged him in every point. Indeed he seemed to swallow up Geminiani's omissions and fill them with something of his own creation which was also fully part of Geminiani's orchestration. When he took the lead he played with exceptional capacity, but without much grace, though there was something in it I confess.

The man played out of a savage passion. The brilliance of his performance was in its fearsome movement, and that alone was its accomplishment. But Geminiani will not understand this. He publicly lauded the man and labelled him with the title 'Carolianus', and laid laurels on him as if he had produced some extraordinary work of genius! Perhaps for a moment I was caught up in that enthusiasm. But in an equally short moment I thought that Geminiani was more blind than the pathetic blind man he had played with.

We must rescue our friend from these affectations of his.

Your companion, Claudio.

September 29th, 1717

My dearest friend,

By now you will have received my last letter. I apologise if it was abrupt, but I was anxious to inform you of the 'entertainment' at our host's home. You will recall how Geminiani seemed enthralled with this man Carolan's harp. I put it down to the excitement of the moment, but since then he has become obsessed. He seems incapable of understanding the stylistic incongruity of north and south. The temper of these northern people is fundamentally alien to Italian genius, but Geminiani insists this Irish harpist echoes the old dance songs of the Italian countryside, frottole, villanete, balletto and canzonets. I can see the associations but not the similarity.

The wonderful Italian madrigal is entirely a new music. Having purged itself of the Flemish music, it has replaced balanced harmonic progression with sensuous alterations and harmonic turns. Though I have explained all this to Geminiani, he is deaf to my reasoning. He refuses to accept that this man Carolan's music is of a different temper and quality than our own. His passion is unruly and perverse, even if it has some brilliance in it. The excitement in our music is inspired, it is imbued with the truly spiritual, but Carolan's harp is drunk with its master's arrogance.

Had Carolan any understanding of the writings of other great theorists, one might give more ear to his music, but he has not. He remains an ignorant peasant knocking at the great cathedral door of art.

Geminiani, with his persistent foolishness compares this peasant harpist to Don Carlo Gesualdo. I was exasperated and informed Geminiani that this Irishman had created a style remarkable for its vigour, handling of light and shadow, colouring and emotional depth, but naturalism, the antithesis of art, marred his genius. Gesualdo was also an experimenter, but in his hands the madrigal became a free sequence of impressions, pictures and musical outbursts. The beauty of his harmonics is remarkable and the boldness of his modulations equals and surpasses Marenzio and even Monteverdi.

I hoped that talking about the work of these masters would replace enthusiasm with reason in Geminiani's head. 'Can we really include Carolan among these names?' I asked him, to which he answered, 'But there is something there!'

I was too tired to tell him what I thought. Turmoil and excited emotion are not the same thing!

And as I am too tired to bore you more with this I ask your pardon and indulgence.

Yours, Claudio

Florence, October 14th, 1717

My dear Claudio,

I have read your letters with much delight. Though I cannot understand fully the situation you find yourself in, I can only say I think you are becoming as preoccupied as Geminiani. I would remind you of one small matter.

You should know above all that the 'dramatic' art is not limited to external happenings. There exists another form of the dramatic which we may call internal, a struggle of forces in the individual soul. Poetry can communicate to us the result of these struggles because it must transform everything into intelligible and concrete symbols. Poetry can represent only momentary mental states or a series of them. Music, however, can present these forces in their very struggle, giving us real pain, free of all material, tangible or visible elements. Music is the language of the soul, it is the expression of actions and experience that take place in the secluded depths of the soul.

I understand what you say about tempers being influenced by their geographical location, north or south. But are you sure your southern soul can fathom the dark depths of Carolan's imagination and that your learning has not made you also blind?

With warmest affection, Adriano

October 30th, 1717

Dear friend,

Your letter reached me on the day we were leaving this depressing western seaboard, and only from you would I take such chastisement!

Perhaps your letter was more timely than you know. I had the fortune to be travelling with a priest who had been staying at Lord Mayo's house. This priest was present at our entertainment and I had seen him speak with both Geminiani and the Irish harper. He is Irish himself and has all the manners, grace and refined intellect of a cardinal. I was intrigued by the man's intellect. He asked me much about Geminiani and I was only too happy to answer him. As he seemed knowledgeable in the fine arts, and with your letter in my breast pocket,

I questioned him about music and the Church and what he thought of the entertainments we had both observed during our stay. I did not, of course, go into detail about Geminiani's fascination.

The priest looked me directly in the eye. I felt he was examining my soul while at the same time preparing his answer. Then he began, 'The Church stands at the dawn of a new era. We understand that the fine arts and music have never forsworn their allegiance to the Church. Their creative power and productive capacity make them the midwives of the faith.

'Human life is not determined by pure intelligence, rather life revolves around the emotions. The Church has nurtured this relationship, encouraging and lending a munificent hand to those who would promote the awe and triumph of the faith and gain mastery over the world. We seek an art that is a response to the new spiritual order that awaits us, an art that is aflame and can convey the passionate inevitability of the new order.'

I knew I was listening to the words of a zealot, so asked him what he thought of Carolan. He spoke with obvious conviction but little emotion, and declared that he perceived a strong metaphysical impulse in the harper, yet it was unfocused or misdirected. He affirmed that the musician might be destiny's man if he surrendered himself to the dark metaphysics of his own personality. The priest stopped to consider, and said that Ireland needed a new voice to hail the new age. Carolan could be the man but even though he might have a sense of enchantment and ecstasy, he was not El Greco. Carolan might hold his audience spellbound, but he was fatally flawed!

I must say I was enjoying this priest, for I felt he was agreeing with what I had said to Geminiani and I felt quite smug with your letter in my pocket. I thought for a moment this priest's impressions were burning your own words from off the paper. As I was thinking, he spoke again but with more excitement in his voice.

'The hearts of the Irish are crying out for a fearless voice to lead them, and an art that is unafraid of dark mysterious depths. One who can excite passions and reveal a longing for the infinite.

'Such an artist will be drawn to unrest and tension. In artistic terms, arbitrary disproportion and excessive measure will guide him as he seeks to create an impression and render a mood. He wants to present us with a profound drama, the components of which are immaterial as long as

his dynamic force is overwhelming. Then we break through the dark into space and light and boundlessness!'

I was becoming breathless with the priest's words when he suddenly stopped and emphasised again that Carolan was incapable of creating the artistic revelation that the nation was waiting for.

So I am sending you this priest's words that you may be less inclined to chastise me.

Your companion, Claudio

PS I have just arrived at our rooms in Dublin. I am exhausted from the journey and the impassioned lecture to which my clerical friend subjected me.

I cannot relate it all, for my head is still spinning. But I will recall two names, which I expect you to fully inform yourself about before my return. Consider it a return of your own chastisement!

My travelling companion informed me that what Ireland requires is a musician or poet who had the vision of the Spanish painter Francisco de Zubarian, who, he said, painted a world set apart. A world which one can only look upon with ecstasy!

Having explained to me something of the work of this man, he then began quoting at length from 'An Essay on the Nature and Conduct of Passions and Affections', written by an Irish metaphysician named Francis Hutcheson! Can you imagine, this priest insisted that had Carolan the wit and intelligence to understand this metaphysician and feel with the passion of Zubaran he might achieve the apotheosis and liberation of this nation!

I must finish. I feel as weary as if I had walked across this country.

Ciao!

Thirteen Miserere

By Charles O'Conor, Son of the O'Conor Don

I have only now begun to realise how much I tended not to see the village and the surrounding countryside. I suppose my father was correct and I did truly live too much inside my head. I remember how he used to berate his brother the bishop for encouraging me in this habit. And they are still at it even today; indeed they have a habit of taking these disputes into Turlough himself. His memory seems so sharp and clear and there is an urgency about him when he speaks. We have to work hard to keep up with him. Charles McCabe is here too, as is Father Fintan O'Hanlon, who was secretary to my uncle more than twenty-five years ago. His status in the Church is more elevated these days, but his years in Europe have not dulled his memory. And, of course, Seamus Brennan is here. I believe there was only one other occasion when so many of us were in this house together.

Mrs McDermott-Roe says that Carolan has insisted on seeing each of us, as though we have been instructed to appear before royalty. I think she is a little jealous of the time we spend with him. She is forever asking what we have been talking about and flies into a tirade if she smells alcohol.

It was clever of him to insist on us all being here together. If any of our memories are faulty then we have each other to refer to. His own memory was always prodigious, but the way he elaborated stories made me doubt the veracity of much that he told me. He was an incredible fantasist!

I spent several hours today with the bishop and Father O'Hanlon. We talked of that strange time many years ago when we were all last in this house. When I spoke with Carolan about it he became animated.

When he was alone with me, his questions never stopped. One

evening, after I had been playing and talking about Vivaldi, he said, 'It's the man that intoxicates me. What and how he played I can understand easily enough. But why, Charles? Who was the man and what was he looking for?'

I had had too much of this interrogation over the previous weeks and answered wearily, 'He was a skinny, red-haired priest who loved to drink and who composed for and conducted an exquisite orchestra of young virgins. And, oh yes, as a cantore, he had, of necessity, to be a castrato. I don't know if that's the right description of his condition.'

Carolan's reaction was strange. 'It's a barbaric splendour he was subject to,' he said.

It was such a strange phrase to use. I couldn't fathom it then. But that was always the way with him. He could say things that unnerved you. I didn't know what to say and watched as he sat frozen. The colour drained out from him. After some moments his eyes began to fill with tears. Almost inaudibly he excused himself and left the room. I walked with him and noticed how for the first time in years he needed to feel out the walls in his room.

After that he spent many nights alone, refusing our offers of company. He later explained he was trying to imagine the man Vivaldi and his female orchestra; he imagined himself there amongst a throng of slight young nuns, convulsed with a need that only music could transform. If quietness had previously been his favourite companion now there was only room for Vivaldi and his virgin orchestra. One evening he even confessed to me how he began to feel the unquenchable thirst behind the music this sad priest had created. Sometimes his enthusiasm made him unintelligible, and on many occasions I put this down to overindulgence in the bottle as much as to Vivaldi.

Occasionally, when he felt he had been spending too much time alone, he would search me out and ask me to read the psalms. He felt that the Italian's music made their despair no less poignant, but somehow less desperate. I enjoyed these evenings, the poet in me was encouraged by Carolan's musing on the psalms.

Poetry and music were the dominant themes of our discussions. I was intrigued by the ideas of a new music and new poetry which were historical and narrative. Carolan questioned me as to whether such a music and poetry could embody the elements of the bishop's lecture to us, which he repeated, 'Art is an ever active progression, your uncle informed us. Do you remember him saying something about how, from the intercourse of all the notes, something new and wholly unexpected, emerges? If art has its own hidden and recreated life, then how can we direct it?'

Before I could answer, he continued, 'Anyway, art is not an intellectual construction.' Suddenly he laughed, 'You know, Charles, for the past few weeks, especially when I am alone, I seem to have Virgil whispering in one ear and Vivaldi in the other.'

'A queer pair!' I exclaimed.

That was the way with Carolan. He was never keen to evolve long intellectual arguments, but there was something he wanted to say and he was, as yet, unsure how to put it. Years ago I had learned not to put words or ideas in his mouth, for he had a habit of throwing my assistance back in my face, with a withering remark if it suited him, or else losing me totally in his ramblings.

'You remember the bishop saying something about art making what is seen reveal the unseen?' he said finally. 'Well, I understand it, the reality of the unseen world, I mean, but it wasn't until I submerged myself in Vivaldi's music that I felt its reality. It was as if he was confirming to me what I already knew, but was unsure how to express it.'

I was even more intrigued, but I still hesitated. I was unsure what would follow or whether I was about to be subjected to the arrogant bravado which he sometimes loved to indulge in; but his confidence seemed drained as he continued.

'I have composed more pieces of music for people than I care to remember. It's my duty as it is my profession. I merely do as I am asked. But there is another side to composition. Sometimes when I am with someone I sense the melody that seems to emanate from them. Everyone has their own inner melody, and only when I play informed by it and in response to it do I truly feel that sense of instinctual creativity your uncle spoke of. I have been pursuing it for years, half afraid of it and half burdened by the constraints of the music that has been handed down to me. Sometimes I can play someone else's inner melody, but I was always afraid to hear my own – until Vivaldi played it for me!'

He paused, waiting for his words to sink in. He was sure I would answer, but I remained silent. I was afraid to speak, as I remember. But Carolan wasn't interested in what I was thinking. 'This new artistic soul your uncle speaks about, well, I think I have found it. Vivaldi has uncovered it, while I have been traipsing the back roads of Connaught too blind to see, but always, somehow, hearing. Now if we can find how our own inner melodies harmonise with others then we will have a new national art,' he concluded in a low voice as if he wasn't sure he wanted anyone to hear.

I answered light-heartedly, 'You're beginning to sound like the bishop yourself.'

A smile spread across his face. 'I could never scale the intellectual heights the bishop has climbed. I am a simple cantore who loves his drink and friends too much to want to be their confessor or their judge!'

'I hope you will tell him that, for the man's as human as the rest of us and he'll be joining us tomorrow.'

As though it was a casual afterthought, I told Carolan the story that the bishop had related to my father. Carolan never moved as I described my uncle's strange and cruel experience on the road, with its terrible refrain, 'Happy now, happy now.'

The following night the four of us sat down together after supper. We had drunk a surfeit of wine and were all in a good humour. The O'Conor Don was complaining to his brother-in-law that since his last visit Carolan had made a recluse of himself and when he wasn't in his 'pantry' or wandering the grounds alone he was locked up with me in the music room for hours on end.

The bishop was generous, 'Just because the man's an entertainer by profession does not mean he has to be constantly at your beck and call.'

My father replied that he always left Carolan and his muses to their own devices, but hoped that whatever they had been passing on to him, he would share with us.

Carolan answered lazily, 'It was mostly poetry we spoke of, as young Charles there is mad keen to make a poet of himself.'

'And he's been having me go over the psalms till I practically know every one of them by heart,' I was quick to point out.

'What attracts you to them, Carolan?' the bishop enquired.

Carolan filled his glass and sampled the wine. There was a slight mocking tone in his voice as he answered. 'Well, the psalmist or whoever he was must have been a terrible old groaner – and a cheat as well.'

Carolan waited for a response, but none came beyond an insistence that he go on from the O'Conor Don. 'Well, the psalms always make an appeal to joy. Joy is their final affirmation, but do they ever expose the fullness or the quality of this joy?'

He was about to say more when I butted in, anxious about his intentions. 'And Carolan now believes that that's the very problem with our music.'

'There may be some truth in that!' the bishop said. 'For I am sure our ancient music has its roots deep in the harp of David. But as for the psalms, when hunger, pain, despair and death await you at every moment, how else should a man appeal to God?'

I could see Carolan was listening intently for any sign of emotion in the man's voice, but the bishop's next remark said more than any quiver in his voice could. 'Whatever the tribulations of the psalmist, guilt and guilt above all was what seemed to wring out his very soul. A man can overcome many things, but when guilt enfolds him in its ghastly shroud, hope and joy desert him completely. . . .'

My uncle was about to continue, but something stopped him. Instead he said, 'Come on, Charles, recite the "Miserere" for us and if Carolan's instruction has been as good as it should be you might accompany yourself. Or perhaps Carolan will?'

'Pour me another drink and let me finish it first,' Carolan answered. 'Guilt, as you say, Bishop, is more deadly than any plague or pain I know and only those who have felt its fingers around their heart can know its fearfulness. We need a heady dose of inspiration to deal with such a monster. Don't you agree, Bishop?'

'Do you mean prayer or port, Carolan? If the latter, I suggest you remember what I said to you of Virgil and Aeneas, "Avoid excess." '

'And you too, Bishop.'

My father understood Carolan's rejoinder as a good-natured rebuke, but I sensed that for Carolan it was very different. He had been deeply moved by my story of the bishop blessing the dead. He wanted to embrace the man and ease the pain out of him. Instead he lifted the harp and plucked out a few notes. 'Slowly now, Charles,' he commanded as he began to find a melody. 'Let me find my feet first!' But it didn't really matter how I proceeded. Carolan had already sensed the melody in the bishop and in himself.

I remember now that at first my voice was low and uncertain, but proclaiming the first verses of the psalm steadied me and allowed me to enter into the great plea at the heart of the 'Miserere'. Carolan's harp accompanied the words like a warm coat being folded around a shivering body:

> Yet since you love sincerity of heart
> Teach me the secrets of wisdom.
> Purify me with hyssop until I am clear,
> Wash me until I am whiter than snow.
>
> Instil some joy and gladness in me,
> Let the bones you have crushed rejoice again.
> Hide your face from my sins,
> Wipe out all my guilt.
>
> God, create a new heart in me,
> Put into me a new and constant spirit.
> Do not banish me from your presence
> Do not deprive me of your Holy Spirit.

Carolan's melody swirled upwards with this plea, demanding rather than requesting and erasing the desperation in the words. I withheld my recitation for a moment, then felt the pull of the harp call me into the poem once more.

> Save me from death, God my saviour,
> And my tongue will acclaim your righteousness
> Lord, open my lips,
> And my mouth will speak your praise.

With an unearthly rhythm Carolan's harp gathered up the

powerful emotions. I seemed to lose all sense of myself and almost fell into the next lines,

> Sacrifice gives you no pleasure.
> Were I to offer you holocaust,
> You would not have it.

The mounting power of Carolan's harp lifted itself in blazing harmony beyond the words. I remember turning to look at my father and the bishop. The O'Conor Don's eyes were fixed, the bishop sat unmoved, as if he had been suddenly frozen, but his eyes were glazed by the fire of Carolan's melody. It was pointless for me to continue. Words were inadequate to the haunting accompaniment Carolan provided. It resonated and pulsed as if everything was drawn into the whirlpool of sound and was then flung from it. It boomed around the room.

I remember turning towards him, paralysed and puzzled by his playing. It was as if he had become part of his harp. Every feature of his face was caught up in the emotion. His eyes spun in the fat globe of his face; their fierce, comic, ugly half-symmetry now disappeared. His mouth moved and his face became a gargoyle mask, grinning, snarling, then his lips would purse for a kiss. The jerky animation of his face was impaled on his eyes. At their inner core the pupils throbbed and swelled. There was a tempo in them that seemed to be something other than the music. It held us transfixed and tense.

But the tension could not hold. Almost imperceptibly, the fire that Carolan had conjured up diminished. Its power evaporated and the music resolved into what seemed like a splendid echo, returning and softening and returning again. Beneath it Carolan spoke the closing words of the 'Miserere'.

> My sacrifice is this troubled heart,
> You will not scorn this crushed and broken heart.
>
> Show your favour graciously,
> Rebuild the wall of Jerusalem.
> Then there will be proper sacrifice to please you,
> Holocaust and whole oblation,
> And young bulls offered up on your altar.

The evocation and celebration that sounded from Carolan's strings precisely echoed what each of us at that moment was feeling. We were all moved in our own way and none of us wanted to be the first to speak. Carolan sat in the silence, nursing the harp as if he, too, was afraid to speak. I could hardly retain the nervous excitement that was welling up inside me. 'There's not much Vivaldi in that composition,' I said, and remember feeling immediately foolish for my words.

'Not yet perhaps, but I wasn't playing it for your Italian friend.' Then, changing his tone, he continued, 'Anyway, I always feel the old music near me when I am in this house.'

The bishop stood up and moved amongst us replenishing our glasses. 'Perhaps you'll play some more?' he asked. But my father was quick to pull him up, 'For God's sake, Thaddeus. Do we have to turn this house into a monastery or something, every time you pay us a visit?'

This was a different Carolan from the one we all knew and loved. He was quite frightening that night. But that was always the way with him. He could soak things up and hide them in some part of himself, only to throw them back at you, sometimes years later. He was an improbable alchemist. His power had to do with cunning and the fact that he kept so much of himself to himself. He loved to play games with people and I wonder if, in that room where he lies dying, he is not still playing games with us all.

Only this afternoon, as I walked about the village, I had sensed the fascination of the man. This countryside has never seen so many people in all its history. And Carolan is the subject of their pilgrimage!

As I passed a handful of strangers drinking by the bridge, one of them declared to his friends that he thought Carolan should be anointed! I laughed at the notion and wondered what the man meant. One of his companions started back at him, 'Anointed! Carolan's been anointing himself for years. The back of his throat must be the holiest place in the whole of Ireland. And it's not holy water, I'm talking about! But there's too many lies and stories that have come out of the back of his throat to allow any amount of holy water to pass down it!'

I have known Turlough for too many years to comprehend this mass of people. In a way I sometimes feel I might be as blissfully ignorant as these strangers, who praise and abuse him in the same breath. To them he is only an image, a story in the flesh. Yet I have known him intimately for more years than I can remember, but now he is dying I doubt what I think I know.

According to my aunt, he has been asking to see me alone. She informs me there is something he wants to tell me and in the same breath warns me that I should not pay much heed to what he says. With comments like that, my poor old aunt could be out there with these revellers, cursing and praising him.

When I told her I had brought Nuala with me, she fixed me with a stare that could have withered me, then declared that there would be no other women than herself and Martha allowed in the room. 'It's no place for a young woman. In any case Nuala has the looks of another young woman about her and he doesn't need any more of those memories right now.'

Her words had as much of apology about them as they had of explanation. In a way I was glad of it, for I had my own reservation about bringing Nuala to see Turlough. Without thinking, I spoke my mind to Mrs McDermott-Roe. 'All those years ago, when he was instructing me in composition, if I mentioned a girl's name he would fly off in a tantrum. "You can't find love in the eyes of a woman," he would declare and if he found me in a young woman's company, he would avoid me and not speak to me for days!"

Mrs McDermott-Roe's answer was easily given, but stunned me. She hinted that some parts of Turlough had never grown up and she warned me that he may have the temperament of a woman. The expression on my face must have told her of my confusion. She stroked my cheek and said that perhaps there were times when I reminded Carolan of his own young life and that maybe I had everything Carolan had wished for himself. I was still perplexed and said so, at which she sighed and said, 'Perhaps you need a woman's temper. You are a better poet than Carolan. You have learning and a sense of your own history and destiny. You have the ability to reclaim your heritage. And you have Nuala! A young woman who loves you more than you deserve! Now apply your man's logic to my words and bother me no more. For as you have Nuala and your whole life before you, Turlough has only me!'

Fourteen Heron's Return

Seamus Brennan Remembers

The whole world has arrived to pitch camp around Keadue and Ballyfarnon. The countryside looks like a battlefield and the village itself has become a rats' nest. Every hustler, half-wit and whore's excuse has brought themselves here and every one of them is pontificating on their good friend Turlough Carolan.

I live here and have known Turlo better than any man for more than fifty years, and I feel a stranger. There are many faces I do know and all of them claim to be real friends to my dying friend, but there is one person who has not shown her face yet. If there is any christian charity in her heart she should be here.

All the rant I hear from the rabble is about what a great carouser and womaniser Carolan was. Sure, the man knew many women, but he loved only one and I'm the only man alive who witnessed the truth of that long love. It wasn't that long ago either, more than a year but no more than three. He was an ill man even then, too sick to be on the road and much too sick to be returning to Lough Derg and the pilgrims' island. It must have been forty years or more since I last remember him going off to 'purgatory'. It's a fitting title for such a place, for it left a scar on my Turlo.

I was worried. For a few weeks he had had a persistent cough. He was also complaining a lot about the cold and seemed to weary quickly. He had taken to drinking his whiskey mixed into a hot punch. At first I thought it was an excuse to indulge himself, but I realised that was not the case when I found him on several mornings, bent double with a lengthy coughing fit. Breathlessly he would ask me to prepare him a hot one to 'flush out his affliction'. But the alcohol held the thing at bay for increasingly short periods. On several occasions he had had to excuse himself from a recital he was giving while I led him back to his room, or into a garden, where he would have prolonged spasms of coughing that left him sweating and exhausted. I had joked about him finding a cure on his pilgrim island when we first set off for Lough Derg. He only said there was no cure for old age.

We had to make several unplanned overnight stops on the route, he was too weary and too ill to remain in the saddle. On two nights I had to be brought to his bedside and spent several hours bathing the sweat from him. I had to strip the clothes from him and bathe his naked body in a cooling potion of herbs. The coughing fits seemed to rack his whole body, leaving him panting like a woman in labour.

He teased me about how I had become his nurse. 'Isn't healing more satisfying than killing?' he would jest, to which I replied dismissively, 'It's only more work!' Carolan laughed through his cough and ordered more drink. I remonstrated and told him his night sweats had little to do with his illness and that if he were truly ill he might do better to rub the alcohol into his body than pour it down his throat, to which he answered that he must nurture the inner man, but I noticed that the laughter which accompanied this rebuke was ill-hearted. I also noticed how the flesh seemed to be hanging off his frame. And that was when I discovered a small leather pouch which he kept tied around his neck. 'What's this, a talisman?' I asked. Carolan's answer increased my curiosity, without satisfying it. He had explained that it was the tooth of an old friend of his, and said no more. For the next few days I tried to persuade him to forgo his visit to the island, but he was insistent, and after a few days seeemed fit enough to travel.

As we stood waiting on the ferryman to collect Carolan, he said, 'Come or stay as you please. But if you come, remember each of us makes this journey on his own!'

I had no intention of going and something told me he didn't really want me with him anyway. I said, 'I'll travel with you but I'll not stay on the island, life's penance enough without adding to it. I will collect you in a day or so, but I'll come here each day in case you return early.'

As the small boat moved out into the lake I felt lonely and anxious, like a mother watching her child go off. I suppose I was embarrassed at the thought, so I called out to him, 'Three days without alcohol, Turlo. It'll kill you or cure you.'

When I think back on it, it was probably the loneliest and most miserable three days I have ever spent. There's not much in that part of the world to keep a man there, but I had to wait on Turlo for three God-forsaken days. I suppose God was punishing me for not accompanying him.

I waited on the landing stage with four others watching the ferryboat arrive. It was a miserable journey over to the island and I was cursing myself for having made it, but I had had enough of my own company and had decided to come over and accompany Carolan back.

Pilgrims were beginning to collect at the landing point, but I couldn't find Carolan among them. Then I heard him call out to me. His voice was broken and hoarse and sounded very old. He called out again and I remember thinking that he seemed lost. I tried to humour him, 'Aye I'm here as I'm bid, but I'll tell you, old man, if you've any notion of dragging me back here again then think on it long and hard, and while you're thinking I'll be gone.'

The boatman and I helped him on board and others helped him to the stern. I was anxious and tried to coax some conversation from him, but he seemed remote. For most of the journey he remained silent, only once declaring that he was tired, cold and hungry. I reminded him that he was alive, for I could see that the world, the flesh and the Devil were back again. I can still remember his reaction. He roared with laughter and the noise boomed out across the lake waters. I thought he had lost his senses and when I asked him what was so funny he answered me, that as I had been his closest friend for all these years it was only right I should be his echo. It made no sense to me, but I chose not to pursue it.

After some minutes I looked at the faces of the other people crushed into the boat. There was something about them I could not quite fathom. They were either silent or spoke in whispers and I had the impression that words were an inconvenience to them. I felt oddly unsure of myself in their company. Then my attention was caught by the sound of voices and I looked behind me. Several other boats were moving slowly through the placid waters and their passengers were singing a hymn.

I marvelled at the harmony they created and mentioned it to Carolan. After a brief silence he answered, 'It's the water, the lake creates a great sound box that levels out and harmonises the voices. If God is our conductor, he is in the depths not in the heavens.'

He was about to continue when a cough rasped out of him. For some minutes it seemed to choke him, then he fell silent again. The lazy splash of oar and the low harmony of the singing voices were everywhere around us. I looked at Carolan. His expression was enigmatic and empty.

I did not know where his thoughts where, but they were not in this boat. He leaned over and in a conspiratorial whisper told me to listen. Then he told me that it was the chorus of virgins of the Ospedale della Pieta being rowed back through the morning mist to their lakeside convent. Their song was full of grace and praise, but their voices were rich and heady with the passion of lovemaking. I thought he had lost his mind completely, but then convinced myself it was only the rambling of a sick old man, hungry, cold and tired from three sleepless nights.

Once more he was seized by a bout of coughing. It was deep and raw and I felt the pain of it. Some of the pilgrims whispered words of blessing and consolation and one wrapped a blanket about his shuddering shoulders. Whatever this island had done, it had not cured Carolan's illness.

The boat bumped as it ground into the rocky foreshore. I was determined to find out just how ill he was. The two passengers in the bow of the boat handed the passengers' belongings on to the beach and then helped them ashore. As the boat shed its load, leaving only Carolan and a woman on board, two sturdy youths heaved it further up the foreshore. The scrunch of the boat on the gravel had the same harshness as Carolan's cough, and I thought that perhaps Carolan had brought more of the island back with him than he knew. I remember looking back at the island floating in the mist. I saw it as dark and dangerous and unwanted. I don't know why, but I knew then that no matter how black and damned my soul might be I would never set foot on it.

Already more pilgrims were gathering to meet friends and family. As I helped with the baggage, I noticed a woman whose gaze seemed fixed on Carolan. It was hard to make out her features. She was wrapped from her shoulders to her feet in a heavy but well-made cloak. Its great black hood shrouded her face completely.

The cloaked figure moved forward as I went to assist my friend, but she reached Carolan before me. She took his hand in one of her own, while her other arm encircled his back. For a moment it seemed as if Carolan was resisting her. His head sprang up on his shoulders as if someone had just thrown cold water in his face. As I walked up to the pair, I heard Carolan speak in a slow, almost timid voice. 'Is this the hand of Bridgit Cruise?'

His words had me confused. I wondered if the island had destroyed his mind for a second time. I was about to go up and lead him away, all the time worrying that if he thought this stranger was Bridgit Cruise then he might not know me. I stopped in my tracks when I heard the woman answer, 'And has Turlough Carolan forsaken his ancient rath for this holy island?'

I was dumbstruck. Though I couldn't see the woman's face, I knew that voice. Age had not changed it. And here she was again, teasing him with that mellow voice of hers. But how had he known after all these years? She had not spoken a word, yet he knew her the moment she placed her hand in his.

I knew my presence would be unwelcome, but I had not seen Carolan for several days and was anxious about him. I called out that I would fetch the horses and our things if he stayed by the boat. Carolan waved his hand in compliance. As I walked off, I heard him say to her, 'It's memory that ages us, not time.'

I took my time gathering up our belongings and pushing through the crowd to where I had left the horses. I never let my eyes stray from them for more than a few moments. All the time I was asking myself, 'Why is she here? Is she real?' The place was said to be haunted by demons and the ghosts of departed souls, and such thinking increased my anxiety. I watched the two of them perch themselves on the boat. Her hand never left his. Then she lifted the cloak to drape it around his shoulders. I still could not make out her face. The gesture seemed somehow evil and I wanted to run down and tear them apart. I was sure that the moment I laid hands on her she would disappear like the apparition I was convinced she was. One part of me was afraid to go back to them and another believed that, ghost or no, Bridgit

Cruise had no claim on my Turlo. I had reserved a room in a hostel a few miles away, but knew the innkeeper would not hold it for long as plenty of pilgrims would be looking for a night's accommodation before setting off homeward. It was a good enough excuse and after some fifteen minutes I decided to return to where I had left them. I quickly fetched our horses and arranged our bags, but when I turned towards them again she was gone. My heart almost burst out of my chest with fear. As I ran to him, I kept saying, 'No, she's real, she would not harm him.'

I found him sitting alone on the side of the boat. The foreshore was empty. I spoke cautiously as I approached, trying to disguise my thoughts, 'Well, here you are, just back in the land of the living and already you have women on your mind. Where did she go?' His answer was neither a rebuke nor did it ease my discomfort.

'That one's been on my mind a long time, Seamus, but she has gone and left me like she did before and I'm too old to be much moved by things of the flesh. Now, if you could get your mind out of that carnal backwater it seems to be wallowing in, perhaps we could get going. Did you find us a room nearby? I have three days' sleep to catch up on and a lot of unexpected thinking to do. And when I have done, I might tell you what passed between us.'

He began coughing again and leaned back on the boat, his hand pressed tight into his chest. I could hear the gurgling in his lungs. He asked if we were far from the water, then spat into the bleached stones at his feet. I looked down and then back to him. He cleared his throat and spat again. My eyes were fixed on the tiny clots of blood floating in the phlegm. I stared for longer than I knew I should, then took his arm. There was nothing to say. The beads of cold perspiration on his face silenced me. The thought came to me that perhaps my premonitions were right. Bridgit Cruise was a demon and I knew then that I would never hear what had passed between them.

When we had been travelling for a while, he suddenly asked me if I had ever really been in love. 'Many times,' I answered, but he pursued it, 'How do you know when it's real love?'

'Perhaps you can tell me, for I seem to remember this conversation from before.'

He was silent for a moment. Then his words came hesitantly. 'I suppose it's as if you have been suddenly carried off by some bird of prey. You feel frightened in case the bird should drop you. But real love doesn't let you fall, nor does it make you fearful. It just makes you content. Now that I think of it, it's like being a bird. You can see the whole world and have any part of it. Yet you choose the high air, happy in the knowledge that the earth is always there waiting to receive you anywhere you choose.'

I thought of the bloody spittle on the beach and tried to lighten the conversation.

'That's too deep for me. Are you sure they didn't have a secret cache of drink on that island?'

'God, I'm dying for a drink and a good sleep. I don't think I'll be much company for you tonight. I'm done to death.'

When we arrived at the inn, Carolan was as good as his word. After only a few warming punches laced with whiskey and a light supper, he retired for the night. His coughing continued as I left him, but an eeriness had taken away its harshness. 'Did you see her face?' he asked me. I hadn't, but said I did. 'Was she still pretty?' I lied again, 'Yes, Turlo, as pretty as ever.'

It was late the next morning when I went to his room. I had supposed he would sleep long after his stay on the island, but I was surprised. Even before I got near his room I could hear the bard's harp pluck out a low melody. I thought he was entertaining himself while he waited for me, but these were verses I had not heard before.

If to Lough Derg you ever go,
Look for the girl with the pearl smooth eyes
For they are an amulet against fear.

Her shape is fairer than a swan,
Her throat and neck are as soft as
A snowdrift in sunlight.
Both the lily and the rose together
Cannot match her grace . . .
It is destroyed I am and poor,
Lying in lack of health.
Relieve me, God, or I will not be long here.

It is discomfited and poor I am,
Lying in lack of health,
And my cure is not to be found with any leech alive.
O secret of my heart who art friendly;
O love of everyone who has seen thee,
Unless thou cross the sea with me I shall not be long alive.

There was something in the bard's verse which made me anxious and angry, yet there was also a premonition that made me uneasy. I would not be content until we were back at Alderford House.

And here we are, many years later, in that very place and all I can think of are his words, 'I'm done to death.' Maybe he was truly dead then or maybe he was dead from the minute he met her and she just came to claim him. No, Bridgit Cruise has no place here. And I alone should be the one to wash him down and lay him out.

Part Three

GOLTRA
The Music of Death and Sorrow

For the dead are not altogether powerless. Dead did I say? There is no death, only a change of worlds.

Chief Seattle of the Duwanish tribe on Puget Sound,
Washington Territory

Fifteen Purgatory II

Journal of Mrs McDermott-Roe

Easter 1738

Easter is full of contradictions, dark days filled with wind and rain are followed by high bright skies and all the promise of spring. But the hopes we had for Turlough have not borne fruit. His health has begun to decline. Breathing is a great effort and he cannot leave the room now. The smell of death is there and I am afraid of it. Blessed Lord, forgive me at this holy time. How can I be moved by Christ's suffering and think to turn my face from poor Turlough? Forgive me, Lord. I am an old woman and death awaits me too. But I have not the strength for it.

1st Day of Easter Week, 1738

I have never known such weariness. The whole house spins around me if I am on my feet too long. My shoulders weigh me down and a searing pain fills my head.

How did our Lord bear his Easter burden and how can I bear to watch Turlough's passing? Sometimes when I am with him my senses become confused. I feel like a young girl, confused and fearful with her first pain of womanhood, then I feel the pain of childbirth and the anguish of widowhood. It is as if I do not want him to leave this world, but he must and the hurt is too great.

I am wrung out of all my emotions, like an old rag, useless either to him or myself.

2nd Day of Easter Week, 1738

Carolan was very subdued today. The bishop visited him with me and he insisted that the bishop read him the passion of Christ. I found it unnerving that he himself, so near to death, should want to think on Christ's own closeness to it. I could not understand it, and prayed quietly as he read.

Yet when the bishop had finished, Carolan spoke to us with such clarity and ease. He told us how he too loved gardens and the peace and inspiration he drew from them, but now in the evening of his life he falls into loneliness and silence, where memory assails him and his only future is an empty space in the earth!

'Christ's pain was that he knew no sense of real belonging,' he declared, then continued to address us in a manner that sounded like one of the bishop's sermons. At Gethsemane his past came to catch up with him full of questions, doubts and anguish. God's face is turned from him.' Then he turned to us both. I swear I have never seen his eyes so bright and his voice so perfectly composed. But when he spoke to the bishop I knew that his composure was only an outward show. I have carved his words on my heart. 'If my heart is a chalice and my altar is my experience, have I performed the Mass of my life? What if God should refuse to drink of my chalice and receive me into himself?'

God forgive my weakness, for I could bear his words no longer and fled from the room. The bishop remained and when he came out I could see that he was deeply moved. I did not need to speak, for the bishop's need to talk was greater than mine.

He confided in me that Carolan had been silent for a long period while he sat with him and prayed. Then Carolan laid his hands on the Bishop's sleeve and told him that each of us should mark the places of pain in our own lives, to see them for what they are, ugly and malformed, creating only loneliness.

He was silent again, then continued. He said that perhaps we each have to pass through that garden and as he spoke he tapped the bishop's hand lightly, almost as if he was conferring a blessing on him. Finally he said in a voice less composed that sometimes he felt as if he had not immersed himself fully in the pain. He had shunned it, refusing to acknowledge how it had marked the world.

The bishop knew he must respond, and said, 'The wine of our life is made up with tears of disappointment, the gems of achievement and power of desire. It is not given to us to renounce life so completely and surrender ourselves so completely. If we have not known joy and not pursued it, then we cannot share it!'

They were the only words he could find in himself and Turlough seemed to find some peace in them. So he left Carolan, for as he explained, it had been an exhausting moment for poet and priest. He whispered to me that he felt he had given Turlough his last confession and had not known that he was doing it. Then he paused and said, as if he had just discovered the fact, 'Or perhaps it is Turlough there who has received my confession.'

I do not think that there is life enough in me to bear this night, yet I feel strangely warm even as I write. I wonder what he is feeling now in his loneliness and his silence.

Feeling the bishop's wet fingers inscribe the sign of the cross on his face and eyes, Turlough remembered back to the three renunciations made long ago. Standing by the water's edge, arms outstretched in the ancient attitude of prayer and frozen by incapacity and defiance, he had mouthed his terrifying apostasy. The world, the flesh and the Devil had been wells of delight in him and any notions of heaven and hell and their dread consequences had long since fallen away. He was drifting again.

About him, he could hear the pilgrims moving like earthbound dreamers, unwilling to break out of the gagging circle of prayer. It had been thirty or more years since he last stood here and mouthed his apostasy. He felt it as if it was yesterday. Its timelessness was suffocating. The bishop's prayers faded. His memories called him back to the island.

About him, the low musical murmurings of innumerable prayers intoned in the flat northern accent was a soporific that lulled emotion. The bead beat and slap of feet on cold stone created an equality and fellowship that conversation could not. The island drew everything into itself, filtered through a sieve of 'Hail Maries' and 'Our Fathers'. He struggled on, remembering the lines of low stone walls on the slope leading to the beds of the saints, Bridgit and Catherine, and beyond them to the schist jutting through the sparse undergrowth. He felt the whole of his history was held here and that this place was the centre out from which his existence had radiated and flowed.

He felt the need to be solitary being slowly drawn out of him, as the warmth of other people pressed about him. Arms stretched out as he stumbled on the loose stones. Each man was his brother's keeper and this physical intimacy confirmed it. He thought that maybe more was bared here than pilgrim feet. Maybe the trappings of the world and flesh were being stripped away and pure soul looked on pure soul.

The church was full. Even in the press of people the place seemed airy, like a vast aquarium of air. Carolan immersed himself in the atmosphere of fellowship as the words of the liturgy called out to him: 'I will go to the altar of God,' with its response 'To God, who has gladdened my youth.' One question preoccupied him: had everything in his life compelled him to return again to this purgatory?

For a moment he thought of the apostles gathered by the waters of Galilee. He too was here in answer to a summons and his thoughts drifted to the words of the sermon on the mount. With its insistence on happiness this was the only Gospel. He found himself mouthing the opening phrases.

'Blessed are the poor in spirit,
Blessed are the gentle,
Blessed are those who mourn,
Blessed are those who hunger and thirst for justice,
Blessed are the merciful,
Blessed are the pure in heart,
Blessed are the peacemakers
Blessed are those who are persecuted.'

His head was suddenly filled with questions. Was there anyone who would recognise and share his feelings? Could he truly count himself among the Blessed? Could anyone be so blessed who was so demeaned? But there was no answer, each pilgrim kept their own council as they received the final blessing, 'Go, the Mass is ended.'

Turlough felt diminished by this command. He streamed out with the other pilgrims, but was sure his thoughts were not in harmony with theirs. Something of the honour of being human had not been elevated with the host. Men were men before they were angels, he thought. As he walked away from the church and the other worshippers, he was convinced that the ghost of his father was with him, he could feel the clutch of his powerful hand warming his own.

He sat on a low wall and breathed in the windborne fragrance of the island's late growth. His thoughts went back again through his life history, and he clung for a moment to the women who had, without him knowing, shaped and formed the man he was. He felt again the close presence of his mother. Her stony face and urgent eyes. She was the all-knowing point of balance in his childhood years, the source of all things before he had any knowledge of the world. Then Bridgit, the lovely smell of her wet hair intoxicating him. She was like the high note which lifted the chorus and around which the harmony constantly revolved. The old bird woman, who beat and abused him, who ground him down, but she had given him the sense to see without his eyes.

Three fine graces who sat in uneasy opposition to the pure, undefiled mother of the Church. He could only return love to love that was given. The body's sensuality was a real delight and the cold pallor of the virgin could not excite him. He wanted his Mary unveiled. He wanted to feel and smell the flesh of her stirring his emotions and making his body sing.

Like his thoughts, the last of the light was leaching out across the lake and the few remaining pilgrims were being herded towards the church. Slowly he rose to join them as a single bell called them to night prayer. He heard its softly booming echo returned to him as if from the lake's bottom, and with it he felt himself being drawn deeper and deeper into the movement of the pilgrimage, but further and further removed from its words.

Re-entering the church, he became alert to the mass of people about him. The sensuous hum of women's voices wrapped around him, and for a moment he felt himself to be in a spiritual harem. It came to him now that all his music, the poems, the harp in his hands, were a way of embracing and exploring the deepest part of himself. His art was always an attempt to speak to people and find communion with them. Yet he felt this same art had cut him off from them.

In these women's passivity and the atmosphere of surrender that was everywhere about him he acknowledged a needful part of himself. He needed to enter into the dark, innermost parts of himself. The whispering voices of the women were tantalising. They were calling to him to join them.

He submitted to the demands of his senses. Attuned to the ritual of the pilgrimage, he lifted his head in weary acceptance as the priest lit the great candle of vigil. He knew the sudden silence about him signified this and unquestioningly he prepared to begin the stations of the mind.

Night had come, bitter and cold, but the pilgrims' obligations must continue. If they could not follow the pilgrim path physically, then they must live its every moment in their imagination. This was no escape from its physical rigours, but a mind-bending journey into the deepest recesses of being. Carolan was pulled into the chanting, circling body as it moved around the walls of the church. Everywhere about him he could hear the constant clicking rosaries, the ancient counting stones of prayer. He felt himself one more rhythmic pulse in this great fleshly wheel of prayer, repeating the 'Hail Mary' over and over. Like a piece of dream music, or an ancient lullaby, he was lost in it.

Within an hour the station had been completed. The circle peeled apart effortlessly and he felt the first numbness of the stone floor on his feet and knees. His old bones dreaded the three remaining stations to come.

He walked outside and sat contemplatively, awaiting the bell to call him back. In the darkness he smelled tobacco smoke and heard young voices laughing. He hoped they were lovers.

As the night progressed, enthusiasm was overcome by effort. The trial of the flesh had begun in earnest. The harmony of the repetitions was now discordant. So many 'Hail Maries' and 'Our Fathers' had been offered up that they seemed to form a great skin against the roof beams, the sheer weight of them pressing down on the pilgrims. The slur of words and forgotten responses, ill-tempered reactions and the growing desire to be finished, measured its weight. And as the pain increased, so did the isolation. Each pilgrim was trapped in his own private purgatory, where the constant ache of sleep and hunger gnawed relentlessly.

His mind was fogged. He felt he was walking in a darkness he had not known before towards some strange destination. Self-accusing and lambasted by memory's constant onslaught, he could find no hiding place in the prayers. His senses swooned as a great black mass of emptiness opened and dropped on him. For some moments he felt nothing and the nothingness was absolute. Then without warning an unearthly pressure seized him as if he was being wrenched from the womb, bloodied with rot and self-disgust. He felt suddenly defensive and then contemptuous. Emotional balance deserted him, as if someone had slashed his harp strings in mid-elegy. He sat, his blind fingers plucking air.

His head was a hive, swarming with loud noise that the vigorous sound of prayer could not penetrate. The single object of veneration was dead. The queen was dead. His mouth was filled with gall and salt traces stung his lips. He gagged. Even the air was bile. Was there no way out? Was there no guide to redirect him?

Awash with sweat and pain, he stumbled through the pattern of his final station. Everything in him screamed to complete it. It was his only way back. Delirious, he uttered his final amen and reeled to the door. Behind him the great vigil candle guttered down into a greasy, congealed lump.

Outside the cold air of pre-dawn penetrated him like the nails he had watched his father shape from his flaming furnace. Maddened by the emotional cauldron his senses had become, he fled to the water's edge. He cupped some in his hands and sank his face into its iciness. He felt the coolness of the flat wet stones on his feet. How many decades of broken feet had worn smooth these stones? He imagined his reflection in the dark waters and his bone-white face looking back. In the vast moving blackness he knew his face alone animated the waters. In this ancient place encircled by water a harmony and resolution awaited, and he gave himself over to it.

The sounds of morning slowly filtered into his shattered consciousness. The dross of the night was lifting. It was as if his self was being returned to him. He noticed his skin becoming itchy and felt the pin pricks of midge bites. Behind him he heard people talking, there was weariness and relief in their voices. He did not know how long he had been sitting, waiting; he only knew he wanted to join them. He raised himself and started towards the church, the pain and numbness of the night was gone. He felt light as he moved across the stone shards, indifferent to their bite on his feet.

The voices that met him on the way offered blessings. There

was a loving harmony in their speech unlike the monotony of the night's whispered repetitions.

His solitary vigil was over but not yet resolved. He knew only that he would not find resolution in questions, but must wait for it to come in search of him. Sleep pressed heavily on him. The ache in his calves and thighs began to ease. He entered the church and found himself a seat. He laid his head back and let sleep take him.

As he sat in semi-conscious oblivion, he thought a young woman approached him. Gently she laid her hand on his forearm and whispered, 'Mister, mister, are you all right?' His smothered breathing reassured her. Another woman spoke to the young girl. 'Come now, let him rest.' She smiled and nodded towards the door. As they walked towards it the older woman said, 'The old ones recover better than the rest of us,' but as she finished the girl turned and darted back to his sleeping figure. She pulled the shawl from her shoulders and carefully wound it about his feet. 'You'll sleep better now,' she whispered as she walked off.

His sleep was brief. He knew immediately the urgency and pain of the vigil hours had gone from him. The night had been full and exhausting. Now he felt drained yet exhilarated, as if the tension had transformed itself into some, as yet undefined, joy.

He knew he must stand and walk again to pump some life back into his limbs. The thought drew attention to his feet. Their numbing ache was gone and they felt warm and comfortable. He thought he could feel the furry warmth of wool against his skin. As he bent to find what it was, the tightening in his back and thighs reminded him of the night's labours. His hands found the rough wool shawl lapped tenderly about his ankles. He unwound it carefully and lifted it to his face. It smelled of woman's hair. Breathing in its scent again and again, he raised himself and laid it around his shoulders. His first footsteps were lacerated with the chill of cold stone.

He finally reached the altar and sought out the mound of wax that was the last of the night's vigil candle. The lingering smell of burnt beeswax and tallow hung in the air. Timidly he laid his hands on the molten lump. His palms and fingers explored its greasy contours. He pictured clay on a potter's wheel, and thought he could shape this burnt-out offering into an elegant vessel from which the lonely and despairing might drink the wine of memory, of life, of love, and that it might restore them after the awful dislocation of the night.

As he stood musing, a drowning, humming sound, soft and intense, called him from his contemplation. It did not belong here. It was a wild noise that was not part of this religious edifice. He listened, mesmerised by its intensity. For a moment the whole church seemed to reverberate with it.

Behind him, he heard someone settle into one of the pews. He asked, 'Where is that noise from?' A voice as old as the church stone and as broken as the gravel it stood on, answered, 'What noise is it you mean?'

'There, that buzzing sound, before me somewhere.'

The old woman to whom he had spoken came to his side and looked at him curiously. Only when she discovered the blankness in his eyes did she answer, 'Well now, would you believe it? There's a great big fat bee dancing and singing away to itself on the very door of the tabernacle.'

'What do you mean, woman?'

'Right there, dancing at the very entrance to the holiest of holies.'

There was delight and mockery in her voice as she added, 'She'll never get out through that door.'

She shuffled off, smothering a cough, but Turlough stood listening intently. It was as if there was some communication between him and the creature. He walked slowly forward, as if into the aura of bee's chorus. Behind the altar, the stained-glass window of virgin and child glowed like a solstice, lighting up the sanctuary of the altar. He walked into its reflected light and stood silent, the warmth flowing over his feet and up his limbs. From the back of the church he looked truncated, his head and shoulders outside the shaft of light that etched his torso. He remembered the window and imagined the rich blues and reds fusing and melting into the features of mother and child. Instinctively he lifted the young girl's shawl to his face. He drank in the smell of woman's hair and flesh. Every sense in him rejoiced. He heard, outside his rapture, the bee's song fade, until it was gone and with it the pain and turmoil of the night vigil. As if in answer to the sensuous flush of wellbeing suffusing him, he heard a chorus of women's voices singing. The words of the hymn did not penetrate, only the melody of human voices wrapping round his senses in sensuous harmony, warming and real. It was like food and drink to him.

Attracted by the singing, Carolan moved out through the door and felt the warmth of daylight on his face and head.

Above him the sky shone like cornflower-coloured parchment. The heat had hatched the lough's store of caddis-fly and birds dipped and skimmed over the water, glutting themselves and calling out to one another. Beside him he heard the slap of flesh on flesh and someone swearing, 'Holy bloody Jesus, these flies would blind you.' In response he heard a young girl's giggling voice. Yes, there were lovers on the island, he thought, and smiled to himself. Hearing the lap of water and feeling smooth pebbles under his feet he sat on a rocky perch. He brushed away the caddis-fly, which landed like soot spots on his face. He thought of the larvae oozing up from the lake's bed, where they had lain waiting for this moment and then bursting into life. For an instant he thought of fishing and his father, the thought which prompted another memory. He was Conan, emerging naked from the belly of the monster. He laughed aloud. The caddis-fly, the story he had heard on this very island, the moment of inexplicable revelation, all mixed in his thinking. Deliberately he dipped his feet in the water and gently rubbed his hands into the cuts and welts that the night had left there.

Across the water the fading sounds of hymn-singing came to him again. Only this time he heard plainly words that seemed to come up from childhood memory, 'Be still and know that I am God.'

The singing voices and the lapping waters were calming. He was caught up in an echo of the intense moment in the church. It had been an incubation. He tried to think through the events of the night, but even as he tried his thoughts were drawn off in another direction. The cold water lapped his feet and the noise of its movements mixed effortlessly with the hymn-singing. Everything seemed to be finding some kind of equilibrium that suggested to him that there was a meeting place in the law of nature and the laws of faith. And what, then, was miracle? For he had first come here so many years ago in search of one. It was neither epiphany nor delusion! It too was a meeting place. A refining of mystery into human meaning. Calmness was spreading over him. He knew that this thinking was its own miracle and he did not want doubt or questions tc separate him from it. Many had embraced him since he had arrived. He felt one with them and without distinction, and the island had done this. Each of us reflected the other, he thought. And his father's words rang in his head a second time, 'In the faces of men you may see the mind of God.'

Sixteen Women and Dreams

Journal of Mrs McDermott-Roe

4th Day of Easter Week, 1738

Today was special somehow. When I took him breakfast this morning, I could feel my own weakness making my step leaden. For a moment I wanted to call Martha and tell her to feed him. But as I approached his room something in me informed me how insignificant I was; perhaps it has been the presence of the bishop and so many priests. I have been told that someone has built a grotto outside his window, people come to pray there and leave little gifts. I know he hears their prayers. I wanted to forbid them, but he would not allow me. I thought it might upset or even frighten him. But he says the rhythm of their prayers and the clicking of rosaries are like a lullaby! When I told him I thought him very brave he said it was not so, and he only wanted to remain conscious. There were things he wanted to tell people. He seems to radiate a kind of energy that strengthens me. I have never felt this before. It's like being in love.

Young Charles calls every day to ask how our patient is. He seems genuinely anxious. I know he had a special relationship with Turlough, but I never thought it was so deep. They used to spend so much time together and I remember that Carolan could be a difficult taskmaster! He could frustrate Charles so.

The bishop has told me he was surprised to see Carolan so alert, but he knew death well and it came in many guises. It was a matter of how men received it. A part of him had expected Carolan to be angry and roar against it. He was surprised at the quiet that seemed to surround the man. He sensed more generosity than Carolan usually displayed. But then nothing is unusual with Carolan.

As the bishop pulled a chair nearer to the bed, Carolan asked him to help him up as he felt the need to walk a little. The bishop was unsure, but knew better than to argue. Mrs McDermott-Roe was so protective of her charge that he could well understand Carolan wanting to spend more time in men's company.

'Have you brought me here to be a crutch?' he asked.

Carolan smiled as he stood and then made his own way feebly towards the window.

'I may have need of your prayers, but it's a bit too late for an old sinner like me to be leaning on the Church.'

'Heaven was made for sinners, master bard.'

'Then there's hope for me yet, though I am unhappy with that title. It carries a great weight. I don't think I am deserving of it, for I am determined to sin a little more. Anyway, I want to have one more drink with my friends before I depart this life!'

As the bishop poured Carolan his drink he informed him that he might be too self-pitying. As he did so, Carolan mentioned the little prayer grotto outside his window, 'A curious accolade for an old dancing master.'

'There are fields full of people out there, and I know one person close to us both who thinks you might be in every measure a bard. I have spent many hours with young Charles and his father recollecting our shared history. The young man has great admiration for you. Indeed there may even be something of Turlough Carolan in Charles O'Conor. I see him often, walking the grounds with his fiancée. He looks lost to me.'

'I think I may have been too hard on him. I am glad he has Nuala. The student may be master of the teacher after all. Pour me a little more.'

After the bishop had refilled the glass, he brought a cover from the bed and put it around Carolan's shoulder as he sat at the window. When he had sat down again, Carolan suddenly asked, 'What is it that you have noticed most in your travels through this land of ours?'

'I don't know what you mean!'

'The women, Bishop, the women,' said Carolan, excited and emphatic. 'Don't you notice the women?'

The bishop was even more puzzled and sat silent.

'My years on the road have been filled with women. I hear them, their voices, laughing, crying, singing, shouting, I smell them, the smell of bread and babies. And from men I hear politics or words. Too many of our youth have gone to the wars and to their deaths and with their heads too full of words. Manhood here is aged and maimed, like an old cockerel with a broken crow.'

For a moment, the bishop thought Carolan had become maudlin and regretted that he had poured more drink. But he listened as Carolan continued, 'So the land itself has absorbed all the passion of women. Its soul is womanised. Even the bleak harshness of it has its own embrace. Underneath the hard rough exterior is something soft and feminine.' Suddenly Carolan's mood lightened and he laughed. 'You know, Bishop, pagan Irish that we are, we cannot accept Christ without Mary!'

The bishop was unsure where the conversation was going, but tried to follow it.

'Old age thickens the blood, Turlough. It makes great romantics of us. But there are those who are still young and can find little to be romantic about. We are a nation enslaved by a heinous law which is not of our making. Youth is hot-blooded, not like us. There are some who say our nation is being reclaimed and reborn in that blood. I myself think . . .'

Before he could finish, Carolan interjected, but a fit of coughing crushed the words out of him. 'This damned law is man-made. It is Herod's law, but it is unsustainable. It has the feel of the sword and the axe and the smell of blood on it. Men make the laws for others that they most fear for themselves. This law is filled with fear, and the fear that has made it will choke its makers. The soul always survives. And it survives at its best in the great houses and homes where I play. These are our safe houses. But we must preserve them, they are the repositories of our future.'

Carolan gave a long sigh, as if to catch up on the words that had come tumbling out of him. There was great urgency in them, as if he were explaining his thoughts to himself as well as to the bishop.

'That's as much a sermon as any I might be expected to deliver!' the bishop said.

'Some men give themselves to life and some to God. I think I prefer an excess of life to one of zeal. Listen, Bishop, I'm too old and too tired to be a revolutionary, but I believe something of what we are will endure. Remember you once advised me to look to our own.'

The bishop found this a strange mix of wistfulness and hard words, but there was also something pathetic about it. He thought that perhaps Carolan was clearing out an old dusty cupboard, but was there something else? Was Carolan asking to be exonerated? An unspoken understanding had grown up between Carolan and himself, but this outburst had confused him. He poured himself another drink and said, 'Perhaps you are too much of a lover to be a warrior!'

Carolan's answer only added to his confusion. 'And perhaps I loved inadequately. What do you make of dreams, Bishop?'

The bishop thought for a moment, thrown by the strange question. 'I don't know, for I am not much given to dreaming. Joseph in the bible dreamed. Perhaps they are visions in their own way.'

Carolan sat silently for a moment, then began recounting his last visit to St Patrick's purgatory. The bishop was confounded as Carolan unfolded the dream he had had there and which had come echoing back to him in these last few days. When he had finished the bishop found himself lost for words. He knew how lucid the dying could be, and he was sure that many people in their last minutes had glimpses into eternity, but this recurrent dream was more than his priestly mind could fathom.

'You make me believe my own words about visions, but as each man's is unique, I cannot fathom yours without more time and you to be my guide.'

'I have too little of the first and don't think I ever had the capacity to be the second,' Turlough answered simply.

Seventeen Dying

Journal of Mrs McDermott-Roe

5th Day of Easter Week, 1738

I felt sick this morning. It's the dread and expectation of what is happening and having to organise for what is coming. Everything has been left to me, and I feel so cut off from everything. I feel alone and I pray to the mother of God that her strength may enter me and show me how to be unafraid. Turlough is never alone now. All his friends are here and are with him constantly. They come to me after each visit and tell me how remarkable he looks and how alert his mind is. I feel excluded. The house and grounds are full of clergy and yet I am so alone.

Only Charles seems to sense my fears. He visits me every day, but sometimes even he is too much for me! He tells me he does not know what to say to Turlough, although there is much that he feels he should. He is like Turlough when he was young, a head full of notions that even he can't understand.

6th Day of Easter Week, 1738

Strange how, though I am exhausted, I draw strength from him. It's as if the nearer death comes to him the more of him there seems to be, as if all the hidden parts of him are being revealed. It is not death that fills the room, just more of Turlough.

Today he wants to be alone with Charles and I am instructed to ensure no one disturbs them. I have told Charles not to worry about what to say, Turlough will have enough words for both of them. He asked if he should read some poems to him. I told him he might, but I felt a little jealous. I know there is a bond between them, but I have been reading to Turlough for an enternity. Has this comfort to be taken from me also!

Turlough lay in a silence broken only by his rasping breath and racking cough. His eyes rolled slowly, but his mind was a spinning whirlpool. At the very edge of life he wanted to drink in all its gaiety and loveliness, but he felt trapped in dejection. Stagnation hung in the air he breathed. It was like bile in his mouth and he wanted to spit it out. He cursed the room and the silence. His mouth curved to a sickly smile and his eyes steadied their focus. Each eye looked away from the other as if staring at two different things. His voice was slow, yet light and dismissive. 'And you, the waiting darkness, I curse you, too.' Forever, it seemed, regret gnawed at the joys of love. That he had lived was insufficient joy for him, but that he had loved and loved abundantly was the consolation that regret could never take from him. But was it enough? The room seemed hot, yet Turlough shivered. His past pursued him like an old sin that would not be absolved. He cursed again, he wanted a drink. 'Christ Jesus,' he spat out, I'm not dead yet.'

Drinking was like living. And living was always running after intimacy. All he had ever wanted was to be embraced by life, to find the balance and stillness of love. Life was a river of love, its ebb and flow traced our engagement with the world. If we were driven by love then the waters would never overcome us. Like a surprised child, he proclaimed to the room, 'No one ever taught me to swim.'

In his delirious state he pictured again the leaping salmon. He saw himself worshipping them at the great rock. He felt his hand tingling as he embraced and fingered them in the cold waters. He saw himself mirrored in their leaping eye. Like the salmon, we must fall back into life. For a moment he imagined the harp in his hands. It felt like a waiting fish. His hands cupped it the way his father had taught him. Then music was flying through his head and his trembling fish were suddenly scudding through the turbulent river.

Images, like little filaments of his life history, flooded his imagination. The opal crescent of the winter moon sparking off the frozen land. The back roads and boreens full of birdsong and butterflies. The physical world in its endless regeneration swamped him: the smells of cut grass, of decaying timber, the pungency of wet turf, the sickly sweet smell of age and the aroma of women. The images came like seismic encounters breaking up and fusing into one another. His mind's desperate search for pattern and significance was pulled into tension by the multiplicity of the images. That was all he knew, the world outside was something he did not feel part of.

He felt hot and a terrible thirst raged in him. His throat was too dry to allow him to swallow the traces of sticky saliva he tried to work up in his mouth. There was little he could do. He was trapped inside this decaying body, but his mind was swimming against the tide. He was swimming upstream to the spawning beds.

From beyond the curtain that enclosed his bed he heard the rhythmic click of knitting needles, it seemed to focus his mind. The quick precision of the clicks drew him out of himself.

Outside the room Charles had begun to climb the stairs. As he entered the corridor leading to Turlough's room, he tripped on a clumsily fitted floorboard. Recovering from his stumble, he stood for a moment suddenly conscious of the purpose of his visit. Then very gently he opened the door and stood on the threshold. The chair in which Turlough had frequently sat by the window wrapped in a blanket was gone. A pockmarked woman was sitting by the bed, knitting drowsily. She looked up at Charles, scratching her head with the butt of the wooden needle.

'What do you want?' she demanded.

'I've come to speak to Carolan,' he whispered.

'Shut the door behind you, he's lying here.' She gave a jerk of her head towards the bed, which was shielded by a curtain, and in some vexation continued, 'The Lord alone knows what business you have with that corpse.'

As she finished, a suffocating cough burst from behind the curtain. Charles looked dismissively toward the woman before going up and drawing it back. Turlough lay curled up like a wrinkled foetus under the neat patchwork quilt. His eyes were vacant and blue-grey like the sea. Slowly, they moved, acknowledging the young man's presence. Charles was struck by the dim serenity of Carolan's gaze. It was the only sign of animation in the faded face where his features were already melting in the placidity of death.

'How are you?' he asked softly.

'Who is that?' Turlough said in a cracked voice.

'Charles,' he answered.

He felt ashamed at the sight of the man and the sparseness of the room. There was an emptiness in it more than its lack of furnishings.

'Aah,' said Turlough and gave a convulsive shiver. 'Sit down.'

Charles looked about him for a stool, but could see none.

'Sit in my place,' the old woman said gathering up her knitting. 'Sit a while with him, I have to go out for a bit,' she continued, as she rolled her knitting and threw it into an old basket at her feet.

'You're in too great a hurry to lay him out, I think,' Charles whispered.

But his words were lost in the empty room as the woman had left before he had finished. The silence of it struck him. He sat down on Turlough's bed. He wanted to be near the old man rather than sit in a chair observing the sickening tragedy before him.

'No, take the stool. Don't disturb me. My hands keep throbbing as if they are the only part of me that is really alive.'

Obediently he drew up the chair. Its scratching noise put an edge on his nervousness.

'I don't seem to recognise people these days, so many people, so many faces. I can't tell one from the other now.' Turlough's voice was feeble and dreamlike.

'It's Charles. You remember, you used to make me recite poems to you while you played. I've come to see you.'

'I remember, but Charles was only a little lad.'

'I've grown,' said Charles, with an apology choking him. Without realising, he started to scratch on the floor with the sole of his boot.

'Don't shuffle,' commanded Turlough. 'Give me a drink, lad, I'm parched. And make it stronger than water. There's a jug about the place somewhere with a real drink in it.'

Charles looked about him and spotted the jug and cup on the mantelpiece. He brought it to the bed, poured a few mouthfuls into the cup and put it into Turlough's hands as he lifted his head to drink. He swallowed and gagged, then Charles propped him further up on the bed.

Taking a deep, but faltering breath, Turlough began to speak,

'A cup a day, that's what I'm reduced to, I couldn't count how many of them I've had in my life.'

Charles noticed an expression of melancholy and pain pucker Turlough's face.

'The cups are running empty and I'm worn out. I remember you now. You forgot me, but I remember you. I remember everything.'

Charles became uneasy, unsure if Turlough was speaking directly to him or if he was simply rambling.

'I'm leaving you my linen, but I'll wear it a while yet,' he warned.

'Oh, you'll live a bit longer. You used to tell me never to hurry when I was reciting. Four score years and ten is man's allotted span.' Charles hesitated. 'That silly old woman of yours has put these ideas into your head. I would chase her.'

'You leave her alone. She's looking after me, though at times I'm sure she wishes she wasn't.'

Silence fell. Charles stood up and moved awkwardly towards the window. The sky was blustery and had cast a grey mist over the hills. Behind him, Turlough mumbled a name he could not quite make out. He only caught the last words, '. . . she doesn't know I'm here.' Charles became more unsure of his own reasons for being in the room. Again Turlough spoke. 'Give me another drink. Nothing tastes of anything.'

Charles replenished his glass and he drank deeply. It trickled from his lips as he tried to chew it. Charles helped him to another. Then Turlough lay back, his eyes rolling. 'I woke in the night,' he paused as if trying to remember, then coughed and gagged, 'and he was standing in the corner . . . waiting.'

'Who was in the corner?' asked Charles, glancing involuntarily to the corner.

'Who? who?' raved Turlough and then more slowly, 'Who?' as if he was asking himself. 'He came for me, but I told him, "You wait a bit yet. I've more days in me, there's something I want to know," and he said, "You'll catch up with me, I'll wait for you!" ' Turlough began to laugh. But to Charles it was not the laugh of a living man.

'It's all your fancy,' Charles said. 'I think you had a few drinks to yourself before I came.' He tried to force a laugh. 'You're tired and maybe you're right, you're a worn-out old man.'

His humorous jibe received no acknowledgement. He felt guilty and ashamed. 'I've written some verses. I want to read them to you. Listen.'

He looked enquiringly at Turlough, but his face betrayed nothing. Charles felt trapped. He began to read. Badly at first, jerkily, at one moment his voice dropping to a whisper and then straining to be a subdued shout, as his eyes raced back and forward to the man on the bed. 'Nearer, lad, come nearer, and don't rush,' croaked Turlough. Relieved and excited, Charles moved to the bed. His voice found a new vigour and pace.

Turlough was listening. His head nodded slowly and the feeble gesture of his hands seemed to be encouraging the words from Charles. The vigour of youth and Charles's trembling voice welled up in the room and seemed to drive death out. Turlough was smiling. He was on the roof again, tempted by the cunning of life. 'Cast thyself down, love will save you,' he mumbled to himself. His eyes were rolling again with the wonder of memory. Charles continued reciting his poem nervously. It was many minutes before he finished, his eyes bright and his heart thumping.

'Well, what do you think?' he asked urgently. 'Should I go on trying?' His eyes were scrutinising Turlough's own for a reaction. There was silence; expectation had blinded Charles to the meaning of the expression on Turlough's face.

'I remember so many times we used to sit together talking of poetry and music. You know the Song of Solomon, that was truly great poetry. And I have come to think that music and poetry are like the bridegroom and the bride. I can imagine what McCabe would think of that. Do you remember the night you played me Vivaldi's music? I remember it as if it was yesterday. Both you and your uncle set my head on fire with words and music that tantalised me. There's something I never told anyone about that time, but I want you to know it. If you are half the poet I think you are, you might give better words to it than I can.'

For the next few hours Charles sat silent as Carolan told him of an experience that dumbfounded him. He remembered the afternoon, but not the way Carolan did. Carolan had insisted on being alone, he recalled.

Slowly and awkwardly Turlough groped under the pillow and held something out in his withered palm.

'Here, take this,' he said sharply.

'What is it?' Charles asked.

'A tooth,' Turlough's voice seemed distant.

'Whose tooth?'

'Mine, there's been no one else sleeping with me, it fell out this morning.' Turlough's face changed. 'Here, take it, lad.'

Charles reached out his hand fearfully. There was a strange brightness in Turlough's eyes. Charles watched fascinated as they filled with tears. He rose suddenly, stunned and confused. 'I'd better be going. I . . . I . . . I think I have wearied you. I'm sorry, I'm sorry. Perhaps you should sleep.'

But Turlough would have none of it. He wanted Charles to stay, for there were things he needed to say to him. Slowly he began to explain.

When people tried to talk to him he heard them as if they were miles away. His mind was too preoccupied for their solicitations. He loved Charles and he didn't want to make him feel unwanted, but his mind was not his own these days. It was a little like when he was a child lying in bed at night, waiting excitedly for the dreams to come. Sometimes he was frightened but he didn't remember being sad. Sadness and regret seemed to move through all his thinking now. Turlough paused for a moment, taking laboured breaths. After another fit of coughing, he asked Charles if he remembered the evening they had spent talking about Vivaldi's music, and how, when Charles had called for him the next morning, he had chased him away. Before Charles could speak, Carolan began to explain.

He had dressed slowly and stolen out of the house before its inhabitants could claim him. He felt an impulsive need to be in the light. The night before had crammed his head full and he wanted to clear the disorder that was still smouldering there.

When he found the garden, he walked away from the arbour, knowing that sooner or later he would be disturbed. Instead he wandered around the back of the house and across the cobbled courtyard that led to the stables. As he passed by them, the smell of horses, leather and the dull, fusty smell of iron reminded him of his father's forge. So intense was the memory that he hesitated for a moment to hear the steady chip and ring of his father's rhythmic hammer.

The stone wall at the rear was overhung by the huge branches of an ancient oak. Light filtered through its leaves, dappling the wall with its heat. The place was littered with barrels and timber. Here and there chickens skittered about and two magpies called out as he found a seat on a small upturned barrel. The smell of old port still clung to it.

Carolan settled himself, listening to the raucous squabble of the birds mingling with the snuffling of the horses. As he sat drinking in the sunshine, he recalled his confession to McCabe and his belief in the miracle of light. He smiled as he thought of the confusion it must have caused him. He was feeling drowsy. The hum of insects and the noise of the wind made his senses leaden.

Briefly, an echo of the night's discussion entered his head. Men hint at things, he thought, Charles and the bishop only knew things with their heads. Memory was the obstacle. It made facts of things. It distilled them from their essence. His blindness had returned to him this essence; it was constantly with him. But he needed to give it form. Was the music Charles had played him a premonition of the form he sought? And what was the wondrous 'truth to art' the bishop had so eloquently spoken of? Both these thoughts seemed to hurl him headlong on to his blindness. It was as if he wasn't ready to answer; these questions demanded a response that he had not fathomed yet. Instinctively he screwed his eyes closed, as if to block out the questions that were nagging at him.

Charles was listening patiently. He wasn't sure if Turlough was simply rambling. But there was something intense about the recollection that intrigued Charles, as Turlough continued.

A long time ago he had begun to learn how to 'see things without his eyes'. 'A blind man must learn to see in another way,' he declared. Turlough thought back to his youth and began to explain his first response to the loss of his sight. In those early months he felt enclosed in a vault that filled him with despair. For a long time he struggled with this unfamiliar landscape with increasing hopelessness and hostility. Then some instinct, like a hand laid on him, redirected him. He did not know how it happened. He thought of it now as a kind of surrender to other impulses within, instead of clinging to the world outside through sight.

Somehow, in a way that his rational mind had not yet found the measure of, Vivaldi's passionate and exuberant music mirrored that moment which he had carried with him as his secret. He felt that Vivaldi's compositions had taken these moments of blind insight and broken in the doorway to them. It was as if the musician had laid a hand on him and was guiding him. Vivaldi's music had the same sense about it as his discovery of his inner light. The Italian's music had a freakish immediacy that drew the substance of his universe together. The music was outside himself, but he seemed to 'see' it from some inner point. It was light, and it was there.

He remembered the indescribable relief and happiness, and the ensuing confidence and gratitude with which he had his first adolescent encounter with his inner light. The experience itself had not remained with such intensity, but something more important had. That was its 'essence'. For it had the feeling of being beautiful, like a dream or an enchantment. Paradoxically, blindness had bathed him in another light. He could feel light rising, spreading, giving form to things. This light had no opposite. Darkness was a word that those who looked outward, those who could see, used. For too many years he had kept this light hidden. It was so contrary to what people understood that he felt unable to share it. Even if he wanted to, he couldn't find the words to explain it, for he didn't understand it himself. But he knew instantly that Vivaldi did.

Why was this awareness of an inner light associated with the fantastical music that was spilling through him as he sat behind those stables?

He remembered he was tired and wanted to shut out his thoughts. Automatically he closed his eyes. But the light remained. It was less bright, like reflected light. He tried to will the sense of it from him, but it was impossible. The more he tried the more he felt a disturbance, as if he was doing something forbidden. It was as if he was a prisoner of light.

It reminded him of how he had felt when he first tried to cope with his blindness and had encountered this light. He remembered how, if he refused the sense of confidence it occasioned in him and hesitated at a door, or a wall, fearful of the injury he might cause himself, then undoubtedly he would stumble. Fear and apprehension made him more blind than his sightlessness. Impatience threw everything into confusion. During those first months when he was learning the harp he could never afford to be anxious or apprehensive. His hands would refuse to obey and as he became more frustrated they seemed to leave him entirely, as if they had been cut off.

He had learned slowly, under the cruel chastisement of his old bird woman, not to force his will on the instrument. Even now he felt the sting of her stick as she rapped him on the hands. 'Your hands are learning to be wise, leave them to their freedom!' she would yell out at him. Sometimes she would snap the instrument from him and hold his hands in hers. Then she would tell him 'not to command his hands with eyes that he had not got'.

Even as he sat there, in the sunlight and silence, he could hear old Fionnuala's cracked voice berating and coaxing him. She had insisted that rhythm could not be understood by the eyes. They run over the surface of things. The eye is satisfied with appearances. For them the world is transitory. What they see lacks substance, and what they value is distorted.

Only when he learned to leave his hands to their own devices could he understand the substantiality of rhythm. The hands were always in earnest, touching, covering and testing every object they encountered. They explored intimately the bulk, the resistance and the regularity of every substance. His fingers became new creatures. They felt out the vibrations of everything and answered with their own pulse. This amazing tactile sense rediscovered the world for him. He did not need to go out to meet things, but only wait to receive them. Strangely and rapturously he sensed how, at times, if he surrendered to it, the universe became his accomplice.

As this thought came to him, he suddenly realised why he had been driven to contemplation. This was the connection that had bewitched him into Vivaldi's fantasy. The Italian's melodic landscape was an image of his own sightless world. There was no darkness and the music was blasted with the 'light' that he understood so intimately. The music had swept away the mist from the window and everything was revealed in its shameless beauty.

Vivaldi's music was like an exchange of pressures, which spilled out and gathered themselves together, in shapes. Each shape had its own meaning and flowed with those around it. It created an unending panorama, and Carolan felt himself on a rooftop, this time looking out on a celestial city. He seemed to lean into this exchange of pressures that the music brought him and in that gesture felt a satisfaction too deep for words. This was the secret that old Fionnuala Quinn had tried to impart to him. Only blindness could release him to see more fully. Blindness allowed him to stop living in front of things and begin to live with them, as a part of them. Only now was he beginning to understand that this was what he had searched the psalms to find.

Charles did not know how long he had been listening to Carolan, nor did he know how to respond. He desperately wanted to say something but he didn't know where to begin. He looked towards Turlough. He was relieved he was blind and could not see his confusion. Carolan's confession had blasted all words from him and he felt that he hardly knew the man. For an interminable period both men sat in silence, with the emptiness of the room pressing in on them. Charles felt himself smothering in the silence and was relieved when Carolan gently asked him to leave. He did so, without speaking, but not without squeezing Turlough's hand. Though he was relieved Charles was going, Turlough knew he didn't want to be alone.

But it wasn't long before Mrs McDermott-Roe entered his room. 'Young Charles didn't stay long?' There was enquiry and some rebuke in her voice.

'You must have been reading my thoughts!'

'Why so?' she asked.

'I was beginning to feel lonely and very bored with myself . . . and before you ask, I didn't chase Charles away. I think he was only too happy to leave. Death makes people very uneasy.'

'Enough! You're only as dead as you want to be. . . !'

Chastisement was rising in her voice as she tutted and pottered about the room. 'Where did Martha go, anyway?' she demanded.

'Never mind Martha. Lazarus wants up. Help me to the window. I weary of this deathbed. I feel like I am adrift in an old curragh and I can't swim!'

Mrs McDermott-Roe was about to say something, but was too

delighted to see him wanting to get up to scold any longer. 'A man shouldn't die in bed and I have a drought on me that's driving my mind to distraction. I'll manage. Fetch that jug and cup to me.'

Mrs McDermott-Roe steadied him and watched him for a second as he palmed his way towards the window. She had no sooner left him to collect the drink than she heard him curse and collapse almost where she had left him.

'Mother of God!' she exclaimed. 'You're as wayward as a wanton child.'

She rushed to him and helped him to his knees, but had not the strength to lift him further. 'I'll fetch Martha, and then I'll tell her a thing or two!' she said breathlessly.

'Never mind Martha,' said Turlough, crawling towards the window. Her breathlessness seemed to double as she watched the pathetic scene. His night-shirt was caught under his knees as he inched forward. 'You've made a woman of me in these skirts and as sure as Christ's in his heaven I'll not be found dead in them!'

She rushed to place the chair for him and tried to help as he pulled himself up.

'The drink, woman, the drink!' he commanded as he settled back into it. Quickly she brought the jug and cup and poured for him.

'You want everything at once and are too impatient to wait for any of it,' she scolded.

Turlough took a long drink and laughed as he spoke, 'You see what would have happened if I fell out of that curragh. I would have sunk and drowned dead . . . and . . .'.

He was about to continue when she concluded for him, 'And you would have had plenty to drink then, and it would have served you right!'

There was relief and comfort in her scolding now and he knew it. In response he simply held out his cup. She filled it, tutting. He drank deeply and sat staring out the window. 'Young Charles still fancies himself as a poet and I think he might have it in him. Is he still courting that Nuala?' he asked.

'He is, though he doesn't know it! He thinks marriage and poetry have nothing in common. He said they are two odd bedfellows.'

Turlough bristled. 'Then he is a damned fool. He'll never string two words together unless he knows the passion of a woman. He'll never be a poet unless he has a bedfellow!'

'You're an irrepressible old rascal! And you are singing with a new tune now, for I remember that it was you, Turlough Carolan, who first put that notion in his head. And how it maddened you if ever you heard he was in the company of a young woman.'

They both laughed aloud like naughty children. Mrs McDermott-Roe announced, 'You're an old corrupter and I'm going to drink from this cup of corruption with you!'

Turlough simply smiled, then he said, 'It took all these years for you to finally succumb to me. Now, when I'm too old, you surrender!'

She looked at him and wanted to touch him. But he looked too frail for the embrace she wanted to give him. His face had no animation in it, no matter how he teased her. She drank quickly. But the alcohol could not contain her feelings. She moved to the window. 'Let me open this. This sun's no use to us, shut out by the window,' she said as she pushed it open. 'My old bones want to drink in the sun like you want to drink this vile brew.'

She expected him to come back at her with some dismissive response, but he sat silent. The bright sunlight on his face served only to heighten the contours of his skull. She felt a desperate need to stroke his head.

Turlough leaned toward the window and rolled his head in the sunlight. He began to speak. 'When I was a child I used to spend many long afternoons away from home. I was always alone, but never felt alone. When my mother asked me where I had been I made some excuse – usually fishing! I could not simply say I had been watching the sun. How, as it moved across the landscape, it was not like the flow of water, for it seemed to be everywhere. It came from nowhere in particular. It was just like the air. It's there and we never question it.'

Turlough shifted back into his chair. She was sure he would ask for another drink and was about to reach for it when he continued, 'You know, I never looked for the sun as it moved across the sky. I was always looking for it elsewhere. I always looked for it in its echo rather than its source, its moving shadows which transformed the very shape and texture of things. That was its echo. It entered into me. It became part of me. I was eating sun!'

He paused at this last remark as if he had just discovered it and it had surprised him. Then after a moment he turned to Mrs McDermott-Roe. The movement of his face against the sunlight gave his words a strange prescience.

She wanted to believe that the alcohol had fired his imagination or that a combination of exhaustion and alcohol had induced this kind of reflection. Turlough's mood seemed to change as he spoke again. 'Have you brought fresh flowers with you? I can smell them. When I picked flowers with my mother it was as if I was holding light in my hands. I still feel the echo of their colours.'

Suddenly he stopped as though the words and the thoughts behind them were too much for him.

'I think perhaps you may be a little tired!'

She knew the expression sounded mundane, but what he had said had drained her. As if sensing her anxiety, he made a mock-serious face and said, 'Death concentrates the mind wonderfully!' She had heard him say it before and she forced a little laugh, enough for him to hear. Slowly and softly he responded, 'I should remember what I preach. First the music then the words! Words encumber us. Bring me my harp. There is something I have been thinking about these last days and as you are my favourite audience and dearest friend I want you to hear it first. But fill my cup first, I fear it is running out.'

'It's too much, Turlough,' she said simply.

'Hush now, it's only too much if it's immodest. And I'm hardly that!'

She didn't answer him, but poured his cup full and turned to fetch his harp. Turlough turned back to the window and drank slowly, but deeply.

She found the instrument and paused with it, looking at him. The silhouette of his head and back set against the light seemed to wash away all the age from him. But for his yellowy-white hair, he could have been a young man. She agreed that the nightshirt did not suit him. She handed him his harp, taking the cup in exchange. 'You've finished, I see,' she said in a matronly tone.

'Yes.'

His voice was distant, as if his mind was somewhere else and these questions were an impediment. She knew her place and his petty fussiness. She walked with the empty cup to the bedside table and sat down quietly.

Turlough nestled the instrument into his shoulder. There was something very businesslike about his movements. She remembered how he used to make such a show of preparing and positioning himself and his harp, as if announcing that the great Carolan was about to play. But the showmanship was gone now. Instrument and man found a quick accommodation. This was a private audience and there was no need for ceremony.

He began slowly at first, but clear notes appeared as if to announce and declare themselves, and having done so they almost joined hands, as in readiness for a harvest dance. Quickly a harmony was established. Although it was delicate, it was not devoid of impulse. The dance was about to begin and the music opened up. It was as if a lone woman was dancing in a place of boundless light. As this image danced around her mind, Turlough laid out before her the different vistas that had been part of his memory. But now they were no longer memory. He filled the room with them and she felt herself looking out on them. His music was a gossamer curtain being slowly pulled back.

For a brief instant she pulled herself out of the music's embrace and looked at him. She saw something she had never witnessed before. Turlough was not playing this music to anyone or any audience, whether herself alone or ten thousand other ears. The music had swallowed him up completely. It was as if he was gone from the place and the form of Turlough before her was itself an image, or a fragment of memory!

At moments the tempo slowed, like an eye alighting on different things and focusing in on them. Turlough was gathering all the meaningful moments of his life around him. He was walking among them, to see and touch and finger them again. It was as if he wanted to thank them for having been part of him. His mellow flourishes across the strings seemed strangely charged. Instantly she remembered his statement about everything having its own vibration. She was almost afraid to admit it, but she felt the sensuality of these flourishes.

Turlough was entranced. His fingers travelled the strings with easy assurance. His harmonies were full but subdued.

She could not take her eyes from him. There was possession in the music. The man and his instrument were one and single and unique, caught up in this quiet outpouring. The last notes emerged tremulously. They seemed to fall off strings that were pure crystal and beyond human manipulation.

She thought of a flickering candle and a prayer. She thought of a hand waving. Joy and a deep sadness had found reconciliation in this music, but she hardly knew how!

Anguish and acceptance hung about the room as Turlough gently lifted his fingers off the strings. For several minutes he held the instrument to himself. The atmosphere was almost unbearable yet he showed no sign of emotion. He simply sat in silence, nursing his harp.

She dreaded that he might speak. She wasn't ready for him, or anything he might say. She was weak and afraid. There was a power in him she had not encountered before.

Eighteen Last Rites

Journal of Mrs McDermott-Roe

7th Day of Easter Week, 1738

I think I am beginning to understand this calmness that everyone sees in Turlough. I think it won't be long now. People are avoiding me. I hate it. It makes me feel like death's handmaiden. But it's death they are afraid of. I am too, but not when I am with him.

I sat all night with him, but I felt that someone other than him and I was there, like a warm and gentle presence. I looked at him in the moonlight and he seemed to be glowing.

I hate to leave his room. When I do I feel old and unloved.

Charles walked through the shadowy lanes towards the dimly lit village. He was embarrassed with himself for the haste with which he had left his old friend. He had stood on the threshold of the room and looked back into it. The smell of age and death was everywhere. It was suffocating and stuffy. He remembered Turlough staring back at him and mumbling something. His voice was no louder than the thin rustle of a page turning in a prayerbook.

Charles bent his head and shoulders against the cold and dark. His hands were buried deep in his coat pockets. In one of them he turned and rolled the tooth he had been given. 'A queer payment for poetry,' he thought and laughed. The laughter was instantly swallowed up in the cold air. It made him feel small and mean. Was he condemned to carry this obscene relic about with him for ever? He was angry; but he was angry with death and not the man whom he had just left.

He stopped at the small bridge before the village. The cold

stillness of the air lifted and carried the noise of the river to him. He stood contemplating the events of the evening. The noise of the water seemed to flush out and wash away the anger and sadness that were confusing his senses. He pulled his hand from his pocket and looked at the tooth. It looked like a piece of dried wood with its bark peeled off. An impulse to fling it into the river seized him, but it passed and he knew he never would. He knew too that Carolan had given him something more than this tooth, but he did not fully know what.

That evening Charles sat alone in the quiet of his room, peeling back layers of memory. He had always found Carolan unpredictable, even irate. He was frequently moody, which everyone put down to the effects of alcohol, and Charles had learned to be dismissive in return.

As he undressed, he took Carolan's tooth from his pocket and turned it over in his hand. He thought of Carolan's declaration that he intended to bequeath him his linen. He laughed at the thought, for Carolan had a ridiculous vanity about his appearance and could be as fussy as a woman about his clothes. Was there some omen or curse in this bequest? And what did he expect him to do with the gift? No one wanted to walk in a dead man's clothes and who would dare wear Carolan's! Already myths were in the making about him. Even as he was thinking this, Charles spoke out into the empty room. 'They're already burying you with stories, old man.' As the words died in his mouth, the thought suddenly crystallised that perhaps that's why he had put off visiting Carolan until now.

He didn't really know the man, only bits of him. Consequently he didn't know how to talk to him. As quickly as this admission confronted him, another followed. Was that why Carolan had made his strange confession to him? Was Carolan trying to give him a part of himself, just as he had done with the gift of his tooth? But what of the linen, what did it mean?

Before retiring, Charles lit a candle. As he lay in bed he laughed. 'I'm developing his habits even before I put on his linen,' he said to himself. The laughter began to unleash other memories. He remembered how on so many occasions when Carolan was teaching him he would round on him and roar, 'Will you never remember to be your own man and never surrender to fancy, either in poetry or in music but particularly when it's in skirts!' Charles was always confused and sometimes frightened by the passion behind these words.

But he remembered many other occasions when the tables were turned and Carolan had become his pupil. He had an intense curiosity about things. His father, the O'Conor Don, had once pityingly described Carolan as a haunted soul. But when Charles asked him to explain he answered that the past was everyone's inheritance, as it was Carolan's and his own and would be Charles's. Then he concluded that the past is ever in front of us tripping us up. Charles had thought little of it then, but wondered about it now. His contemplation resolved nothing, for the night was too full of too many memories.

It was a long night as he remembered all those times he had been with Turlough. He realised that he was a man whose presence excluded a past. Whatever world Turlough inhabited, little of it entered into his relationship with others, or did it? Charles wondered if anyone else knew the man. He also wondered if he could tell his father or the bishop or anyone else what had been explained to him. Another part of him questioned if Turlough was simply playing a game with everyone. Performer to the end.

As he pondered over these things he heard voices and people moving about the house. He glanced towards the divide in the shuttered window. Outside it was still night. But the confirmation of night and the restless house hinted that what everyone was waiting for had happened.

Charles rose and walked to the window. He could see torches moving in the nightscape and below him the house lights had given a glow to the grounds nearest the building. Doors were banging and horses were moving along the drive. He was about to go down, when he heard his father announce to whomever was in the house, 'There's little we can do now but marshal ourselves for tomorrow.' He knew his father was right, for the vault of memory seemed the proper place to be right now. He retired again, but slept a troubled sleep filled with Carolan's ghostly presence.

In the morning Charles learned that Carolan had died at about the time he had stood on the bridge. He could not bring himself to visit the corpse. He didn't want anyone to say, 'He called for you.' Instead he paced about his room, listless and indifferent. It seemed to him that the very air and the food he ate smelt of coffin wood. It tasted bitter and sickening.

He remained at home, unwilling to be part of the business and bustle that death brought with it. But now his conscience began bothering him. He threw on his coat and tossed his hair back with the flat of his hand. As he arrived at the door and opened it he saw Nuala waiting, her face and shoulders draped in a creamy white shawl.

'I was coming for you. You can't stay here,' she said.

'I can't bear it at home any longer,' he replied.

'I'm going with you, and I don't want any arguments.' Her voice was resolute and Charles shrugged.

A cloud of silence accompanied them as they walked to Alderford. Occasionally they nodded greetings to people who stood moodily in the doorways. Funerals were always a kind of performance, Charles thought. People attended to be seen. But grief sometimes exposed parts of people they might prefer to leave hidden. Charles was anxious about the nature of his own grief; and no matter how hard he tried to resist, Nuala insisted on holding his hand as they entered the house.

'You wait here, I'll go first. You know what they're like. There'll be no end to the gossip.'

'Let them!' she answered, angry with him as she trailed him after her.

The room was crowded and filled with the smell of incense and stale tobacco laced with alcohol. A tall scrawny-necked priest was handing round the thin candles that Charles knew Turlough had kept close to his bed. Turlough lay dressed in what looked like new but cheap clothes. In repose his chest seemed puffed out and a small saucer of salt sat on it. Charles whispered to Nuala, 'Such dignity for a dead man.' There was a hint of sarcasm in his voice and Nuala ignored him. A bald old man who was a stranger to Charles was mumbling a psalm. As he shifted from one foot to another his boots squeaked, they were new.

The man's voice was low. It was as if he was reciting only for Turlough and from time to time he glanced at the dead man to ensure he was listening attentively to the bitter complaints of Job in his affliction. Charles watched him and thought of his own attempts to read to Turlough a few days before. 'At least he heard me!' he said to himself and gave a dismissive sigh.

'What's the matter with you?' said Nuala impatiently.

'Nothing!'

Charles looked towards the priest. He was angered at how the censer greedily devoured the store of incense that had been kept with the candles in a little lacquered box under Turlough's bed. Charles lit his candle from a neighbour's and then waved Nuala towards the window. The priest whining his prayer noticed them and twisted his neck to follow them.

'Let me light your candle.'

'Look out, you're dropping wax on to my dress.'

With all the candles lit, the heavy atmosphere of the smoking censer lifted a little. To Charles, the bearded faces of the men and wrinkled faces of the women bore the stamp of dull, uncomprehending wisdom. They were neither saddened nor astonished by death. Though it was a mystery, they were not awed by it. Its mystery was diminished in their unquestioning acceptance of it. Amongst them Mrs McDermott-Roe seemed to direct the proceedings with a commanding protective glare; occasionally she would dart to the coffin and straighten the pillow or fix Carolan's hair. Another woman was placidly trimming the candle wicks, ensuring that they would burn ever brighter.

Charles stood with his eyes downcast, fearful to look too long into the women's faces. He felt the need to pray, but there wasn't a prayer in him.

'Life ate you up, Turlough, just like it's eating your candles and incense, but if there had been twice as much of both, you would still have wanted nothing left over. Never waste the day!'

He glanced towards the coffin. Turlough seemed to have shrunk, as if intimidated by the ritual being whispered around him and the field of eyes staring vacantly on him. But Charles could not lift his eyes off the corpse. He wanted to warm the cold body or, if he could, receive some last sign or word of life.

'Look at us,' whispered Nuala. 'We're standing together with candles in our hands as if we were getting married.'

It was true. Without fully knowing it, Nuala had warmed his own cold soul and perhaps had given the sign and word of life he wanted desperately to draw from Turlough.

The whispering and shuffling in the room were brought to a halt as the priest declared, 'Peace on all here.' His words drew all attention to himself as he perfunctorily began the ritual; first setting oil on the table, then extracting the crucifix and taking up the vessel of holy water, he moved about the room. He sprinkled the corpse before him, then turning away from Turlough and making a sign of the cross, he sprayed the room and everyone in it.

When he turned to whisper inaudible words of spiritual consolation into Turlough's unhearing ear, Charles bristled. This final parting excluded him. As he heard the prayers mumbled around him, he felt more excluded. Somewhere outside himself he heard the priest call the bystanders to prayers while he administered the final sacrament, 'In the name of the Father and of the Son and of the Holy Spirit.'

Charles watched the priest's hands describe a cross in the air. It was as if he was pushing everyone away for the moment, as if he was marking them as unwanted.

'May all the power of the devil be extinguished in thee, by the imposition of these our hands, by the invocation of all holy angels, archangels, patriarchs, prophets, apostles, martyrs, confessors, virgins and all other saints: Amen.'

Dipping his thumb into the oil and making a cross on Turlough's eyes, he prayed that all sin committed by them might be forgiven. Somewhere behind him a man's voice announced quietly, 'It's a long time since those eyes might have seen, never mind sinned.' There was no humour in the remark, but Charles smiled, relieved. He knew the sincerity with which Seamus Brennan spoke.

The priest continued his eerie ritual undisturbed. He took a white cloth and wiped the oil from the eyes, then moved to the nostrils and to the lips, from there to the hands, at which point Mrs McDermott-Roe started, then quickly bowed her head. The priest continued down the body to the feet, constantly praying for forgiveness and absolution of the sin committed by each part.

After a few prayers he concluded the sacrament of extreme unction. Then lifting the saucer of salt from Turlough's chest he cast its contents dismissively on the floor, and with one of the candles set the white cloth alight. It burned with a black pungent smoke.

At this point, many of those assembled quietly filed out of the room. Death was entering in and they felt its dread. Only those who knew him intimately remained. Like Charles, they sensed that Turlough could not bear to leave this life alone and companionless.

The priest looked at the faces of those remaining. To Charles there seemed to be a hint of irritation in his face that he could not fathom. Was he angry because people had left and would not witness his final priestly performance, or was it that Turlough's friends chose to remain, oblivious of the priest's indulgent ceremony?

Finally the priest turned back to Turlough and mumbled something between his teeth. Dropping dramatically to his knees, he adored the host, then lifting it up he held it before Turlough. Under his breath Charles hissed, 'Didn't he hear Seamus? Doesn't he know he's blind?' Mrs McDermott-Roe heard his desperation and gently took his hand. The priest's voice had a grating monotony as he intoned, 'Behold the lamb of God, which taketh away the sins of the world.' And with this he put the wafer to Turlough's mouth. 'Take, this viaticum of Christ's body, which may preserve thee from the evil enemy and into eternal life.'

And with that he fell silent, as did everyone else. Charles felt like weeping, but anger would neither let him weep nor pray. Was this all that Turlough had become – a carcass of sin, described in the incoherent babble of this pathetic priest? He remembered someone saying that the man had been trained in France. 'A pot scrubber in a convent,' Charles thought to himself, 'one of those who clung to the Mass book with all the piety of an ignoramus.' As these thoughts were about to boil over, he felt a movement behind him.

Mrs McDermott-Roe moved forward with the grace of a young woman. In her arms was a massive bunch of wild flowers. Without a word she laid them gently along the length of Carolan's body as if she were covering him with a blanket. Lightly she kissed his mouth, then turned and walked from the room. Her face was as inanimate as Turlough's. Charles looked again at the corpse. In his hands he held a rosary of coral stone, Carolan's 'musical abacus'. He smiled at the double significance of the act.

'Young man,' a voice snapped, 'time to collect the candles. It's all over.'

The mourners drifted out in twos, whispering and crossing themselves. Through the open door came a burst of cold air, but it could not dispel the sour smell of the extinguished candles. In the corner the goose-necked priest was removing his vestments and questioning some of the mourners about Turlough's last days. They answered with childlike obedience and he listened to them, nodding silently as he folded his shabby chasuble, the way sailors fold a flag. The psalm reader blew his nose loudly into a red handkerchief as if to say, 'Well, there you are, Turlough, that's your lot for the night.'

Charles was the last to go. He turned again at the threshold, as he had done some days before. But it was dim and empty. The coffin candles glowed grimly and his eyes turned to the corner. The bed on which Turlough had lain only a few days ago had been taken to pieces. Only a little heap of dust and rubbish remained, as if the room had been hastily swept. And there, too, Turlough had left his dust, he thought to himself.

As Charles and Nuala stood in the hall trying to find some kind of conversation, Mrs McDermott-Roe came towards them. She smiled kindly at Nuala, then turned to Charles. Her voice was weak and Charles leaned towards her to listen, 'This will be a lonely house for me tonight, more lonely than I think I can bear. God knows he made it his own. Charles, will you stay a few days with me?'

She turned swiftly towards Nuala, seeking her approval also. Nuala smiled, understanding, and took her hand. Charles took her other hand, 'Of course I will.'

Later that night he slept uneasily. For many hours he lay awake wanting the night to be over. He could not come to grips with the room in which Turlough had spent his last hours. The weight of its emptiness pressed in on him. It was as if the air had been sucked out of it. The night too was suffocating and restless.

Morning came suddenly. Charles rose and sat exhausted on the end of the bed. He didn't want to leave the room, but the day seemed to be clawing under the door and calling him to the ceremonies ahead. As he began drowsily to raise himself, he stopped abruptly. A sudden remembrance of a dream that had gripped him in the night flashed into his head. He saw himself bent over the sleeping figure of Turlough, shouting at him to wake up and listen. The thought made him shiver and laugh at the same time. But his laughter quickly subsided. This remembrance had been only a part of his night's unease. Slowly it began to unfold again.

In his sleep he had imagined he saw a figure sitting with his head bowed. Though the figure sat far off from him, he sensed that the eyes were closed and the figure had no hands. The arms simply faded away at the wrists.

Its presence disturbed him enough to wake him. But before his consciousness was about to recognise the room he was in he heard a voice: 'I am the voice of the blind harper. When he was young music came naturally to him, people loved him and found great peace in his music. He brought healing to them with his harp. But as he grew older poetry arose in his heart and he became a poet. Art must come first from the heart, poetry adorns, but the heart feels. He chose to live passionately. For he sought to create a symphony of the heart.'

Charles now remembered he had lain awake trying to wash the figure and the words out of his mind. He didn't know for how long. But now he remembered how, just before awaking in the morning as darkness gave way to the first hints of colour, he had seen a head held high and the eyes filled with a dazzling brightness. The face was vague and unclear, but he knew it was smiling.

Charles sat on the end of his bed trying to understand what had happened. He was angry and more upset by Turlough's passing than he cared to admit. He had desperately wanted his approval for his poetry. But he could not make sense of the night's drama. He only knew it was significant. As he sat trying to dismember the dream, he became aware of noise outside and with it the smell of burning. Sleepily he moved to the window.

From where he stood he saw the smouldering remains of a large fire. Around it a group of men and several women were gathered. The noise was that low but disturbing keen of grief which confirmed the death of Turlough Carolan. The smouldering fire flared into life as an occasional breeze fanned it. Charles saw clearly now that it was a mattress that was burning. Turlough's mattress. The sight, for a moment, calmed the searching questions that had so perturbed him. He remembered that the Romans raised loud outcries at the death of their friends in hopes of them recovering. As a young child he had heard many stories of the dead being called back to life by displays of outlandish sorrow. But there was no hysteria in these mourners' grief. He was sure Mrs McDermott-Roe had forbidden such displays. He walked back to his bed. He wanted this final confirmation to sink in. He needed to steady himself because the house would soon be filled with people. He wanted to remain alone for a while. He was not happy with such communal grief, for no matter how much these people acclaimed him Carolan was always his own man.

He pulled a cover from the bed and threw it around him before sitting back in a stout chair. Outside a cockerel announced the morning. It was fitting, he thought. He felt exhausted and empty. Even the dream of the night could disturb him no longer.

Suddenly a pile of soot fell from the chimney and spread across the hearth in his room. Amongst it were old papers and rags that had been stuffed in it to keep out cold drafts when the fire wasn't lit.

Nineteen Laying Out

The house had never seen a day like this, with the coming and going of so many people. Some would not enter, but rather stood about on the gravel driveway or sat in groups talking and laughing. Here and there, those who had travelled a long distance lay sleeping. In other places young children ran and played while others slept or wept by their mothers' sides.

Charles stood, still wrapped in his bed cover, watching the scene from his window. There was a carnival atmosphere about the grounds and he was grateful for it. It seemed to him much more appropriate than the dreadful obsequiousness of the previous night. Even now he thought that someone, some stranger, would be washing down Turlough's corpse. The 'laying out' they called it. He could envisage them handling Turlough's naked limbs. He saw them spreadeagling his arms and wet cloths slapping against his skin. He winced at the thought. 'They must be careful with his fingernails,' he mumbled to himself. Suddenly a flash of the handless figure in his dreams returned momentarily. He turned to the crucifix above his bed and crossed himself. He dressed quickly. It was time to go, his own company offered him no solace.

As he walked into the grounds, he was grateful for the warm sunlight and more grateful for the noisy crowd. He knew some faces from the village and surrounding farmlands. He nodded to them in recognition and they, in turn, acknowledged his greeting. It was like a secret signal. There were so many strange faces. They must have been on the road for days before Turlough's death. 'Bad news has Mercury's winged feet,' thought Charles, but as he looked around him he began to question his own thinking. These people were all here for a reason, and he decided it was not that kind of morbid curiosity that attends so many funerals. They were here because of the person who had died, it was an act of homage and honour. This was a pilgrimage as much as it was a carnival.

The stables were full of the carriages of the gentry for whom Carolan had played for more than forty years. The parlour of the house Charles knew to be filled with clergy, and everywhere about the place he saw musicians, farmers and tradespeople. Rank or station did not matter here, only honour, and to his delight, humour.

Passing a crowd of unknown faces, he paused to listen to what had occasioned their curious laughter. In the middle of them a man wearing a brightly embroidered waistcoat and velvet knee breeches that had seen better days held his small knot of listeners entranced. 'And he was such a womaniser that it was inevitable. Lewd women can make a man terrible sick, you know. Anyway, his condition, shall we say . . .'

The speaker made an ambiguous gesture with his hands, suggesting just what part of the male anatomy he was speaking of. Charles saw the smirks and low laughs that the word 'condition' had occasioned, and he smiled himself. 'So they put the poor creature into their powdering tub as they call it. I tell you, I would rather swim through a lake of fire than sit in one of those things. Anyway, when the treatment was near its height, the unfortunate creature's whole face and tongue swelled so much that he could be neither recognised nor understood!'

The storyteller stopped at this point and nodded his head in mute sympathy. After a few moments he looked eagerly into the face of his audience and continued.

'A priest who came to visit him, for he was as good a Christian as anyone, finding the man passed out, and without a word in him, concluded that death was on the way. Off he went, fast as a hunted fox, and comes back with all his priestly paraphernalia to perform the last rites. And such a show as he made of it . . .', for a moment his voice dropped into a conspiratorial whisper, 'knowing full well the nature of the man's disease and the sin he had committed to catch it, the priest insisted on performing the unction on the poor man's sinful member, eventually pronouncing forgiveness to "Quicquid per Lumborum Delectationem Deliquit".'

At the pronouncement of this grandiose absolution the crowd stood momentarily silent, but as each of them began to picture the scene, Charles saw them choke back the laughter. But the storyteller was not going to miss his moment, 'And so much did he rant and rave about scarlet women, carnality and perdition that the poor man, who was no more near death than you or I, God forbid! and who was unable to call out to any one, because of the swollen tongue in his face, lay in silence getting colder and colder, while the priest roared on about hell fire and burning.'

At this point the man stopped suddenly and looked forlornly at the ground. Slowly he began again, picking out every word as if handing it to each person as he looked at them, 'Between freezing cold and swollen suffocation the poor man passed away where he lay!! The way I see it, the unfortunate Christian died from suffocating on the priest's piety!'

This conclusion released a torrent of hysterical laughter, Charles himself was no exception, his convulsive laughter in complete contrast to his anger at the previous night's ritual.

Whenever Charles went among the milling mourners he caught snippets of similar ribald conversation. It was humorous and warm-hearted and everywhere, by innuendo or by direct reference, Carolan was at its heart.

'Holy God, he'll be loving it now for sure, with himself laid out on his bed and a bunch of women washing and wiping him!'

'Turlough Carolan never had an eye for the women!' called out someone defensively, to which another voice replied, 'You're right there, sure he had no eyes at all!' And another voice rejoined, 'Well, someone should have told that to the priest when he was rubbing the oil of absolution into them!'

Laughter and celebration seemed to be everywhere. And always behind it, there was music playing, some tune or other of Carolan's. Amidst the music was the banter and discussion of the musicians.

'It's no time to be playing a drinking tune!'

'And why not? The man never refused a sup in his life – and his life was the better for it!'

Everyone claimed a part of Turlough. As Charles listened and laughed, he thought how the rumours that might have brought some of these people here were already taking wings. The tapestry of tales and anecdotes had already begun to etch Turlough into history.

But how, puzzled Charles, would he remember Turlough? His

mind was full now of all the days and hours he had spent in his mentor's company. They were too many and he felt he could not lose any of them by singling out only one. He turned to walk back to the house, as if called. Inside the house was as full as the grounds. But the faces here were more familiar. Each person he passed expressed condolence. There was a quiet and genuine sadness about the place as he looked around him. Never had he seen so many noble families, however history had reduced them, gathered under one room. Here were the St Georges of Carrick, the Bradys of Ballinamore, the Nugents and O'Reillys of Granard, the Featherstones of Ardagh, the Cruises of Edgeworthstown. Conor Fahy and Mrs French stood in a corner of the hall talking together. The Dillon family from Loughglinn stood with the O'Kellys and the Drurys. All the great families of Roscommon were somewhere in the room.

The eminent Dr Harte was obviously comforting the McDonough family from Sligo. In another corner near the stairs he saw his father and his uncle, the bishop, and gathered around them more members of the clergy. As Charles walked towards them he thought how Carolan had written so many of them into history in his compositions. In his own way he had preserved them in his music. He had lifted them out of their crumbling history. He had made life richer and more meaningful, even if he wasn't a saint. Without engaging them in conversation, he asked where he might find his aunt. Quietly his father answered, 'In Turlough's room and she will allow no one else there.' Charles nodded and left to join her.

She was sitting by the window and hardly turned to see who had entered. Her head was already covered in a black mantle and her eyes were fixed on her open hands. Nervously she fingered something. 'I must remember to give him his silver buttons.'

Charles walked forward and stood beside her with his arm around her shoulders. He was having difficulty finding words of consolation, 'Aye,' he said softly, 'but keep something for yourself.'

'I have my memories, Charles, and even they are too much.'

He was sure she was about to break down, but instead she turned her face up to him. She had aged since he spoke with her last night, but there was a light in the vast chasm of her eyes. She began laughing as she spoke, 'I think I'll keep his cup. He won't need that now!'

'No,' laughed Charles in return, 'for they're drinking enough toasts to his memory already. Wherever he's gone he'll be floating on a sea of alcohol!'

'He talked about floating on a raft, you know.'

Then suddenly she jumped up. 'Oh God, Charles, I must make sure we have enough food and drink.'

'Sit down now. Unless you think you can perform the miracle of the loaves and fishes, I don't think you should worry about it. They'll bring their own or provide for themselves somehow!'

'It will be a long wake.' Then looking directly at Charles, she commanded, 'And the gates must be shut to no one as long as he is in this house!'

'Then prepare for a siege! Now, enough of this, I want to speak with you.'

Mrs McDermott-Roe sat back and looked out of the window at the gathering mass of mourners. Charles looked over her shoulder.

'I've spent the last few hours walking amongst them. Some might call it blasphemy, but I have never laughed so much. The things they are saying about our bard . . .'

He was about to continue, but the word 'bard' redirected his thoughts. Slowly, without taking his eyes from the window, he explained about his troubled sleep and the confusing dream. Mrs McDermott-Roe listened attentively while keeping her eyes fixed on the scene beyond the window. When Charles finished, she raised her arm in a backward motion and softly patted the back of his hand with the palm of her own before speaking. 'And you say this spectre, or what ever it was, was finally smiling and had his hands returned to him?'

'As I remember it, yes.'

'And those people there, you found them all laughing and enjoying themselves?' She turned her body in the chair and looked up at him. 'Then why are you confused?'

Her logic was too devastatingly simple for him to fully comprehend. She turned back to the window again and asked him to draw the curtain. As he did so, she got up and walked about the room as if looking for something. Then she began to speak as she rolled the silver buttons in her hands. 'He was often troubled, you know, especially in these last months before he became ill.'

Suddenly Charles's confusion came flooding back to him. He had on many occasions been aware of an unease in Carolan, but thought it weariness or the aftermath of a long night of carousing. He waited patiently for her to explain.

'It's difficult to understand, really. There were parts of Turlough that he hid away from the world – on many nights as we sat together he talked of how his music troubled him. Sometimes he felt he had been somehow dishonest.'

'Dishonest!' Charles exclaimed.

'Yes, dishonest, though he used other words for it, I suppose. You see, at times he felt he had turned his back on the pain of the people. There were some nights when guilt and alcohol overcame him and I would hear him call out, like a frightened child, "I'm afraid of the dark!" '

Charles wanted to speak, but couldn't. He could only wait. She walked towards the vase of wild flowers standing on a small table. 'He always insisted on these being in his room. He used to pick them with his mother. He knew every flower that was in the room by its scent. He didn't need to go near them.'

Her hands were busy rearranging the flowers. She paused to smell one or two. 'I think he was not made for pain. Other people's suffering affected him deeply, but he would never show it or discuss it. I think he knew it, yet could not bear it; his loneliness was his own. I suppose blindness had made him independent – yet he loved people so.'

She stopped and once more looked around the room. 'There now, enough. I feel him scolding me already for this confession, though from your dream I'm sure he would not mind you knowing. Come now, Charles, we have a lot of preparation to take care of. We must do him proud, for if we don't! . . . Well, you know what a temper he had if he was not done justice to!'

For two nights Carolan's body lay in Alderford House so that his closest friends and patrons could take their last farewell. Each day brought more and more pilgrims to the house and the lands about it. There was not a house in the village of Keadue that was not crammed to the gills. In the grounds of the house itself people had set up tents and rough shelters. It was a royal wake. A chieftain had died and the whole island, it seemed, was on the move towards him.

On the evening of the second day it was decided to move Carolan into the great barn. Mrs McDermott-Roe had declared that no one should be denied access to Carolan and ordered the barn to be made ready. Charles thought of her confession to him in Turlough's room: she was giving him back to the people whom Carolan was so worried he had denied. As dusk set in, the corpse was mounted on Lord Mayo's carriage and made its short journey from the steps of the house.

Inside the barn and at one end a crude altar had been thrown up by laying the door of Alderford House, which had been removed for the occasion, upon several barrels. A swathe of black curtain hung down from the hayloft above. Turlough's body lay on the door covered in a white sheet. Mrs McDermott-Roe had ordered that large brass candlesticks be brought from the great house and set up around the body. The remainder of the barn was lit by smaller candles, strategically placed. The floor was covered with rushes and fresh straw. A makeshift auditorium of barrels, planks and anything that would serve as a seat was made up. Already people had found places for themselves. There was a constrained silence. Those who had brought children with them were busily instructing their offspring how to make crosses from the straw stalks. Everywhere, St Bridgit's circular symbol was being fingered in many hands young and old.

Everyone who entered made some sign of reverence towards the corpse; kneeling down, they repeated a 'Pater Noster' or an 'Ave Maria' for Carolan's soul. In a semi-circle behind the body, a group of six musicians and singers sat like sentinels. Fronting the altar some sixty clergy in cassocks and surplices were in constant attendance. The atmosphere at times was that of a primitive cathedral and the occasion could have been the investiture of a cardinal. In odd contradiction to this atmosphere, two barrels of whiskey stood on each side of the entrance. The moment they became empty, they were replenished.

Twenty Interment, Oration and Homily

It had been five days since Turlough died and for three of them he had lain beneath that white sheet in the glowing barn. So many people had entered and left its confines that Charles wondered how it could ever be returned to its usual function again. Great tubs of drink and tables of boiled meat had been constantly replenished. The miracle of the loaves and fishes which he had joked of had come about. Charles had visited the barn with Nuala, not knowing what to expect, but fascinated by the thousands who made their way there; ragged peasants and the remnants of Ireland's nobility mixed in easy communion. Turlough was the leveller and silent reconciler.

During the evenings Charles and Nuala strolled through the village. It had been transformed by the countless mourners, some drinking or singing or sleeping where they sat, while others, to sustain themselves, were fishing in the rivers. The more enterprising had set up crude stalls selling rabbits, hares, chickens, cheese and bread and some on the outskirts of the village had cows and goats, waiting to be milked. At the entrance to Alderford House one old woman sat with great baskets of roughly made candles, which many of the mourners purchased before paying their respects.

On these occasional walks they would sit amongst a group of musicians or other mourners and listen to their animated conversations. One of these groups was drinking and arguing in equal measure when they joined them. As they sat, they heard someone pronounce with authority, 'I tell you, the man would never have been half the man nor half the musician without it. The drink was the making of him.'

At this the speaker raised his own jug and Charles watched his Adam's apple roll up and down several times before he set it down again. He immediately started speaking again with a frown on his face. 'And he had a scathing tongue to any who complained of his drinking or was stingy with their pouring hand.'

Everyone laughed and as they laughed a fiddler took up one of Carolan's rollicking drinking songs. Charles knew the tune and smiled as the music spurred the drinkers into song. Carolan was generous in his praise of alcohol's special qualities. The song lifted them and the singers caroused through the words. Charles listened as they praised the virtues of drink. It made the miser generous, it made the slowcoach quicker and gave brains to the dunce, but when they came to the line about making the bashful man amorous Nuala laughed momentarily and the old man sitting opposite her winked and smiled through his black teeth. Through her laughter she whispered to Charles teasingly, 'It might not do you any harm to drink some more!'

Immediately she leapt up and filling an empty cup placed it in his hands.

'Go on, then!' she challenged and as she did so the whole party cheered and took up her challenge. Charles forced a wide smile. He was embarrassed and felt his smile made him look like the dunce or the slowcoach in the song. He drank quickly, trying to hide his face. As he set it down again, it was filled once more and another one of the group said with a wide smile, 'We wouldn't have Carolan's curse on us for only giving you half a cup!'

Charles could not refuse, but looked towards Nuala, his eyes half-scolding her. Nuala smiled her challenge back at him. He surrendered, called a toast, 'To the Bard', and drank back the rough whiskey to more cheers from his new companions.

As the musicians returned to their drinking and arguing about the right words to some tune, Charles signalled to Nuala that they should leave. As they stood to go a voice behind them called out, 'Blessed Jesus and all his miracles, that's fast working stuff!' Neither of them could resist laughing, but only Nuala turned to wave goodbye.

As they walked off, Charles felt the charge of the alcohol beginning to work on him. 'It may have all the magic they say!' he said. Nuala simply mocked him for not being used to it. Charles would not argue and they wandered through the darkening village, talking briefly with those they knew and listening and drinking with those they didn't. They met Seamus talking with a few other grooms. He had been drinking heavily and the drink had made him morbid.

'They wouldn't let me prepare him,' he slurred. 'They insisted it was women's work! Women's work!' he spat out. 'Haven't I been lifting and laying for him better than any woman could for more years than I can remember? He's cantankerous and contrary and he's not half the saint the world and his sister here want to make him out to be. But he was terribly modest, you know. Aye, he would have loved the idea of half a dozen women washing him. But if he was living now he would not have wanted their touch on him.'

Suddenly Seamus began weeping. There was no outburst. His face became awash with tears. Quickly he wiped his eyes with the cuffs of his coat.

'They shouldn't have denied me that last service. They made me feel useless and unwanted. My God, I could take that abuse from him, but that coven of shrivelled witches. What were they to him?'

Charles and Nuala tried to console him. It was true. He had been so much a part of Carolan that people sometimes forgot him. Poor Seamus knew Turlough Carolan better than any man or woman ever could. For a moment Charles felt a pang of jealousy, then he suggested to Seamus that perhaps he would like to go for a walk, but Seamus replied, 'I'm going to drink the insult out of me. Here, both of you, you must drink with me!'

Without further comment, he pushed his jug towards them. Charles's resentment was transformed into pity. He drank lustily as a sign of sympathy.

Seamus ranted on, 'Look at them. There's some out there never knew what the man looked like, probably never heard any of his music before tonight, and look at them. Every one of them is singing or talking about him like he was their next-door neighbour. And you know what! He would love it. He'd be right there in the middle of it, drinking and singing and shouting for them to dance.'

He looked at Nuala, as if suddenly realising she was there. He blinked his eyes then held them closed for a few seconds. Suddenly they burst open and Seamus lurched drunkenly towards her. 'And he would probably fill your ears full of the greatest cock and bull stories.'

It was obvious what Seamus was leading up to, but Nuala cut him short, finishing the story for him, 'He was a great charmer of women, Seamus, and sure, don't we deserve it?'

'Aye, charmer! he was a greater charmer all right.' He paused for a moment. 'But he really worshipped women. I mean every one of them could have been the blessed Virgin herself. Walk round these fields and half the music you'll hear playing was dedicated to some woman or other. Aye, charmer, he was a charmer!'

They had another long drink with Seamus, and leaving him to his own devices began to wind their way back to Alderford. The alcohol had confused Charles's senses. In the darkness, with strange faces emerging from the braziers that had been set up everywhere, he kept thinking of Seamus's statement that Turlough would be right there in the middle of all this confusion, drinking and singing along with everyone else. He whispered this thought conspiratorially to Nuala, 'He's here, you know, he's here tonight.'

Nuala just looked at him and smiled. Perhaps the drinking had not been a good idea. 'It may make people happy but it also makes them morbid,' she thought. But Charles's thoughts were concentrated on the ribaldry of the evening. Its carnival appeal was beginning to dim. His sense of Carolan's presence was rapidly vanishing, now it was a sense of finality that seemed to be overtaking him. While Carolan was alive, everything seemed possible, but now it was all disappearing. He was feeling lonely and he did not enjoy it. Turlough had spent a lot of time on his own. He often insisted on it and Charles had thought he understood the necessity of it, but now he wasn't sure.

The glow of small fires lit up the grounds everywhere as they approached the barn. Nearing the entrance, they heard the strains of a lamentation being played. It struck Charles how often Carolan had played such tunes for others. He wondered how happy he would be with this performance.

As they entered, it was almost impossible to see through the thick atmosphere. Around the walls the candles guttered low and the altar itself was no more than a haze of blurred light. They walked forward, clutching candles they had collected from the old woman at the gate. It seemed to Charles that she had sat there for three whole days and nights, wizened but awake. She had not moved from the position she first took up. Hundreds of people had purchased one of her candles, yet miraculously her baskets were always full.

Some minutes later they returned to the house. Every window was alight and many lanterns had been set out in the front. Outside the entrance a group of young men and women had formed a circle and were dancing to the accompaniment of a loud set of pipes. Beyond them, other young men hoisted their friends on to their shoulders and span around in abandon as young women and children chased after them. As they entered, they met Mrs McDermott-Roe standing in the hallway. It seemed she too was watching the antics of the people. Charles and Nuala went to her and Charles arranged the heavy wool shawl she was wearing. There was a weariness in the old woman's words as she spoke, 'I have carried my mortality too long and you, young man, have had too much to drink. I'm an old woman, resigned to the fact. But they loved him, Charles – oh, how they loved him.'

For a moment he watched as she fought hard to speak again. Her eyes never left the scene before her as she continued, 'If you have learned anything from that corpse out there, remember that the gift of love cannot be refused. No matter how else he treated them, he never refused them that.'

Her eyes were burning as she turned on him and her words cut into him, 'Don't waste what's given, take it, live it and regret only what you didn't take. Now go, both of you. The night's too long and this entertainment suits me fine.'

Nuala pulled Charles away gently and he followed almost afraid to speak. Mrs McDermott-Roe's last command had seemed to come from the mouth of Carolan himself.

He wanted to talk, but Nuala was too tired and insisted she would get no sense out of him anyway. Like a scolded child she directed him off to his bed. He had a funeral to attend and if his present state continued he would, by tomorrow, look more like a corpse than the one being buried.

Charles woke at about ten o'clock, but was unable to move any further than the window. If he had visited hell last night, then he had surely brought its hot ashes home in his stomach and his throat. The thought of entering that evil-smelling barn made his stomach churn. He hobbled from the window to a basin and jug laid out for washing. Like a man possessed he set the jug to his mouth and gulped down great mouthfuls of water, while the rest of it flowed over his face and down his chest.

Slowly, like a man recovering from a brutal assault, he dressed himself by the window. It still looked like a vision of hell to him as he watched the plumes of smoke from last night's fires and saw body after body emerge, as if out of the air, and make their way towards the barn. It was the final Mass before the interment, but he could not face it. He wanted to laugh but he couldn't. Carolan, in his day and especially when he had been drinking a great deal, would have had no hesitation roasting the clergy with his fiery tongue. Instantly as the thought came into his head he found himself parading about the room imitating Carolan as he proclaimed pompously, 'You clergy who never give way to drink but censure our errors from first to last. However severe your correction, I think that none of yourselves ever died of thirst!'

No sooner had he ended his performance than he sat on the bed and swore again. Then he appealed pathetically to the empty room. 'A mouthful of water after a night drinking that devil's brew and I'm more drunk than I was when I was drinking it.'

It was obvious to Charles that he would not be going to Carolan's Mass. He felt too intoxicated and found himself laughing again as he thought of all those priests scurrying around the barn trying to bring some order to the proceedings. Turlough in his last moments had made little black beetles out of them all. Completing dressing was an effort, but walking from his room down the stairs and into the open air was even more of an effort. Every few moments Charles felt sickness rise in him and choked it back.

Outside, it was bright with a light breeze blowing, which quickly rid his eyes of sleep and he joined the last stragglers walking towards the barn. Either they were in no better condition than himself or else the gravity of the occasion had already settled on them. As he walked he was met with contradictory greetings, 'It's a fine day, for the day that's in it,' said one. Someone nearer the barn called out to him, 'It's a black day for us all!' Charles felt too ill to indulge in conversation and simply nodded or answered, 'Aye, indeed it is.'

A huge crowd had gathered outside the barn and there was a constant babble of conversation. He pushed his way to the front, tempted to go in to the Mass, but he stopped to look around him, and as he did people started filing out. The crowd surged forward and for a moment he felt intimidated by them. He had never been this close to so many people. It was as if the pressure of them was squeezing out the memories that were bubbling in him. They would trample them in their ignorance and leave him nothing but the smell and noise of themselves. Gasping, as if suffocating, he pushed himself free and found a clear spot from where he could watch.

A clutch of peasant women emerged from the barn and seemed to hold up the proceedings for a moment as they huddled together and pulled their scarves over their heads like cowls. One or two of them, Charles was convinced, drank covertly from small green bottles before forming a phalanx at each side of the door.

Then, without any more ceremony, Turlough's body was carried out. For a moment there was silence. Charles could see only a little of what was happening. Six black-cassocked priests lifted the sheet-covered body off the door and raised it in the air as another group of roughly clothed labourers slid a coffin under it. Slowly the sheet descended and delicately Turlough was set into the coffin. In his intoxicated state Charles thought the act a parody of the Mass, with Carolan himself the host.

No sooner was this completed than the group of women lining each side of the coffin began to moan in low voices. As it was lifted on to the shoulders of those who were to carry it, their chant grew in volume until, as the coffin moved off, the crescendo reached screaming pitch. It was an awesome and terrifying last farewell, but it broke the tense silence of the multitude of mourners. They moved off as one, carried on a wave of sympathy that was distilled in the white keening scream of the women who walked alongside the coffin.

The burial place was about two miles from the barn. Charles was convinced that the road would not hold the mass of people who were following the coffin. As he looked around him, it was as if the fields had suddenly risen up and were moving inexorably towards Turlough's grave. The mass movement was irresistible and Charles fell in with it, to be swept along like a leaf on water. His fear of these people had gone. He was glad to be received by them.

When they reached the small graveyard the crowd immediately broke up and swarmed over the landscape. There wasn't a hill, rock, tree or gravestone that was not covered by them. They sat there, silent and waiting. Charles stood not far from the grave. The trees around them were filled with rooks and crows. Only their raucous cawing broke the silence.

Movements around the grave announced the arrival of the clergy and musicians. Charles knew the ceremony would be short. Turlough had been lain out for long enough and the Reverend Daniel Early, the parish priest, quickly delivered the 'Benediction' and the prayer for the dead. Without prompting, the harpers who waited in attendance began another dirge over the coffin. They kept the volume low to allow the priest's closing words to be heard.

> 'Even so, thy memory should now die away.
> 'Twill be caught up again in some happier day
> And the hearts and voices of Ireland prolong,
> Through the answering future,
> Thy name, Thy song.'

At this the music swirled up and the priest left the musicians to their own elegy. It penetrated every ear and froze every face into solemn and glassy-eyed concentration. Charles stood mesmerised by the atmosphere, then watched as his uncle, the bishop, walked to the graveside and began to address the crowd.

'I have few enough words to say. Each of us here today shall make his own oration in his heart and in his prayers. But I will say only this. It has been acknowledged in every nation that music was cultivated in Ireland when melody was scarcely known in other countries. Music may well be considered the essential element of our nationhood. The Holy Father himself has called Ireland the mother of sweet fingers and none was sweeter, none more loving than the hand of Turlough Carolan. He is first among the musical genius of our age, a self-created phenomenon in the cultivation of his chosen art. Let us, then, who are gathered here, commemorate him as a chieftain of our race.'

Immediately the graveyard became alive with applause and cries of agreement. If the bishop had more to say, neither the mourners nor the musicians would allow him. Instantly they broke into Carolan's composition, the famous O'Neill. The bishop was content and bowed his head for a momentary prayer, before crossing himself and walking slowly to join his nephew. Both men stood in silence and listened to the lament. The persistence of the harps soon quelled the enthusiasm of the crowd. As the music concluded, the bishop whispered, 'It was kind of Daniel Early to keep the service short. But I think they're still not happy to let him go!'

Charles nodded in agreement and then nodded again, pointing to someone moving through the crowd. He spoke slowly, 'This one will be the last to let him go!'

Through the crowd the upright figure of Charles McCabe moved towards the grave. Though his stature was upright, he walked as if he was trailing a plough behind him. He had the appearance of a farmer rather than a poet, and he carried an old tattered volume awkwardly in his hand. He stopped before the grave and slowly turned his head to take in the sight in front of him. His voice was craggy and weak, as if the words died in his throat before they left his mouth. But however inaudible, he commanded silence.

'Many's the night I've spent in this man's company and listened to his ludicrous wit and his barbed tongue abuse my words.'

A gasp of surprise and some words of dismissal were shouted at him. But he heard none of them. McCabe had long since drowned his sorrows, but was determined that he would not be silenced. 'No other man would I allow to speak to me as Turlough Carolan did. For no other man did I love as I loved this one. Many are the nights we read and discussed the work of the great poet Virgil. So now I will once more read to my friend.'

McCabe turned his head, slowly taking in the sight of the multitudes surrounding him. Then he declared with a low shaky voice, 'Here our own Aeneas lies!'

With his great hands he raised and opened the book. His voice found its steadfastness.

'It was the hour when divinely given rest first comes to poor human creatures and creeps over them deliciously. In my sleep I dreamed that Hector stood there before my eyes. He looked most sorrowful, and was weeping plenteous tears. He was filthy with dust and blood, as he had been that day when he was dragged behind the chariot, and his feet were swollen. Harrowing was the sight of him: how changed he was from the old Hector, back from battle wearing the spoils of Achilles, or that time when he had just flung Trojan firebrands on to the Greek ships! Now his beard was ragged and his hair clotted with blood, and those wounds which he had sustained fighting to defend the walls of his homeland could still be seen. I dreamed that I spoke first, weeping, forcing myself to find words for the sad meeting: "Light of Dardan land, Troy's unrestful hope, what held you from us so long? How we have waited for you, Hector! From what boundary do you come? We are weary now, and many of our fold are dead. We and our city have had many adventures, many trials. To think that we may look on you again! But what can have shamefully disfigured your princely countenance? And why these wounds which I see?" He made no reply and gave no attention to my vain questions, but with a deep, choking sob, he said, "Son of the goddess, make your escape quickly from the fight around you. Your walls are captured and all Troy from her highest tower is falling; Priam and our dear land have had their day. If any strong arm could have defended our fortress, surely mine would have defended it. But now Troy entrusts you her sanctities and her guardians of the home. Take them with you to face our destiny, and find for them the walled city which one day after ocean-wandering you shall build to be great, like them." '

For a moment McCabe hesitated, then stumbled where he stood. Emotion and alcohol had overcome him completely. Then gathering himself together, he snapped closed the book from which he had been reading. He bowed his head over it for an instant, then faced the crowd with great solemnity. When he spoke again everyone listened.

'Turlough Carolan in his life and art has given us a cornerstone on which we might build this nation again.'

When McCabe had concluded he turned abruptly and brushed through the mourners. Many of them were confused and dumbfounded by his words. Virgil and Aeneas and Hector meant nothing to them, but something of the sense of his words stirred them.

'I don't think they know how or why, but McCabe has given them their hero!' the bishop said to his nephew with a hint of a smile on his face. Then before Charles could say anything, he continued. 'Good; Daniel Early had the sense to seize the moment. They're making ready to bury him now.'

To the melody of a plaintive slow air and in stunned silence Turlough Carolan was lowered into the grave. Both Charles and his uncle felt the urge to leave and quietly pushed their way through the crowd. When they were clear of it and walking on the empty road near Alderford, the bishop spoke once more of Carolan.

He said that Carolan's life had touched more people than he knew, but his death had moved the bishop more than he had expected. In a way he couldn't fully explain, these last days with Carolan had helped him to take death into his own heart. With his voice low but serious, he said that his sense of life had been revitalised. He felt that if we could marry living with dying fearlessly it could affect the quality of our daily lives, our whole existence even, for we would be able to look back and feel no regrets.

He was sure that Carolan was not free from such regret, yet he could not fully understand the cause or source of such feeling. 'To die believing that the world might be a better place for our having lived in it would require us to live more intimately with ourselves and with others. Perhaps Carolan lived too much with himself!'

The bishop stopped and looked about the landscape. His head turned slowly as if he was drinking in every last detail. Then he continued, 'There are very few men I have known who had a more vigorous mind than our dead friend. Yet it was like this old landscape here. It was undisciplined through the want of proper cultivation.' He laughed momentarily. 'Mind you, for all that, he could be as sharp as a butcher's blade. Our Turlough was, at heart, absolutely the child of nature. If indulgent caprice was his mother and an abiding sense of a deeper and richer life was his father, then with such parentage his imagination could not fail to be eccentric in its poetic flights. But when he employed his unbounded imagination in the harmonic arts, he found a new mastery which compelled us all. His inspiration may have come from a highly charged imagination about the Irish people. I think he genuinely believed that our spirit could be reawakened or perhaps reworked, but I think he was less concerned about the details of the myth of an Irish identity, so long as it worked. Inspiration, provocation and even intimidation were his tools and he played them all. McCabe's drunken oration at his grave may have more truth in it than he knows. Carolan had all the characteristics of a warrior chief and might have died happy in that life, but there was something more to him. His heart was bigger than that!'

As he finished, his eyes again surveyed the scene in front of him. Then he suggested they walk a little further. As they moved further away from the noise of the mourners, the bishop began relating a dream that Carolan had first experienced on his last visit to St Patrick's Purgatory and which had been preoccupying him in his last days. The bishop said he wasn't sure of its significance, but that he remembered every detail of it for it had all the power of a prayer expressed out of the very depths of his soul. Slowly, never once taking his eyes off the lake waters that formed the backdrop to Carolan's grave, he related the dream as Carolan had told it to him.

In this dream he looked out over an old city that time had worn into a quiet elegance. A man was running through the streets. His feet and clothes were filthy and ragged and fear and jubilation were mixed in his features. The streets seemed empty, but were filled with the sound of festive bells. Around him the windows and doorways were hung with bouquets of flowers and religious icons draped in blue and white.

The man seemed to be a stranger who knew only one destination and he darted like a frightened lizard towards it. He found what he was looking for and knocked urgently at a small door framed in a long wall. The door opened and he hurried through. Once inside he was ushered through three sets of locked doors. It was a convent and he was being received into the strict enclosure of women.

In a small room lit by a single window the man sat enclosed by a group of nuns, veiled in black muslin draped over white habits. His torn shirt was about his waist and a nun's white hands bathed the welts and sores that stood out on his back, while another pair of hands cut off the thick patches of matted hair from his head and beard. Everywhere the perfume of scented candles and wild flowers bathed him.

The quiet of this scene was suddenly broken by loud banging and the clamour of angry voices demanding entrance. Some of the nuns left and told the protesters that they must go away, as no man may enter an order of women.

In a broken voice the man told the nuns that he had been travelling the countryside for many years but that he had forgotten why, and only knew that he was searching for something. As he could not explain himself to people he had chosen to hide himself away from them. For many years he had forsaken the world of people and lived a solitary life in a cave near a river. People thought him deranged and dangerous and avoided any contact with him. Only a few of the village children brought him food which they left outside his dwelling. His one consolation was the river that flowed beside his cave. It alone was his companion. His solitary life was measured and lightened by the movement of the river as it ran over its rocky bed. It eroded his despair. As the seasons changed, so did the note and volume of the river. He knew the rumble of the snow melt, the fast sparkles of spring rains and the slack sluggish summer waters. The man paused, as if hearing the sound of it still, and then he spoke again.

Once, when he was very ill and near to death he had strayed towards the village. As he lay exhausted near the fields that surrounded it, he could hear the wondrous melody of women singing their harvest songs. Then one plaintive voice sang a love song. The song was simple and unadorned, but set against the orchestra of the sounding water it was a divine chorus in which his soul was forever immersed and uplifted. The man's speech faded again. About him the unquestioning eyes of the nuns glowed like candles, reflecting his own intensity.

Having cleaned and fed him they told him he must go further

into the convent confines, and find the room at the centre of the convent. They pointed to a door and told him to leave his tattered clothes and go. Without questioning he left the roomful of women and walked across a cobbled courtyard. It was bright and filled with butterflies. The air was laden with the smell of wood sorrel. The man stood and listened. Again he heard the peasant song, plaintive and full of exile and longing. It seemed more than human. It was compelling and intense, and pulled him to the great door of the waiting room. He surveyed the cracked symbols and figures carved on wood. To him the door was a manuscript of sound. He seemed to hear its meaning, like a great sounding board reverberating in his senses. As he stood before it, it opened silently.

Beyond it was a swirling fusion of unformed colour. He fell to his knees, overcome by humility and veneration. The altar was melting and evaporating and with it the divine love song faded. Everything was dissolving and reforming, each time returning richer and more elaborate.

Inexplicably the man was transported from the open door to a landscape in high summer. The bronze of the oaks blended into blotched red and blue-black of the wild berries. Everywhere yellow and lilac erupted from the profusion of green.

As the colour took form and shape, he found himself standing near a rough stone wall hidden behind some haw and blackthorn bushes. He passed through a small but magnificently wrought-iron gate and entered into a circular graveyard. He walked through the sloping and rolling drifts of willowherb and long summer grass and into a circle of small headstones. All around him the mossed and weathered gravestones leaned as if in fixed adoration. He seemed to recognise the names inscribed on each of them. At their very centre, one squat two-faced stone stood alone, as if calling everything into itself. The twin faces stared wide-eyed and open-mouthed. Slowly the man knelt and fingered the features of each face. The eyes were huge globular protrusions, unblinking, all-seeing. The mouth was pouting and sensuous. His hands followed up the shape of the body. Its crossed arms held and embraced whatever sex the Godhead was. His fingers trembled, he raised himself and circled about the image, studying its enigmatic symmetry. The two faces took in opposite views, but the energy of the stone was in its composure. It stood as if suspended in perfect harmony.

The man's hands traced the contours of its form like a blind man and found at the centre of the effigy, crowning the faces, a hollow filled with rainwater. Tentatively he dipped his fingers in. The water cooled the burning sensation in his flesh that the stone had imparted to him. Somewhere inside himself he could feel the love song, resonating.

When the bishop had finished, he simply walked on in silence and Charles followed, feeling awkward but grateful. After some minutes the bishop spoke again.

'Purgatory is supposed to be a place of spiritual nurture, but I am more interested in that pagan idol of Carolan's with its Janus-like face. Janus is the spirit of the threshold, of things both inner and outer, of all beginnings. In its centre is a purifying pool of water where Turlough dips his hands. Those same hands that gave us his music. I think our friend was like his idol. Standing between two worlds looking backwards and forwards, but always looking into the light. And perhaps that is where he is standing now – somewhere between us and the light.'

ACKNOWLEDGEMENTS

Noleen Gernon who typed this manuscript over and over and over again, and whose fingers must have the numb dexterity of Carolan's own; Robin Robertson, my editor, who convinced me there was merit in my imagining; Senator Maurice Hayes who picked me up and set me down to this project; Nicholas Carolan who knows more than I could write and who was ever helpful; David Hammond and Neil Martin whose jovial encouragement was invaluable; Michael O'Suillibhan who dismissed my musical illiteracy in one magical afternoon; Paddy Maloney for the loan of his books which began this enterprise; Joan Trumble from whose upstairs landing I was passaged back to Carolan's Enniskillen; Derek Bell who sent me into the mystic one night in Nobber; Luke Gibbons and his family for introducing me to Keadue; Janet Harbinson for lecture notes and articles; American Ireland Fund; staff of Traditional Music Archive, the National Library, Dublin and staff at Trinity College Dublin Library; Dr Thomas Mitchell, Provost, T.C.D.; Staff at English office T.C.D.; the Inuit woman who wrote to me from Alaska on several occasions, convincing me that Carolan was a Dreamwalker, and showing me blindsight-edness; and finally, all the perchance people who without their knowing it prevented the whole card-house from tumbling down.